B

The Sad-Faced Bank Robber

Clive F Sorrell

authorHOUSE®

AuthorHouse™ UK
1663 Liberty Drive
Bloomington, IN 47403 USA
www.authorhouse.co.uk
Phone: 0800.197.4150

Published by AuthorHouse 04/27/2017

ISBN: 978-1-5246-8066-4 (sc)
ISBN: 978-1-5246-8064-0 (hc)
ISBN: 978-1-5246-8065-7 (e)

IN MEMORY OF
MY BELOVED WIFE

Sophia Catharina Sorrell

My sincere thanks to
Piet and Kay
David & Carolyn,
Terry and Liliane,
Rob and Carol,
Alan and Pat,
Syd and Marah,
Gideon and Toni,
Ken and Ann
Brendan
Jonathan and Sarah
and all close and distant friends
who gave me great comfort.

Siddiqui
Kawthar
Jumana
Duress - The Life and Death of a Ton-Up
Ingrid's Children
The Distant Cousin
The King's Charter
The Sad-Faced Bank Robber
Stories For Dark And Stormy Nights

BOOKS BY CLIVE F SORRELL – PUBLISHED BY AUTHORHOUSE

CHAPTER 1

A rather unfortunate beginning.

GERALD LATIMER HAD LEFT school at the early age of fifteen years, three months and two days precisely. This was for the reason that his father thought it was time the good-for-nothing earned his own living instead of, as he put it, "Swotting for damned whatchamacallit-Levels, playing computer games and generally being a bloody nuisance and financial drain on the family resources."

Just before his calamitous accident Mr Arnold Latimer had been the senior power-press operator in a car factory that was only ten minutes from number six Fiesta Avenue. His main responsibility had been to operate one of the six giant hydraulic presses that shaped sheet steel into a specific form; on this particular day a die for the rear offside passenger door of a popular family saloon was being used.

Mr Latimer was a drinking pal of a particularly important foreman who was capable of pulling strings and Gerald was taken on as a trainee in the cutting section of the factory. This was contrary to the Protection of Young Persons (Employment) Act, 1996, as he was, by this time, only fifteen years, three months and five days old. Like the last trainee, who coincidentally was promoted to assist Mr Latimer on the power press, Gerald was assigned to making an unending flow of tea for ten plasma-cutter operators.

'You've got the most important job in the factory lad,' he was told by the stubbly-faced foreman as he handed Gerald the electric kettle, a box of extra strong Yorkshire tea bags and pointed to the workers' tea room.

As mentioned, the previous tea boy had automatically been promoted and unfortunately became the prime instigator of the following event that gravely affected Gerald's future and the continuing health of his father.

It was 7.00 a.m., the first shift of the day, when Mr Latimer began his boringly repetitive procedure which was as follows;

1. Raise the safety barrier
2. Place a large sheet of 0.8mm steel into position
3. Lower the safety barrier with the orange button
4. Activate the press with the red button.

When the press gave two rapid alarm signals the assistant would raise the safety guard by pressing the green button and remove the sheet of metal that, due to pressure of one thousand tons per sqare inch, would have been moulded into what would become a car door in one-point-seven seconds flat.

However, what actually happened that particular morning was;

1. On raising the safety barrier Mr Latimer spotted a paper cup that had blown between the mammoth dies.
2. He climbed into the press to remove the offending item.
3. His assistant then bent over to watch and carelessly leant the palm of his hand on the orange button.
4. The safety barrier was then lowered, trapping the assistant's mentor.
5. The mentor began shouting; *Raise the barrier! Raise the fucking barrier you bloody bastard!*

6. The bloody bastard, who was screaming *How? How? How?* fumbled
    with the controls and in blind panic missed the green button with
    his shaking forefinger and pressed red.

It goes without saying that the subsequent funeral was a closed casket
affair as the 0.8mm remains of Mr Latimer had to be scraped from the
dies like old lead paint. The fare was familiar to two other widows who
attended; egg and cress sandwiches with crusts removed, Mrs Latimer's
own fruit scones, clotted cream, bottles of Hardings brown ale and clean
glasses were laid out on the sideboard table during the wake.

As a mark of respect, the scones were denied any strawberry jam.

It should be mentioned that the young power press assistant had been
so traumatised by the sight of his boss being squeezed into the shape
of a rear offside passenger car door that the balance of his mind was
disturbed and he was officially sectioned by two psychiatrists and placed in
a sanatorium where he remained for the rest of his life. The other patients
were maddened so much by his repetitive reciting of *Green button, not
red button, green button*, that he was subsequently transferred to solitary
confinement, strapped to his bed and classified as a potential suicide.

Over the next two years Gerald moved on from tea boy to minor parts
assembly where he remained until he was upgraded to the position of major
parts assembler which involved the installation of very large engines with
a very small increase in wages.

It was on Gerald's nineteenth birthday, an overcast Friday afternoon,
that the foreman told him, with a grim expression, to report to the main
office. The carpet had a lush pile and he wished he had left his oily boots
outside the door. Without looking up the elderly receptionist directed him
to room number three in a corridor lined with photographs of alien looking
cars that seemed to date back to when roads were still waiting for Edgar
Purnell to patent tarmacadam. It was there he was coldly informed by a
blonde secretary, whose roots were beginning to show a definite shade of
ginger, that he was now redundant. Gerald was suddenly glad he'd left his
boots on and he made a point of shuffling his feet on the pile as, without a
word, she handed him a biro to sign the receipt for a small brown envelope
with a glassine window that contained two weeks notice in cash, his P45

and redundancy money represented by ten twenty pound notes and odd silver and copper coloured coins.

Gerald left the office clutching the envelope that had terminated four years hard labour and would now completely change the direction of his life. Whilst emptying his locker Gerald was further aggravated when he learnt from one of the small parts assembly workers that his replacement was a nifty little royal blue robot called JP/2/XN5a.

To install a car engine within the mandatory three minutes was a reasonably specialised skill. Robots it appeared were now capable of doing it faster and he soon discovered that new jobs as an engine fitter were impossible to find. Most car factories throughout the land had installed the same if not similar robots to carry out major assembly work on their cars.

Competition was fierce with hundreds of car workers seeking employment so Gerald thought he'd play it clever and apply for a job as an JP/2/XN5b robot assembler. He believed he was demonstrating his ability to think laterally but his smug expression instantly evaporated when he was informed at the local Job Centre that all JP/2/XN5-b robots were made by JP/1/XN5-a in a factory at the foot of Mount Fuji on the island of Honshu.

Having left school at fifteen, three months and two days with only limited knowledge of the world these were not names Gerald was familiar with and on visiting the town library he learnt Honshu Island was five thousand eight-hundred and seventy-four miles away, as the crane flies, from number six Fiesta Avenue and therefore beyond a reasonable daily commute by bicycle or No. 43 bus.

Since first working at the car factory as a small lad, Gerald Latimer, now twenty-two, had risen to five feet eleven inches tall with broad shoulders, light brown hair and average good looks. After three years of job hunting he was still collecting social security cheques and living at home with Mrs Stephanie Latimer, his mother, who constantly relived the way her husband had died. This tended to make sleeping difficult and she was prescribed a powerful sleeping pill by the doctor to help her through the night but when he said she was exceeding the time allowed for continual usage of the drug and could no longer issue any more presciptions Stephanie had to travel further afield to find another doctor and then another, until she could no longer receive any medical help without leaving the country.

Stephanie's dreams were constantly filled with people shaped like car doors who rapidly slammed shut or dissolved into grisly images of her husband. When Stephanie was awake she reached the point when she could no longer look at a rear passenger door opening without screaming. She was perfectly normal with any other train, coach, bus, or car door but rear off-side triggered horrific pictures in her mind. Gerald loved his mother dearly and was driven to ignore all NHS refusals to medicate his mother to seek a more reliable drug source on the street.

It was in one of the scruffier pubs near the factory that, after discreet inquiries across the bar, Gerald was directed to a sallow-faced youth who could offer pills in all colours of the rainbow. Uppers or downers, he had them all and at a price Gerald could just afford. He bought fifty that were the product of an amateur pharmacologist and had undoubtedly been concocted in a New Cross lockup garage; or somewhere similar.

As she was now able to take the little yellow tablets to her heart's content Stephanie became calmer but so addicted to the mystery substance that she began suffering from unexpected side effects. Not only did her beautiful brown hair slowly turn silver but her normally youthful appearance faded and her face became deeply lined. Even her disturbing nightmares returned making her wish in her imaginary world that she could wake. These generally involved becoming wafer thin beneath the weight of colossal flat irons wielded by pigtailed men in a Chinese laundry.

Gerald was painfully aware of his mother's detriorating condition as he noticed she was suffering frequent dizzy spells, unsteady walking and her trembling hands slopped most of her tea into the saucer. Stephanie's screams of abuse when he advised her to stop taking the yellow tablets and her heart wrenching wheedling for just one more when he threatened to cease going to the supplier became impossible to endure.

After a few months on the home-made drug Stephanie began feeling, seeing and hearing things that didn't exist and she developed a habit of rising in the early hours of the morning to search the house for 'those people' who were spying and trying to control her.

It was when Stephanie started to believe her son was one of "those damned door people" persecuting her that she began eyeing him with suspicion and he found it impossible to give the hands-on care she so desperately needed. He began studying the advertisements for nursing homes in the untidy stacks of old women's magazines that are part of the interior decoration of every waiting room throughout the land.

It was losing his part-time job as a sorter at the recycling centre on the day before Good Friday that became the last straw for this had been followed by his mother attempting to carve him instead of the roast lamb on the following Easter Sunday. Gerald summoned the courage to contact some of the homes he had listed in a little notebook and after two frenetic days of phoning whilst dodging the occasional missile thrown by Stephanie that he found the perfect place, a nursing care home called Shady Trees. The name was a trifle inappropriate as the nearest trees were a good half-mile distant and severely pollarded to avoid the overhead power lines emanating from a noisy sub-station; however, these became trivial considerations when weighed against the feasible fee he would be paying.

Gerald had always known that moving his mother to a care home would be costly but it was something he was unable to avoid if she was to receive professional care. Transporting his mother to Shady Trees was also the next problem to overcome for on leaving the house Stephanie would scream at the rear passenger doors of every passing car. She flatly refused to go anywhere near the Shady Tree's Volvo and the car had to leave with a rather disgruntled Eritrean nurse at the wheel. The only solution was to administer strong home-made sedatives, that Gerald illegally obtained from his dodgy supplier at the pub, and pay for an ambulance and two burly paramedics, who seemed more suited to nightclub bouncing, to persuade his mother to take the short journey.

Regular visits to the care home became irregular within a short period of time for Stephanie began to receive him more and more as a stranger. She rarely recognised him and on a few occasions she even objected to the weird man who wanted to hold her hand. Gerald was accused of being a sex pervert and there was a time he had to leave hurriedly after she could thrown a recently used bedpan at him. Gerald became more depressed and yet he was able to manage financially for a further eight months before yet another disaster affected the Latimer family.

It was on a dismally overcast day when a White Paper was rushed through Parliament and the House of Lords adding a bylaw to *Schedule 2 of the Immigration Act 1971* which dealt with restricting the number of illegal migrants entering the Green and Pleasant Land. Unlike normal implementation of a new law this particular bylaw took effect immediately. Agents of the UK Border Agency, in full riot gear, raided businesses and homes across the country seeking illegal aliens. Hundreds of addresses were raided in alphabetical order which made it a number of days and three o'clock on a Tuesday morning before the doors of Shady Trees were battered open. This was followed by twenty-two minutes of shouting, screaming and swearing by the rudely woken nursing staff; all of who proved to be of foreign origin. They were without work visas and completely unqualified to care for the elderly. All were given five minutes to dress, gather their things together and they were then taken for questioning, internment and immediate deportation.

The Shady Trees Care Home was bereft of any care and the surviving staff member, the manageress, was left to face twenty-five elderly, and decidedly daft women each of whom angrily demanded personal attention. What made matters worse was that the owner and his wife had also been taken for questioning and the manageress had no option but to telephone a local nursing employment agency and with panic in her voice urgently request properly qualified staff. Seven SRNs instantly materialized at an eye-watering pay-rate, excluding agency commission that, when she telephoned her decision to her employers, had them climbing walls with rage.

While their manageress had been spending their money like there was no tomorrow the owners had been sitting in an interrogation room. The bad news had been texted to their mobiles before their cross-examination by the officers began and they began scribbling figures on the sheets of paper that had been supplied for their written statements. Their final calculations coincided when a large deficit in the profit column was presented. They agreed there was only one solution, they would have to increase the resident's fees and by a considerable margin if they were to continue enjoying their Sandy Cove beach house in Barbados.

When the letter dropped onto Gerald's doormat two days later he was devastated. He could not believe that the figure picked out in bold type could be justified by the list of reasons given for the increase. Even the concluding apology failed to make the annual fee acceptable for the sum demanded now amounted to a forty percent increase. It was a major disaster and he knew that even if he appealed to the Department for Social

Security they wouldn't bother to reply. They might even question why his mother was in such a home and not only that but in a care home that had been raided by the UK Border Agency. Gerald was already rationed to surviving on one can of baked beans on toast every day, except for Sundays when beans were replaced with spaghetti, and unless he was able to beg, borrow or steal some money his mother would be returned to a loving stranger and her own hell of perceived persecution at number six Fiesta Avenue; due to the financial benefits of being close to a major car factory the council members had been obliged to name the streets after automotive models; trees, flowers, battles, politicians and freedom fighters were in the next borough.

Gerald decided to have a word with the yellow tablet man and sound him out for any ideas on how to make a little more than twenty-three thousand pounds and seventy pence per annum. The disastrous direction his life had taken and this latest misfortune would now collaborate to unsurprisingly make Gerald thoroughly sad and yet surprisingly happy within a few short weeks.

Reginald Barnett, for that was the full name of the sallow-faced youth with rings in his ears and nose who preferred it to be shortened to Reg, listened to Gerald's tale of woe, nodding his head knowingly as though he had been through it all himself. His father was the manager of the town's only bank who refused to advance loans to young men in the morning or, to his own penniless son at any time of the day, knowing that the money wouldn't be used wisely. The one and only time he had advanced Reg three hundred pounds for text books on neuroscience, nutrition, biophysics, physiology and other similar 'ologies he learnt that the money was used to purchase a stock of recreational drugs from a rather dubious character in London. These had fallen into unprofitable hands during a rock concert in the O2 Arena when two plain-clothes policemen and a sniffer dog called Archie arrested him.

Reg's father, a highly respected freemason, skillfully pleaded to convince the local magistrate that it was a case of youthful impetuosity that was now deeply regretted and his father's emotional address reduced Reginald's sentence to a Community Service Order of sixty hours.

This was completed in record time at an all-night soup kitchen for the homeless where Reg soon picked up a lot of new tricks from the old lags in the queue. He then made the decision to leave home and the incessant lectures on living a law-abiding life behind him. Another reason for making his own way in life was that his self-righteous father was revealed to have given one of his bank tellers a bun in the oven. Reg's mother packed her suitcase and after a peck on his cheek she left to go and live with her mother. Any amiable home life was now made nigh on impossible. Reg didn't bother to return to the university for he had made many new friends down at the soup kitchen who had 'bags' to sell and although he was no longer a paying customer, thanks to his father cutting off his allowance, he had been invited to kip down in the empty house they had commandeered.

The carefree, undisciplined life in the squat suited Reg down to the ground and distributing drugs for Mr Goldenstein, a man you never argued with, provided him with enough money to stay independent and in a constant semi-high state; his father gave up on his son and didn't bother trying to rehabilitate or even to try to find out where he lived. His mother lost all interest, took an Australian lover, manufactured two new sons and emigrated to Mutawintji National Park to care for joeys orphaned by road-trains.

When Gerald stopped talking to take a long draught of Hardings finest ale which, incidentally, was perfectly harmless now that the original contents of the fermentation tank had long been sold, Reg stopped plucking meditatively at his lower lip, looked furtively round the noisy bar and in a whisper, made Gerald a life-changing offer. This he had to repeat when Gerald shouted that he couldn't hear and Reg moved in closer and put his lips against his ear, inviting a few odd looks from drinkers standing nearby.

'I like you Gerry, we could go into business together and make whatever your mum likes.' He paused as though considering a better idea. 'Move in with me and I'll show you how to make something similar to the 'yellows' and flog them. Then we'll be able to give some to your mum to keep her happy. With you doing the marketing and distribution while I make the product we could make a bloody fortune.'

There was a long silence as Gerald considered the offer. 'Why do I have to move in with you?' he asked.

'Security, mate, I can't risk you blabbing off, even to your old mum. The closer you are to the factory at all times the more I can control things. Okay?'

Gerald thought about what Reg had said, asked if he could go home to collect the post and tidy up and on receiving a nod he accepted the offer before adding, 'Where do you live, is your laboratory close by?'

'Close enough, it's on the other side of the old abandoned gasworks.'

Gerald accepted that piece of information with a grimace for it was a rather rundown part of town that prided itself on colourful graffiti that illustrated various body parts of both genders with creative copywriting that made full use of the Anglo Saxon dictionary. He gave a nod and asked the most important question. 'Do you think I can make twenty-three thousand and seventy-pence in the first year?'

'That's a lot of dosh, mate, why that exact sum?'

'That's what the Shady Trees' sharks demand to keep my mum safe.'

'Shady Trees? Sounds more like a cemetery to me.'

'Pretty close, it's a nursing home that's proving to be a whole lot more expensive than a hole in the ground.'

'Don't worry, you'll make more than those vultures are asking.' Reg said as he held his hand up for a high-five that Gerald missed the first and then the second time round; Harding's ale was beginning to take effect.

Not wanting to rock the boat about such a bold scheme Gerald couldn't help having vague misgivings. Reg didn't exactly promote himself as a successful clandestine chemist when wearing a threadbare jacket and grubby shirt with a frayed collar but beggars couldn't exactly be choosers and they shook hands rather than miss another high-five.

'Okay, I'll give it a go,' he said and they left the pub together. Gerald was embarking on a venture that would either make or break him and his vague misgivings began to manifest themselves as Reg took a bicycle from a rack and nodded for Gerald to take the next one.

'Are these yours?' Gerald inquired innocently.

'Don't be a bloody fool, why pay for transport when you can get it for free.' Reg cycled off into the gloom. Gerald considered running after him but curiosity prompted him to mount the remaining bike in the rack and pedal furiously to catch up. As he drew alongside Reg laughed for Gerald had taken a woman's bike. He then recalled the young couple that had been cuddling in a corner seat with glasses of cola before them. The plastic straws remained untouched for their lips were fully occupied elsewhere.

'You gonna be my bitch now, Gerry?' Reg laughed and Gerald blushed and wondered if he seriously meant for him to be available in that way. They crossed town and entered a warren of terraced streets that stretched behind the gasholders that could no longer be seen. The massive containers had long been emptied and were fully depressed leaving only the lift bracing columns and the open support frames silhouetted against the ash-grey early evening sky.

Forty-one Delphinium Road was a pre-war two-up-two-down clone of numbers forty and forty-two. All the estate streets were named after flowers to supposedly offset the constant whiff of rotting cabbage that after five years still hung in the air like a stagnant pond. As they entered the house Gerald noted that the original fan shaped window over the front door had been replaced by a piece of cardboard.

'From time to time kids thought it was fun to take pot shots with their air pistols at the three saints in the stained glass,' Reg explained as he closed the door, waved to a grimy face with a bushy beard that had appeared at one of the doors in the hallway and led the way through the house and into the backyard.

Reg jerked a finger back over his shoulder. 'That was Big Ed. He used to be a chartered accountant until the auditors discovered he was keeping a separate set of books from all his clients. Syphoned off a fortune and opened sixteen bank accounts throughout the Caribbean before they caught up with him.'

'Does anyone else squat here?'

'Old Monty dosses down in a back room. He's generally known as Ali-Monty from his days when he maintained two ex-wives until every penny he had was gone in alimony and he had no choice but to disappear. Some say he's a toff with a really fancy title and that he had gone off the rails when his country house had been sold.' Gerald learnt later that this was only a fanciful rumour. 'Sexy Sue has the room on the top floor and is an ex-exotic dancer but I wouldn't bother visiting her because she's in her sixties, has lost all her teeth and her ability to dance vertically and horizontally as well. She smells high to heaven which is why most of the windows in the house are left wide open.'

'What about winter?'

'We've found nose clips and sucking extra strong mints helps.'

A monstrous black and white cat slipped between the towering nettles that had destroyed what had once been an attractive little garden and Reg, followed closely by Gerald, weaved his way through the slowly swaying sunflowers to what appeared to be a large greenhouse with all the glass panels painted black.

'Don't want anyone looking in, do we?' Reg muttered as he glanced up at the bedroom windows of numbers forty and forty two. 'Doesn't look too suspicious from the air either.'

'From the air?' Gerald rubbed his arms where the nettles had touched them.

'Drones. Cops frequently patrol this area for any youngsters causing trouble with their bloody street racing,' Reg said. He opened the door and stood to one side for Gerald to enter. 'Welcome to Paradise, Gerry.'

It was impossibly dark in the greenhouse until Reg tripped the light switch and Gerald was dazzled by row upon row of glittering glass jars, beakers, plastic trays and Bunsen burners on a workbench that stretched the length of what could only be described as a homemade chemistry laboratory. There was a four-ring gas cooker standing at the far end of the greenhouse with stainless steel pots hanging above that he could tell were brand new.

Pointing to one of the jars Reg said, 'Those are Morning Glory seeds that produce lysergic acide amide and the box next to it contains ergotamine tartrate. At first I thought about using ergot fungus itself, which is the other reason for painting the glass black as the fungus decomposes rapidly if exposed to bright light. However it was virtually impossible to get and far too expensive.' He picked up a flask carefully. 'Anhydrous hydrazine is incredibly dangerous as it can explode if heated and it's also a deadly poison, just like the argot fungus.'

Gerald was confused by Reg's technical explanations as he continued to point first at one container and then another and another while spewing out unmemorable and impossible to pronounce names. 'You sound like my old science teacher. What do you actually make with all this stuff, the yellow tablets?' He waved his arms to encompass all the bottles, boxes and jars.

'LSD blotters, mate. It's the current trend in all the clubs.'

'LSD? Blotters?

'S'right, I dip sheets of blotting paper into the LSD solution and then dry them. That's where you'll come in. You first rubber stamp the sheets with my design which I still have to draw and then you cut them into half inch squares which it's reckoned should give five hundred doses per sheet.'

'And then what?'

'We go out and sell them for a bloody fortune.'

Gerald picked up a flask of clear liquid. 'How many have you made already?' He tossed the flask from hand to hand and Reg flinched.

'I wouldn't do that if I were you, Gerry, that's chloroform and it'll knock us both out for days if you drop it.' He took the flask with a guilty look. 'Look mate, I haven't actually made any blotters yet which is why I need your help.'

'What! You dragged me all the way here to make a fortune from something you haven't even tried doing yet?' Gerald shouted and Reg patted the air in an effort to shut him up before the neighbours overheard and began to get nosey.

'I've got all the instructions here,' Reg said with renewed optimism in his voice as he picked up two foolscap pages and ran a forefinger down the top sheet. 'It took me ages but I managed to get all the ingredients on this page, you can check them all yourself,' he said as he waved a hand airily at the jars. 'And this page is a guaranteed recipe. Got it from a kosher guy in Primrose Place.'

'Recipe! This isn't Master Chef,' Gerald growled. 'Look Reg. if you can't make yellow tablets then where the hell did those you've been selling to me come from?'

'I bought them from Mr Goldenstein, a bloody big dealer in the area and then sell them on in pubs and clubs at a pittance of a profit. It's not much of a living and that's why I thought I'd take a shot at making the damn things myself. Cut out the middle man so to speak.'

'If he's such a big wheel in drug distribution won't your Mr Goldenstein object to you making your own drugs and selling them to his customers?'

'He'll be bloody furious if he finds out and if he does we'll have a bloody big guy called Dozer calling on us which is why you must be particularly careful when distributing them. For God's sake, you don't tell anybody where you got them from and you make sure you're not followed back here.'

'I get it, Reg. I take the biggest risk of being arrested by the police or having my head bashed in by the local mafia while you remain safely tucked away in this godforsaken back garden.'

'Put that way it does sound a little trickier for you than for me,' Reg said as he slowly nodded his head. Gerald grunted with a grim look on his face, took one last look at all the dangerous chemicals littering the greenhouse, shook his head at Reg and stormed out to abandon his new career and cycle back home. It looked like mum would be coming home after all.

It was only a week later that he read in a local newspaper of a large explosion behind the old gasworks that completely destroyed a semi-detached house, a greenhouse and a large patch of wild sunflowers. Even though nobody was hurt the detonation and resultant destruction to property was heard and felt a mile away and was initially believed to be the result of a major gas leak even though all the houses in Delphinium Road had electricity.

What wasn't mentioned in the news item was that three people were affected by the blast; these were two slightly scorched men and a smoking bag-lady who squeamish paramedics refused to handle without gloves. Furthermore, a large black and white cat had been launched into the air to land safely with claws unsheathed on the head of a bald gardener who was mowing his lawn four gardens away. They had all been reduced to a homeless state again. There was no mention of a laboratory, drug-making equipment or anyone called Reginald Barnett. He, it would seem, had disappeared completely.

Gerald put the paper down with a sigh and tried to think of new ways of making twenty-three thousand pounds and seventy pence.

CHAPTER 2

Yet another unfortunate beginning.

AT PRECISELY THREE O'CLOCK, three days after Elizabeth Shank's seventeenth birthday, her formal education came to an abrupt end and her path through life took a totally unexpected and sinful direction. She hadn't been expelled for any of the usual reasons like smoking hash, reading pornographic literature or inappropriately touching the science mistress – Miss Plath had only recently come out as a lesbian and the head mistress was currently considering whether to ask her to leave or to breakfast – the prime reason for terminating Elizabeth's analytical chemistry, French and media studies was simply the cessation of her college fees; the teenager could no longer be kept in Clattenburg College for Young Ladies for one reason only; her two parent family had, without giving her any prior notice, suddenly become one parent.

Mr Brian Shanks, her father and chief brewer at Hardings Ales had, at that ill-fated hour of three, placed his size ten rubber-soled shoe on an inoffensive little member of the *Cannabaceae* family of hemps, commonly known as hops. With arms flailing he slipped wildly on the overhead catwalk before performing a perfect swallow dive into the new seven-thousand litre fermentation tank. This had only recently been installed at the brewery after being purchased from a German manufacturer in Munich for nineteen-thousand euros. Until that precise moment in time, when their doomed brewer disappeared beneath the thick foam, it had been the company's pride and joy.

On that very same joyless day, soon after the unfortunate man reeking of wort had been unceremoniously gaffed, fished out through the top access by fellow workers, rushed to the nearest hospital, briefly examined and sent on to the morgue Mr Cyril Partridge, who had been busily 'sparging the wort', was also unceremoniously rushed to the boardroom.

The moment the managing director of Harding's Ales had heard that his Chief Brewer could no longer brew he knew he would need a scapegoat to answer any questions on health and safety should they be raised by the coroner. He called an emergency meeting of the Board and it was put to the assembled directors that this would be the right time for their Senior Sparger to be given more responsibility. This was immediately seconded and the subsequent vote unaminously promoted Cyril Partridge to Chief Brewer and the company's official Can-Carrier.

To justify the directors' faith in their choice, Partridge, without bothering to do any laboratory studies of the cooling and partially hopped wort, revealed his derisory knowledge of biological safety matters by declaring that there was absolutely no reason to drain and sterilise the fermentation tank. This decision would undoubtedly have been challenged by Mr Shanks, if the man were still alive to do so, but as he was regrettably absent from the meeting Partridge was able to set a lot of heads nodding around the boardroom table for his course of action would undoubtedly save the company a goodly sum of money.

Partridge further explained, in his newly acquired white-collar tone of voice, that apart from drowning the careless and rather slipshod Chief Brewer – some chuckles from two or three of the directors – the alcohol in the wort had attained a high enough ABV level to destroy any dangerous bacterium. Partridge did not know this for a fact for he hadn't tested the wort with a hydrometer but the company directors weren't to know this and burst into applause and endorsed his decision with one voice provided news of this course of action would never reach the ears of the press or, in any other way, become public knowledge.

What Partridge could not possibly have known however was that the shock of finding himself airborne and plunging into tepid wort with his mouth wide open was so great that it caused Mr Shanks to lose total control of his large intestine and sphincter with calamitous results. Three weeks later those results became very evident when there was a sudden outbreak of *E.coli* poisoning across the county and even further afield. The origin of this rather unpleasant bacterial outbreak was a complete mystery and, despite extensive testing of all food types by the Department of Health, the deaths of a plumber, hairdresser and life insurance agent, who had never bothered to take out any insurance on himself, were never attributed to the county's finest ales.

Never had Harding's Brown Ale – *Made to a 150 year old Secret Recipe* – been more aptly described on its barrels.

On the demise of Mr Brian Shanks, Elizabeth's mother, who was a children's piano teacher of mediocre ability had been compelled to take a job as a waitress come barmaid at The Old Pig and Whistle; this didn't compensate for the loss of her dead husband's income. It was suggested by some members of the Board that the Shanks family should be held responsible and sued for the cost of production downtime but this was overruled when the financial condition of the widow was revealed. We must always consider the company's image the Public Relations executive added which set heads nodding again.

Mr Shank's fervent belief that *life-insurance was just a bloody capitalist trick to squeeze working people for every penny they had* meant Alice Shanks had no hope of any extra pennies for herself.

At the inquest the coroner also ruled, after a pejorative testimony given by Cyril Partridge, that it was a freak accident brought about by the carelessness of the deceased and that Hardings Ales could not be held legally or financially culpable. Without any insurance payout or compensation from the overly gleeful board of directors and only a pittance from her widow's pension, Alice soon found she had to work double shifts and sleep a lot less to barely make ends, if she could find them, meet.

Customer tips from waitressing meant she was able to earn a little more than from teaching six-year old wannabe contestants for BGT – *Britain's Got Talent* – but considerably less than the sum required to meet the mortgage repayments and the daily bottle of gin she had begun drinking since Brian had downed his last, long drink. Working in a public house helped with the latter expense as she only needed to purchase one small bottle of spirit for a nightcap on arriving home. During the day she furtively kept herself topped up from the optics. Naturally this resulted in Alice finishing the day in a rather inebriated condition and she soon became unsurprisingly generous with her spirit measures. It was only human nature for the regular customers to take advantage of her condition by changing from half pints of beer to hard liquor as the evening wore on.

As a child Alice had been raised by strict, God-fearing parents who had both died pure in spirit – not of the alcoholic kind – and penniless in purse. Sundays had always been strictly observed with fasting, morning services in church and evening prayers in the living room after listening to *Songs of Praise* on the radio.

In her early teens the unsuccessful fumblings of adolescent boys behind the school cricket pavillion had left Alice confused and ill-informed on the correct sexual procedures and it was a number of years later before Mr Shanks became the only person to know Alice in the full biblical sense. The first clumsy moments when she painfully lost her maidenhood – and all dreams of romantic love – occurred on their wedding night and thereafter every Friday night, when the bedroom light had been blushingly extinguished. Why it had to be Friday was never explained to her but the concurrence with religiously eaten fish, and only fish on that day, may have had something to do with Mr Shanks' choice of time for coitus; he always preceded each climactic end by gasping; *with what you're about to receive may the Lord make you truly fertile.* The man wasn't averse to changing the words of a prayer to achieve his goal of a son. When Alice finally revealed she was pregnant he no longer felt the need to say grace and all physical contact was terminated with his wife until the child was born. On seeing that certain dangly bits were absent on the infant he resumed saying grace on Friday nights but without success.

Now that Alice was a widow, and a reasonably attractive middle-aged widow with woman's needs, she had reached a crossroad that could either strengthen or undermine her deep-rooted moral upbringing. Unfortunately, without her husband's constant lectures on God's will and how it should be done Alice ignored all signposts and raced down the wrong road, tripped over a secular thought and allowed the Devil to catch up with her. As was expected of his sort, he directed her along the iniquitous path on which she should travel and in no time at all Alice found herself hopelessly lost, along with all the inhibitions her parents and husband had branded onto her mind.

Long after the *last orders* bell, when the inebriated were forced to stumble out of the pub and the doors bolted behind them, one of Alice's principal tasks was to clean the guest rooms that had been vacated during the day. It was only three weeks after the death of her husband and two weeks since starting work at the pub that something stirred in the widow, something she hadn't felt since the last time Brian had said Friday night grace in the darkened bedroom. It was a familiar physical stirring that had been aroused by one of the last drinkers to leave; he was a ruggedly handsome man who had occasionally given her a knowing eye and as she watched the broad-shouldered farm worker leave she felt a strong need for the touch of a man again; preferably one who didn't need a prayer to gain an erection.

Alice had been tripped and the Devil – or was it the landlord of the Old Pig and Whistle – led her to discover that any empty guest room upstairs could become a discreet way to earn the extra money she so desperately needed; money that would help her send Elizabeth back to Clattenburg College for Young Ladies.

It was not long after hiring Alice that Mr Entwhistle, the publican, began making a point of personally checking her work upstairs. His love of beer, preferably Harding's brown ale, had resulted in a pot bellied, constantly sweating, hirsute caricature of a man who was commonly known as Pigwhistle by the women he had known intimately.

It didn't take long for this malodorous man to learn through casual pub gossip that Alice was in dire financial trouble and it was in room number two that he finally tore down her last moral barricade, as well as her underwear, to seduce her with inordinate gusto. Mentioning a sum of money that Alice calculated would pay her electricity bill for a month had been his opening gambit to overcome any opposition to his advances and the simple act of opening his pig skin wallet opened her legs. Matching the rythmn of the old pub sign hanging outside the window, that coincidently squealed like a piglet when the wind was blowing, Entwhistle was soon snuffling, snorting, grunting and living up to his nickname until he was physically and financially spent to the tune of fifty-pounds; his customers, oblivious to this seduction of their favourite barmaid, unsteadily weaved their way home singing her praises while she moaned her downfall into the pillow.

It soon became clear that no matter how often she performed horizontally for the beer-reeking landlord Alice's income still didn't meet the costs in running such a large house. Even inviting the muscular farmhand up the stairs for greater intimacy than a knowing eye failed to meet all her monthly bills; although she readily agreed with herself that the physical experience was something to remember. However, college was an expense she couldn't possibly afford and she was compelled to make the painful decision to end her daughter's education and put her to work; this could help satisfy the stream of final demands that frequently flowed into the letterbox.

Thanks to her youth and attractive appearance Elizabeth soon had job offers from all sectors of the market; this included a pizzeria, a cancer charity shop, the local bank and a rather steamy massage parlour. She had seen the latter pinned to a newsagent's notice board and in her innocence had phoned for an interview. She was told to come immediately to the parlour, which after numerous directions from pedestrians who winked at her in a rather strange manner, she found was in a narrow alley that led down to the sluggishly moving river. This was a part of the town unknown to Elizabeth and the leers of two men idly standing either side of the door, watching her lithe legs striding youthfully towards them beneath a thin cotton dress, gave her a moment of anxiety which was soon replaced by an unexplained shiver of excitement as she pressed the button beneath the *Eden Health Studio* etched brass nameplate.

The amount of a possible weekly wage whispered into Elizabeth's ear by the middle-aged, garlic-breathed manager with designer stubble was considerably higher than those offered by the other businesses who had already interviewed her. His unsubtle hints about additional money that could be earned by convincing her clients to try the expensive 'extras', less *Eden Health Studio's* thirty-five percent commission, made it curiously attractive yet mysteriously repulsive at the same time. When Elizabeth, in all her innocence, revealed her age the manager began to repeat the number *seventeen* beneath his breath whilst perspiring heavily. As he rested his hand on Elizabeth's thigh and mopped his brow the manager tried to convince her to join his team of girls by promising she would make a fortune from gentlemen who regularly patronised the establishment and had a particular taste for young girls. Elizabeth gently removed his hand and said she would think about it and left as the manager was asking her to audition for the vacancy; *in any position you choose,* he said. Now clearly understanding the man's real intentions Elizabeth ran down the corridor and out of the building with the knowing chuckles of the men at the door floating behind like tempting demonic satyrs.

Elizabeth's mother was appalled when told about the lecherous behaviour of the manager. Contrary to her own immoral after-hours activities at The Pig and Whistle she sat the girl down and repeated one of her own mother's Calvanistic lectures. This repeatedly embodied the merit of keeping the knees tightly held together until a reasonably solvent, good-looking man of strong moral and religious fortitude had said the words *I do.*

Alice concluded by telling her daughter that she could meet just as many, if not more wealthier clients whilst working in a bank. She explained there was a slim chance that these same men may also frequent the *Eden Health Studio* but when doing business in the bank they would at least be fully clothed with hands clutching money and not Elizabeth's derrière.

Alice ended her lecture with the thought that although bankers may currently be disliked by everyone and believed to be as corrupt as the girls in the massage parlour Elizabeth would nevertheless be involved in a completely legal, tax-paying occupation with no risk of pregnancy or sexually transmitted diseases.

Elizabeth was old enough to appreciate the wisdom of her mother's words and although she had always found algebraic equations difficult to understand, let alone answer, and that she was desperately shy in the company of strangers – this was due to a coughing fit when she was eleven that caused her to wet herself during a friend's birthday party – she decided to take the job at Crampton Bank.

These two worries about working in a bank as a teller soon faded to the back of her mind when the manager, Mr Percival Barnett, told her during the interview that she would be a perfect bank employee and explained to Elizabeth that being in direct contact with people and working with money on a daily basis would soon overcome any lack of skill and personal fears. Barnett didn't add that he had also found Elizabeth more desirable than Cynthia Witherspoon who had been the same age and whose position Elizabeth was now taking at the main counter. She was also a great deal more appealing than the women at the *Eden Health Studio*.

It would seem that Cynthia Witherspoon had suddenly been embarrassed by an unexpected pregnancy which unbeknown to her was due to a condom being stretched far beyond its use-by-date. The unfortunate mother-to-be steadfastly refused to tell her parents who the father was. This was due to the perverse pleasure she gained from blackmailing Mr Percival Barnett for a monthly sum he could just afford without alerting his wife; Mrs Barnett rarely checked their joint banking account. It was from a minor sense of guilt over Cynthia and a major stirring of desire for a possible carnal replacement that Barnett immediately hired Elizabeth on a slightly higher salary scale than the position and her lack of experience merited. He planned to rectify the latter failing in the filing room at the earliest possible opportunity.

Neither Mrs Shanks or her daughter possessed a driving licence which meant the sky-blue Ford Fiesta was destined to remain in the garage to depreciate in value and gather several layers of dust. To reduce the long commute to the bank Elizabeth found a bedsit on the top floor of what was once a Victorian school for mentally-disadvantaged children. Despite the lack of any planning permission the large loft had been converted into three living quarters and was only an eight-minute bus ride from the bank. Elizabeth was attracted by the low rent but soon discovered she had to climb four storeys to her tiny living room, coffin-sized bedroom (with a single and remarkably hard mattress) and the bathroom. This was a tiny room that she shared with two other tenants on the same floor.

One was a middle-aged insurance agent who, despite the wall-banging by his immediate neighbour, spent most evenings listening to Verdi operas at full volume. The wall-banger was short, moustachioed like Hitler and unashamedly revealed to all and sundry that he was a salesman in ladies erotic underwear. Unknown to all who met him he took secret pleasure when wearing his company's products. As he was squeezing past Elizabeth in the narrow passage one morning he asked in a whisper if she would like to model the latest crotchless samples he had in his room. Elizabeth told him what he could do with the loofah he was holding and slammed the bathroom door in his face.

Like her enforced routine at school Elizabeth rose at six forty-five without the need of an alarm clock and wearing her favourite white slippers with pink pompoms, she brewed coffee instantly, toasted bread darkly and spread marmalade thickly before smothering herself in a thick, terry-towel dressing gown. After the meagre breakfast, the seven o'clock news and the shipping forecast she went and used the draughty bathroom at the end of the corridor. One tap spurted hot water from a geriatric gas boiler mounted over the end of an old roll-top bath. The enamel was a leprous colour of black and brown stains caused by water from corroded iron pipes. If the pilot light in the boiler went out there would be a panic filled period finding a dry match with wet, soapy hands. On successfully striking it and offering the flame to the collecting gas around the burner there would follow a small ear-popping explosion and after a long, expectant silence a thick clod of soot would suddenly plop into the end of the bath; this would rapidly spread on the surface and creep towards the horrified bather who was forced to retreat before leaping out of the bath to avoid the black, incoming tide.

Three ceramic bowls, also chipped, were labelled with a magic marker and used by each tenant to carry water to the small washbasin beneath the window that overlooked the local council dog pound. Elizabeth didn't mind the odd pit bull terrier, Bohemian shepherd or friendly looking mongrel looking up at her perky breasts but her window was in turn overlooked by rows of voyeuristic dark windows in the towering tenement beyond. It was after spotting the occasional glint of binocular lenses that she regained her modesty by draping a stained tea towel over the naked curtain rail.

Whenever Elizabeth found the ceramic lock on the door reading *Occupied* there was a good chance she would be late for work for the other two tenants always took an inordinate length of time with their ablutions. If *Vacant* showed, she was able to keep to her timetable by brushing her teeth in two minutes, washing her hair in six and showering in the bath for five (sans clods of soot) using her favourite herbal bodywash. After making sure the closet transvestite salesman wasn't lurking in the passage Elizabeth returned to her room to dry and brush her short hair to the same style she had been using since first attending Clattenburg College for Young Women.

When the bathroom was unoccupied she was able to finish her toiletry in double quick time and the brief bus journey would end outside Crampton Bank, in the High Street, at six minutes to eight precisely. Elizabeth would then wait with four other staff members for the bank manager to arrive. Mr Percival Barnett drove an old black Vauxhall that had never been serviced and although this saved him a great deal of money it also resulted in the vehicle frequently emitting a large cloud of black smoke. This was accompanied by spasmodic backfiring that set dogs howling and alerted shop and business owners that the bank would be open in fifty-five minutes precisely.

Barnett was not the nicest of bankers for he was one of those gluttonous managers who tended to be over generous when giving loans to businessmen who gave gifts and entertained him at the most expensive restaurants. In fact, he had been so liberal over the last fiscal year that Head Office was covertly investigating whether he had any financial interests in the recipient companies.

Apart from rich food Barnett had one other shortcoming, his uncontrollable libido and Elizabeth's curves and pretty looks convinced him that the young woman would more than satisfy Crampton Bank's needs as well as his own. He had no sense of guilt and only felt stirring below the waist when it came to women and, if she was very young, rather than suppressing his urge to seek pleasure, it further increased his carnal interest.

Excessive makeup was frowned upon in the bank and consequently it took the female staff very little time to touch up during the day. However, Mr Barnett wanted Elizabeth to look more grown-up than she was and encouraged her to exceed the limitations set out in the Crampton Bank's rule book that was entitled; *Correct Behaviour for Female Staff.* This sexist catalogue of rules had been compiled in the London head office by a junior clerk who, being gay from an early age, had very little experience of the opposite sex and contained forty-two rules which, along with number five headed, *Use Very Little Makeup*, accompanied by illustrative examples, also included a ban on gum chewing, the proper disposal of sanitary products, the correct skirt length and a prohibition on cleavage-revealing tops. Naturally, any cross-gender familiarity that was not work related would result in instant dismissal. Unsurprisingly, this rule, the last in the book and printed in bold capital letters, didn't apply to Mr Barnett who had immediately begun his programme of seduction by patting Elizabeth in an overtly familiar manner at every opportunity.

Elizabeth had been morally influenced throughout her childhood by her mother and her exceptionally devout grandmother and had always abided by the Shank's knees-together edict; even when the science mistress tried it once. She seethed on every occasion she was touched by Barnett but as a new and very innocent employee she believed this sexual harassment was normal behaviour in an adult place of work and possibly the only way to guarantee permanent employment and possible promotion.

The other staff members who arrived early and waited outside the bank with Elizabeth were Mr Roger Wilton; he was head cashier and nearing retirement, Ms Marjorie Tander, who was a teller like Elizabeth but thirty-seven years wiser and twenty two inches wider. Mr Bernard Sisson from Foreign Exchange was of an indeterminate age and sexual preference. Arthur Watts, the bank's sole security guard was, like Mr Wilton, greying at the temples and soon to be discharged. It had always been company policy to dismiss staff for reasons of incompetence or tardiness before entitlement to a full company pension. Mr Wilton was frequently ten minutes late no matter how many times Mr Barnett told him that professional bank security had to be in place before the doors were even opened to let in the staff and therefore Crampton Bank had a good case for dismissal. This branch of the bank was rather small and, as the day revealed, not very well organised.

After a never-ending queue of black, white, yellow, sallow, fat, thin, spotty, scowling faces and one particular year of soul destroying tedium that

Elizabeth arrived home to find that her mother had upped and died from a sudden cessation of the heart. Finding she was financially embarrassed by the meagre salary that couldn't stretch to pay the mortgage as well as the rent on her bedsit Elizabeth was forced to sell the family home and put the Fiesta in a friend's lock-up garage for a rainy day. The outstanding mortgage and death duties was paid and she was left with very little capital.

The funeral was attended by some of the men from the brewery who knew her husband; a broad shouldered and rather glum farm worker, an obese publican who sweated all through the service and a few drunkards from the Old Pig and Whistle who would only miss her large spirit measures. Most had come expecting a good feast and beer after the interment but left early on discovering there was only three plates of egg and cress sandwiches and a pot of Earl Grey tea. Whilst mouthing condolences and sympathetic platitudes Mr Entwhistle furtively pressed a sweat stained envelope containing money into Elizabeth's hand. She didn't know what it was for and didn't bother to ask for the sum was quite considerable and would comfortably cover the cost of laying her mother in the cemetery; something Entwhistle had done on numerous occasions himself.

When all the egg and cress sandwiches were gone and the mourners had filed out of the Sea Scouts hall that had been hired for the occasion, Elizabeth returned to Strawberry Close with Ruby Wexford, her landlady. She was a rather shapely woman who not only had Elizabeth as a tenant but four men she regularly entertained in the early hours of the morning. Elizabeth's bedroom was directly over Ruby's and on many occasions she was able to hear, over one or another of Verdi's overtures, bedsprings protesting *accelerendo*, accompanied by a chorus of giggles, groans and moans. Far from exciting the listener this tended to emphasise the strange feelings in Elizabeth that were more akin to a cold emptiness than any hot passion. This empty sensation grew stronger with each passing day as she was forced to return after work to sit in the silence of the bedsit until squeaking springs began their nocturnal rhythm.

Elizabeth had resisted the bank manager's persistent groping for she instinctively knew that succumbing and losing her virginity to the much older, lecherous man would be degrading and an insult to her mother's memory. What's more she learnt from Majorie, the teller working at the next counter, that Cynthia Witherspoon had not been a willing particpant in the creation of her baby. Over a cup of tea in the staff room Majorie described how she had been in the filing room at the time of the conception and heard violent scuffling, tearing of cotton and Cynthia's pathetic cries coming from the next aisle. Waving a biscuit in the air she warned Elizabeth about being alone in any room with a man who held the power of employment or unemployment over the willingness of every female staff member.

In the course of a working day Elizabeth met and spoke on average to forty-six customers and yet was still unable to strike up a meaningful conversation that would lead to something more personally exciting. Initially, she was a little disheartened by her loneliness but then she slowly sank into a deeper, depressive state after each customer curtly thanked her and walked away tucking their crisp banknotes into a wallet or purse as they hurried back into their busy lives. She would, with great enthusiasm, tell the younger men to 'have a nice day' but this rarely evoked anymore than the curt lift of an eyebrow and an echo of the same throwaway words.

It was the day following her twentieth birthday, which Elizabeth celebrated alone by downing a whole bottle of Pinot Grigio in her bedroom, when her whole life was turned topsy-turvy and some say took a turn for the better. However, most people, if they had known the facts, may have said that it was the time when she made the biggest mistake of her life and possibly become a danger to herself and others. Nevertheless, Elizabeth thought it was a wonderful day for it was the day when her depression lifted and life had meaning again.

This was pure assumption on the poor girl's part for Elizabeth would soon find she would lose her heart to a very strange stranger indeed.

CHAPTER 3

CRAMPTON BANK WAS EXPERIENCING a slow Tuesday and there were only six customers at the counter when Mr Percival Barnett imperiously strode across the marble lobby and used his fingerprint to enter the bank's inner sanctum. He walked past the tellers, patting Elizabeth on the behind as he went by and entered his office where he took a bottle of twelve-year-old malt whisky from a desk drawer, poured a capful, downed it and replaced the bottle. He would perform this ritual every thirty minutes until noon when, as was his other habit, he would cross the street to the King's Head for two or three decent measures in a proper crystal tumbler to accompany his steak and mushroom pie.

Customers who frequently used the bank for commercial reasons were aware of his daily weakness and would only apply for business loans in the afternoon when Barnett was more likely to be in one of his mellower moods. Head Office was also unaware that a daily intake of alcohol and the occasional complimentary slap-up lunch at the Cosmopolitan Hotel followed by Napoleon brandy and a fine Cuban cigar were the reasons why this particular branch manager approved so many unsecured loans.

Barnett's alcohol dependency had it's origin when Doreen, his wife, walked out on him after twenty-three years of marriage. There had been a growing number of circumstances that motivated Doreen's sudden departure from hearth and home.

The first was when she had caught him watching a pornographic film on his computer screen while totally naked nude and had invited her to join him in imitating what was being colourfully demonstrated in high definition.

After the first shock had passed Doreen became aroused by the situation and had stripped completely. She was in the middle of performing what might pass for, in some lower-class nightclubs, an erotic dance routine when the second circumstance became clear, literally; Percival had forgotten to close the curtains and the Walkers, their sanctimonious neighbours who had decided to pay them a visit were staring at Doreen's cavorting nudity with eyes that could only be best described as well and truly goggled.

The curtains were snapped shut and there followed a furious argument interrupted by a very brief phone call that proved to be the third circumstance that broke the camel's back. The poorly disguised voice of Roger Wilton, Crampton's head cashier, informed Doreen through a grubby handkerchief stretched over the phone that Cynthia Witherspoon was putting on a few pounds due to her husband's energetic activities in the bank's file room.

Doreen had only paused long enough to get dressed, pack a bag and shred Percivals best shirts and undershorts with a pair of pinking shears. Apart from destroying her husband's wardrobe while waiting for the taxi Doreen had also appropriated the joint account chequebook and credit cards.

As Reginald had completed his obligatory community service and left home, taking his Groov-E boom box and a backpack filled with Metallica, Iron Maiden, Judas Priest and Black Sabbath, it left Percival Barnett in a silent house with the privacy to do as he wished without any recrimination from members of his family. His first act on arriving home from work every day was to close the curtains in the living room to avoid giving another free show to the Walkers. He then spent his evenings washing pizzas down with six packs of beer while watching one of the many DVDs he had purchased from a specialist shop in the seedier part of Soho.

It soon became normal practice to take one of the films to his office where his personal laptop and a few capfuls of 12-year-old whisky enabled him to fantasize Elizabeth in the leading role. Barnett became more and more determined to get to know the young woman in the Biblical sense and as the level in the whisky bottle dropped he grew more confident at the thought.

While Percival daydreamed about his imminent conquest the object of his carnal arousal was serving a sad-faced young man with dark brown hair and hazel eyes. She had noted his appearance from the very first moment he entered the bank. Despite his youth he walked like a much older man who carried the cares of a lifetime on his shoulders as he crossed the lobby to the only available teller. When the dejected figure stopped before Elizabeth she was tempted to ask why he was so depressed but knew it would be highly offensive to address a customer so informally and if Mr Wilton overheard her she could be dismissed.

'Good morning, sir, how can I help you?' she asked cheerfully in an effort to put a smile on his long face.

'I wish to ask for a bank loan, whom do I see about it . . . ' he leant forward to read the bank nametag on her regulation white blouse, ' . . . Miss Shanks?'

'That would be Mr Barnett, the manager,' she replied with a smile. 'He deals with all matters concerning loans.'

'Can I see him?'

'If you'd like to wait one moment I'll go and see if he's free.' Elizabeth stood up and went to knock on Barnett's door. All staff had been instructed to wait until they were asked to enter before opening the door. A young teller, Tony Simpson, had been dismissed after walking in without waiting for permission and caught Barnett with his hand under Cynthia Witherspoon's dress. Nobody knew what Tony had seen but most made their own guesses when Cynthia left the bank a few months later with a slightly swollen belly.

Elizabeth emerged after a couple of minutes followed by the manager who went into the interview room. The depressed young man was shown into the same room and Elizabeth, once more making an effort to remove the creases on his forehead, offered him tea or coffee. He shook his head and Barnett's hand at the same time and sat down. When Elizabeth had left the office the manager took a sheaf of forms from the drawer and with pen poised began his questioning.

'I understand you wish to make a loan from Crampton Bank, Mr errrr,' he paused waiting for the young man to fill in the blank gap.

'Latimer, Gerald Latimer,' Gerald said and waited.

'You're a customer of this bank, Mr Latimer?' Barnett looked the young man up and down and then up again.

'Yes.'

'And you'd like to make a loan?'

'Yes.'

'For how much, Mr Latimer?'

'Twenty-three thousand pounds and seventy-pence.'

Barnett gulped and sat more upright. 'For what reason?'

'To keep my mother in Shady Trees nursing home for a year.'

'A very admirable objective, Mr Latimer, and can I assume that in a year's time you'll want another twenty-three thousand pounds and seventy-pence plus the three percent CPI?'

'Most probably.'

'And that would be after you've paid off the first loan within the year?'

'Possibly.' This was said with a certain amount of hesitancy.

'Where are you currently employed and what do you do for a living, Mr Latimer?'

'I'm not and I don't do anything at the moment.'

'Ah, so what kind of collateral will you put up to secure this rather sizeable loan?'

'Collateral?' Barnett was scrolling through accounts on the computer. 'You obviously cannot use what you have deposited in this bank so far as that is only a grand total of five pounds and twenty three pence.'

'I am hoping to add to that very soon.'

'Do you have an insurance policy . . . pension . . . property?'

'No . . . no . . . and my home is in my mother's name.'

Percival Barnett looked around the office, trying to find the hidden cameras that would reveal he was the subject of a practical joke but when he was unable to see any he lost his temper. He'd only had a chance to down three capfuls of single malt and watch ten minutes of his favourite film since arriving at the bank and he was far, far, far from mellow.

'Do you expect any bank to advance twenty-three thousand pounds and seventy-pence to anyone who walks in off the street, has a current account worth five pounds and twenty three pence, is unemployed, has no collateral and cannot guarantee repaying the first loan before wanting another of the same amount?'

Barnett had ticked off the salient points on his fingers and was searching for another point to start on his other hand when Gerald answered. Unlike the canny businessmen who used Crampton Bank and knew precisely what time in the afternoon would be best to gain a sympathetic ear on borrowing money Gerald simply said, 'Yes.'

Barnett shot to his feet and pointed to the door. 'Get out, Latimer, if that's really your name. I don't appreciate practical jokes so get out before I call the police and have you locked up.' His countenance had changed from a mild pink to wild beetroot. 'You've got a damnable nerve entering my bank and asking for a loan. . . . ' He didn't get any further for Gerald had left the room and closed the door behind him. Looking even more dejected Gerald crossed to where Elizabeth had just finished with a customer and shook his head.

'I didn't know you had to give something to the bank to get something back,' he said softly and Elizabeth immediately felt sorry for the good-looking man with the sad, brown eyes and no sense of finance; she had also looked at his account balance while he was with the manager.

'It's called security, sir,' she replied. 'The bank has to be assured that you can repay a loan, plus the interest, within the time period set.'

'Is there another bank in town I can ask?' Gerald inquired hopefully as he gazed into her long-lashed eyes. Rich auburn hair flowed down to frame the unusually symmetrical features of her pretty face.

'I'm sorry, sir, this is the only one and if there was another one they would undoubtedly insist on the same conditions as Crampton's.' Elizabeth glanced down when something glinting caught her eye and saw the signet ring with a tiny ruby set in gold. 'That's a nice signet ring, sir,' she said taking his hand and he felt his heart accelerate to one hundred beats per minute.

'It was my father's,' he croaked, without taking his eyes from her face, 'I was told it was the only thing that wasn't flattened to 0.8mm in thickness.'

Elizabeth was puzzled by his words but didn't ask what he meant.

Gerald noticed the little frown that gave her brow a very sexy appearance. 'I'll tell you the story of my life some other time but . . . ' he stopped for Barnett had stormed out of the interview room and was staring at Gerald and Elizabeth holding hands with eyes flashing dangerously. He pointed to the main door and Arthur Watts, noting the object of his boss's anger, tugged to straighten his uniform jacket and started to cross the lobby. Gerald didn't bother to wait to be escorted from the premises and after removing his hand he gave Elizabeth a brief smile, which pleasantly surprised her and sadly left the bank virtually penniless. He paused at a pawnbroker's window and fingered his father's ring for the briefest of moments before walking on. He would regret and, strangely enough, celebrate this decision later.

Gerald crossed the street, lured by the smell of charred beef and fried onions and stopped in the doorway of the fast food outlet while he checked his resources. Posters of heavily retouched pictures of meat patties and golden fries ganged up against the measly two pounds twenty-five pence in his trouser pocket to mock his raging hunger.

'Go in, I'll treat you,' a voice said at his shoulder and he turned to find the grinning face of Reginald. It was a face that had acquired four more rings and a tattoo of a skull on the left cheek since last seen in the greenhouse of forty-one Delphinium Road.

'My God, I thought you were dead,' Gerald gasped as he grabbed Reg's forearm to reassure himself that he wasn't hallucinating.

'Nah, I was walking back from the boozer and a good hundred yards from the front gate when the whole bloody shebang went up. It was great that I had my iPod 'cos I was listening to a Black Sabbath track just as a humungous cloud of yellow smoke shot up from where the greenhouse used to be. It was perfect and when the second blast shook the ground and the squat collapsed in flames I was belting out Metallica's *Fuel*.'

'I recall the local paper reporting that fiery missiles had been fired into the air to hit the old gas holder and set off pockets of trapped gas that had lingered in the main container since nineteen-fifty-six. There was a rumour that they were rockets and it was the work of terrorists.'

'Must have been some of the chemical flasks I had stored.'

'Now that I come to think of it there was always a whiff of something whenever I walked past that monstrosity but at the time I thought it was you.'

'Nah, it turns out there was still a thousand cubic feet that burnt beautifully until three fire engines spoilt the whole bloody effect by smothering it under acres of foam.'

'Never mind the gasometer, what about the other guys?'

'Ed, Sue and Monty were just leaving the house when it all happened. Big Ed thought his flight over the opposite house and landing in the canal was the result of a huge meth hit he'd just had. He only had a few burns and Sue's habit, whenever she went out, of wearing all her clothes at the same time helped to protect her from the splinters of flying glass. She bounced off the garden wall and only broke her left arm.'

'And Ali Monty?'

'Dead lucky 'cos he landed on the road just after the shock wave caused it to collapse. Monty fell into the main sewer and on finding he was unhurt, apart from a small cut on the cheek, he avoided his ex-wives from reading newspaper reports that he was still around by wading downstream for a good mile. He emerged at a primary screening tank in a purification works smelling like a herd of incontinent cows.'

Nobody saw Monty climb out of the tank, walk three hundred yards and steal a brand new Porsche off a dealer's forecourt. The owner had deservedly left the keys in the ignition when he went in to complain about a squeaking windscreen wiper. Although Monty's forty-one inch waist was a tight squeeze he was still able to put on three thousand pounds in traffic fines plus thirty-six points on the owner's license as he put distance between himself and the fire. Monty reeked of sewage all the way to London where he left the car on a double yellow line in Oxford Street. The traffic police had traced the vehicle's hair-raising progress by helicopter and the owner had the awkward task of explaining why he was racing at one hundred and thirty on the motorway and how his car came to be reeking of faeces.

After a casual stroll that turned many heads and twitched even more noses in Regent Street and Trafalgar Square Monty arrived back at his old dossing-down spot under Charing Cross Bridge where he was greeted like a returning crusader.

'It was fortunate that nobody was killed, Reg, but what caused the explosion?' Gerald asked.

They entered the brightly lit restaurant and joined the shortest queue.

'I worked it out later, Gerry. As it was starting to get a bit nippy I think I put the paraffin heater on before going for a drink. Well, it must have been too close to the six flasks of anhydrous hydrazine and naturally, when that went off so did the chloroform and every other bloody chemical I had; what are you going to eat?'

Gerald glanced at the backlit posters and opted for the quarter pounder with cheese and black coffee. 'You are buying, Reg, aren't you?' he asked and Reg reassured him that the meal was on him. When they were comfortably seated in a corner booth Gerald devoured the meal and idly stared at Reg's fries until the failed drug baron felt morally compelled to slide the plate over the table and lie, 'Dig in I'm full, Gerry.'

Gerald finished them before muttering, 'I'm dead broke, Reg, I only have two pounds and twenty-five pence to my name and I still have to find twenty-three thousand pounds and seventy pence by the end of the month.'

'That only gives you sixteen days.'

'Don't I know, mate, it looks like I'm going to have to care for and feed my mother and myself on two pounds twenty-fi . . .'

'Okay, I get it.'

'The bank chucked me out when I asked for a loan.'

'I'm not surprised, you can't rely on banks to help you out of a fix, you've gotta make your own money.' Reg lowered his voice to a whisper and leant over the table. 'There's a bloke I know who sets up real money-making jobs for a percentage.'

'Sets up jobs, is that what I think it is?'

'Yeah, he tells us where and when to go and for that we give him fifty percent of what the fence will flash for the goods.'

Gerald shivered. 'You're talking burglary.'

'Shhh, keep it down. If you're game we can go and see him tonight. Look, I'll give him a call now and see if he has anything for us.' Reg dialled and after a brief moment of murmuring and listening he began to smile until he hung up. 'Let's go,' he said with a wink as he slid out of the booth. 'He's got something that he reckons will be right up out street.'

Gerald also stood but with his normally rare nervous tic ticking like crazy in his left cheek whilst his face grew longer.

Wellington Street was a five-minute walk and both men were soon standing before the portico of a terraced Georgian residence in the Palladium style. There was the threat of rain in the air but the gentle glow of the setting sun gave the sandstone a pale, yellow hue that was warmly inviting, belying the nature of the business conducted within.

The door opened within seconds of the doorbell chiming and a man almost as wide as he was tall wearing a dark suit waved them into the front room. 'The boss'll see you now, Reggie,' he rasped from a throat that had been marinated far too long in brandy and cigar tar. He stared suspiciously at Gerald as they entered and approached the large desk behind which sat a contrastingly small man. He was roughly fifty years old and had a wide, shiny runway through his grey hair and a black Stalin moustache above pale wet lips. He was so thin he threatened to lose himself in the folds of his expensive mohair suit. Gerald was immediately conscious of the covert cruelty lurking within the man's steel-grey eyes. They weren't invited to sit and were obliged to remain standing.

'So you and your friend would like a job, Reg?' The ends of his bushy moustache fluttered playfully in contrast to the humourless voice.

'Yes, Mr Goldenstein.'

'And who is your associate?'

'Gerald, his name is Gerry and he can be trusted to keep his trap shut.'

There was a long silence as the little man fiddled with a gold cufflink before leaning forward to study Gerald from his tousled hair to the roughly scuffed shoes.

'I have a little thing I'd like you to do, Reg. Usual rate is sixty percent?'

The intake of breath by Reg revealed his surprise. 'The *usual* rate has always been forty percent, Mr Goldenstein'

Gerald watched the big man slowly and wordlessly move to stand beside his miniscule employer with one large hand buried deep in his jacket pocket. The other toyed with a large medallion hanging by a gold chain around his thick neck.

'It's the cost of living, Reg,' Goldenstein said in a silky tone and went on to familiarize the two men on the current dismal state of the national economy; virtually non-existent interest rates, low inflation level, the rise in business taxes, incomes barely meeting pre-crises levels and the drop of international confidence in the United Kingdom before finishing up with a veiled threat. 'Expenses, they're going up all the time, Reg, but if you can get a better rate on return elsewhere then you are very welcome to leave without any hard feelings whatsoever.'

There was a deathly moment of silence as Reg considered what was meant by hard feelings. Did he mean 'hard' as in bulldozer buckets and was it really 'with' hard feelings. Reg made up his mind and replied through clenched jaws. 'We'll do the job at your new rate of sixty percent but would like you to kindly consider a different figure for any future jobs.'

'I will consider it but I cannot say that it will change, will I Dozer,' he laughed, looking up at his enforcer as he tossed a manila folder onto the desk.

Reg nodded, knowing that he would always have to accept Goldenstein's greedy nature and stopped the sliding folder before it went over the edge and onto the carpet.

'In there you'll find a job that is worth ten grand.' He stood and walked to the door. 'Take the item you retrieve from the first address on the piece of paper in the folder and deliver it to the second address in two days time. Dozer will pay you forty percent of what it's worth, if the item is still in perfect condition, less his own expenses.'

Even though he knew he was skating on thin ice Reg asked why Dozer would have to estimate the value of the item if it was already known. There was a long menacing silence and Dozer's hand twitched in his pocket before Goldenstein informed Reg coldly that Dozer had to make sure the item had not be damaged and deduct his own travel expenses and various other incidental expenses from their percentage. Then without another word he stood and left the room and Dozer indicated with a grunt that it was now time for them to leave and get on with the task.

While walking towards the centre of town in the light drizzle which, according to Murphy's Law, had started the moment they stepped out of the front door, Gerald asked Reg why the bodyguard was called Dozer as his friend had previously warned him that it was Andrew Lawson. As they slowly became saturated Gerald learnt that the enforcer's favourite method of making troublesome people untroublesome was to bulldoze a hole, put the troublesome person in it and bulldoze the earth back in until all troubles disappeared. He was even known to pat the soil down with his lucky baseball bat as a final gesture of farewell. Gerald didn't comment but made a mental note not to be of any trouble to the man.

'What's the job?' Gerald asked when they arrived at his home and had changed into dry clothes and were sipping a weird concoction of five-year old Assam and Oolong. The leaves had been found on a top shelf and the penniless Gerald had grown to like the taste but Reg was finding it impossible to swallow without a large quantity of sugar.

Reg flipped the folder open and began to read to himself. He gave the most relevant details; these were to go to an address owned by an elderly man who lived alone and regularly drove to his office in Norwich every day. They also noted that a contract house cleaner arrived Thursday mornings at 8.30 a.m. and stayed until 1 p.m. at the very latest. Finally, they were to obtain a single bible page kept in a locked display cabinet in the library that was located on the ground floor.

'Does it say which page it is and whether it's from the Old or the New Testament?'

Reg read the note again this time aloud and he shook his head until he stumbled over a word he wasn't familiar with and read the word twice.

Gerald held his hand up to stop him from going on. 'Gutenberg, I've heard of that name,' he said and made a mental note to look it up at the public library. 'It's believed to be the first book printed with moveable type a very long time ago.'

We're taking a bloody big risk for a single book page, Reg thought. 'Four thousand pounds for a piece of paper, does he think we're morons or something?' he exclaimed.

Gerald ignored him for he knew that it must be worth a good deal more than the figure they'd been told, but he could only hazard a guess at how much more until he visited the library and had done a little research. Gerald picked up his raincoat and informed Reg where he was going but was told, in no uncertain terms that it would be a waste of his time. Gerald ignored the sulking man, which was now becoming a habit and left the house. Reg immediately took a small plastic bag of giggle weed from his pocket and smoked his last supply of Jamaican Gold until he was euphoric and thoroughly zoned out.

A middle-aged brunette and her work experience assistant were at the front desk stamping small stacks of books when Gerald entered the library. He enquired about the Gutenberg Bible and was told that all library copies were out on loan thanks to the Archbishop's impending visit to all local churches and directed Gerald to the Reference section and the three computer terminals. Muffled laughter followed him down the musty aisles that were lined with rarely read books but no rare books.

After five minutes he was able to fire up one of the computers and Google that the bible was first printed in 1450 and that the 1455 copies were known as the Mazarin Bible, or B42s. They had been highly praised at the time for their high aesthetic and artistic qualities and he also learnt that they had forty-two lines on each page and were amongst the most valuable books in the world. There were only twenty-two copies known to exist and that a single copy had been valued at between twenty and thirty million pounds. A single page had been bought at auction for fifty thousand pounds. Gerald calculated that it was a bloody sight more than forty percent of ten thousand pounds. He shut down the computer and left to hurry home and give Reg the news that he had to tell Goldenstein the figure was now fifty percent.

'You want me to tell *that* man that we'll only do the job if he gives us twenty five grand?' he shouted, still convinced that they should only take the agreed four thousand pounds despite being told the true value of a single page. His mind kept visualizing a yellow Caterpillar looming over him and he wasn't thinking of a nice furry, multi-legged adolescent butterfly.

Gerald went through a lengthy explanation that it represented fifty percent of what they would be owed and that it was almost exactly what he needed to pay the care home for another year and keep his mother from being evicted and returned home.

It was then Reg's turn to explain that one of the cardinal unwritten rules when working for people like Mr Goldenstein was that when they told you how much you'd get for a job then that, or possibly less, is what you'd get. If you wanted to be troublesome and argue about it then there was a very good chance that Dozer would be given permission to play with his big yellow toy in the nearby quarry.

'Then let's do the job and worry about the financial rewards afterwards.' Gerald said to put a stop to what had become an unwinnable argument. 'When we've got the page in hand we'll have another discussion before telephoning Mr Goldenstein,' Gerald summarized neatly and Reg reluctantly agreed with a curt nod.

The first problem the two men encountered was transport. They couldn't exactly take a taxi to the scene of their impending crime without increasing the risk of being caught. Gerald's father had driven a second hand Polo with dodgy brakes but he had been forced to sell that to raise some of the money required by Shady Trees. Reg suggested that they follow Monty's example and steal some form of transport that was easy to take but Gerald didn't think a bike would make such a good getaway vehicle. They immediately set off on their quest to find any car with its ignition key left in the lock and hit the jackpot only two hundred yards from Gerald's front door. It was a dark grey BMW 3 series and not only was the key in the ignition lock but both doors were wide open. In a flash Reg had slipped into the driver's seat and was waving to Gerald who was looking up the gravel drive to the house the car was parked outside. Two burly men were pounding on the door shouting something he couldn't quite make out.

'C'mon, Gerry!' Reg tried to shout in a quiet voice and Gerald was spurred to climb into the vehicle a split second before the car shot forward with screeching tyres. He looked back through the rear window and was in time to see the two men running into the road and waving their fists in the air before Reg slid the car round the first corner and put his foot down hard. Gerald sank back into the soft leather and buckled the seat belt as they swept through town and filtered onto the main road heading north.

Colchester was sixty-three miles away and they had only travelled two miles when Gerald slowly became aware of the huge, glowing dashboard that aggressively sat between him and Reg. It had a giant screen with two mini-screens on it and a side panel stacked with orange, green, red and blue buttons that glowed like a Christmas tree lights.

'Bloody hell, Reg, you've stolen a police car.'

'I know that now, mate, and incidentally, it's not *I* who stole a police car but *we* who stole a police car and it's a bloody good idea 'cos *we* can use the siren to clear the road if at any time *we* need to get a move on.' He had kept emphasizing *we* to clarify the point that they were now well and truly in it together, literally, and he laughed loudly.

Gerald told him that there would be an all points bulletin out within minutes and that they should ditch the vehicle as soon as possible but Reg argued that they should put as much distance as possible between them and the place where they nicked it. They had travelled twenty-five miles north on the A12 when a police car passed them going the other way. Gerald turned to watch the car fading into the distance before the blue and red lights started flashing and a cloud of pale blue smoke rose from braking tyres. He gave this latest update to Reg who nodded and took a right hand turn that sent them across four lanes and down a small street and into the wilds of the Essex countryside. They were entering Tiptree, home of the famous fruit jams, when Reg spotted a road sign for Colchester outside a supermarket car park. He drove in and left the police car unlocked with the door open to look for another careless driver. An Audi with a *Baby on Board* sign was ignored out of courtesy for any infant or infants being wheeled down the nappy and baby powder aisles and a Ford Mondeo chosen. Reg checked the Norfolk address, punched it into the sat-nav and found they were fifty miles away from the house they had to burgle. They pulled out of the car park just as the owner, a mother with a bawling three year old in tow, left the supermarket laden with groceries and found her Mondeo missing. She snapped at the child, telling him he couldn't have the box of Ferrero Rochas she had returned to the shelf for the umpteenth time and started dialling the police.

The partners in crime followed the directions given until an electronic voice that had a rather sexy timbre announced they had arrived and saw they were at the entrance to the grounds of a small estate. Wrought iron gates that had an obscure coat of arms in the centre were closed and the pillar to one side had a brass plate etched with *White Friars*.

They cruised slowly along the narrow country lane circling the high-walled property until they arrived at what could only have been the tradesmens' entrance. Reg stopped and they inspected the iron-gate set into the red brick wall and saw that it was locked, which Reg announced confidently could be picked in a matter of seconds. It was while they were standing by the gate that Gerald spotted a black shape rushing towards them and was able to jerk Reg back before ninety pounds of pure aggression slammed into the bars with jaws agape. The Doberman didn't bark but simply snapped his jaws together within millimetres of Reg's face before dropping to the ground where it stood with hackles raised and gums bared, revealing fangs that could puncture a rhino's backside.

'We need a pound of raw steak,' Gerald observed as the animal sat with its head cocked on one side eyeing the two men as though *they* were the juicy steaks he would prefer. Reg agreed and they drove on to the next village where they purchased enough sirloin from the butchers to feed a dozen man-eating Dobermans and a packet of rat poison from the handy hardware store across the road. Gerald objected to this purchase until Reg explained that a ninety-pound Doberman would finish the sirloin and be enjoying his second course wrapped in jeans long before they could get in and out again. Gerald shrugged and they drove back to the rear gate of the house. The sirloin was cut with a pocketknife and powder was applied liberally before closing the incision. Checking that the lane was clear he went to the gate and hit the bars with a rock before swiftly stepping back. Within seconds the same black shape raced towards him to crash into the old gate in a furry blizzard of flying foam and snarling fangs. Reg held out the bloody offering and the dog snapped and growled when unable to reach the meat no matter how hard he forced his jaws between the bars.

'For God's sake,' Gerald said and told Reg to get on with it. No sooner had the slab of sirloin thrown between the bars landed on the ground than the Doberman was upon it and they sat in the car and witnessed open-mouthed the animal tearing a two-pound steak apart in a matter of minutes. When the animal had gulped down the last morsel its head turned slowly and the almond shaped eyes fixed on the two occupants of the car as though expecting them to offer a nice piece of buttock or neck. They waited and waited and waited but the dog stood firm, apparently unaffected by the liberal dose of warfarin.

'Looks like he'll need another steak,' Reg observed as he generously dosed another large piece of meat and tossed it through the gate where, once more, it was pounced upon, swiftly torn to shreds and devoured. Once more they waited as the Doberman stared back at them with baleful eyes that never blinked until Gerald observed that the owner would be returning within the hour. It was as he made this warning that the Doberman swayed, closed its eyes, gave a small sigh and fell over. Gerald felt his eyes prickle as he looked down at the magnificent animal sprawled in the dust. It was a terrible deed they had done but it was essential that they gained entrance without losing any bits of their own vital anatomy.

Reg soon had the lock opened and they ran through the large garden and across an immaculate lawn to where the French windows opened out onto a back terrace. Reg worked a few miracles on four contact points before attacking the lock and entering the drawing room. Gerald followed, recalling that their destination was on the same level and they sped across the hallway and into what was clearly the library. Glass cabinets filled with Moroccan leather-bound tomes lined three walls and there was a single large display cabinet in the centre of the room with two books lying open beneath a protective glass cover. Gerald crossed to the customized cabinet and was amazed to see first editions of *Through the Looking Glass* and *The House at Pooh Corner*. The latter was opened at a page showing Pooh trying to distract bees whereas the other was opened at a page showing the Cheshire Cat grinning rather mysteriously at the two intruders.

Reg had gone to the other side of the sloping display case and was looking at Gerald with an inexplicable expression on his face. 'The one we want is on this side,' he said and added, 'and it isn't what we were told to get.'

Gerald walked around the large case and gasped for the single page they had been instructed to retrieve had multiplied into a 1455 first edition of the complete Gutenberg Bible that had to be worth millions.

'What now?' Reg whispered as he lifted the glass top and used the prop to hold it in place. 'Do we tear one page out or take half a dozen and make a bit on the side for ourselves?'

Gerald was horrified. 'You can't desecrate a book like this by ripping out pages,' he whispered as he reverently touched one of the illuminated decorations with a fingertip.

'Then what shall we do?' Reg asked as he closed the bible and lifted it out of the display case.

'We take the whole book you idiot. It'll keep my mum in Shady Trees for a very long time.' While Gerald was dancing a victory jig across the library a large black Mercedes was sweeping up the drive while a large black, and rather angry, Doberman was running towards the back door of the house.

CHAPTER 4

J UDGE GEORGE ATKINSON HAD caught the earlier train
due to a mistrial caused by an incompetent prosecution counsel failing
to disclose a prime witness to the defence. Even the traffic lights were in
his favour and the electronic sensor in the car opened the gates on his
approach to allow the black Mercedes S-Class to silently sweep up the drive
at a much earlier time than normal.

He was disappointed when Satan didn't bound round the house by
the time he had unlocked the front door for it was his Doberman's habit
to greet him on his arrival home. The judge was unaware that his dog was
preoccupied with savagely attacking the back door in the vain hope of
getting his teeth into the strangers who had locked him out. It was only
when the judge was hanging his hat and coat on the hallstand that he heard
Satan's ineffectual efforts to guard his master's property. He called out
as he walked down the hall and the furious scratching and pounding on
the solid oak door ceased. This silence was then followed by an almighty
crash and the door shivered on its hinges. Satan had used basic canine
intelligence to come to the conclusion that his master was now in the house
with two strangers and therefore in great danger.

The two strangers crept to the library door and peered into the hallway
just in time to see the portly figure of the judge in his grey pinstripe suit
striding towards the back door. They had heard the pounding on the
door and although they didn't know what was causing it they did know
it meant trouble. With the Gutenberg Bible clutched beneath one arm
Gerald sprinted to the front door and opened it at the same time as the
judge opened the back door. Both men saw a dark shadow leap into the

hall, knocking the judge to one side and streaking towards them. Reg slammed the door and felt the resounding impact of the 'deceased' dog on three inches of solid New Forest oak.

'He was dead, I'm sure he was dead,' he stuttered as Gerald ran across the drive to check the Mercedes and found it had been left unlocked. It must have the constitution of an elephant Reg assumed as he opened the passenger door. It was that or there had been two Doberman's and the other had been guarding the main gate. They men got in and as the car accelerated down the drive Gerald looked in the mirror in time to see the front door fly open and the resurrected canine bounding past his master to race after the car.

'Whatever it is his bitching mother must have mated with a greyhound,' Gerald said as he watched the animal gaining on them. Thanks to the judge's expensive gadget the heavy gates opened automatically and they screeched out onto the road to narrowly miss a No. 70 bus to Colchester. It was rather ironic that the Doberman, in closing the gap fast, was unable to stop in time to miss the bus and the double rear wheels of the thirty-eight thousand pound vehicle succeeded where diphacinone, bromodiolone and warfarin had failed.

Gerald assumed, incorrectly, that the owner of the bible would be alerting the police to the theft of the Mercedes and that they would have to get rid of it very soon. He accelerated and on spotting the next bus stop he parked in a side street. After a very brief argument that Reg lost, his jacket was wrapped around the heavy bible and they walked in the light rain to catch the approaching bus, the same vehicle that still had the vital parts of Satan wrapped round the rear axles.

It was on discovering that the only thing taken by the thieves was his much-venerated bible that the judge's lightly-held belief in forgiveness and true mercy for those less fortunate than himself went out of the window. As he stood at the open door looking down the long drive at Satan's hopeless chase he swore he would inflict a greater harm on the perpetrators than the fangs of Satan could ever do. The bible had been the result of a hunt on every continent and exploration in ten countries, questioning one rare book dealer after another for clues until he achieved success in a grubby sheesha café in Marrakesh. In a remote corner of the ancient souk George finally met a handsome Lebanese who had illegally acquired one of the last of the 1455 Mazarin Bibles.

The evenly-tanned man had crossed his hand-tailored slacks, sized up the podgy young man facing him whose eyes gleamed with religious fervor and promptly doubled the price. The gigolo, for that was his vocation, had brought his wealthy matron to the table who, having a devious sense of humour, decided to prolong the agony by tripling the original price. The couple was playing a game they knew the young man could never afford but decided to amuse themselves until the real buyer, a Vatican agent, arrived with his bank draft for thirty million euros. They kept teasing the young man until he realized what they were doing and that they never intended to give him the prize lying on the table between them. The all-purpose Swiss army knife, a birthday present from Aunt Phyllis, brought their tedious teasing to a satisfactory conclusion; not that the gigolo from Byblos or his older lover would have agreed. The corner chosen by the man from Lebanon had been sufficiently dark and smoky and the café adequately noisy to preclude any curiosity about a young man leaving his parents in a silent and motionless embrace.

George was at Menara airport with the bible safely stowed in his luggage when the two foreign tourists were discovered dead in the café. They were reported by the local radio as being the victims of a terrorist attack and police were put on full alert at bus terminals, train stations and airports three hours after George's flight had already taken off for Gatwick. He had been cleared by customs at both airports by wearing a clerical shirt and dog collar, a simple ploy George had used in various meetings with dealers in the far-east and South America, to lull them into a false sense of trust. The book was shown to the customs officials at Menara and Gatwick as his personal bible and despite being an elaborate and very expensive looking tome it was in fact a cheap facsimile that his parishioners had presented to him last Christmas.

On his arrival in London the book was placed in a safe deposit box and George Atkinson was able to finally focus on his career in law. In the graduate years that followed he completed and passed the Bar exam, was accepted for pupillage and practiced in chambers for a number of years. He married a young woman of twenty-two when he was fifty-four and was divorced twelve months later when she found he didn't want to regularly ski in Montreux, spend late nights in Annabel's nightclub or pop pills in the King's Road jazz clubs. To expedite matters she agreed to seduce the gardener, which she did with an enthusiasm suggesting it wasn't the first time she had enjoyed his carnal company, and name him as the co-respondent. It was not long after the decree absolute restored the barrister to bachelorhood that his good listening and communication skills were brought to the attention of the Judicial Appointments Commission and he was recommended for higher office.

At sixty-three, and by now more than podgy, Judge George Atkinson, forty years after his first successful hunt in Morocco, had been launched into another hunt to regain the exact same book. Although he was a man who lived by the letter of the law he was now suitably maddened to pay or do anything to recover the bible and to punish the thieves in a manner that befit their crime. George Atkinson was at heart a judge who constantly longed for the 'good old days' when capital punishment demonstrated the true power of a High Court Judge. He would regularly hold forth on this subject in the privacy of his private club in an attempt to gain converts from the other legal members. Most, no, all considered him to be politically dangerous and made sure they gave him a wide berth.

Having originally acquired the bible by a double act of murder that was never solved Atkinson was unable to go through the normal law-enforcement channels for fear awkward questions would arise. His library was the one room in the house that was restricted to everyone, including the cleaner, for the book was strictly reserved for his eyes only. It was his daily ritual, before retiring to bed, to lightly place his palms on the glass above the book and pray for forgiveness. He had performed this penance for more than thirty-nine years and had received not the pardon he craved but a visitation from two common thieves who had caused him more suffering. He was reminded of Gestas and Dismas the two common thieves crucified on either side of the Lord and the judge fell to his knees on the doorstep to pray. Would one of them be the good thief and be penitent when caught, he thought after closing his prayer with a plea for their speedy deaths and the safe return of his holy book.

'I'll crucify the buggers if they ever appear in my court,' he said aloud as he closed the door and went to the phone on the hallstand knowing full well they would never be legally punished. Rasmus Psomas answered the phone immediately and after he had been briefed he told the judge he would start putting out the word, assuring the judge that the two would be apprehended within twenty-four hours. The judge hung up and nodded his head for he knew that his man had never made a promise he couldn't keep.

Rasmus had been brought before him three years previously on a charge of 'accidentally' causing death in the pursuance of gain but a motion was made for the court to dismiss the Cause of Action when two vital witnesses failed to make an appearance. They had both suffered unfortunate accidents; one was the victim of a hit-and-run driver while pruning roses in her front garden and the other fell from the tenth floor of her apartment building while standing on the balcony in stiletto heels, supposedly adjusting her dish aerial.

The charge against the Greek had been that he demanded money from a shop owner and when refused had 'accidentally' discharged a weapon, a shotgun, which for unaccountable reasons had had its long barrels illegally shortened with a hacksaw. The witnesses had been two women who had run out of the shop when Rasmus began emptying the till. There were no other witnesses and two 'friends' of Rasmus were able to supply him with a watertight alibi. The judge also considered that the defense attorney appointed by the state had been patently inadequate in putting forward a proper case for his client's innocence. This may have been due to an envelope, stuffed with fifty pound notes, that was slipped into the barrister's letter box on the eve of the trial with a simple note that read 'He goes free. Or else'.

The jury was dismissed and from that day Rasmus was of the opinion that the judge was now his friend and, although it was never proved, the shooting of the shop owner and the fatal accidents were never attributed to the Greek.

This unspoken friendship became very useful for the times when the judge needed information or tasks carried that concerned the underworld and this was one of those times and one of those tasks. Rasmus immediately began contacting associates who could help hunt for the men who had robbed his 'best friend'. When he caught up with them he vowed to make a point of cutting off their privates and sending them to Judge Atkinson.

Twenty-two gangland bosses were spoken to by Rasmus, one of those being Goldenstein; all made the usual clucking sounds of disapproval with their tongues before giving the word to their men to listen for any word on the street. Goldenstein clucked along with the rest of them but inwardly rejoiced for he soon expected to be the owner of a sixty-five thousand pound piece of vellum that would cost him only four thousand. It came as a big shock when the next phone call he received was from Reg who now demanded twenty-five thousand for a complete Gutenberg Bible; not just one page but the whole bloody book which he knew would be virtually impossible to sell on. The buyer he had lined up was only prepared to go to sixty-five thousand pounds for one page, not six hundred and forty-four pages that he was unable to sell. As he explained this very slowly to the amateur burglar Reg could hear the rumbling in Goldenstein's magma chamber threatening to surface.

'There wasn't a single page there, guv, God's truth, only the complete book.'

'Then tear out a couple of pages and take them to the address I gave you; Dozer will be waiting for you.'

'Gerry won't let me do that.' Reg apologized and explained that Gerald forbid him from doing that as it would be tantamount to an act of sacrilege.

'I don't give a monkey's, do as I say, tear them out and burn the rest of the book.' Goldenstein said in a low ominous voice and clarified his words by growling that it was too hot to handle, especially as he hadn't any provenance to convincingly get an auction house to accept the damned thing; the wrong word to use when describing a bible. Goldenstein then paused, wondering why he was being so patient and having to excuse himself to an addicted worm like Reginald Barnett and he ended the call by shouting. 'Do as I told you or Dozer will be told to go out and play with his big toys.'

There was a long silence, although it wasn't quite silent as Goldenstein could hear nervous breathing. Suddenly the connection was cut and the gang boss was left holding a dead receiver. However, it wasn't as dead as Goldstein believed for the Organized Crime Division had been tapping his landline for the last two months without too much success.

Detective Inspector Austin Cooper, thoroughly confused by the conversation, removed the headphones that had been making the sides of his head uncomfortably hot and turned to the detective constable who had been seconded from vice to assist him in finding evidence against the crime boss.

'Did you make any sense of that, Teal?'

D.C. Teal shook his head. 'Sounds like he's moved into the market of selling hard pornography, sir.'

'One page at a time, constable? There's no money in that little caper and it would have to be pictures of William and Kate making a spare heir to convince any gutter-press tabloid to hand over sixty-thousand pounds. And what's all that talk about a complete book that's too valuable? It doesn't sound like our nice Mr Goldenstein to turn down an opportunity to make a lot more money.'

Teal perked up and mentioned the fact that they did have three new names; Reg, Gerald and someone called Dozer who likes playing with toys. 'Could be a possible paedophile, sir. The book may show celebrities or politicians with children for blackmail purposes.'

Cooper gave a desperate sigh. 'For your information, Teal, Dozer is Goldenstein's chief enforcer and there's a rumour that he likes to bury Goldenstein's competition with heavy plant machinery but so far we haven't been able to catch him playing his games. He's also happily shacked up with three Polish pole-dancers, suspected of being trafficked illegals, which discredits your paedophile theory. Finally, we haven't any chance of finding the other two as we don't have the actual address they've been told to go to or their full names.'

Suitably chastened Teal put on the headphones and looked to his boss for the next move while a jacketless Reg also sulked in the back of a bus that was stopping on Colchester high street. Gerald had told him that there was no chance of them tearing a page out of the bible and that they would have to go into hiding for a while until Goldenstein had cooled down and Dozer was no longer looking for them. Their first task was to find a shop where they could purchase a container that would accommodate the twelve by seventeen inch leather-bound tome that was painfully pulling at his shoulder joint. Reg perked up because it meant he could have his jacket back and be warm again.

It was sheer coincidence that a young man called Alfred, happened to be Goldenstein's nephew as well as the manager of all travel luggage in the Walters & Garfield department store when two men entered. He watched them as they began opening a number of the smaller suitcases and trying to put the same, very large book, in each one of them. Alfred strolled over to inquire if he could be of assistance and was promptly told by the shorter one to fuck off while the other politely said that the brown case with the double-lock would be fine. The lid was quickly closed and the book was hidden from Alfred's curious eyes but not before he glimpsed the front cover of a rather elaborately bound book. Working to become the manager of a luggage department meant that Alfred was well read on the subject and he had instantly recognized the quality of the hand-tooled leather. The gilt decorations in each corner and total lack of any lettering gave no clues as to the title or content of the book but it was definitely something of interest to gossip about in The Dead Goat later that night. Alfred was surprisingly given cash in payment by Gerald and on asking if he could giftwrap the purchase was abruptly informed by Reg that the damned thing didn't need wrapping in water soluble paper.

'It's a bloody suitcase, for Christ's sake, it's meant to get wet.' This was said with a dismissive sneer as Reg buttoned up his jacket and picked up the suitcase. The two men promptly strode from the store leaving a rather startled manager.

Gerald, Reg and the Gutenberg Bible went to the station to take the first train to London and were well on their way back to Gerald's place when Alfred finished work. He slipped into The Dead Goat for his usual free pint of bitter, bag of salt and vinegar crisps and a bit of a gossip with his uncle, who, incidentally, owned the pub. He had also intended to chat to some of his friends before heading home to the steak and mushroom pie his wife had promised but his casual mention about two men with a fancy book that needed it's own suitcase put paid to all his plans.

'What did the book look like,' Goldenstein asked even though he didn't know what it looked like himself. Alfred described it as best he could from the brief look he had been allowed before the lid slammed down and then followed that up with a fairly accurate description of the two men before his uncle impatiently asked for their names.

'The man who paid, a rather polite fellow with a very sad looking face, was called … ' he paused, his face screwed up in concentration ' … I can't remember, Uncle, but his friend, a foul-mouthed little man, was definitely Reg; at least that's what his mate called him.'

'Reg what?'

'No, I don't think Watt was his name.'

Goldenstein rolled his eyes and asked his nephew if he knew the man's last name. Alfred shrugged but on seeing the disappointment in his uncle's face he told him, rather lamely, that he would try his best to remember something by the morning. His uncle clapped him on the back and told him not to mention the book to a soul and although he knew Alfred wouldn't remember anything of any use, he told him to meet him in the pub at lunchtime tomorrow but to go straight home now and enjoy his steak and mushroom pie before it dried up in the oven.

When Alfred left The Dead Goat his uncle phoned Dozer and told him to stand down for the day and to wait for new instructions tomorrow. The big man nodded without saying a word, cut the connection and returned to the one-way mirror to watch one of his three pole-dancers wrap her legs round a naked pet shop owner. He then checked that the camera was still running before turning to look into the second room where his other girls were using floor-to-ceiling poles to arouse the passion of a wealthy Chinese client. Dozer had a thriving business that didn't really require the use of his Tonka toy or any interference by Goldenstein to turn a swift profit.

Gerald and Reg walked down Fiesta Avenue, taking turns to carry the heavy case, until they were outside number six. The house was in darkness and they both looked round before opening the gate and going to the front door. Still nothing stirred in the avenue apart from Mrs Bolton's black cat that ran across the lawn, making Reg touch his grubby collar in deference to his superstitious beliefs. Gerald showed Reg to the spare room and then hid the case on top of his own wardrobe before returning to the kitchen. He knew he had to find a more secure place to ensure nobody could find it and an idea was slowly unfolding.

'Reg, I need to go and visit my mother for an hour or two,' he said and before his partner could open his mouth he went on, 'and while I'm gone you can begin negotiations with Goldenstein. Tell him he can have the whole bible for forty thousand.' Gerald didn't wait for an answer and hurriedly left the room. In the silence that followed the door slam Reg realized there was a big difference between four thousand and twenty-five thousand pounds. Gerald now wanted him to ask for a further thirty-six thousand while he nipped off to mummy to sip G&Ts on the lawn. 'No way!' he exclaimed and ran out of the house only to find Gerald had already vanished. Reg rushed back into the house and Gerald's bedroom where he searched frantically for the Gutenberg Bible; that also had vanished.

While Reg become more and more frustrated in his fruitless search Gerald had taken a bus that dropped him right outside the massive gates of Shady Trees Care Home. When he arrived he could see his mother in the conservatory that doubled as the residents summer lounge, and he went directly to her room. It was a very basic, furnished bedroom with a double wardrobe, dressing table and en-suite facilities. Gerald chose the hiding place and slid the case under the bed knowing his mother had difficulty with bending and wouldn't be likely to see it there. He then went to the conservatory to legitimize his visit and although Mrs Latimer greeted her son warmly, if not thankfully, for a little company, she had a distinct problem remembering his name.

'It's Gerald, mother. Gerald Latimer, your son,' he prompted and she snapped back in an irritated tone that she knew his name and didn't need reminding she had a son. However, she did need a reminder that her name was Stephanie, her husband was dead and that she was in a care home and not in her own bedroom at number six Fiesta Avenue. As usual a one-sided conversation then developed and progressed along the same lines for thirty minutes while Gerald attempted to bring her up to date on the family history, from the day she was born, before he saw that she had, as she always did, nodded off. He sat for a few minutes studying the lined features he loved so much before the spell was shattered by an explosive expulsion of air. Stephanie had begun to snore and Gerald tugged the tartan-travelling rug around her body, took the spectacles from her lap to put on the side table and left quietly.

It was late and there was only the memory of a pleasant day in the sky. Clouds streaked with orange and crimson were drifting overhead when he arrived home to be greeted by an extremely irate Reg whose first words concerned the whereabouts of the bible. As Gerald began making tea he reassured his partner that the volume was in a safe place and then asked him, before Reg inquired where the 'safe place' was, what Goldenstein's reaction was when he told him the revised deal.

'All he said was there's a Dozer coming our way.'

'Didn't he want to negotiate a price?'

'Yes. His offer was, and I quote verbatim, our lives for the Gutenberg Bible.'

Gerald switched the kettle off. 'Then I suggest we immediately find alternative accommodation because it won't be long before that bonehead turns up and parks his bloody big Tonka toy outside.'

Reg was in full agreement and they hurriedly packed a small suitcase with Gerald's toiletries, shirts and clean underwear, some of which Reg would have to borrow, and took the first bus without checking where it was going. As they, and the few passengers on the bus, rubbernecked the remains of what had once been a possible drug concern at forty-one Delphinium Road Dozer arrived in Fiesta Avenue and kicked open the door at number six. He soon found it was deserted and after a thorough search came to the conclusion that the two men had taken the bible with them. A leaflet left lying in one of the bedrooms gave him a clue to where he should look next. Dozer called his boss and before he communicated his hunch he was ordered very loudly, and in no uncertain terms, to find them and the bible. He was also told to inflict as much suffering before slaughtering them in his typical trademarked manner.

Dozer was in the hallway, about to leave, when a man who was obviously of Greek origin and equaling his own height confronted him. They both stopped dead to study each other for a millisecond before the swarthy assassin loudly demanded the Gutenberg Bible. When informed by Dozer that he didn't have such a thing Rasmus Psomas produced a rather formidable pistol.

'You will give me that bible, Mr Latimer, or you will die,' the Greek hissed.

'I'm not Mr Latimer and if you don't stop pointing that ridiculous thing at me I'll wrench your arm off,' Dozer snarled.

Psomas' face registered surprise, 'You're not Latimer?'

'He's gone.'

'And who are you?' The barrel drooped in disappointment.

'I represent Mr Goldenstein. I'm known as Dozer.'

'Never heard of him or you.'

'My boss also wants me to retrieve the bible and take it back to him.'

The barrel was raised again and the Greek took a step back. 'I have no wish to shoot you, Mr Dozer, but my boss has paid me to return that holy book to its rightful owner who happens to be His Honour, Judge George Atkinson.'

Dozer took a step forward despite the pistol aimed at his chest. 'Not if I get to it first,' was the last thing he said before being shot. There was a powerful thump in the chest, he stumbled backward and all went black. Psomas sneered at the prone figure and swiftly left the house to continue his hunt for Mr Latimer.

CHAPTER 5

————————

T HE TWO MEN CHANGED buses three times before arriving
at Charing Cross Bridge to begin their search for Ali Monty. They
found the big man fast asleep beneath a blanket of broadsheet newspapers.
His snoring echoed off the raw concrete structure above their heads and yet
he awoke in a flash when Reg touched him on the shoulder. Tossing the
papers to one side Ali reared up with a large cider bottle in his fist. With
an unintelligible 'umurmph' be began swinging the bottle in the belief
that he was being mugged by thieves.

Reg stepped back to avoid having his skull crushed as he shouted, 'It's
me, mate. It's Reggie.'

Ali's eyes opened wide as he checked the shadowy figures standing
over him and the bottle was put down and he grinned with perfect teeth
that glinted orange in the light from the sodium street lamp. 'Reg,' he
exclaimed. 'Is that you?'

Reg confirmed it was indeed himself and accepted the invitation to
sit on a copy of the Daily Express beside the big man; Gerald was given a
nod and a copy of The Guardian. To the gentle sounds of the night traffic
above, men's snores punctuated by the occasional farts below, Reg related
everything that had happened to them since forty-one Delphinium Road
was turned into forty-one Hole-in-the-Road.

'To sum it up.' Ali said meditatively tapping his forefinger against the
dried cut n his cheek, 'You had been instructed to nick a single page from
a high court judge but took the whole book which you can't sell because
it's so valuable and yet it's desired by someone called Dozer who also can't

sell it but has an urge to put you both in the ground using a large piece of earthmoving equipment?'

'In a nutshell, me old china,' Reg said and fell silent. The three men sat in the gloom beneath the bridge pondering the problem set by Ali's outlined set of incidents.

'Yet you still need to raise twenty-three grand to keep your mum in the nuthouse?' Ali said suddenly.

'And seventy pence –,'

Gerald began to protest about Shady Trees being referred to by Ali as a nut-house but was interrupted. 'The only thing you can do is to seek out a new source of revenue.'

They all fell silent again until Reg looked both ways, held a finger to his lips and then whispered, 'We could try robbing a petrol station.'

'Without a getaway car?' Ali said sarcastically.

'We could steal one,' Reg added.

'We'd be nicked before we even got close to a petrol station.'

Gerald was inwardly horrified at the thought of carrying out another illegal act so soon after the burglary and yet the idea sent a chill of excitement through his whole being. 'What about a big supermarket? Twenty tills must hold quite a bit of money,' he suggested, shocked by his own shame at proposing such a deed.'

'Same problem, mate. No rapid means of getting away without thieving a car and most shoppers use credit cards not cash,' Ali said and then he clicked his fingers. 'Mind you, what about stealing three bikes from the railway station while the owners are travelling to work and then rob a bank?'

'Make our getaways on bicycles?' Reg exclaimed in horror.

'But it's clever, Reg,' Gerald asserted. 'Who would take any notice of three men riding bikes. When the police get the alarm they would race past us none the wiser that thousands of pounds was pedalling in the other direction.'

All three sat nodding as they thought about the simplicity of the idea.

Reg suddenly piped up. 'What about disguises and weapons?'

'We can shoplift toy guns and children's masks,' Ali volunteered.

Our crimes are adding up to a life sentence, Gerald thought with a fearful shudder as he looked at the big man. 'You don't have to do this, Ali,' he said. 'Why should you take such enormous risks?'

'I like you, Gerry.' Then Ali Monty's serious tone of voice changed to excitement as he went on. 'Also it's my idea, brilliant as it is, and I'd like to see it through just for the fun of it.'

Gerald was flattered by the stranger's comments and his willingness to undertake such a dangerous task for someone he'd never met, an elderly woman who had trouble remembering her own son's name. He also thought the man had to be a little touched to think breaking the law was fun. There was an awkward silence before Ali spoke again. 'When the shops open we'll go to Oxford Street to collect our tools.'

Reg chuckled. 'Now go to bloody sleep.'

Making themselves as comfortable as chewing gum speckled concrete would allow they prepared to sleep. Reg waited until the others had dropped off and then fished a folded piece of paper from his pocket and poured a line of cocaine onto the back of his hand. A short length of drinking straw was used and he lay back sniffing and unable to close his eyes as he tried to think of the right bank to rob. Suddenly, the drug kicked in and his mind became crystal clear as Crampton Bank appeared, like a Holy Grail, in his head; at least, it wasn't the bank so much as the manager, his father. He became so thrilled with the thought of teaching his father a lesson for all his past neglect that he sniffed another line and was unable to drop off until noisy pavement cleansers trundled slowly past his legs. This woke the other two who immediately shook Reg and reproached him for sleeping so late.

'Let's get something to eat and then make our way to Regent Street,' Gerald said. Ali nodded and tidily folded all of the newspapers and put them in a rusting supermarket trolley for future use. Reg yawned and wearily pulled himself to his feet to follow the two men who were already heading to the soup kitchen on The Strand.

'I reckon we should hit Crampton Bank first,' Reg said as they walked up Craven Street.

'That's your father's bank.' Gerald said with surprise.

'Your dad's got a bank, Reg?' Ali said with amazement. 'You never told me or anybody in the squat.'

Reg ignored them. 'Crampton's has few staff who can give us any trouble and I happen to know that Tuesday is the slowest day for customers.'

'But it's your dad's bank,' Gerald repeated.

'You never told me your dad had a bank, mate,' Ali repeated.

'Very few staff makes it perfect,' Reg repeated.

'And it's not that very far from Oakwood police station,' Gerald pointed out.

'It's a few miles,' Reg said dismissively. 'And we'll be in and out and cycling away before the wooden-tops can get their car started.'

Gerald suddenly envisioned the young woman behind the counter who had spoken so kindly to him and his heart fluttered. I can't rob *her*, he thought and then recalled that Reg's father had been the one who had refused to give him a loan, thrown him out of the bank and started him off on his path of crime. This changed his mind and it suddenly became a very good idea that it was Percival Barnett's bank they planned to rob, provided the guys promised there'd be no violence.

'Naw, we'll show the toy guns and they'll all wet themselves and fall over like possums,' Reg said.

'Possums?' Gerald repeated.

Reg explained that he'd watched every David Attenborough programme and that he learned that the possum was able to keel over and play dead whenever threatened.

Ali was still repeatedly muttering beneath his breath 'you never told us' when they arrived at the soup kitchen and broke their fasts with corned beef and pickle sandwiches and mugs of hot, strong tea. Ali continued to be of the opinion that if a mate's dad was a bank manager then the aforesaid mate should have unlimited access to cash to share with his mates.

The world famous toyshop was open when the trio arrived and as they had already discussed how they would steal the guns they went straight to the fifth floor and found that it was a children's restaurant. A security officer eyed the three disheveled men with suspicion. They look like they've been sleeping rough on the street, he thought, not knowing how right he was and asked Ali what they doing in a children's area without a child in tow. Ali swore that when he was seven years old the Al Capone cap guns were kept on the fifth floor. The man's suspicion grew and they and were shown the way out. They descended the stairs, searching floor by floor, without any success until another suspicious staff member asked if she could be of any help.

'My little boy wants a toy gun for his birthday,' Gerald said and then asked where they could find the replica pistols. The young woman, a university student paying her way through a psychology course, was shocked and explained that it was contrary to the store's policy to stock such aggressive items. Had they not read in the papers how terrorists and thieves were running rampant throughout the country and that law-abiding citizens should teach their children that guns are dangerous because policemen will shoot anyone holding what appears to be a weapon.

It took five minutes before they could finally thank her for the wise parental advice despite the obvious fact that she was many years from being a parent herself and secretly disliked young children. They had a quick conference outside the store and agreed to try the other big stores along Oxford Street that, four hours later, proved to be a total waste of time – toy guns that generally required the user to shout 'bang' were now *out* and ultra realistic computer war games that fostered gory nightmares were *in*.

Gerald couldn't understand the logic as they all taught extreme violence as being the sole solution to any of life's little problems. Ali then pointed out that it would be stupid to be caught stealing the kid's masks if they couldn't nick any guns. They agreed and went to buy burgers and coffee using the money Reg had taken from a handbag left on a Barbie doll counter while the owner was berating an assistant about the unrealistic long legs and size of the pneumatic breasts.

'What now?' Gerald mumbled through a mouthful of burger and tomato relish. His companions shrugged and they all finished eating before turning their minds back to the problem. Ali then said, 'I've been giving it quite a lot of thought and come to the conclusion that most bank guards only have batons and surly expressions to ward off bank robbers.'

'So?' Reg said. 'They can still bloody hurt.'

'Yes, but everyone, including the guards, are scared witless by big sharp blades.'

'Like choppers, machettes and very long knives,' Reg said excitedly.

'We can use stockings as disguises,' Gerald suddenly said. 'Ali can get those when he's finished eating.'

The other two nodded and Gerald, mid nod, noticed the two teenagers at the next table who had frozen, colas in hand, and were giving them very strange looks.

'We're scriptwriters on *EastEnders*,' Gerald explained in a confidential tone and watched their faces change to one of relief. The three stood as one and left before the youngsters started asking awkward questions about the programme and when they could expect to see their hero, Grant Mitchell, raiding a bank.

'What size should I get?' Ali asked as they stood outside a department store.

'Size? What size should you get?' Reg echoed. 'Does it really matter what size they are.'

'Get the one-size fits all, Ali,' Gerald said and the tall man went into the revolving door only to instantly re-emerge.

'What colour would be best?'

'Make it dark brown,' Gerald said quickly before Reg lost his temper and said something he would regret and Ali rode the revolving door again. This time it took him six minutes before he rejoined the two who were pretending to study the artistic window dressing.

'What about big knives,' Reg inquired. 'Did you get those?'

'You only asked me to get tights, not knives,' Ali complained.

'Stockings, Ali, we asked you to get stockings otherwise we'll have spare legs dangling over our shoulders like right idiots.'

'Too late now,' Gerald said. 'We'll make do with what Ali's bought. Give me some money and I'll go and get a couple of carving knives.'

'Out of money, mate,' Reg exclaimed, checking the woman's purse while Ali held his hands out. 'She obviously kept her credit cards elsewhere so you'll have to lift them.'

'That's great. So you two do all the no risk legal buying and I end up doing the big risk stealing.'

'It's *your* mother you want to keep in that care home, Gerry.' Reg said with a broad grin.

'I've got a better and much cheaper idea that's completely legal,' Ali said grinning.

'We're planning to rob a bank and you've got a legal idea on how we can go about it?' Gerald said scornfully. 'This I've got to hear.'

'We put on our tights and burst into the bank with our hands in our pockets as though we're holding guns. We tell everyone to lie on the floor or they'll be shot and get one teller to ransack the tills before we scarper.'

There was along silence before Reg spoke with an arched eyebrow. 'We go into a bank and pretend to have guns?'

'Right,' Ali said with pride at coming up with a solution.

'You must be bloody nuts, mate.'

Gerald had been thinking and suddenly interrupted. 'D'ya know, it might work,' he said, 'it could *really* work and what's more nobody gets hurt.'

'And if it doesn't work?' Reg snapped.

'Well, we make a run for it and if we're caught we can't be charged with armed robbery.'

For a few moments the trio stared silently at the size zero mannequins in the window wearing diaphanous nightwear that only much larger matrons with matching bank accounts could afford.

Ali quietly asked, 'Shall we do it?'

His partners in crime nodded and they strode off to make their final plans beneath Charing Cross Bridge.

CHAPTER 6

'GET DOWN, EVERYBODY GET down,' Ali Monty screamed. An elderly man holding a walking frame and a young woman holding a designer shoulder bag joined the bank staff in looking round at the three scruffy men standing at the revolving door. They wore disguises that brutally flattened their noses to one side like well-kneaded putty.

Bernard Sisson, Foreign Exchange, put a fist to his mouth and with eyes wide-open gave a small squeal while Roger Wilton, Head Cashier, looked at the men with a rather bewildered expression.

'Get down, and nobody will be hurt,' Ali shouted again as he made a threatening movement in the pocket of his ragged raincoat. Now that the robbery was taking place he suddenly felt his empty fist was a trifle inadequate to the task before them. He looked round and was a little reassured that Reg also ha his hand in his jacket packet as though he was also holding a hidden weapon.

'Down, down, on the floor,' Ali croaked and Arthur Watts, who had taken only one unarmed combat lesson in thirty-three years and was six weeks from retirement was nobody's hero and he flopped onto the parquet floor. Old Marjorie struggled to lower her weight followed by Roger who creaked with arthritic slowness. The elderly customer gripping his walker defiantly remained standing, as did Bernard who was unable to move being frozen with fright with eyes wide open. Elizabeth simply looked on in amazement at the ridiculous sight the three robbers presented and, almost reluctantly, pressed the red emergency button beneath her counter.

This was connected to the local police station that unfortunately wasn't that local being nine miles away in Oakwood.

The one who had done all the shouting was tall and Betty could see that he was exceptionally thin by the way the raincoat loosely hung. The other two were of average height but Betty couldn't help giggling for they were all wearing ladies tights in a completely different way. The tall one in the grubby raincoat had pulled it down until there was a gathering around his neck and under his chin and the crotch gusset covered his left ear. Silken legs had been tossed over each shoulder and as the material was tightly stretched it not only twisted his nose to one side but clearly showed he had sustained a recent cut on his cheek. The man with a hand under his jacket had only pulled the tights down sufficiently to cover his face and wrapped the rest of the tights around his neck. Only the third man had shown any sense by cutting a short length from one of the legs to disguise his face before discarding the rest. His light brown hair curled in an unkempt fashion through the opening at the top.

'You!' Ali shouted, pointing at Elizabeth. 'Stop laughing and start emptying the tills.' He threw a supermarket shopping bag over the counter. 'Put the money in that, notes only and no loose change.'

Elizabeth gave the motley gang an occasional glance and with a fixed grin went from one till to the other, taking only a few notes from each drawer and dropping them into the plastic bag. The robber with the neater disguise went to meet Elizabeth at the last till and took the bag, his father's ring twinkling red beneath the neon lights. It was gold with a tiny ruby that Elizabeth instantly recognized as belonging to the rather nice young man who had come into the bank seeking a loan.

'Would your mother want you to help her this way, sir,' she whispered as she released her hold on the bag. Gerald stepped back, shocked that the girl had identified him, and in doing so stumbled into Ali who, to keep his balance, took his deadly clenched fist out of his pocket. It was then that two things happened in quick succession: One, Arthur Watts glanced up to see the empty hand emerging and two; Gerald tripped over Ali's large boot, dropped the shopping bag to reveal that neither of his hands were clutching anything more deadly than nervous perspiration.

Gerald hit the ground, rolled away from the guard losing his wallet in the process, which skittered under the chair that Foreign Exchange had just sunk into with eyes still staring. The guard continued to get to his feet while pulling a truncheon from the special pocket in his trouser leg.

'They're unarmed Mr Watts,' Majorie called out to the security guard who was well aware of the situation and already considering which of the three robbers he should whack first.

Reg considered tackling the guard but on seeing the shiny metal of the very long truncheon emerging from a very long pocket he turned and ran to the exit. Mr Watts saw Reg open the door beside the revolving door and disappear and was confused when the other two saw their chance and also began making a rapid escape. Gerald had leapt to his feet and reached the door just ahead of Ali who decided to use the revolving door. Reg had disappeared but Ali was suddenly jerked back as the legs of his tights were caught in the door mid rotation. He was trapped and before he could think clearly enough to push the doors counter clockwise the security guard had shot a bolt and the revolving doors were well and truly locked.

Gerald and Reg reappeared outside and tried to push the doors either way but distant sirens ended their attempt to free their friend and they ran to the nearest bus stop where they were fortunate enough to leap upon the platform of a doubledecker just as it was pulling away. With presence of mind Gerald had snatched the disguise from his head whilst running but the conductor gave Reg a strange look as he went up the stairs still wearing his tights.

Ali Monty calmly sat down on the floor between the locked doors with two customers and all the bank staff staring down at him through the glass as though he were a dangerous zoo exhibit. Elizabeth saw this as an opportunity to retrieve the young man's wallet from under the chair. On the other side of the locked door Gerald had glimpsed her doing this just before he turned to flee and he patted his hip pocket to confirm that it was his wallet.

It was a simple black-leather billfold with a section for credit cards that held no cards and Betty slipped it into her jacket and strolled to the entrance to have another look at the man who had tried to hold up Crampton Bank with a pair of woman's tights and a clenched fist in his pocket.

While the police were putting Ali Monty into the squad car and gathering odd bits of evidence that amounted to no more than one Tesco shopping bag and three-hundred and twenty-two bank notes, Gerald and Reginald were being thrown off the bus by a conductor who had discovered they hadn't any money for their fares. This wasn't the only problem for Reg had also removed his tights and the conductor had been able to commit the faces of both would-be bank robbers to his memory.

The river was glittering with South Bank office lights when they arrived under Charing Cross Bridge and after convincing the more troublesome homeless people that Ali Monty would be arriving soon they flopped down unchallenged onto their friend's usual pitch.

'What now?' Gerald asked as he rummaged through his pockets for any odd coins missed during his search on the bus. 'How can I raise the money now?'

Reg didn't respond because for in a similar rummage through his own pockets he found he had used up all his 'bags' and he began sweating with fear. 'I've got to go back home,' he moaned and stood up. 'Now!'

'And so must I,' Gerald echoed, realizing that the pretty teller he had seen pocketing his wallet may be foolish enough to go to his home and there was a good chance there would only be one person waiting there and it wouldn't be himself. Police sirens wailed behind them as they hurried up the street to the railway station and entered the concourse that was now crowded with late night revellers. Reg told Gerald to wait by the main exit before disappearing into the currents of people flowing chaotically like white-water rivers to catch the last trains of the day. It seemed an age before Reg materialized beside Gerald like a malodorous wraith wearing a devilish grin.

'Okay, let's go catch our bus,' he said triumphantly as he surreptitiously showed Gerald a cherry-red ladies purse. 'That's for you, mate,' he said, 'and this one's for me.' He produced a brown wallet and pausing briefly beside a rubbish bin, removed all the money and credit cards before discarding it. Reg then nodded at Gerald who guiltily took bank notes, coins and two ultra-sensitive condoms from the unfortunate woman's purse before dropping it in the bin.

As they strode to the nearest bus stop Reginald counted and found he had successfully 'dipped' seventy-five pounds. Gerald flicked through his notes to find he had one hundred and ten pounds and he couldn't help returning Reginald's broad grin as they boarded the late N15 night service for Romford Market where they were able to hail a cab for the rest of their journey.

Fiesta Avenue was in darkness when the taxi driver dropped them at the end. They walked cautiously, studying every parked car until they reached number six. The gate creaked open as did the front door when Gerald used his key and opened it slowly. The two crept in and began checking each room on the ground floor until they were satisfied that they were unoccupied by any thugs. Reg flipped a coin and Gerald went up the staircase, taking care not to step on number ten as that invariably squeaked whenever pressure was applied. Each room was inspected with extreme care until Gerald called down for Reg to join him.

'Someone's been here,' he said when Reg walked into the room where Gerald was waiting. That's an understatement, Reg thought as he looked round, for every drawer had been removed and emptied on the floor, wardrobe doors were wide open and clothing was also randomly scattered.

'The other rooms are the same,' Gerald said gloomily. 'This is my mother's room and I think they may have found what they were looking for.' He held up a slickly produced brochure proclaiming that Shady Trees offers the most care for your money. 'Whoever tore this place apart knows where my mother is and that's a big problem.' Gerald said softly as he went to the corner of the room and rolled the carpet back.

'What yer looking for, Gerry?' Reg asked with sweat beading on his forehead.

'Something of my dad's,' Gerald said. 'Show you later.'

'It'll have to be tomorrow, 'I've got to go and see a friend of mine.'

'Okay, Reg. Will you be coming back?'

'Tomorrow morning, mate, promise,' he called out as he pounded down the stairs and left the house, slamming the door behind him. Gerald prised a short piece of floorboard up and reaching into the cavity took out a bundle of cheesecloth. He unrolled it and stared at his father's grease-smeared revolver. Ignoring King's Regulations he had kept his Enfield Service Revolver after the war and hidden it beneath the floor, telling Gerald of it's whereabouts only when he came of age. The robust weapon had six .38 calibre cartridges loaded and another dozen wrapped in a separate piece of material. Gerald put it in the bedside table and replaced the floorboard and carpet. As he stood up he caught a glimpse of himself in the mirror and he become conscious of how much both he and his clothes were reeking. He found the boiler still switched on and after flinging his filthy clothes into the washing machine he luxuriated beneath a hot shower until the room was filled with steam. After shaving Gerald went to bed and fell into a deep sleep.

After the police had finished questioning the staff, Percival Barnett, on the advice of a police counsellor, closed the bank and sent everyone home. He had not felt it necessary himself since he was unaware a robbery had taken place as he had been in his office watching one of his favourite films with the door locked. It was when earphones prevented him from hearing a knock on his door that a rather heavyset police sergeant in full riot gear broke it down. This immediately revealed his habit, which was in his hand, and his ignorance of the situation.

When she left the bank, with the wallet deep in her coat pocket, Elizabeth felt a shiver of excitement. At home she sat on the settee for a few moments to calm down and then took it out. The billfold was a few years old and slightly scuffed and on opening she found it contained three one-pound coins in a loose change pocket and despite a thorough search she couldn't find a single banknote. He was telling the truth when he said he didn't have any money, she thought as she removed an expired library card and read the owner's identity. She had at the time asked Mr Barnett who was the good-looking young man so the name on the card came as no surprise and it was simply confirmation that he was the amateur bank robber.

As she tossed the wallet onto the settee a small piece of folded pink paper fluttered to the floor and on picking it up she found it was a lottery ticket. She turned it over and found that Mr Latimer had been very optimistic for he had filled in his name and address. 'Six Fiesta Avenue,' she murmured, making a mental note to pay the sad-looking bank robber a visit very soon. She tucked the ticket into her own purse and had soon forgotten it.

Ali Monty was conveyed to the local police station in Oakwood and taken to an interview room by a rather pleasant constable and a senior officer, who did most of the talking, soon joined them. Ali gave his nickname

'Who?'

'You know me, Gerry. You tried to rob my employer with an empty fist yesterday.'

Gerald winced on realizing she had found his address in the wallet. 'Are you alone? Are the police with you? What do you want?' he asked without taking breath.

'Let me in and I'll tell you.'

'Let her in, Gerry,' a familiar voice said.

Gerald immediately opened the door with a look of surprise on his face when he saw Ali Monty standing closely behind the young woman with an equally surprised expression. The two entered and Gerald checked the street before putting the gun on the hallstand table and following them into the kitchen. Questions for both of them hovered on his lips until Ali quickly explained how he had escaped from the police. Gerald shook his friend's hand and then turned expectantly to Elizabeth and held his hand out.

She took his wallet from her bag and handed it to him. 'Not a very wealthy person are you,' she teased with a smile as he slipped it into his pocket. 'How do you get about without any money?'

'We manage, now tell me, what do you want?' Gerald asked as he switched the kettle on to make tea.

Elizabeth studied the young man's face and felt again the same strange sensations when he had entered the bank for the first time to apply for a loan and the second time he appeared to carry out his abortive robbery. 'I thought you and your friends were very brave to attempt a bank robbery without anything more dangerous than a pair of tights. I should also mention that, in my opinion, you and your friends are bloody useless at robbing banks.'

'That's a bit unkind,' Ali responded sulkily.

'But true,' Gerald said.

Elizabeth explained that from her viewpoint a bank robber who gets his pair of tights caught in revolving doors and looks like a throttled goldfish when he could have used a perfectly ordinary door shouldn't exactly lay claim to being a professional criminal.

Ali continued to sulk and Gerald tried to ease the tension.

'It was our first time at doing such a thing and we didn't want anyone to come to any harm,' he said by way of an explanation for their behaviour.

We would never claim to be professional at that sort of thing and the only reason we did it was to raise twenty-three thousand pounds and seventy-pence and no more.'

'Why that exact figure?'

As they drank their tea Gerald told her the whole sorry tale that she listened to in silence, only occasionally clucking her tongue as he related his father's death and his mother's subsequent mental degeneration. Like their first meeting in the bank Gerald was captivated by the young girl; his eyes slowly moved down from the soft curls brushing her forehead to the wide, intelligent eyes, petite nose and generous mouth which revealed even white teeth when she smiled.

'Was robbing a bank the only option you could think of?' she asked when he had finished. She hadn't been embarrassed by his staring, quite the contrary, she had been flattered and returned the favour by inspecting him.

'Reg had suggested that we could make and sell drugs but his factory blew up unfortunately.'

'Actually, that was fortunate for if I catch you anywhere near drugs I'll turn you in to the cops. There are many more ways to raise cash other than by destroying children's lives with that filth,' she said softly.

'Such as?' Ali said rattling his cup to attract their attention for he had been a little rattled himself by the way they had overlooked his presence.

Elizabeth frowned as she sank into deep thought. 'Give me a bit of time and I'll come up with something. In the meantime you can both do a bit of thinking yourselves while you rustle up breakfast.'

Ali groaned and held his stomach. 'Not for me, I've had enough already.'

Gerald looked at him in amazement and then went to answer the doorbell. He looked through the side panel and the silhouette was that of a man. Gerald picked up the revolver and held it behind his back as he opened the door to find an impatient, bright-eyed Reg standing on the welcome mat. He entered and on seeing the revolver held his hands up in mock terror.

'Don't kill me, don't kill me,' he pleaded with a broad grin and Gerald replaced the weapon on the hall table. 'Is that the surprise you wanted to give me last night?' he asked.

'It's my old man's service gun and it's never been fired.'

'And never will be,' Elizabeth said, emerging from the kitchen, and she took the Enfield and dropped it into her handbag. 'I'll have nothing to do with men who have guns either.'

'Who the hell is this?' Reg exclaimed, pointing at the girl in alarm.

'She's the bank teller, Reg. The girl who works in your father's bank.'

Gerald's reply further shocked the addict and he rushed into the kitchen and poured himself a large measure of 21-year-old whisky. It took another hour of argument and almost half the bottle to mellow Reg's anger and convince him that it was safe for Elizabeth to stay. 'But only if she can come up with some good ideas for making money,' he asserted, determined to have the last word.

Elizabeth nodded and then asked him if he really was Percival Barnett's son and when he said he was she looked puzzled. 'Why rob a bank when your father is a bank-manager and clearly not without a few pennies?'

'He refused to finance my habit and kicked me out last year,' Reg mumbled, ignoring the fact that he had been the one who had left without being told, and Elizabeth could see that the conversation wouldn't be going any further.

They all fell into a silent truce as Reg poured another whisky while Ali, Gerald and Elizabeth returned to their tea. Gerald ended the silence by asking Reg where he stayed the night and was informed that he had visited an old friend, a fellow street pusher who worked for Goldenstein and was able to score a quality 'hit' and a bed for the night.

'That was bloody dangerous, mate,' Ali exclaimed. 'Knowing that you need to shoot-up from time to time Dozer will have his gang watching every one of your old contacts.'

'For all we know *you* could have been followed back here,' Gerald added, the cup rattling in his saucer as he put it down. They were unaware that one of Dozer's pole-dancers had already spotted them in the street and was telling her boss where Reg had gone to ground. Dozer's grin had never reached his eyes; they simply narrowed as he pocketed the bulldozer keys, took his favourite metal baseball club from the umbrella stand, and left the house.

CHAPTER 7

J UDGE ATKINSON HAD JUST received a report from Rasmus Psomas and he was in a foul temper. Rasmus hadn't caught the burglars and the only piece of information the thug could give him was that he had the feeling a top organized crime boss called Albert Goldenstein may not have told him everything he knew and was possibly involved in the theft. The name seemed familiar and the judge, while checking the court listings, noticed a case he was hearing later that day which could have some bearing on the matter.

Tim Holt, a well-known addict had been up before Atkinson on numerous occasions for possession but never for dealing and was known to have worked for Goldenstein. The judge made a call requesting his private secretary arrange a covert meeting with Holt before the hearing. After impatiently tapping his fingers on the desk for two minutes she rang to give him five minutes in one of the court holding cells.

The scrawny twenty-something looked up with lazy eyes as Atkinson entered the cell and then dropped his head again to contemplate his death's head belt buckle. The bright red shirt had faded to a pretty pink and was stained down the front with dried vomit. 'Whatcha want?' he mumbled as Atkinson sat down at the table to face him.

'In thirty minutes I will be the judge who'll either grant you a suspended sentence or put you away for five to ten years in one of Her Majesty's hotels,' Atkinson replied softly and Holt's head snapped up, his eyes fixed fearfully on the judge. 'That's better, now I want you to tell me a little about Mr Albert Goldenstein.'

'Can't do that, he'd give me to Dozer,' Holt whined.

'If you don't tell me something, Tim, I will have no option but to give you the maximum and you know how they like new talent, lads as young as you, where you would be going.'

Holt thought about it for three seconds before answering every question put to him. It was all Atkinson wanted to know but the judge knew this new knowledge could never used against the crime boss for it had been obtained under duress from an addict who was still affected by his last drug hit. However, the rumour among Holt's friends that Goldenstein had made a deal with someone in London for a single page from a bible for thousands of pounds was enlightening and Atkinson made a note to pass this tidbit on to Rasmus.

'Thank you, Tim,' Atkinson said when the lad had run out of words and he left the cell to hurry up to judge's chambers where he prepared himself for court. It was forty minutes later that Tim Holt was found guilty of possessing class-A drugs with the intention of selling the aforementioned class-A drugs to a young under-aged person or persons unknown and was sentenced to ten years. Atkinson had phoned Rasmus before the brief trial and informed him of the link to Goldenstein and ordered him to find out if he was the man behind the theft of his precious bible.

Rasmus soon found out where Goldenstein lived by beating up a few street peddlers and it was late evening when he drove past the brightly illuminated wrought iron gates to reconnoiter. He spotted the CCTV camera mounted high in a tree, just inside the encircling wall and he drove on. When the wall ended he parked the car in a small layby and set out on foot to follow the wall round the house.

It was a densely wooded area with thick undergrowth that made progress tediously slow. The number of burrs attaching to his trousers increasingly irritated Rasmus. He reached inside his jacket to unbutton the automatic's holster and to check that the heavy combat knife was still snugly sheathed at his waist. The wall was less tended at the rear of the property and strong vines were covering the bricks. Rasmus used their thick stems to climb up and peer over the top and found to his dismay, and a cut thumb, that it was covered in glass fragments set in a bed of cement. A vast lawn stretched up the slope to a ha-ha and beyond that he could just make out a large floodlit terrace stretching the width of the Lutyens styled house. Looking directly down he was pleased to see that the wall was less in height than on the outer side and he balled up his jacket, placed it on the glass and rolled over to drop into the herbaceous border. Rasmus tugged his blazer free and winced on hearing the sound of torn material. 'Damn!' he muttered.

Using hunting skills learnt in the Greek mountains he dodged from one small tree to another as he made his way towards the light. The ha-ha presented no obstacle and he slowly crawled to the low stonewall surrounding the patio until he could hear voices. He was about to raise his head to look over the parapet when he heard a strange rumbling sound. This developed into a growl and then a snarl before a forty-kilogram Doberman Pincer sprang and knocked him to the ground. He gave a cry of surprise and struggled to his feet only to be knocked sideways as the attack dog sprang out of the darkness and clamped its jaws on his arm.

'Petal, down Petal,' a reedy voice called and the animal stopped growling but kept on tightening its painful grip on his arm. Rasmus looked up to see through tears of pain a silver-haired woman looking down at him with slight concern in her eyes.

'Petal, down Petal,' she commanded once more and just as softly as a mother would her baby and the savage power of the dog was slowly released and his arm was freed to hang in the tattered remnants of his fifteen-hundred pound Armani blazer of which he had been inordinately proud.

'I'm sorry if Petal frightened you but she does take her work seriously. I must add that you did frighten her a bit by creeping up the lawn like that,' the woman said as Rasmus climbed over the decorative wall. I frightened her? Rasmus thought as he looked across the terrace to see a second elderly woman. She had remained sitting at a small table holding a sherry glass by the stem between finger and thumb as she studied the swarthy-looking man through a Victorian pince-nez.

'Who are you?' she demanded.

'More to the point who are you?' countered Rasmus loudly, surprised to find two dotty old women instead of a bunch of heavily armed bodyguards and then froze on hearing Petal growl beneath her breath.

'We're the Waterstone sisters,' the one holding a sherry glass snapped back. 'And you should watch your tone of voice when Petal is around.'

'Where is Goldenstein?' Rasmus asked softly, with a smile that he turned to show to the beast that was slowly circling him like a wolf. It stopped and sat only five feet in front of him with dark unblinking eyes fixed on his face.

'We bought this house three months ago through our solicitor and if that was the name of the previous owner then we have no idea where he is living. Now, perhaps you would be good enough to give us your name and tell us why you visit your acquaintances like a burglar?'

'Michael Hinkley,' Rasmus lied. 'I'm sorry to have troubled you but could you show me the way out?'

The woman in tweed pointed at the holstered gun that had become visible when he swung round. 'And what's that for?'

Rasmus thought fast and explained he had been invited by his friend to a novel murder dinner party and had thought it would be fun to make an entrance in the most unorthodox manner he could think of. The Doberman growled when he took the gun from its holster and was explaining that it was only a replica which clearly the Doberman didn't believe for the animal launched itself and it's jaws snapped shut on his wrist. Once more Rasmus gave a loud cry of surprise and dropped the weapon that discharged and a .38 bullet went through the head of the sherry drinker. The dog, confused by the deafening explosion, released its grip and Rasmus quickly took advantage, retrieved the weapon and shot the beast before it decided to try for his throat next. This time it was no accident and he knew that the other woman, who was sitting with a dumbfounded expression, would also have to go.

After he had done the deed he took no chances, returned over the back wall and retraced his steps to the car, making sure the cameras were unable to see or identify him. The drive back to his accommodation was uneventful and he was able to slip into his apartment without anyone seeing his muddied, torn appearance. He quickly changed into a dark suit and was soon out on the street and accosting the young drug peddler who had given him the wrong address. After he had extracted an apology and beaten him senseless he left the unconscious youth in the alley. No sooner had he stepped out into the street when he was approached by a skinny pimp and his equally skinny girl and asked if he wanted a good time. Rasmus asked if they knew the address of a man called Goldenstein and when they said yes, but couldn't tell him, he beat the pimp until the hysterical girl gave him two addresses. Rasmus asked if she knew which one was the right address and was told that she frequently went there on business. It was only the threat of the large knife and his clenched fist that extracted every detail about a Docklands penthouse and Georgian house in Wellington Street before leaving her minus two front teeth and cradling the pimp's head in her lap.

Judge Atkinson had been sitting beside the phone and was able to answer instantly when it rang. Rasmus gave a report on what had taken place and for his pains he received lengthy verbal abuse before being ordered to go and do as he was originally instructed. The phone went dead and Rasmus went into the bathroom to run cold water over his knuckles and cool his anger while twenty miles to the west Judge Atkinson threw the phone across the room and made a mental note to increase the punishment he had prepared for three perpetrators of misdemeanors. He was sentencing them the following morning.

The sun had only just risen when Rasmus left his apartment and, using the car sat-nav, drove into London to locate the new tower block in Docklands. The rising sun glittered off the wall of glass as he walked along the south dock wharf. He entered the large atrium and casually approached the circular reception counter that he tapped with his gold ring to attract the concierge's attention.

'May I help you, sir?' he asked.

'Yes, does Mr Albert Goldenstein live here?'

'I'm terribly sorry, sir, but I am unable to give the names of residents but if you would give me *your* name and telephone number I will check and . . .'

'Don't bother.' Rasmus had considered thumping the man but instead turned away and strode out of the building with a grim expression, almost running into a heavy-set man topped with a crewcut and a similar scowl. Both men wore identical dark suits, as if there was an official uniform for hired enforcers and they looked at each other with suspicion clearly showing in their eyes. Rasmus was unknown to the man entering the building but on passing each other the Greek noticed the hearing aid and the distinctive bulge under the armpit and guessed that the aurally challenged thug was another of Goldenstein's men. Due to the concierge's stonewalling and the working girl's story Rasmus was confused; was it Goldenstein or the big enforcer who lived in the glass tower and if it was the latter he planned to extract a couple more of her teeth for misleading him.

Rasmus parked the car to wait until his target left and then he planned to follow him until he had the opportunity to have a quiet talk to him alone. He was soon rewarded for his patience when a black BMW rose out of the underground car park and whispered past. At the wheel was Mutton and in the back sat a small corpulent middle-aged man with a wispy moustache. 'That has to be Goldenstein,' he murmured. 'Maybe they're gay and live together.' He followed the Mercedes at a discreet distance until it turned into Wellington Street and parked in the drive of a rather imposing Georgian residence. Rasmus searched for cameras and noted every other detail of the property as he drove past and kept going until he was able to turn a corner and park the car out of sight. He had just settled down for a long wait when the black BMW screeched around the corner and braked alongside him. A very surprised Rasmus saw that the car was empty apart from Mutton. He was behind the wheel and pointing a disturbingly large, semi-automatic weapon at his head. Goldenstein had clearly instructed his minder to dispose of the troublesome man who had been following them.

The driver's side window exploded a split second after Rasmus threw himself sideways and the shot lightly creased his temple before exiting through the opposite window. There was a sudden roar and the Mercedes took off while Rasmus struggled upright, hand reaching for the automatic as blood streamed from the shallow scoring on his head. The black car was rapidly pulling away and, with a lap full of glass fragments, Rasmus started the car and accelerated after it, tyres smoking.

Mutton was an experienced driver and he used the full width of the road to his advantage and the detriment of other road users. They were forced to swerve onto pavements or the central reservation when seeing the BMW approaching on their side of the road. Rasmus followed using the same tactics, leaving a trail of devastation in his wake until they both turned into a *cul de sac*. Having seen the No Through Road sign Rasmus had smiled triumphantly but his expression soon changed when he saw that the BMW had stopped at the end of the road. Large bollards marked the edge of the river and Mutton was already out of his car which he'd parked beside another and two men in black suits had joined him. They all levelled automatic weapons at Rasmus who, seeing the firepower about to be unleashed, slammed on the brakes and jerked the shift stick into reverse. Once more he threw himself sideways and put his foot down as a hail of bullets shattered the windscreen, the seating headrests and the rear window. The car shot out into the main road narrowly missing an ambulance as Rasmus sat up, spun the wheel and raced back to Wellington Street with four road traffic cameras clocking him for the second time. He had a reason for speeding since he had a hunch that Goldenstein had sent all of his men to deal with him which meant he was now unprotected and had created the perfect occasion for Rasmus to pay him a friendly visit.

The Greek parked his bullet-riddled car fifty yards from the house and strolled the rest of the way to the front door and rang the bell. The porch was sheltered from the road by a large rhododendron bush, ablaze with flowers, and he slipped the automatic from its holster and held it by the side of his leg. Footsteps could be heard approaching the door and it swung open to reveal the same small man with the whispy moustache. His eyes widened at the sight of Rasmus and became even wider when the automatic was placed against his forehead and he was propelled backwards. As the door closed a black-suit appeared at the top of the large staircase and taking in the scene reached beneath his jacket. In one well-practiced motion Rasmus shot the man and replaced the warm muzzle against Goldenstein's forehead before black-suit had finished tumbling lifelessly to the bottom of the stairs.

'I don't have much time, Mr Goldenstein. Just tell me where the book is and I'll leave you in good health.' Rasmus said, pushing the muzzle harder, forcing the little man back and into a room that had a large window overlooking the driveway. 'If I am still standing here when your men return it will be the last thing you will ever see.'

'I don't have it,' Goldenstein stuttered. 'I sent my man to track it down but he has yet to return.'

'What's his name?'

'Dozer.'

'He's dead, I shot him for trying to impersonate a man called Latimer who I believe stole the book from my boss on your orders?'

'No, no I didn't . . .'

Rasmus looked into Goldenstein's terrified eyes and saw the lie before stepping back to avoid splatter and pulling the trigger. The crime lord collapsed like a wet sack of flour onto the Pietra Firma tiles followed by the oil painting of his mother that had been hanging on the wall behind him; she had also been neatly shot between the eyes.

Rasmus removed the silencer and was about to leave the house when he saw yet another black-suit walking up the drive. He reassembled his weapon and stepped out onto the porch just as the man came around the rhododendron bush. Rasmus indicated that he should keep coming and told him to go into the house where a single, barely heard report placed him beside the man he'd come to see. The door was closed and the killer returned to his car and drove it down to the river where he found a quiet place to safely roll it over the bank and into fifteen feet of water; the gun and silencer followed. He then walked two miles before risking a taxi and returned to his apartment to consider his next move. It was only when he watched the ten o'clock news that he learnt of the police officer who had been found with a very dead Albert Goldenstein, a known criminal. His mouth fell open when he heard that the black-suit who had come up the drive had been a detective constable called Henry Teal and he'd been visiting to interview Albert Goldenstein.

'Vlacas!' The Idiot best expressed how he felt, knowing that the whole of the Metropolitan police force would now be a trifle agitated.

Elizabeth looked at each of the men who seemed at a loss as to what to do next and she took Gerald's hand and pulled him towards the door. 'It's clear that we can't stay here but we can go to my place to plan what to do next.'

'First, I've got to go to Shady Trees and retrieve the book otherwise my mum will be in danger from whoever ransacked my place,' Gerald said with such determination in his voice, she couldn't argue.

She quickly scribbled her name on a scrap of paper, took some money from her purse and handed them to Gerald. 'Take a cab to the care home, get the bible, and come straight back to my place while I go by bus with these guys,' she said.

Gerald ran an eye over the cards thumb-tacked to the kitchen notice board and dialled one of the numbers for a mini-cab company while the others left to catch a bus. The cab arrived and he was driven to Shady Trees where he went directly to his mother's room and found she was sound asleep. He sat on the only available chair and watched the bed sheet rise and fall with each breath while her pale waxen features remained immobile. He remembered the happier times when he was a child, long before his father's accident, and the magical trips to Margate when his mother giggled and laughed with carefree abandon as she ran from the little red bucket he had filled with seawater. Gerald sighed and knelt beside the bed to retrieve the suitcase.

'What're you doing? Who are you?' his mother said sleepily.

'It's me mum, Gerald. Go back to sleep,' he said and stroked her hand lying on top of the sheet.

'That you, Arnold?' she mumbled and slipped back into sleep. He quickly slid the case out and walked out to the taxi he had asked to wait. The journey to Elizabeth's apartment was filled with melancholic memories that saddened him more than usual and when the door was opened Elizabeth was troubled by the way he looked.

'What's wrong, Gerry,' she asked as she closed the door and led him into the living room.

'I'm still worried that someone will visit my mother and really frighten or even hurt her,' he replied dejectedly. Reg and Ali had made themselves comfortable on the settee and were finishing the last of her Rich Tea biscuits with mugs of tea. They both remained where they were and Ali suggested that they all put their minds to achieving their original goal of raising twenty-three thousand pounds and seventy pence.

'I've been thinking about that,' Elizabeth said. 'I used to watch the security van that came every Friday to Crampton Bank to collect the excess and saw that there were only two guards. Usually the company puts three men in each armoured van, one to drive, one to remain in the back of the van and the third guard to enter the bank and pick up the boxes.'

'Does that mean the guard outside opens the back of the van himself?' Ali asked with curiosity in his voice.

'No, I think the driver has access to the back of the van and unlocks the rotating repository from the inside. The guard places his box inside and it is rotated by the driver who takes the box out and awaits the next until all cash boxes are in the van before he returns to the front and unlocks the passenger door for the guard.'

'So we wait until *that* door is opened and leap in?' Reg said excitedly.

'Not quite, I saw your father's service revolver, Gerry and we'll use that to intimidate the guard the moment he opens the door. However, I insist that it isn't loaded and that we carry no bullets with us.'

'I agree to that, but why don't we just hold the single guard up and take the boxes from him?' Gerald said in a puzzled tone.

'There is more than one box and he brings them out one at a time. If we want them all we have to be able to get into the back of the van and the only access is the way the driver uses. We order both guards out of the van and . . .'

'We get in and drive away,' Reg interrupted excitedly. 'Your Betty's a bloody genius, Gerry.'

Elizabeth blushed and Gerald glanced at her before going to make himself a coffee. 'She's not my girl, Reg,' he muttered, whacking the back of Reg's head as he passed the settee.

'Oh c'mon, Gerry. I've seen the way you two look at each other.'

'Leave it alone, mate,' Gerald snapped, growing angry at the thought of being caught ogling the girl. 'Let's get some rest, we have a big day tomorrow.'

Reg continued grinning as he left the room to use the toilet and snort the two remaining lines in the paper packet. Ali was unable to disguise the smile as he agreed and settled himself down in one of the old armchairs. Elizabeth left to go to her bedroom and paused briefly to look at Gerald in a way that could either be interpreted as an invitation to join her. He modestly chose to remain and with a sad expression listened to her climb the stairs, enter the bedroom and close the door. He reluctantly stretched out on the settee and prepared to sleep. Reg returned and slumped, slack-jawed to the sound of protesting springs into the other armchair and was soon lost to the world. Gerald was still awake on the settee when Ali began emitting stentorian snores accompanied by the regular sniffling of Reg's cocaine-affected sinuses and he rose to his feet and prowled around. He stopped when he heard a distinct clicking noise from upstairs and Gerald looked up the stairs to see a faint line of light appear on the ceiling; a bedroom door had opened a fraction and he instinctively knew which one it was.

Gerald stealthily climbed the staircase and just before he reached the door the light on the other side went out and the door was opened wide.

He entered the room and was stopped in the dark by warm arms going around his neck and moist lips pressing against his own. He put his arms around her waist to find he was holding a naked body and as his hands slipped further down he found himself being aroused. Elizabeth briefly pulled away to close the door silently before pulling him towards the large bed. There she clumsily stripped him of unfamiliar clothes that buttoned on the wrong side until he too was naked and pulled him down onto the soft duvet cover with her lips stilled fastened to his, a tongue beginning to explore.

It was Gerald's first time and when they touched, stroked and caressed each other his body experienced new sensations and at the point when he exulted at being a man and Elizabeth became a woman, her passionate cries of joy muffled by the pillow, alarmed him greatly until she tenderly caressed and kissed his fears away. They lay clasped in each other's arms, feeling perspiration trickling between them as they murmured their love for each other and fell into a deep sleep of satiated contentment.

'Wakey, wakey,' Ali shouted as he pushed the door open and stormed into the bedroom. He three the duvet to one side exposing the two naked lovers to the chill morning air and left, slamming the door behind him. Gerald sat bolt upright with shock and Elizabeth couldn't help giggling at the expression on his face.

'I guess your friends definitely know what we've been up to now,' she murmured as she pulled him down to her. Gerald examined the whole length of her perfect form with his fingertips and, unable to remain angry at Ali's crude wake-up call, began making passionate love to her once more.

Ali was smiling in a knowing manner when the lovers finally emerged from the bedroom to ask if anyone had bothered to make breakfast. Ali volunteered to toast some bread and fry a few eggs while Reg wearily stood up and announced irritably that he had to go out for a while. His nerves were shot and his hands were vibrating like A Flat tuning forks. Drug withdrawal always made him suspicious and his paranoia compelled him to open the small case and check if the Gutenberg Bible was still there. He gave a small grunt, put the case on the table and without another word left the apartment.

'Where's he gone to?' Elizabeth asked, fearing the answer.

'To get his own kind of breakfast,' Ali said.

'Cocaine,' Gerald explained.

Elizabeth's disappointment was clear to see. 'The last time he went out he brought trouble back to your place do you think history will repeat itself?'

'God, I didn't think of that,' Ali said as the slices were ejected from the toaster. 'We'd better get ready to move on again. We'll wait for Reg to return and then leave to do the armoured car.'

The two nodded and Elizabeth looked round the small room that had been the only home she had known for more than a year. 'I'll have to give up any thought of returning to the bank,' she said with a nervous laugh and the joys of the night evaporated to be replaced by a strong sense of insecurity.

'No place to live and nowhere to work is a fine way for us to begin our lives together,' Gerald muttered and Elizabeth put her arms around him and kissed him lightly.

'We'll manage,' she whispered with a touch of hope in her voice.

CHAPTER 8

THERE WAS A LIGHT drizzle in the air and pale grey clouds were stretching from one horizon to the other when they left the apartment for the last time and caught the bus that would take them past Crampton Bank. Reg had returned in a state of euphoria with eyes sparkling with excitement. It was on seeing his good spirits that it was agreed Ali should fetch Elizabeth's blue Fiesta from the lock-up while the rest went ahead and found a good spot to wait for the armoured van to arrive. Gerald had put the unloaded gun in his pocket after Elizabeth had checked that all bullets had been removed from the chambers. He was also carrying the case containing the priceless book.

The rain had begun to dampen their spirits by the time Ali arrived and parked the Fiesta in a side street before joining them. They had planned that after they had hi-jacked the armoured van and driven it to an isolated place they would unload the cash boxes, put them in the boot of the Fiesta and drive north into East Anglia. There they would divide the money and stay at different hotels until the police uproar had died down.

'What time did you say,' Reg asked Elizabeth as he flicked drops from his hairline.

'Eleven thirty on the dot,' she said. 'They're always very punctual.'

'The moment the van arrives I want you to go and wait in the car,' Gerald said. 'You must not be seen with us just in case someone recognizes you.' He fingered the filmy piece of silk in his pocket; Elizabeth had professionally cut the tights down to short lengths from the thigh that would cover their faces without the farce of the last attempt. 'You'd better go now,' he said giving her shoulder a light squeeze as a dark green van turned into the high street and halted outside the bank. An overweight security guard wearing a padded jacket, visored helmet and carrying a baton in his hand climbed out and, with one quick glance in each direction, waddled into Crampton Bank.

'Let's get ready,' Ali said and Gerald felt a shiver of fear as they hurried across the road and stopped to study the display in the shoe shop next to the bank. They made sure to stand with their backs to the van as the guard emerged from the bank carrying a steel box that he put in an opening at the back of the van. This closed and re-opened empty to reveal that the box had been taken inside. Reg began to fidget impatiently as the guard repeated this process four times until he thumped the back of the van and went to the nearside door. They quickly slipped the tights over their heads and rushed to be at the guard's side as the door swung open.

Gerald produced the gun, told him to back away and then instructed the driver to get out and join his partner who was now fearfully backed against the bank wall. The trio leapt into the van and locked the door while Gerald familiarized himself with the controls. They pulled away and after a few fitful leaps and jumps Reg mastered the clutch and they swept round the corner to briefly stop beside the Fiesta to allow Ali to change vehicles and follow the van.

'My God, that was so easy, Gerry,' Reg exclaimed elatedly as adrenaline and cocaine pumped through his system and he jumped two red lights, narrowly missing a motorcyclist and an arrogant senior citizen on a mobility scooter who had jumped the lights himself.

'Slow down,' Gerald warned. 'You'll draw attention to us and then we've had it.'

The armoured van slowed to well below the speed limit and after travelling ten miles Reg turned into a leafy layby hidden from the main road. The Fiesta soon caught up and pulled in behind them. When Ali climbed in Gerald turned to the small opening between the seats that led to the back of the van and the moneyboxes and stared at the heavy metal door.

'C'mon, Gerry, open it up and let's see what we've got,' Ali said gleefully.

'It's locked,' Gerry said sadly.

'What do you mean, it's locked, open it,' Reg shouted.

'It's a combination lock and we don't have the number,' Ali said mournfully as he leant past Reg to see the type of lock.

'Bollocks,' Reg exclaimed as Elizabeth arrived at the open door.

'Is something wrong, Gerry?' she asked on being confronted by a collection of frustrated faces looking down at her.

'Can we break it open?' she said innocently.

Gerald thumped hard with the palm of his hand on what could only be a thick, solid steel wall lying between them and a lot more than twenty-three thousand pounds and seventy-two pence.

Knowing it was only a matter of time before the van was traced to the layby they all climbed out, piled into the Fiesta, and drove out onto the main highway that was heading north.

Gerald had failed his mother again.

Detective Inspector Austin Cooper, his parents had had a sense of humour at the time of his christening, pulled up at the bank and went in to question Mr Percival Barnett. He was in the blackest of moods and had been since constable Teal was gunned down unmercifully in Goldenstein's house. As instructed in the car the three accompanying constables remained outside and began questioning the curious bystanders and local shopkeepers about the three bandits and any other suspicious characters loitering near the bank.

'Mr Barnett, did you see anything that may be of help to the investigation?' the inspector asked, shaking his head when he was comfortably seated in the manager's office and being offered tea.

'I'm afraid I was inside the bank and never saw the robbery taking place. The good news is that . . .'

'There's good news, Mr Barnett?' the sarcasm didn't go unnoticed.

'Yes there is good news. The security company was automatically notified and as the van has a transponder it shouldn't be long before it's location is pinpointed.'

'How could three professional guards working to a strict routine be so easily overcome?'

'That's the fault of the security company who only sent two men. One guard drove the van and the other did the pickups.'

Cooper stared at the manager suspiciously. 'Why only two?' he asked as the thought that it may have been an inside job crossed his mind.

'It's one of the bank's financial cutbacks during this recession. It's quite simple, if the bank waived the Premium and chose the security company's Economy service the increase in insurance would be less than the additional cost for increased manpower.'

The inspector shook his head in wonder, stood up, and without saying another word left the bank. Two of the constables were still questioning the local traders while the third was waiting by the revolving door with a small, petite woman in her middle forties.

'Excuse me sir, but this lady said she saw something of importance,' the constable reported and Cooper turned to the woman with one eyebrow arched questioningly.

'And what was that, madam?' he asked.

'Well, I always come this way to pick up fish fingers and milk and when I went past there –,' she pointed to a small street fifty yards away and across the street. 'I saw a green … no, it was a blue Fiesta, parked with the engine running. I knew the engine was going because there was steam coming out of the exhaust pipe.'

'How did you know it was a Fiesta.'

'My husband makes cars and he bloody well doesn't stop talking about the latest models he's been working on; he fair drives me potty he does, what with camshafts, gearwheels, inlet valves, carburetors etc. etc.,' she paused, took an exasperated deep breath and added, 'we also own one ourselves.'

'Did you see anybody in the car?' Cooper held his breath for the woman's answer.

'Yes, it was a woman with longish auburn hair. She was sitting in the passenger seat as though waiting for someone to join her.'

The inspector thanked her, told the constable to get a full statement and address details and reentered the bank. The manager walked across the hall to meet him with a puzzled expression.

'Did you forget something, Inspector?' he asked.

'Are all your staff present today?'

'As far as I know, yes.'

'Sure?'

Barnett went to the counter to ask Roger Wilton, the head teller, the same question. There was a brief irritable reply and the manager returned to the inspector to report that one member hadn't turned up for work and hadn't bothered to call to say why.

'Who would that be, Mr Barnett?'

'Miss Elizabeth Shanks, a junior teller who'll have a lot of questions to answer when she does honour us with her presence,' he replied angrily.

The inspector was thinking along the same lines. 'Would you happen to know if she has a car?'

'I don't think she does, she can't drive and goes everywhere by bus,' Barnett said and was surprised when the inspector simply turned and addressed the constable with him.

'Check Vehicle Licensing for any cars owned by a Miss Elizabeth Shanks or any members of her family,' he snapped and went to his car with a distinct feeling that the whole thing had been an inside job.

Barnett felt as though he had been hit in the solar plexus for the young woman he had been planning to seduce would now have to be fired for being an accessory to the robbery. With fingers crossed he returned to his office to begin writing a lengthy e-mail explaining the theft to head office. Although he had interviewed an inexperienced girl (in all matters) because of her curvy figure and angelic lips he had hoped to put to work he nevertheless wrote that it had been the Head Cashier's final decision to give her a trial period.

Inspector Cooper was halfway back to the police station when the answer came back on his smartphone, confirming his suspicion. Elizabeth Shanks didn't own a car but her deceased father had done, when he was alive, and it was a sky-blue Fiesta. Cooper instructed Traffic Control to find the car *poste haste* before passing the registration's listed address to the driver and telling him to get a move on.

It turned out to be a rather modest Victorian house and surprisingly it no longer belonged to the Shanks family. Elizabeth had given her address to the new owners for the purpose of forwarding her mail; the inspector took the piece of paper, thanked the woman and handed it to his driver with yet another order to break a traffic law.

Cooper was completely out of breath after the nerve-shattering, white-knuckle drive and taxing climb to Elizabeth's apartment but the driver right behind him was calm, cool and unaffected by the four flights of stairs. Cooper indicated the door and the large constable threw a shoulder at the door, breaking the flimsy lock, and staggered into the living room.

It was clear that the birds had flown and that the apartment had been thoroughly ransacked as though somebody had been looking for something very specific. The inspector made his way to the bedroom and was searching the wardrobe when the call came in that the armoured van had been located in a layby on the A12 running north; the transponder was activated and still working.

'They must have had another car waiting for them,' the traffic officer said and the inspector was reminded of the girl waiting in the blue Fiesta with the engine running.

'Any news on the Fiesta yet?' he asked and was informed that no vehicle with that registration had been spotted yet. 'Put checks on the whole length of the A12,' Cooper instructed before inquiring how much had been stolen.

'That's the weird thing, sir.' The traffic cop answered. 'They got away with nothing at all. The rear door was undamaged as was the access hatch in the driver's cab.'

The inspector shrugged and thought what kind of bizarre hijacker would hijack a security van loaded with cash and not, at least, try smashing the door open to steal it.

While thirty police cars were being allocated to create roadblocks along the length of double highway for the sole reason of apprehending a Fiesta that very same car was cutting across country and making a point of avoiding all major roads. Gerald had correctly assumed that the blue car may have been spotted at the scene and a quick police check would reveal the identity of the deceased owner. Gerald explained to the others that a member of staff, seen sitting in a car with the engine running while an armoured car was being hi-jacked didn't require much mental activity to reach the obvious conclusion that there was a link between the two. They agreed to his plan to leave the A12 and take a more devious route north which was why they were now lost in a complex matrix of Suffolk lanes.

'We need to stop and buy a road map,' Gerald said as they recognized a thatched cottage they had passed for the third time.

'Could you tell me why you chose to head this way?' Reg asked.

'The A12 was the nearest major road to the bank apart from the M25 and as you know that's monitored by scores of traffic cameras. However, we'll have to stop at some stage or other and decide on how we can make twenty-four thousand pounds and seventy-two pence and find a safe place for that.' He jerked his thumb at the case standing between Ali and Reg.

'Why don't we simply bury it,' Ali suggested.

'The case isn't waterproof and would rot in no time at all.'

'We need to hide it in a weather resistant building and I think the ideal place where it wouldn't be noticed would be in a dry church and in plain view,' Elizabeth said with a hand gesture that had implied *voilà!*

'What a fabulous idea, Betty,' Gerald said patting her on the knee. 'It will have to be a church big enough to make the book seem at home on its lectern.'

'Why not a cathedral?' Reg said with a curled lip.

Gerald ignored the sarcasm and thought for a while before speaking again. 'Let's get a map first and then decide which way to go.'

Ali stopped outside the general store in a tiny village they had already passed through twice and went in to emerge carrying a large road atlas and a paper bag filled with meat pies and cans of cola; Gerald and Ali had agreed that they were both hungry.

The map was spread out over the steering wheel and Gerald leant forward to study it over Ali's shoulder while eating one of the pies. 'Did this village have a name?' he asked, spilling pastry flakes and steak gravy on the shoulder of his friend's suit.

'Birdbrook,' Elizabeth said. 'I've read the sign three times so far.'

Gerald ran his finger up the page until he stopped and muttered, 'Of course, that's perfect.'

'What's perfect,' Reg snapped between sniffles. His desire for cocaine had now exceeded his need for food and he had become extremely irritable.

'Ely, mate. It's a medieval town with a magnificent cathedral.'

'It has all the essential grandeur to match a Guttenberg Bible and it will fade into the tapestry of the place if put on the right shelf,' Elizabeth said. 'However, I read all about it at school and I can't recall that the cathedral had any bookshelves inside that we could access.'

'They all do,' Gerald countered. 'Cathedrals have their own archives where they keep hundreds of religious and theological books as well as historical records on the history and people concerned with the cathedral and the surrounding region.

'So we look for the archives, pop our book on one of the shelves and hightail it out until we need to retrieve it at a later time.' Reg was still not convinced by the plan and felt that they could do better if they tried to sell it on the inter-net to the highest bidder.

'Without proof of ownership we'd have cops pounding on the door in no time at all.' Ali said sourly and Reg huddled down into the rear seat with a sullen expression. He desperately needed a happy moment and having used up his precious supply he wasn't looking forward to the unpredictable side effects of withdrawal that could begin at any time.

Ali started the car and following the map they were soon speeding from Suffolk into Cambridgeshire and heading for the island city of Ely. It was when they stopped to take on petrol in Bury St Edmunds that Reg left the car to use the men's room and make a phone call. His friend, still recovering from the beating he had received from Dozer, made a solemn promise to post a sniffer dog-proof packet of cocaine to the Ely main post office for Reg to collect. The supplier then promptly called Dozer to tell him where he could find Reg and his friends.

Reg, whose hands had begun to shake, returned to the car as Gerald came back from paying for the fuel with the debit card Ali had stolen. They continued their journey until one of England's most beautiful cathedrals greeted them in majestic style, rising above the surrounding fenland, soaring into the sky and marking the end of their journey.

Despite losing his employer Dozer was still determined to rescue the Gutenberg Bible. Rasmus' bullet hitting him in the chest and yet not killing him had motivated Dozer to continue the hunt. On recovering consciousness he found he was alone with an excruciating pain in his chest. Dozer tore his shirt open and found his solid gold medallion of St Christopher had been impressed into his flesh. He carefully prised it free, revealing a blood-red intaglio image of the Saint standing in water and bearing an infant on his shoulder.

This was the precise moment that a professional hit man who loved burying people alive with bulldozers had his epiphany and found God. He fell to his knees to give thanks and promptly promised to return the holy book to the church no matter what it took to do. Which church he had to take it to he wasn't sure but he felt God would let him know when the right time arose. Dozer knew it had to be a catholic church as his parents had begun raising him in that faith and from the age of four the family priest and his father's calloused hand had drummed righteousness into his head until he could take it no more.

The phone call from the small-time drug supplier was now seen as yet another instruction from above to ignore the physical abuse of his father and return to the faith. Once more he fell to his knees and this time he vowed to take confession at the nearest church before setting out to find the book that promised everlasting glory.

The total silence and the chill air as he entered St Marks seemed to foretell a death and he quickly used the holy water kept by the door. From a long-ago memory he was still capable of genuflecting before entering a back pew to recover from his guilty nervousness from entering a place of worship after so many years. Dozer tried to recall the prayer his mother repeated over and over again as he tried to sleep. This was after she had sat by his bed reading from the Old Testament, a black shawl covering her plaited hair. This had happened when he was only eight years old and no matter how many times his mother repeated *Actus Contritionis* his father's approach to religion would knock it out of his head the next day.

Dozer sat in silence for ten minutes.

'*Deus meus, ex toto corde paenitet me omnium . . .* ' O my God, I am heartily sorry for having offended Thee, and I detest all my sins . . .

Only the first line of the prayer in Latin returned and he had begun to whisper it under his breath when a black figure stopped beside his pew.

'Are you all right, my son,' the priest asked softly.

'I wish to confess, Father,' the thug said and the priest walked to the confessional and with a slight, almost imperceptible movement of his hand invited Dozer to enter the other side. The musty curtain instantly transported Dozer back to his childhood and he began to regret his decision as he sat on the hard seat. His buttocks were more cushioned than his youthful bony arse but the plain oak still proved to be just as uncomfortable. The small connecting panel was pulled back and beyond the latticed screen he could see the priest's shadow that began reciting a prayer as it made the Sign of the Cross.

'Bless me, Father, for I have sinned.' Dozer stuttered.

'How long has it been since your last confession, my son?'

There was a long pause before Dozer, who had been counting on his fingers, said, 'Forty-nine years, Father.'

A slight intake of breath and a couple of 'tuts' was the only encouragement for Dozer to continue.

'Is it true that whatever I say to you cannot be repeated to anyone else?' Dozer asked.

'Only to God, my son.'

'Then here goes, when I was nine I shot my father with an air-gun and ran away from home.'

'Was he badly hurt?'

'Apart from losing an eye he was okay,' Dozer said as though it was a minor event.

'Any sins a little more recent than that?'

Dozer wasn't going to be hurried by sarcasm. 'At eleven I stabbed a drug pusher and then . . .' Dozer went on to relate his whole life story with every sin carefully recalled and confessed. There were times when the sinner had to run back through the chronology of his life and confess to some earlier crimes he'd recalled.

The priest glanced down at his watch and realized he had been sitting in the confessional for nearly three hours with the devil's right hand man sitting no more than two feet distant. Dozer had only reached his eleventh assassination at the age of thirty-one when the priest called a halt for reasons of nature.

'I have to take an urgent break, can we continue this tomorrow?' he asked, shifting his painful buttocks that had been increasingly chafed by the edge of the wooden seat.

'I'll be here when you've finished what you have to do, Father,' Dozer snapped irritably and true to his word he was still waiting to continue the next twenty-eight years when the priest returned after a quarter bottle of twelve-year old Jack Daniels and a cheese sandwich. Dozer didn't finish until early evening and no sooner had the priest said, 'I absolve you of all your sins in the name of the Father, the Son and the Holy Spirit,' than Dozer was out through the curtain before the priest could suggest a suitable Act of Contrition.

Now feeling much lighter and completely cleansed of his sins as a bully cum thief cum blackmailer cum rapist cum murderer he ran down the church and paused briefly at the lectern where a very old and battered copy of the bible lay open. One particular passage struck a chord and he memorized it before going to the car to begin the long drive to a city called Ely. He was not familiar with that part of the country and had to rely on sat-nav to put him on the right road to a specific post office that wouldn't be open until the next morning but when it did he'd be ready to carry out his own act of contrition on the person he planned to meet.

CHAPTER 9

A FTER A RESTLESS NIGHT the motley band of friends abandoned the Fiesta in one of the city car parks, took a meagre breakfast at a reasonably priced café and used the rest room to wash and see to other natural needs. Suddenly Reg announced he had to go and see a friend about borrowing some money. Ali volunteered to go with him but Reg angrily insisted on going alone and darted out before any objections could be raised.

'See you at the post office.' It was this last remark at the door that had puzzled them all.

'Why on earth would he choose the post office as a meeting place?' Ali mused.

Gerald thought for a moment and then a wave of panic crossed his face. 'He's asked someone to post something to him,' he deduced.

'Cocaine,' Elizabeth assumed. 'He's been very fidgety since yesterday.'

'In which case he would have called the same peddler who would probably have informed those people we don't particularly want to meet,' Ali added in an anxious tone that made his voice crack.

'And they'll be waiting for him there,' Gerald ended the thought on everybody's lips and all three stood in unison and hurried from the café to catch up with Reg before he could reach the post office. When they turned the corner into the High Street they were immediately overwhelmed by the sheer majesty of the Cathedral soaring high into the washed-out blue sky. They had trotted fifty yards with eyes fixed on the beauty of the Church of St Etheldreda and St Peter before Gerald spotted Reg running across the road with a rather burly figure in black close behind him.

'That's Reg,' Gerald said.

'And that's Dozer,' Ali observed drily. 'We'd better find somewhere to lay low for a while,' he added before Gerald expressed the same sentiment. They retraced their steps until they stood outside the café where an extremely angry woman wearing a pink pinafore rushed out and grabbed Ali by the arm.

'You didn't pay for your coffees,' she exclaimed, turning the heads of customers within the café. 'I'll call the police and have you arrested.'

'Madam,' Ali said in his most rounded, well-modulated tone of voice, 'we had realized our oversight when we were on the way to join our party in the cathedral and immediately returned to rectify the situation.' Ali took a wallet from his pocket, one he had lifted three days previously, and extracted a twenty pound note. 'Will that cover the bill,' he asked innocently.

'I'll get your change,' the waitress mumbled remorsefully.

'Please, madam, accept any change as our apology for giving you so much trouble.' Ali touched his forehead and led the others away leaving the waitress undecided about whether to smile or scowl.

'Now what?' Elizabeth asked when they were out of earshot.

'We can go back to the Fiesta and see if Reg managed to dodge Dozer and if he's not there we can wait in the car for him to turn up before making any decisions,' Gerald said and they both nodded. The walk to the car park took the best part of an hour and the case in Gerald's hand was becoming heavier with every yard they covered. They turned into Brays Lane and immediately saw the patrol car blocking the exit to the car park. The walked closer and saw another car parked by the Fiesta with four officers discussing whether to break into the car or leave it until the chief superintendent arrived.

'I think we have to consider whether we should loiter near the car park until we spot Reg; then head him off before he runs into that heap of trouble or head straight for the cathedral and hope he doesn't get caught,' Gerald suggested and on their agreement not to let their friend fall into the trap they split up to avoid being too obvious and wandered to the junctions of the three roads around the car park.

Ali was the first see Reg walking fast towards the entrance, oblivious to the patrol car blatantly obstructing the entrance. He increased his pace to catch up with him but stopped, scratched his head as though remembering something he had forgotten to do and walked back the way he had come. Gerald spotted Ali's about turn and saw his reason, Reg had gone straight to the car and two plain-clothed detectives who had been waiting nearby were approaching him.

The friends met up at the next intersection and Gerald pointed towards the cathedral and told them it was imperative that they go ahead with their original plan to hide the bible in the cathedral's library before they themselves were caught.

They were only two streets away from the main entrance and after a brisk walk, constantly checking for any stalkers, they entered the cool interior of the Gothic Galilee porch without being seen. They walked down the longest nave in Britain, marveling at the rich colourful decorations far above their heads.

'It's so beautiful,' Elizabeth whispered craning her neck as far back as possible.

'And the most apt place to hide the Gutenberg Bible,' Gerald replied in an equally hushed voice.

Ali remained silent as they paused briefly beneath the famous octagonal lantern before going through the North Transept and into the magnificent Lady Chapel. They found no sign of an entrance to anything resembling a library and moved on to spend the next twenty minutes exploring the whole cathedral before admitting defeat and collapsing into a pew.

'I would have thought Ely had a huge library,' Gerald muttered.

'Why don't we ask someone?' Elizabeth asked.

'It'll draw attention to why we are here,' Ali whispered as a cleric walked past with cassock swishing lightly on the stone with each step.

'I'll do it,' she replied and without waiting for an objection she went after the tall man and tapped him on the arm.

He stopped and looked at Elizabeth with pleasantly brown eyes. 'Can I help you, miss?'

'Could you direct me to the cathedral's library.'

'We have a variety of books in the gift shop.'

'No, I meant the proper library or the archives where you keep all the old books.'

His pleasantly brown eyes had changed and were now unpleasantly suspicious. 'And why would you want to go in there?'

'I have a great interest in old books,' Elizabeth answered, her mind racing as she tried to preempt his next question. 'I have a college project that is all about the development of the English language through religion.'

The cleric studied her face for a few seconds before nodding. 'That's very interesting but I cannot help you as the archives are not open to the public and you would need to make an appointment with our Cathedral Archivist to get special permission.'

Elizabeth made a brief remark of disappointment, asked how she could contact the Archivist and thanked the cleric before returning to the pew.

'A-n-d?' Gerald asked.

'No luck, we'll have to think of somewhere else to hide it.'

'There is one place we could try,' Ali said hesitantly.

'And where is that?' Gerald asked.

'My place.'

'You don't have a place, Ali,' Elizabeth said. 'You've only got Charing Cross Bridge and a bundle of old newspapers.'

'I admit that Ali doesn't have a home but Sir Alistair Montague does,' he replied holding his hands up apologetically when Elizabeth and Gerald, struck dumb, found they could only stare at their friend in disbelief.

'Is that your real name?' Elizabeth finally whispered while looking towards the west tower where a familiar silhouette was framed in the main entrance by shafts of sunlight.

'I became known as Ali Monty because of the alimony payments that almost reduced me to penury,' he replied. 'Is that Reg?' he added as he also squinted the length of the cathedral at the small figure looking their way.

'Yes.' Gerald stood up and raised his arm to gain his friend's attention. 'I don't know how he did it but the clever sod escaped that police trap and even more farfetched is expecting us to believe you're a knight of the realm?' All three watched as Reg strode down the nave towards them with a grin as wide as a whale shark feeding.

'I'm sorry, Gerry, but yes, and I have a small place in Norfolk that might be an acceptable hiding place for the Gutenberg Bible.'

'You could have told us that earlier,' Gerald muttered.

Reg grabbed Gerald and then hugged the other two in turn, spending a little more time holding Elizabeth than necessary until Gerald tapped him on the shoulder. 'How did you get away from the trap in the car park?' he asked.

'When they asked for my name I asked for their identification and I made a point of studying both warrant cards before explaining I was undercover and couldn't take any risks.' Reg then told them how he explained away his shabby appearance by giving the two detectives a cock and bull story that he was part of a local operation, codenamed Hotcarski, that was out to trap a ring of car thieves who transported luxury cars to Lowestoft for shipping to Murmansk and the lucrative mafia markets in St Petersburg.

'They bought it all, hook line and sinker and wished me good luck,' Reg concluded. 'That's the good news but I have some bad news too. Dozer is in town and he spotted me leaving the car park but I lost him in the back streets. Did you find somewhere to stash the bible?'

'No, and we'd better get moving,' Ali said.

'And I'd better get us some transport,' Reg added as they went through the main entrance and out into the bright sunshine. 'Walk down to the roundabout and wait,' he pointed down Gallery Road. 'I'll join you in five minutes.' Reg went back into the cathedral and disappeared from sight in the gloom of the Galilee Porch.

True to his word he pulled up beside them in a dark green Citroën C3 and invited them to get in. They left Ely and headed northeast on the A10 as Reg told them how he had managed to steal the car so swiftly. Ali took up the narrative and gave them his family history. By the time they had bypassed King's Lynn and were heading towards the Norfolk coast they had learnt that the Montague family had farmed in the region for more than twelve generations. Ali had been knighted for his agricultural services to the nation and had risen to the rank of Colonel with the 1st East Anglian Regiment and been awarded the DSO for bravery in Afghanistan. Although his whole family had warned him about the money-grabbing woman he chose to marry he still went ahead and was taken to the cleaners. All she left him was the small farmhouse near a village called Cley next the Sea; this she couldn't keep for Ali had signed the deed over to Margaret, his older sister.

'My younger sister is married to a millionaire sheep farmer and living in Alice Springs,' he finished and lapsed into a meditative silence as they passed through one village after another that dotted the drained fenland stretching to the North Sea. With Ali navigating they finally passed through Cley next the Sea and on to a small side road that led to a large set of wrought iron gates. On the pillars that stood either side were stone gryphons with one paw raised as though warding off invaders from the sea.

'It's been our family crest since the sixteenth century,' Ali said on noticing them looking up as they swept through the open gates. They were rendered mute as the Citroën glided along the long drive lined with giant elm trees that had escaped the Dutch elm disease until a country house suddenly appeared before them.

'This is your small farmhouse?' Reg croaked as he braked on the gravel forecourt before the broad set of stone steps that led to double oak doors carrying the same legendary symbol of divine power and guardian of treasure as the gate pillars. One of the doors opened and a willowy, dark haired woman stepped out with a grim expression on her handsome face.

'Where the fucking hell have you been, Alistair?' she shouted the moment he left the car. 'You've been gone for three years and not a word to let me know where you were or what you were doing and then you pitch up out of the blue.'

'Please meet my sister, Margaret,' Alastair said by way of introduction. 'This is Gerry, Elizabeth and Reg.' One by one the woman firmly grasped their hands and Ali asked Reg to hide the car in one of the garages at the rear of the house before he truned to lead the others into the house. As they entered the vast drawing room Ali was slightly concerned that he may have put Elizabeth at risk. His sister had remained unmarried for one reason and that was because she preferred her own gender. Ali had noticed the way she had eyed Elizabeth up and down when she was getting out of the car. Elizabeth, innocent of her hostess's disposition, dropped into the soft upholstery of one of the chairs and carelessly crossed her legs, revealing a little thigh that Margaret's eyes pounced upon like a feral cat.

Ali distracted his sister's attention by pouring brandies and giving her a brief history of the last three days. Margaret was compelled to shift her gaze away from young woman and to look at her brother in total disbelief.

'You've been blown up by a drugs factory, robbed a bank, hi-jacked an armoured car and now you're being chased by killers and the police who want a valuable book that your friend Gerald burgled from a high court judge; all in three days?' she spluttered and put her glass on the side table.

'Afraid so, sis, although the police know nothing about the Gutenberg Bible' Ali said as though that forgave him for everything else.

'And you've come back home to hide for a while?'

'And to hide the bible; is the old priest's hole still there?'

'Of course it is.'

'We can put the book in there, Gerald, and then we can relax a little,' Ali said pointing to the case at Gerald's feet before turning back to his sister. 'Is that okay with you, old girl?'

Margaret frowned at her brother and looked across at Elizabeth's pretty face and her hard expression melted. 'We've still got dad's old Purdeys in the gun cabinet and we've got your old BSA air rifle from when you were a boy,' she said without looking at her brother.

'That should be enough,' Reg murmured as he stared through the large leaded window at the long drive disappearing into the avenue of elms as though expecting something to appear at any moment.

He was unaware that the two gryphons guarding the main gate were blindly watching as a dark car stopped in the road and a large man got out to read the brass plaque attached to the left-hand pillar.

No Hawkers, Canvassers, Double-glazing Salesmen or Religious Instruction sent him to the pillar opposite that was engraved with a conflicting message; *Welcome to Montague Hall* and he knew he had arrived at the right address.

The moment Rasmus shot Goldenstein in the head Mutton joined the nation's ranks of unemployed and now there were only two things he wanted; first, to be the head of Goldenstein's business and second, to avenge his employer's death. For eight years after his departure from Wormwood Scrubs Mutton had been fully employed as a nightclub bouncer, protection enforcer and occasional assassin. He was well rewarded by Goldenstein and Mutton's warped sense of honour now put the onus on him to take an eye for an eye.

He had learnt about the Gutenberg Bible from Dozer and knew the only way he could find Rasmus would be by hanging around Gerald Latimer. The word doing the rounds in the clubs was that Gerald had joined up with two down-and-outs called Reg and Ali Monty. Reg Barnett had led nowhere and Gerald proved to be a dead end, literally. Mutton and an associate called Rodney, another ex-employee of Goldenstein, continued probing until one of the dropouts under Charing Cross Bridge mentioned that Ali spoke 'real proper like' and had the look of an officer. This led Mutton to an odd reference in *Who's Who* that had a photograph of the young uniformed man and revealed Ali's true identity to be one of the landed gentry with a farm and manor house in the county of Norfolk. Mutton decided to investigate the address and Rodney would follow to lend a second heavy hand should it be needed.

Who'd have bloody believe it, Mutton thought as he sat outside the impressive gates; the man slept rough and looked like a tramp when all the time he had this. He drove through the gates and along the avenue towards the house on the basis that Rasmus would come to him if he wanted Gerald and the bible. Mutton had no time for religion and church books meant even less for his prime objective was to remove Rasmus from his short list of rivals for the gang leadership.

Gerald had been daydreaming about making love to Elizabeth when he was rendered speechless by a black car emerging from the tree-lined avenue and driving slowly towards the house until it stopped outside.

'We've got visitors,' he managed to gasp and the others rushed to the window to watch as the car door swung open and a burly man in a camel hair overcoat got out, his bald pate glinting pink in the setting sun. Margaret had disappeared into the next room and as they watched the man stomping towards the front door she returned and handed Gerald one of the Purdey shotguns. He clumsily broke the gun and both unused cartridges were ejected onto the carpet.

Margaret scowled at him. 'Haven't you used a gun before?' she asked tersely, taking it and reloading it in a manner that showed her familiarity with weapons.

'Not exactly the tool needed to make sedan cars,' he retorted as she returned it and pointed to a small lever on the top.

'That's the safety and it's on. Just push it with your thumb when you're ready to fire,' she explained. 'But only when you're ready to shoot, got it?' she snapped and Gerald nodded. Margaret tossed the other gun to her brother who caught it, professionally broke it to check the load and hung it over the crook of his arm.

The doorbell clanged and everyone froze.

'Who is he?' Elizabeth whispered.

'It's Mutton,' Reg said as he stood the air rifle against the wall. 'I know him and he's one of Goldenstein's men.'

'He'll be after the bible then,' Ali said closing the Purdey with a satisfying clunk as Reg went to answer the door. 'He's a tough one so be ready for anything,' Ali added following his friend into the grand hall with the weapon ready.

'Reg! Didn't know you'd be 'ere,' Mutton exclaimed as the door opened and then he took a step back on seeing Ali with the Purdey.

'I know why you're here Mutton and you can't have it,' Reg declared defiantly.

'Don't know what you're talking about mate. I'm hoping to catch that bloody Greek who wasted my boss.'

'Goldenstein?'

'Who else.'

'Someone's killed Goldesntein?'

'How many times do I have to say it and aren't you going to invite me in?' He began entering the house and only stopped when the barrels of the two Purdeys were touching his overcoat. 'It's been a long drive and I could murder a drink.'

'Why are you really here?' Ali interrupted as he lowered his gun.

'To wait for Rasmus Psomas,' Mutton said with an impatient sigh as Gerald did the same.

'Not for the bible?'

'If I'm going to shoot somebody for something you can be bloody sure it ain't no bible.'

'Come in . . . e r r r, Mutton,' Ali said. 'Is that really your name?'

'Cyril Catchpole, pleased to meet you, Sir,' Mutton said in a mock Oxbridge accent as they entered the living room. 'They all call me Mutton because of this.' He pointed to the barely visible hearing aid.

'Mutton?' Elizabeth asked.

'It comes from Mutt and Jeff. Deaf. Cockney rhyming slang,' Reg explained while the big man slipped his coat off and accepted a large gin and tonic from Ali. 'He's here to see to a Greek killer who is looking for us, and the book. It seems that fellow had murdered Goldenstein, who used to be my boss and his, and he's not too happy about it.'

Margaret had come to the conclusion that an extra gun, should the nasty fellow called Rasmus turned up, may come in handy. 'We have plenty of bedrooms, Mr Catchpole, if you should wish to stay the night,' Margaret offered as she collected the Purdeys to return to the gun cabinet.

'That's nice of you lady, I'll go and tell my girl the good news.' Mutton said and left the room with the glass still in his hand. They all rushed to the window to see him open the car door and a very attractive blonde climbed out wearing the shortest and tightest of skirts and a blouse that visibly struggled to contain its silicone contents.

'This is Lilly-Ann,' Mutton announced as they returned to the room. All eyes fixed on the beautiful young woman with the reddest lips, that were no strangers to Botox, and the longest dark lashes they had ever seen. 'Great isn't she?'

'Sensational, Mutton,' Reg said with eyes saying a lot more.

'Hi everybody,' Lilly-Ann said in an east London accent. 'It's so kind of you to put us up for the night.' She sat on the sofa and crossed her long legs in a casual yet well-rehearsed manner that far excelled Elizabeth's demure posture and drew every man's eyes to the expanse of nylon exposed. Margaret was not unaffected herself and she hurried to make a drink for her sixth houseguest who looked long and hard into Margaret's eyes when she took the cold glass, their fingers touching briefly. Margaret left hurriedly to prepare a simple meal for everyone before her beating heart became too dangerous.

Ali sorted out bedrooms to everyone's satisfaction and after a quiet word with Gerald about his position regarding Elizabeth Ali gave him the most comfortable double bedroom in the house.

They finished eating and returned to the living room just as the moon began to rise and the grounds were bathed in a silvery light; creating an artistic monochromatic image with the black lawn and white drive being swallowed by the blackness of trees. They held a council of war resulting in all the men being given four hours for sleep and four to patrol the grounds. Margaret volunteered to look in on the girls to make sure they were okay while Mutton and Reginald were on duty and apart from a suspicious look from Ali it was agreed.

The heavy drapes were closed and more drink was circulated before Ali called it a day and retired to his room. Gerald and Mutton were on first watch and they took the Purdeys and went out into the grounds while everyone else went to their rooms; Margaret lingered to check that all windows and doors were securely locked.

The large clock on the landing had just chimed twelve thirty when a ghostly figure swept along the corridor and paused outside the room given to Gerald and Elizabeth; it paused and then continued on to tap on the door to Mutton's room. Lilly-Ann opened it wearing a gossamer nightdress that hardly reached her knees and then unhesitantly stood to one side to let Margaret enter.

'Is everything okay, nobody under the bed or in the wardrobe?' Margaret said with a grin as she sat on the large bed.

Lilly-Ann chuckled and sat beside her. 'How much time do we have?'

'Almost two hours.'

'That should be enough,' Lilly-Ann murmured as she leant close to smell Margaret's long hair.

The large clock chimed two o'clock when the door opened again and the shadowy figure resumed her walk through the house to arrive at the front door that she unlocked to admit Gerald and Mutton who, covered in night dew, had just arrived.

'Is my girl okay?' Mutton asked as he handed the shotgun to Ali who had just come down the stairs.

'Wonderful,' Margaret said with an enigmatic smile. 'You'll also find Lilly-Ann is fast asleep as the long drive from London has thoroughly exhausted her.'

Ali looked at his sister with the suspicion of a smile and rushed from the house before he was unable to prevent himself from laughing out loud. Reg followed more slowly with the second Purdey, trying to remember if the safety had to be pushed forward or back to render the weapon safe. Ali waved him off to the right while he headed across the lawn on the left hand side of the house. Reg mistook his instruction and trotted across the lawn to the trees where he began working his way through the undergrowth to where he believed the boundary wall lay. After a few minutes of being painfully scratched by the brambles and aching from the effort to make any headway in the wilderness he retreated back to the lawn. It had occurred to him that it would be easier to spot any intruder by constantly walking around the house like Ali and he had just turned the corner and was heading into the courtyard when he spotted a shadowy figure dart across the cobbles and into one of the garages. Reg didn't believe it could be Ali being so furtive and he brought the gun up to his shoulder and began walking towards the dark opening. Suddenly a figure emerged from the shadows and Reg could see that he was a perfect stranger and that he was taking a gun from his coat pocket. The Purdey remained silent when he pulled the trigger and Reg realised he had pushed the safety lever the wrong way. There was a sharp sound and an even sharper pain in his side when the stranger fired. Reg dropped to sit on the cold cobbles and without thinking slid the safety lever and with the gun by his side he tried pulling the trigger once more. Four things happened all at once. One, the stranger was thrown back by a 28g piece of shot in his chest; two, his automatic fired again and killed the female peacock that always roosted on the courtyard wall; three, the loosely held Purdey had recoiled out of Reg's grasp and shot back across the courtyard; four, the mahogany butt of the weapon struck the wall to discharge the second barrel which felled the male peacock roosting on the roof of the garage ending the breeding pair's happy relationship.

Ali came running round the corner of the house to find Reg staring in shock at one dead man and two dead birds. Ali knelt beside the sitting man and on seeing the blood soaked through the shirt his mind ran back the years to his time in Afghanistan. He tore the shirt open to find a single seeping hole in Reg's side and a quick look revealed that it was a through and through in the fleshy part of the waist. He used a clean handkerchief to create a pad and instructed Reg to press it against the entry while he made another with his cravat for the exit wound. Gerald and Mutton ran into the courtyard to find a scene from Gunfight at the OK Corral and they helped Ali get Reg onto his feet.

As they walked past the fallen man Mutton looked down and shouted a profanity. 'My Gawd, you've killed Rodney,' he exclaimed as he dropped to his knees beside the ex-unemployed gangland enforcer. 'Wotcha do that for,' he yelled into Reg's ear on standing up.

'He tried to shoot me,' Reg said and winced from the pain in his side and Mutton's stiff forefinger poking his chest.

'Whoever he was he *did* shoot you, mate,' Ali corrected. 'Who was he?' This was directed at Mutton who had turned and was looking down at his former colleague.

'That was Rodney, he was my partner and had come to help me deal with Rasmus, whenever he bothers to turn up,' Mutton mumbled. He turned and stumped off back to the house and Lilly-Ann who had remained dead to the world when the big man leapt from the bed on hearing gunfire.

'Oh, damn, I think you've pissed him off, Reg,' Gerald said and they went into the house to be greeted by Margaret and Elizabeth who immediately began fussing over the wound like hens with a cracked egg. Reg suffered liberal amounts of iodine, four painkillers and Elizabeth's neat cross-stitched needlework in relative silence and when dressings had been applied fell asleep in an instant.

'He'll need to get proper medical attention and soon,' Elizabeth said.

'That goes without saying, but what do we do about the corpse?' Ali benoaned.

'You do nothing, I'll handle Rodney,' Mutton said on entering Reg's bedroom. 'You must know of a good place to dump a body. Some god-forsaken spot where he wouldn't be found for a very, very long time?'

Ali thought for a moment and then clicked his fingers. 'There's the old well that hasn't been used by anyone for over a century; some say it's over one hundred feet deep.'

'Show me,' Mutton demanded curtly and he strode from the room.

With Rodney rolled in a horse blanket and draped over Mutton's wide shoulder they strode out of the courtyard and over to the farmyard. Montague Hall had long ceased to be a livestock farm and was primarily used by a tenant farmer for the arable land and the dry-stone enclosure was bereft of animals; the well that had once been used for the pigs was situated in the far corner and was covered with a heavy wooden cover.

'How deep is it,' Mutton asked as Ali struggled to slide the cover to one side.

'I don't know, as a boy I used to drop stones but I never heard them hit water or the bottom.'

Mutton sat Rodney on the edge. 'And it's never likely to be used again?'

'No, it's completely dry now.'

'Goodbye, Rodney,' Mutton muttered and pushed the dead man who toppled backward into the blackness. Both men listened and within a second a loud splash was heard as Rodney hit water that was very close to the top of the well.

'I thought you said it was dry and deep.'

'It is, or it was,' Ali stuttered and as he tried to see something in the darkness the moon emerged from behind a cloud and he saw the glitter of rippling water and the white face of Rodney looking up at him in recrimination.

'Bloody hell, I can see the tosser, he's only ten feet down.' Mutton exclaimed angrily. 'How did that happen?'

Ali shrugged. 'Maybe air was trapped in his coat.'

'What I meant was where did the fucking water come from?'

'It must be the heavy rain we've had this year, it's raised the water table considerably and that's helped to fill the well.'

While the two men stood in silence looking down at the face that seemed to mock them another stranger to the Montague estate stood by the farmyard gate looking at them. He had no idea what was interesting the two men in the well but being unarmed he was taking no chances with a shotgun and automatic pistol and he silently returned to the car and his own armoury stored in the back.

CHAPTER 10

RASMUS HAD BEEN AT A COMPLETE LOSS in his hunt for Gerald and the bible until he telephoned Judge Atkinson and told him the latest events and how he now had a cold trail. After a curt 'Wait' the line was cut and Rasmus was compelled to sit on his hands for thirty-five minutes before the call was returned.

'I've been checking with my police contacts and it appears that Inspector Cooper has driven to Ely to investigate a car that had been abandoned there by suspects who fled after failing to rob an armoured car. They are undoubtedly the people you need to find so you must go there to pick up any leads and if I hear more I'll call you.' The line went dead and Rasmus shrugged and went to the rented Mondeo to programme the sat-nav for the historic city in the fenland.

As he drove towards Ely he received another call from the judge informing him that a dark green Citroën C3, belonging to one of the cathedral clerics, had been reported stolen and was last seen by traffic CCTV cameras heading towards the Norfolk coast. Inspector Cooper had received the same message from central traffic control and was also driving towards King's Lynn on the off-chance he would either receive another report of a sighting or possibly catch up with the stolen car himself.

At a discrete distance behind Cooper's car was a dark green Volvo with Dozer behind the wheel. He had fortuitously arrived at the car park when uniformed police from two patrol cars and what appeared to be a plainclothes detective were discussing what to do with the Fiesta. It was only after he had parked that he recognized the untidy plainclothes cop and when, after waving to the police, Reg hurried away from the scene

Dozer followed, knowing he would lead him to Gerald and the holy book he craved so passionately. He lost his fleet-footed quarry in the smaller streets and had returned to the Volvo when the phone rang and Mutton's instantly recognizable bellow forced him to reduce volume. Mutton had a habit of compensating for his impaired hearing even when his hearing aid was switched on.

'Where are you Dozer?' the voice shouted.

'Ely, where are you?'

'I'm at a place waiting for Rasmus Psomas, the man who killed our employer.'

'Does he know where you are?'

'He'll soon work it out.'

Dozer had heard of Rasmus and he respected the Greek's reputation for dishing out death at the drop of a coin, preferably gold Britannias. It was rumoured on the street that a High Court judge was using him to intimidate witnesses, jury members and any other dirty little tasks his judicial hands shouldn't be seen touching.

Dozer listened to silence for a moment and then repeated his question. 'Where exactly are you?'

'I'm at a place called Montague Hall with Reg, Gerald and Ali Monty.'

Dozer knew he was being lied to for he had just lost Reg in Ely and the other two may well be with him. 'Where's that?' He growled.

'Just outside a town called Cley next the Sea.'

'Does Gerald Latimer still have the bible?'

There was the briefest of pauses before Mutton confirmed he did and Dozer felt a frisson of excitement at the thought of being so near to the Holy Grail. He was then told that there were three women in the house and Dozer was disappointed that he couldn't just crash in and demand the book. His sudden enlightenment after confession had also included a new respect for women and he had shown his sixteen-year-old Chinese pole dancers the door with instructions to find righteous employment or else he'd make sure Allah's wrath removed their heads; his recent re-introduction to the faith and the latest news on terrorist activity tended to confuse his knowledge of religious punishments.

Mutton could sense Dozer's indecision. 'Just come and I'll get Reg to introduce you to everyone as his ex-colleague. Then we'll work out a way to locate the hiding place of the bible and be on our way. Would forty percent of the take be okay with you?'

'You think I'm going to sell it?' Dozer snapped. 'That's a sacred book that belongs in the Lord's house and that's where I'm going to put it.'

Mutton was amazed by the man's passionate reaction and tapped his earpiece thinking he'd misheard. 'Why nick it if we're not going to get anything for it?'

The words Dozer had read in the battered bible came back in a rush. 'Render to Caesar the things that are Caesar's, and to God the things that are God's.'

'What the heck is that meant to mean?'

'It's enough for you to know that we'll be getting the Lord's blessing for what we are going to do and that should be enough.'

'For you, mate but not for me. It's only a damned book and we should get whatever we can for it.'

Dozer's intake of air on hearing such blasphemy whistled down the line before the connection was abruptly broken. Mutton knew he'd said the wrong thing to a man who was obviously one storey short of a bungalow and he would now have to warn the others. They weren't surprised by his news that Dozer was on his way as Mutton's voice had carried through the oak bedroom door as though it was tissue paper. The men and the women were gathered in the living room when Mutton entered and before he could say anything Ali tapped the side of his head and told him that they had heard the complete one-sided conversation and that he should get a new battery for his earpiece.

'Dozer's not happy and it sounds like he's with the fairies,' Mutton mumbled.

'Why on earth did you phone such a man?' Elizabeth asked.

'We need help if Rasmus turns up and he will, you mark my words.'

'Not the kind of help that a man like Dozer hands out,' Reg snapped, wincing from the stab of pain beneath the tight dressing on his side.

Ali wandered over to the window and looked up at the bright moon. 'We need to make a plan for when your mate and that other man called Rasmus turn up,' he suggested and they all sat down.

Margaret sat next to Lilly-Ann and took her hand. 'The house is well protected with strong shutters on all the windows and heavy locks on the door.'

Mutton had seen the way the two women looked at each other and he knew Lilly-Ann was lost to him. The young woman was clearly enamoured by the Margaret and he mentally shrugged and innocently bellowed in his normal voice, 'Where's the bible hidden?' The room went quiet and all eyes were fixed on the criminal. 'Dozer is only coming for the book and if we give it to him nobody will be hurt.'

'Like hell we will,' Gerald growled. 'And where it's hidden is none of your damned business.'

Mutton bristled and rose to his feet only to sink down again when the men stood, one with a casually held Purdey. He had considered using the automatic in his pocket to threaten the men but the twin barrels that lay across Ali's arm and his determined expression put paid to that idea and he decided to wait for better opportunity to arise. Reg volunteered to go round the house and close all the shutters and Margaret gave him the keys for all the outside doors.

Margaret and Lilly-Ann went to the kitchen to make a late night snack for everyone. It was when the last cheese and pickle sandwich had been put on the plate by the younger woman that Margaret suggested she stay and live with her at Montague Hall. Lilly-Ann's answer was to embrace her lover and to kiss her with a passion that aroused Margaret. Lilly-Ann placed a sandwich to her lips and told her they would have to wait until after they had given the others their meal.

Heavy knocking at the front door separated them and Margaret hurried to see who had arrived at such an early hour of the morning. Gerald and Ali, both carrying shotguns, stopped her from unlocking the door and her brother called out, 'Who's there?'

'I want to speak to Mutton,' a voice shouted back.

'Come back at a respectable time in the morning,' Gerald said.

'It is morning.'

'Later, much later,' Gerald insisted. The only response was a deathly silence that went on until Margaret, who had gone to an upstairs window, shouted down the stairs that a large burly man in a long overcoat had just driven away.

114

'He'll be back,' Mutton warned on walking into the hall. 'The stupid bugger has become all religious and wants nothing more than to give that bloody book to the first priest who'll make use of it and I have a feeling he'll kill anybody who gets in his way.'

Margaret rushed down the stairs. 'There's someone else out there,' she said breathlessly. 'Almost as big as the other one and dressed in black.' There was a sudden bang on the door that added credence to her words.

'Let me in,' a man with a faint foreign accent demanded angrily.

'That's Rasmus,' Mutton exclaimed in what he thought was a whisper but was clearly heard on the other side of the door.

'Rasmus Psomas to be exact and I've come for the bible.' There was a sound of metal on metal and Ali pushed Gerald to one side as a large gun blasted a one-inch diameter hole through the three-inch oak panel. Across the hall a ceramic vase, standing on a jardinière, exploded into a thousand fragments.

'Open the door or I'll blast it and you to kingdom come,' Rasmus shouted.

They all ducked back into the living room and Margaret looked round for Lilly-Ann but couldn't see her anywhere. She felt a growing feeling of impending disaster as she saw her new love emerge from the kitchen on the other side of the hallway and start walking towards her with a nervous smile. Margaret and Ali both held their hands with a cry of warning to prevent her coming any further but they were too late. Another blast rocked the front door and a bright scarlet blotch appeared in the young girl's side as she was thrown to the floor. Margaret instantly knew she was dead and a plaintive wail of despair left her throat, chilling the hearts of everyone. Elizabeth looked through the doorway at the fallen girl in horror while Mutton bellowed pure hatred for the Greek assassin.

'I thought you said it was Dozer who would kill anyone who got in his way,' Gerald cried out. 'Now we've got this psychopath after us as well.'

'We've got to leave,' Ali stated coolly and went into the adjoining library. The others reluctantly followed without fully understanding how they could escape the lunatic outside without going out into the dark themselves.

'I have a feeling our shotguns and an air rifle will be a trifle ineffective against the weapon he is using,' Gerald said as he caught up with Ali who was standing in front of a large bookcase packed with leather-backed tomes. 'This is the sort of place I was thinking of to hide the Gutenberg in.' he added as he gazed at the floor to ceiling collection.'

'And so it was,' Ali said climbing the library ladder to remove one of the books.

'That's the bible, isn't it,' Mutton asked taking the automatic from his pocket.

Reg stopped behind him. 'I'll take that, Mutton,' he said, prodding the man with his Purdey and he took the weapon and dropped it into his own jacket pocket and waved the big man away. 'What's next, Ali?'

'Yes, how are we going to get away from Rasmus?' Elizabeth added.

'The same way our family priest got away when the roundheads came a-visiting with chains, faggots of wood and flaming torches,' Ali said enigmatically.

'The priest's hole,' Margaret said as she looked back over her shoulder towards Lilly-Ann with tears glistening on both cheeks. She then walked to another section of the library, pulled a copy of Shakespeare's sonnets from the shelf and pushed against the massive bookcase. To the amazement of those watching a small section of the shelving turned on a central pivot to reveal a dark hole in the wall behind.

'It was originally concealed by a simple cupboard that two servants manhandled whenever there was a threat and their cleric had to disappear swiftly,' Ali explained and taking a torch from a shelf within the cavity he lead the way with an instruction for the last person to close the bookcase. Margaret volunteered to do that for it afforded her with a last look at Lilly-Ann and soon they were all following the weak pool of yellow light along a dank passage lined with ancient bricks.

'How far does this stretch?' Gerald asked.

'Three-hundred yards and it comes out in a small copse on the other side of the hill,' Ali replied and then told them how he and Margaret used to play in the secret passage whenever there were boring dinner guests or visiting children they couldn't abide to play with. The floor was running with water seepage that ran down the walls and their shoes became covered in mud that began seeping through leather and material until their feet were uncomfortably dampened.

Gerald was starting to feel claustrophobic when they finally arrived at an iron gate interwoven with dense ivy. Ali produced a large key and it turned easily in the well-oiled lock enabling them to leave the passage and push through a wild hedge to a small clearing in the copse. They stood in a group wondering what their next move should be when Margaret, seething with hatred for the man who had destroyed her new love, spoke in a flat, toneless voice that her brother had never heard before.

'I don't know about you, Alistair, but I refuse to be driven from our ancestral home by a psychopathic murderer of young women.' She snatched the automatic pistol from Reg's pocket and before he could react she had stepped back, challenging him to recover it; needless to say, Reg backed away with his hands held up.

'It's much too dangerous, Margaret,' Elizabeth said and as if to underline her words a loud explosion rolled across the estate as Rasmus sent another round into the door to smash the heavy lock.

Ali went to take his sister by the arm but she evaded his hand and slipped away into the trees, disappearing in the darkness. 'I'll have to go after her,' he said with a shrug of the shoulders and took the shotgun from Reg and held his hand out for extra cartridges.

'Then I'm with you, Ali,' Gerald said as he checked to see if the shotgun he carried was loaded.

Mutton watched the two men stride off and shook his head. 'You'll not get me going up against the Greek,' he said but unable to hear himself because the battery in his aid had died he repeated himself in a shout. Elizabeth who had decided to walk after the man she loved turned briefly with a disparaging look and disappeared into the darkness of the copse; Mutton sneered and quickly left the clearing heading in the opposite direction; his target was Dozer and not the Greek.

Although Margaret was in a hurry to exact her revenge she took care when crossing the wide gravel drive and approaching the front door for it was hanging open on one hinge like a thick slice of Emmental. She could see remnants of the iron lock lying on the doorstep but of Rasmus there was no sign. Margaret could also see the crumpled form of Lilly-Ann still lying in the hallway and she knew it would be foolish to enter the house before knowing where Rasmus was and she decided to circle the house and check the rear doors first.

There was a flash of bright light at one of the upper windows at the same time as a loud shot that echoed out through the open doorway and Margaret knew the killer was venting his anger on one of her precious artefacts. She quickly circled the house and waited at the corner that overlooked the courtyard and the two garages. She had been drilled from childhood on gun safety and had carried the weapon broken over one arm but now Health and Safety was the last thing in her mind and she was ready to exact blood for blood. Margaret checked the cartridges and closed the weapon firmly before sliding the safety into the fire position.

A shape moved at the opposite corner of the house and she crouched down and aimed the shotgun. She had just begun to tighten her finger on the trigger when a big man lurched out of the backdoor and trotted silently towards the garages; it was Rasmus and Margaret shifted her aim but was too slow and the Greek disappeared into the open garage containing the Citroën before she could fire. She stared into the darkness to the spot where she'd last seen movement but nothing stirred. Her eyes began to water from constantly focusing, unblinking, across the courtyard but she continued to wait for her target to emerge.

Suddenly she heard a loud slam of wood on wood and Margaret guessed that Rasmus had left the garage by the side door and was probably going to check the farmyard that lay on the other side of the garage. She slipped her shoes off and raced across the cobbles in time to see her target entering the flint-walled enclosure, clearly with the intention of checking the pigsty and the cow biers.

She crept up to the wall and peered over the top to see the shadowy figure of Rasmus standing by the well. He briefly looked down but a heavy cloud obscuring the moon showed nothing and he turned to retrace his steps.

'Don't move a step you bastard,' Margaret shouted, startling the man into almost dropping his gun; it was a semi-automatic Russian Saiga 12K, one of the most powerful shotguns in the world. The shock of Margaret's voice so close to him tightened the finger that had been loosely resting on the trigger and he blew the front half of his left foot to pieces. His shriek of agony mixed with the booming gunshot and echoed across the estate to be heard by four poachers who fled to their homes believing gamekeepers were firing at them.

Having lost most of one foot Rasmus, standing on one leg, looked down, lost his balance and fell sideways. He hit the wall of the well and toppled over the rim. Still sighting along the barrel of the unfired Purdey Margaret watched him disappear from view in complete surprise. A movement beside her made her jump and she turned to find Ali had also been lining up his weapon on Rasmus when his sister materialized out of the gloom, delaying him in pulling the trigger.

'Where did he go?' Ali asked, for the abrupt detonation of the Saiga had caused him to blink and look away at the moment Rasmus vanished.

'He's in the well,' Margaret said emerging from her shock.

They both walked across the farmyard, Ali with his gun at the ready, until they reached the parapet and looked over. It was pitch black but they could hear splashing and a sudden shriek, not from pain but this time from horror, for what the brother and sister could not see was that on surfacing Rasmus had found himself staring into the dead eyes of Rodney. He splashed away from the floating corpse and attempted to get a grip on the slippery, algae-covered bricks but it was futile and the pain in what remained of his foot was unbearable. Rasmus frantically looked up and saw the silhouette of two heads against the night sky and he screamed for a rope. The disturbed water soon began to affect Rodney who slowly sank as the air trapped within his coat was dislodged.

'Don't leave me here with him,' Rasmus yelled in fear as the sinking corpse knocked against his shattered foot.

'Shall we drop him a line, sis,' Ali asked looking at her grieving features. Margaret shook her head and walked away from the well with Ali's comforting arm around her shoulders. Reg and Elizabeth turned the corner of the house and rushed across to the farmyard as the siblings slowly emerged with the distorted cries of the Greek rising from the well in a hollow ghostly manner.

Reg pointed, Ali shook his head, Elizabeth shivered and they all returned to the house for warming brandies and to take Lilly-Ann from the cold hallway tiles and place her on a silk bed coverlet with her hands crossed upon her shattered body. Margaret kissed the generous lips that were losing their warmth and spread a small lace handkerchief over the pretty face she had so quickly come to cherish.

With brandy still warming his throat Gerald went back to the underground passage to recover the leather suitcase he had placed in a small niche in the wall. He stretched his arm into the darkness and he found emptiness, the case was missing. Mutton had been nobody's fool, for on joining the others in the clearing he had seen that Gerald's hands were empty. That was when he told them that he wouldn't be returning to the house and went in the opposite direction. When Mutton was sure they had all left the clearing he went back to the iron-gate, which had been left unlocked, and searched the passage until he had located the hiding place. As he was unable to return to the house to retrieve his car without alerting the others as to what he was carrying he ran across the estate until he reached a small door in the wall and proceeded to smash the padlock with a heavy rock.

Mutton hiked along the road until the sky lightened and the first glow of the sun illuminated the treetops. A car appeared on the road behind him and he held his thumb up and gratefully watched as the Dark Green Volvo slowed and pulled to a stop beside him. A silenced automatic appeared at the passenger window to point at his head.

CHAPTER 11

G ERALD RUSHED BACK TO the living room and gave his companions the bad news that the Gutenberg Bible had disappeared.

Ali shrugged. 'Thank goodness we're rid of that albatross,' he said in a surprisingly unperturbed manner and Elizabeth agreed.

Reg was crest-fallen. 'Damn, that was worth a great deal of money.'

Ali contradicted him. 'No it wasn't, Reg. It would have been impossible to sell as we had no ownership papers or provenance of any kind whatsoever.'

'The moment we showed it to anyone and tried to sell it we'd be arrested,' Ali added as he poured himself another brandy. 'The most important thing right now is what do we do about poor Lilly-Ann upstairs?'

Margaret bit her lip and instantly decided on a solution that was considered by her to be perfect. 'We'll honour her by interring her with our ancestors,' she murmured reaching for the tissue box.

'Shouldn't we inform the authorities?' Elizabeth asked.

'That's a can of worms we should leave untouched,' Ali added in support of his sister. 'We'd have to tell them about the two in the well and that would lead to a million questions and a rather long imprisonment for drug peddling, burglary, robbing a bank and taking an armoured car without a licence, insurance or the owner's permission.'

'What's putting a deceased girl in your own family vault compared to that little lot?' Margaret added with a finality that made the room fall silent. 'Anyway, she told me that she doesn't have any living family so she'll never be missed except by us.'

'Let's do it,' Gerald said and Elizabeth nodded her head.

With all due solemnity Lilly-Ann was wrapped in a white winter duvet and carried from the house. They crossed the main lawn to a small granite edifice that glowed in the moonlight. Gerald thought it was some kind of Victorian folly but Ali explained that it had been the family vault for twelve generations. A large iron key was produced and the door screeched on corroded hinges to admit them to a large room that was lined from floor to ceiling with stone shelves; on each rested coffins and ceramic jars containing the final remains of the Montagues.

'Don't let the door close as it cannot be opened from the inside,' Ali warned. They lay Lilly-Ann on a central dais and unfolded the goose down duvet so that each could take their turn to kiss the young woman on the forehead goodbye. Margaret remained to hold the face between her hands until her lingering kiss on the lips was sealed with teardrops only then did she draw back to let Ali close the duvet. They all filed from the vault that was dimly lit by moonbeams filtering through the small apertures in the high domed ceiling.

'What now, Gerald,' Ali asked as they solemnly walked back to the house.

'I still need to get twenty-three thousand pounds and seventy pence for my mother's care home,' Gerald murmured dispiritedly and Elizabeth squeezed his arm in a feeble effort to comfort him.

'What about a Post Office?' Reg suggested. He was beginning to feel the effects of withdrawal again and knew he would be useless to the others within a couple of days. Margaret wasn't ignorant to his addiction and on arriving back at the house she took him by the hand and led him into the kitchen that was enormous compared to any normal English home. Copper pots and pans shone and twinkled in the electric lights as she reached up to take a stone jar from the highest shelf. Reg gave a puzzled expression when she winked at him and slid it along the scrubbed pine table until it stood before him.

'Please accept this as a gift for I no longer have a need for it.'

Reg lifted the lid, found the jar half-filled with fine white powder, and asked why she thought he needed flour. Margaret wet the tip of her finger and transferred a small amount of the 'flour' to his lips. Reg licked and went white with shock and then pink from sheer delight on tasting such high quality. No matter what name it was called whether flake, snow, toot, basa, pearl or coke Reg knew she had given him a fantasy gift, one that could only have come from one of his more fantastic dreams.

'It's for me?' he said huskily, touching the jar again to check that it really did exist, and when Margaret nodded he immediately tipped a small amount onto a handy Jamie Oliver cookbook. He then used a chef's knife to create a rail and took a clean tampon applicator that he always kept in his pocket and snorted; a look of sheer pleasure swept across his face and he turned to thank Margaret but she had gone. He snorted three more rails before returning to the others with a euphoric expression and carrying the jar in his arms like a much-cherished infant.

'What did you mean by Post Office?' Gerald asked and Elizabeth frowned.

'I think we should keep a long way away from doing anything more that is illegal,' she said.

'Do you believe any job will pay me twenty-three thousand pounds and seventy pence for three weeks work?' His harsh tone hurt Eizabeth deeply and she turned away to hide her disapproval.

Reg was on a high and excitedly explained that one person normally managed a small village post office and that there were no security guards like a bank. 'Walk in with one of those,' he pointed to the Purdeys leaning against the end of the settee, 'and we'll have the money in no time at all.' He sat down with a smug look that was softened by a very dreamlike expression and as they watched, waiting for further post office information, he slowly sank back and into deep sleep.

'He does have a point,' Ali said. 'They are a very soft target. We would only need to do three or four to raise the money you need, Gerry.'

'Listen to yourselves,' Elizabeth interjected. 'You're talking about armed robbery and scaring people half to death to steal hard-earned money from people who deserve a lot more respect than you could ever command.'

Gerald suddenly felt unclean. 'You're right, Betty,' he muttered, feeling angry at how low he had fallen since first listening to the mad ideas of a drug addict who was now beginning to snore like a Gloucester Old Spot sow. 'I'm going to see if I can do something about Margaret's front door and then I need to sleep too.'

'I'll join you,' Ali said. 'I know where we can find some bits of timber and the tools.'

The two men left the living room and then returned walking backwards with the twin barrels of a Saiga 12K following.

'Thanks for leaving the door open,' Dozer said. 'I did say I would return in the morning and when I did I found this lying on the ground by the well. It's one helluva monster of a gun which is undoubtedly the one that made a mess of your front door and I know it doesn't belong to that little weasel.' He pointed the barrel at Reg. 'So, who does it belong to because I can see you have all your weapons here?' This time he pointed the Saiga at the two Purdeys.

'Rasmus Psomas,' Margaret stated boldly. 'And he'll be coming back.'

'Judging by the way the gun had been carelessly discarded I'd say Rasmus no longer has any need for it.' Dozer studied the faces one by one. 'I would presume that you killed him and dumped him down the well. Am I right?' he snapped.

Elizabeth nodded and blushed with guilt, eliciting a smile from the big man.

'Good, I hate foreign competitors contracted by High Court judges so, you can hand the bible over to me and I'll be on my way to St Marks.'

'We don't have it,' Gerald said quietly.

The gun fired and the oil painting of three wood nymphs hanging over the fireplace was reduced to two nymphs. 'Don't play games with me,' Dozer bellowed.

'We're not playing, it was stolen from us only two hours ago by a man called Mutton,' Ali said coolly and he noticed the black eyes of the weapon drooping with disappointment.

'Did he leave in a car or on foot?' Dozer snapped.

'On foot and if I hazarded a guess he is probably returning to London,' Ali said.

'May the Lord have mercy on your souls if you're lying to me,' Dozer boomed in a voice that was more suited to an evangelical pulpit than the living room of a country house and he stormed out.

Gerald looked at Ali and Reg and there was an unspoken agreement, they had to rescue the bible, and they rushed from the house and piled into the car Rasmus no longer had any need for. The key was still in the ignition and as the two women shared their surprise at the front door the Mercedes raced down the drive.

'Why would a man like that want to go to church?' Elizabeth asked.

'And was the one in the well really hired by a High Court Judge?' Margaret countered.

The both stood in puzzled silence as the car disappeared into the trees.

CHAPTER 12

DETECTIVE INSPECTOR COOPER WAS sitting in his car feeling immensely irritated. He had just been informed that the hunt for the driver of the abandoned Fiesta had come to a fruitless end and Henry Robinson, the local Chief Constable, had withdrawn his men for 'more important' duties. Thirteen days ago Robinson had signed a lease on a London apartment, on the fourteenth day he been turned down by the committee for a senior position with the Metrpolitan Police and it still rankled him.

Cooper glowered at the back of his driver's head and ordered him to check headquarters for any news relating to the hijacking of the armoured van. He had filled the car with obnoxious fumes and was close to giving the constable lung cancer from secondary smoking when the call came in that Ali Monti, a charged suspect in the bank robbery, had escaped whilst being taken to court.

'It's the same bank the armoured van was collecting money from,' the driver added and Cooper grunted thoughtfully. 'Funny name, though,' the driver added. 'Could be a middle eastern terrorist getting funds for weapons.'

'You watch too many movies, constable,' Cooper snapped. 'Shut up.'

The driver sank into his seat to sulk while his superior developed a new line of thought that investigated the possibility that the man called Ali Monti had also been involved in the robbery of the armoured van and therefore the probable driver of the sky-blue Fiesta.

As his superior pondered the imponderables the driver took a call from the local constabulary to learn that a Citroën C3 had been stolen in a street close to the car park and was last reported heading towards the Norfolk coast.

'That could be Mr Ali Monti, sir,' he guessed, coming to the same conclusion two seconds after his boss. 'He'd need some form of transport after dumping the Fiesta.'

He wasn't used to having brilliant notions but this was one of those times when Inspector Cooper excelled. 'Get the local plods checking the Electoral Register for names similar to Ali Monti who live in the north Norfolk area.'

'You don't think he's a terrorist, sir?'

'Don't be an idiot.'

It took three more cigarettes and the insubordinate driver opening his window to clear the inspector's fug before they learned that the only person of any similarity whatsoever was an estate owner who went by the name of Sir Alistair Montague of Montague Hall that was situated close to Cley next to Sea.

'Get me there fast,' Cooper demanded with a satisfied smirk at the thought that he could have the pleasure of arresting a knight of the realm for bank robbery and an assortment of other offences. Following the coordinates given by the sexy voice of the sat-nav they reached the wrought iron gates and were rolling along the drive in less than forty-five minutes. They were still within the trees and their shadows when a dark car raced past them, removing their wing mirror with a crash that made Copper shoot upright and hit the roof with his balding pate. The constable braked violently to bring the patrol car to a rocking halt and subsequently throwing the inspector forward to hit his face against the constable's headrest. 'For crying out loud,' he exclaimed and then he spun round, cricking his neck in the process, to watch the careering vehicle pass between the gates without any sign of brake lights and turn right to disappear.

The car was suddenly buffeted by the compressed air of a second vehicle passing by with only millimetres to spare. They watched, with mouths wide open as the second vehicle raced to the main gates, turned left and vanished from sight.

'Bloody hell, is this Silverstone, or what?' Cooper said as he gently felt his nose for any damage.

'Do we go after them, sir,' the constable asked as he unclipped the microphone to notify traffic police. It was a long time since his last pursuit and that was only to catch a seventy-year old widow racing to get to the supermarket before it closed at midnight. 'I've run out of milk for Tiddles,' she had said when he finally caught up with her trying to park in the supermarket staff car park. To make matters worse the inspector had a bad case of indigestion and was in no condition for a high-speed chase.

'No, let the local plods do that, just get me to the house,' Cooper ordered, feeling the gastric acids churning inside his stomach. The excitement he was feeling, on realizing that there was a very good possibility he had found the bank robbers and security van hijackers hideout, didn't help either.

The sun was just showing above the tree line, lighting up the sandstone gable of Montague Hall when the patrol car swept up the drive and stopped at the foot of the steps. Two figures standing in the open door could be seen to be women; one older than the other, as the sun illuminated their equally attractive features.

The inspector climbed out of the car and the women went inside the house forcing him to follow. He entered the hallway and couldn't help noticing the crudely repaired front door and the defaced portrait of an old biddy on the facing wall. He wandered from one side of the hallway to the other to find the women comfortably seated in a drawing room that had the same floor area as his own apartment.

'Good morning, ladies. I'm Detective Inspector Cooper of the Metropolitan Police and I would like you to answer a few questions.'

'How d'you do Inspector, I am Margaret Montague and this is my good friend Elizabeth Shanks. How can we help you at such an early hour?' Margaret said as she patted Elizabeth on the thigh to indicate how close a friend she was before offering him a choice of Oolong, Rooibos, Lapsang Souchong, Keemun or chamomile tea with Battenberg, carrot, chocolate or fig cake.

The inspector's stomach rumbled and he kept shaking his head until she finished her recitation. 'Would either of you know of a man called Ali Monty?'

'Good grief no. What a funny name,' Elizabeth said straight-faced. 'Sounds like some sort of a circus clown or one of those disgusting instant puddings.'

'Please, don't take me for an fool, miss, 'What about Alistair Montague?'

'Ah, Alistair, my brother,' Margaret replied smiling. 'and it's Sir Alistair.' This was said in a frosty tone that was at odds with the smile and irritated the inspector.

'Well, I have reason to believe that Sir Alistair has been involved in robbing a bank and hi-jacking a security van.' Cooper growled, indicating to the constable that he was neglecting to take any notes. 'Was that his car that I saw leaving a few minutes ago?'

'No.' The frost persisted.

'Are you quite sure?'

'You wouldn't be calling me a liar would you, inspector?' The frost had now become positively glacial.

'You wont mind me looking round the place will you?'

'Feel free, inspector,' Elizabeth said, knowing that Margaret was on the brink of blowing her top which would achieve nothing except anger a senior policeman who would turn up the next morning with a search warrant and begin to do too much investigating for their own good.

'There's nothing hidden here.' Margaret hissed and stalked away and into the library to stand guard over the secret entrance to the priest's hole.

Cooper grunted and slowly left the living room to begin his search of the whole house. The constable was instructed to check the upstairs rooms while he searched the ground floor and the outbuildings. The two women followed him. Elizabeth held Margaret's hand tightly when Cooper went into the farmyard, checked each stable and wandered across the yard to the old well to peer inside. The women squeezed hands and held their breaths as he leant over the parapet, lingered for a few moments, then gave a grunt of annoyance.

Dawn light was now illuminating the lichen covered walls and the thick film on the water's surface shimmered bright green. There was no sign of Rodney or Rasmus for they had only just descended to the bottom and wouldn't rise back to the surface again until sufficient decomposition produced the right quantity of gas. Cooper looked down at the glutinous farmyard waste that had accumulated on his shoes and made a hasty retreat. The driver was shaking his head when he joined them at the front of the house and the policemen left without a further word.

Despite the uncomfortable feeling in his stomach Inspector Cooper urged his driver to drive faster having wrongly guessed that the car which removed their wing mirror was being driven by Sir Alistair when in fact it was Dozer.

'Check with traffic control and see if they've come up with anything yet,' he said, unaware that the driver had been quietly muttering into the microphone the moment he had turned out of the gates and driven onto the public road.

'Sorry, sir, nothing to report yet,' he said and Cooper grunted in a surly manner as his stomach rumbled noisily and then passed wind uncontrollably, in a series of short sharp blips that went on for an embarrassing length of time.

'Back to London then, and make it quick,' he ordered while thinking that it was clear the thieves were heading that way. He was also thinking of instructing the constable, who was finding it hard to stop himself laughing, to stop at the first service station that had rest rooms.

As Margaret watched the vehicle hasten down the drive and disappear into the trees she sighed, gave Elizabeth's hand a final squeeze before shifting her hand to hold her by the waist and guide her back up the steps. 'I hope dear Alistair hasn't done something foolish,' she murmured with a sense of foreboding.

Elizabeth was beginning to feel somewhat uncomfortable for the hand on her waist was occasionally sliding lower as they walked out of step.

'I'm hoping Gerald is going to be okay, too,' she answered, her discomfort increasing for she was fully aware that Margaret lived in an isolated place that denied her the company of women and any further chances of meeting someone as rare as Lilly-Ann with whom she could freely express herself.

She increased her pace, moving away from what was now becoming a deliberate caress and headed into the kitchen. 'I'll make us some breakfast,' she called out over her shoulder as she closed the door, showing the disappointed woman that she was quite capable of boiling eggs and making toast soldiers without any help. Margaret took the hint and went into the dining room to switch on the coffee percolator and read the morning paper while she waited for Elizabeth to return.

Mutton stared at the gun and froze for he had instantly recognized the big man sitting in the driver's seat with a sadistic grin on his face.

Dozer waggled the automatic. 'Put the case on the passenger seat,' he ordered grimly. 'Then I want you to undo your belt, remove your trousers and toss them onto the back seat. There was a light whir and the rear window was lowered to receive the pair of dark serge trousers. Mutton looked at the man's lips moving but heard nothing. The lips moved again and the gun became more threatening with it's waggling. He tapped his hearing aid and shook his head until Dozer finally understood the problem and was forced to point and mime his instructions. Mutton put the small suitcase through the window and then stood back to await the next charade. Dozer undid the buckle of his own belt, mimed sliding it free from the loops and pointed. Mutton did the same and then went white when Dozer mimed the removal of trousers. The hammer of the automatic was thumbed back and though Mutton couldn't hear the ominous click he understood the action he had to take and quickly slipped his trousers off and threw them into the car. The jacket and shirt were next and Mutton began to shiver with the cold. Dozer waved for him to back away from the car, the windows closed and the car roared away disappearing round the next bend.

Mutton stood by the side of the road, in flat-battery silence, with a vertical thumb boldly held up. It seemed a rather optimistic action for a very large man dressed only in white undershorts embroidered with brilliant red hearts; a gift from one of the go-go girls he had slept with at the late Mr Goldenstein's nightclub.

He stood by the roadside for what seemed a lifetime without realizing that Gerald Latimer had drawn the short straw by turning left and had driven for twenty minutes before realizing he was going in totally the wrong direction for London. I'll never catch up with Dozer, he had thought and Reg gave an impatient tut as he slowed the S-Class, did a U-turn and drove back the way they had come.

Ali laughed suddenly and then fell silent.

'What's the joke, mate?' Reg asked.

'I was just thinking how brave Gerry is.'

'Brave, why do you reckon the plonker's brave?'

Gerald looked at Ali in the rearview mirror. 'Yes, why am I brave?'

'You've left your lovely girlfriend alone at Montague Hall, that's why.' Ali said and he laughed again.

'So what, Ali, she's got Margaret with her and they've got the shotguns. Betty's well protected.'

'It's Margaret you should be worrying about, Gerry,' Ali said with a broad grin. 'I think losing Lilly-Ann has hit her hard and she'll be needing a shoulder to cry on, someone to hold and comfort her.'

It was putting the accent on 'comfort her' that made Reg exclaim, 'Wow!' and burst into laughter. 'I think you've got a bit of a problem there, Gerry,' he spluttered. He shifted the flour jar to prevent the arm from fully going to sleep.

'I trust Betty and one thing's for certain she isn't batting for the other side.'

'You know nothing about women, mate,' Ali said. 'When they're suffering an emotional loss they'll bat for any side if it helps them recover that feeling of being needed and loved.'

Gerald responded by telling him he was spouting a load of bullshit but inside he had a disquieting premonition that his friend could be right and on seeing the gates ahead he slowed down and turned into the drive causing his companions to burst into laughter again. As they walked up the steps to the front door Gerald glanced through the living room window and his blood chilled for he saw, as Ali predicted, Elizabeth and Margaret hugging each other.

'Looks like you're too late,' Ali said and on seeing Gerald's face he couldn't laugh and simply remained silent.

The trio entered the living room and the two women drew apart. Margaret's cheeks were wet with tears and Elizabeth had sadness written all over her face as she rushed to Gerald and, burying he face in his shoulder, put her arms around him. Gerald pushed her away and looked from one woman to the other expecting an explanation for their intimate behaviour.

Elizabeth didn't know if she should be angry at his notion that she and Margaret could be lovers or glad that he was so much in love with her that he could be jealous. 'Margaret went to the mausoleum for a last look at Lilly-Ann and it upset her more than she thought it would,' she explained. 'I hadn't realized she'd gone until I brought the tea tray from the kitchen and discovered that Margaret wasn't here; when she returned to the house she was in a terrible state of shock.'

Ali went to his sister and wrapped his arms about her trembling shoulders. 'Could you get a fresh pot that's extra strong?' he asked Elizabeth who simply nodded and left the room. 'I think we can all do with some tea.'

'I'll be okay, Alistair,' Margaret murmured as Ali led her to the settee where she sat with a deep sigh. The cushions sighed sympathetically. Reg wasn't one for extreme emotions and he opted to follow Elizabeth and seek release from the melodrama by snorting a couple of lines from his jar. Gerald sat in one of the armchairs and remained silent while Ali murmured soothing words in an effort to calm his grieving sister and was relieved when Elizabeth reappeared with the tea tray.

'We have to decide what to do,' he said taking one of the cups.

'I suggest we go back to London and try to get the bible back from whoever has it, whether that's Mutton or Dozer,' Reg said, having followed Elizabeth back to the living room with bright eyes and fully dilated pupils. 'Knowing those two thugs they'll go back to where they came from to fight for, or divide up, Goldenstein's territory.'

Ali nodded agreement. 'Then I suggest we get going as soon as possible.'

'We'll use Mutton's Mercedes again as it has plenty of room for all of us,' Gerald said without mentioning his passion for luxury cars that had drinks cabinets and heated seating.

'And we take Margaret with us as I don't want to risk any of those fellows returning here,' Ali added and after a moment's hesitation Gerald agreed. The men cleared the plate of chocolate biscuits and finished their tea as the women went to collect their overnight cases. With Ali's permission Reg put the Purdeys in their leather, monogrammed gun cases, collected a box of cartridges from the kitchen along with a small packet of cocaine from his jar and took them all out to put in the boot of the car. They were taking a risk but it was better to be armed when confronting the type of people Dozer and Mutton mixed with. The house was locked, as best it could be with hardboard panels nailed over the perforated front door and then they left for London.

They had only covered a few miles when they saw the most amazing sight. Standing by the road, bold as brass, was a large hairy-chested gorilla of a man wearing nothing more than a pair of boxer shorts covered with red hearts. He was holding his thumb out on the off-chance that someone would be brave enough to stop for such an unnerving character.

'It's Mutton,' Reg said on recognizing the shorts for he had been given a similar pair by a go-go dancer at Mr Goldenstein's club after they had smoked four splits when sharing her bed.

Gerald slowed the car to a crawl until he was sure the man wasn't carrying any weapons that could be secreted in the scanty shorts, which on getting closer, didn't leave anything to the imagination, and then pulled up beside him.

Ali pointed one of the shotguns as the window whirred down. 'Where's the case, Mutton?' he shouted and was answered with a dumb look and a finger that tapped his ear. Ali mimed holding a case and when that didn't elicit a response he took a lurid paperback Rasmus had left in the seat pocket, flipped the pages and held it up.

A lightbulb went on in Mutton's eyes. 'Dozer took it along with all my clothes,' he shouted and then pleaded, 'Can you give me a lift to London?' Ali leant away to avoid the fine spray of saliva.

'Thanks for nothing, Mutton,' Gerald shouted back and put his foot down.

'You're not going to leave the poor man looking like that?' Elizabeth asked as the Mercedes resumed cruising to the capital city.

'Poor man, nothing,' Reg said. 'He's evil, Betty, the type who'd sooner slit all our throats and feed us to Tamworth pigs before helping us recover the Gutenberg Bible.'

❧   Reg's character prognosis was spot-on for Mutton was watching the big car diminish in size and thinking about how he would like to borrow Dozer's giant Tonka toy and bury them all alive.

Judge George Atkinson hadn't heard a word from Rasmus for twenty-four hours and had begun to think disturbing thoughts that the shitty crook may have absconded with his precious bible. Thanks to his unique position in society he had acquired a number of contacts on the street apart from Rasmus Psomas. Atkinson had never believed it was a clash of interest for him to associate with criminals as he considered himself to be a true guardian of the law and in keeping law-breakers in check he needed to be above the law himself.

The judge put the word out that he would reward anyone who could tell him where Rasmus Psomas could be found. The lure of money soon had inaccurate reports flooding in from all sorces; pickpockets, muggers, pimps and prostitutes, and it wasn't long before a genuine tip revealed that Cyril Catchpole, aka Mutton, had been seen parking close to Mr Goldenstein's nightclub; at least, his old Ford with a recognizable baseball bat on the back seat had been parked there.

Mutton and Dozer had been brought before the judge a number of times and he knew that they had both worked for the deceased gangster. On his next visit he asked his prime informant if either of the two men had been in contact with Rasmus. At the time, the judge had handcuffs restraining his arms and legs and was spread-eagled, face down, on a bed with an attractive middle-aged woman whacking his buttocks with a length of thin, whippy bamboo; Mistress Candy had been the judge's informant for more than three years and he had always found her very talkative during his Tuesday night sessions of penance.

'I haven't seen Dozer for quite a long time, slave.' *WHACK!* 'Not since he got into the habit of sleeping with those three Chinese pole dancers.' *WHACK!* 'The bastard even had the cheek to take many of my customers with those silicone pumped-up immigrants.' *WHACK!* 'Now, Mutton is a different kettle of fish.' *WHACK!* 'He always comes back to me for a good beating.' *WHACK!* 'Usually after he's been a naughty boy with that little go-go tart from the club.'

'When did you last see him, Mistress?' His Honour gasped.

'This morning.' *WHACK!*

'Ouch! Today?'

Candy ceased raising welts on the white cheeks. 'Yes, he sneaked up here wearing only an overcoat he'd stolen from a roadside café and a silly pair of undershorts covered in red hearts that half the men in town are wearing and asked me to get some clothes from his flat.' She put the cane down and unlocked the handcuffs.

'What else did he say?' Judge Atkinson said as he sat up wincing.

'Don't you want me to finish you off?' Candy asked as he began dressing.

'No, another time, please answer the question.' He slipped a sufficient number of notes from his wallet and put them on the bedside table.

'Mutton said he'd been mugged and a valuable suitcase containing a fortune had been taken from him.'

'That's it!' the judge said, unable to contain his excitement. 'Who mugged him, did he say?'

'That's the weirdest thing, he said it was his old mate called Dozer who done him over and left him naked on a road in Suffolk.'

'And where can I find this Dozer?'

Candy gave the judge a strange look. 'I would think you'd have that on record considering you've banged him up two, or was it three times.'

'What's his real name?'

'Andy Lawson.'

Atkinson slapped his forehead and hurried from the apartment followed by Candy's shout, 'See you next Tuesday, Your Honour?' He winced with every step as he descended the urine perfumed, graffiti decorated stairwell.

It was too late to visit the municipal offices and he had to wait until the following morning before going straight to his chambers and using the computer to search through the court records to locate Andrew Lawson's current address. He then summoned his judicial assistant and gave instructions to cancel any hearings for the day and left without any further explanation.

A large black BMW 7 Series with D10ZER plates was standing outside the terraced house in Limehouse. A small concrete mixer and bags of cement stood on the hard forecourt advertising interior building works were in progress. However, what every passerby did not know was that they were tools of a trade with which Dozer was an expert. Apart from burying people he also had the habit of dropping them in the river wearing concrete filled buckets. Atkinson asked the taxi to wait, pressed the doorbell and impatiently tapped his foot until the door suddenly swung open and Andrew Lawson, a mountain wearing a silk dressing gown and glowering darkly, stood before him holding a bottle of brown sauce waiting for a reason why his greasy bacon and egg breakfast should be allowed to get cold.

'I know you,' Dozer bellowed, his eyes widening in recognition. 'You're the bloody judge who gave me porridge a few years ago.'

Judge Atkinson took a step back as the glowering face rapidly changed to one of dark anger. 'I wish to know if you have acquired a priceless book recently and if so how much do you want for it?' Atkinson asked. Courtroom procedure had ingrained the habit of stating the facts and getting straight to the point, which in this case proved to be a negative ploy to adopt with a man like Dozer.

'What if I do have it and what if I don't want to sell it?' Dozer snarled producing a baseball bat that was very similar to Mutton's favoured tool for chastising troublesome doorstep time-wasters who made breakfasts lose their tasty warmth.

'If you're thinking of using that on me let me warn you that the police will have you in my court receiving another three-year sentence for aggravated assault.'

'Maybe.' There was an ominous pause. 'Only you won't be there to hand out the sentence because you'll either be dead or having numerous bones pinned back together before you leave hospital to live in a wheelchair for the rest of your life.'

Judge Atkinson prided himself on his appearance and athleticism and he took another step backward before speaking with a wavering voice. 'I will have that book Lawson or your life.' He turned and ran to the taxi shouting non-judicial anglo-saxon instructions to 'get a fucking move on.'

Dozer threw his bat after the taxi and cracked the rear window that the driver said Atkinson would have to pay for. On arriving at his home in the country the cab door locks refused to be released. The judge conceded and wrote a cheque for an estimated figure before he was allowed out of the vehicle. He had silently vowed to phone his bank and cancel the cheque the moment he was in the house but the taking of his Rolex Submariner as surety had put paid to that plan.

Instead of phoning the bank he dialled Candy. 'Do you know of anyone who could retrieve an errr item that belongs to me from a man called Andy Lawson?'

'Who?'

'He's known as Dozer.'

'Bloody hell, you're going to need a real heavy who possibly has a gargantuan grudge against that big bruiser.'

'Such as?'

'Well, if Dozer took the errr item, from Mutton, then I would suggest you ask *him* to get the errr item back for you.' Candy then gave him the telephone number and last known address of the deaf enforcer.

The logic of using the actual victim of a mugging overwhelmed the judge and he couldn't fault it so he thanked the woman and promised to keep his usual appointment; by which time the marks and stinging pain of his last penance may have faded.

Atkinson dialed the number and waited for it to be answered. He waited a long time before hanging up, not realizing Mutton couldn't respond to the ringtone until he had replaced the dud batteries in his hearing aid. He decided to drive back into town and go and visit the man himself.

The address was a little seedier than Dozer's apartment that was further to the east. It was a ten-floor apartment in a tower block estate that was notorious for breeding the next generation of career criminals. The taxi driver, knowing the area, at first refused to take him and then only after prepayment of an outrageous sum of money. To rub salt into the wound he promised to wait and then unashamedly didn't but instead accelerated away the moment the judge stepped out of the vehicle. All done in a twinkle and before any of the local lads could consider nicking the wheels.

The door was wide open and the lift in darkness. Atkinson stepped into something soft and squidgy and was immediately overwhelmed by the stench of urine and faeces. To see what he was doing he lit his cigar lighter and pressed the tenth floor button. Nothing happened and when he looked down saw the Out Of Order sign lying in the filth. Obscene words and graphic pictures had been drawn on the walls and he fled to use the stairs where childish, sexually explicit drawings followed him up all ten floors.

Atkinson was gasping when he arrived at number twenty-two and he rang the bell still reeking of lift. He heard the sound of numerous locks being unfastened and the door opened a fraction to reveal a single blood-shot eye.

'Whatcha wan?' A voice croaked suspiciously.

'I wish to speak to Cyril Catchpole.'

'Shit, you're Inky Smudge Atkinson,' Mutton exclaimed in surprise on seeing the face and hearing the voice for he had only just restored his hearing with new batteries.

To the sounds of chains and bolts the judge rapped on the door until it opened once more. 'You put me away once,' Mutton said morosely.

'Three times, actually, but that's not what I've come to see you about.'

'What is it, then?'

'It's about a book that was stolen from you by a man called Andrew Lawson.'

'Who the fuck is that?'

'You know of him as Dozer.' There was a sudden rattling of the chain being removed and the door was opened wide. 'He stole a suitcase and its contents from you and I'd like to discuss the return of those items.' Atkinson added.

With his hearing restored Mutton beckoned to the judge, much against his natural instincts, to enter his home. 'How you do it is entirely up to you but if you can give me the contents –'

'The book?' Mutton interrupted.

'Yes, the book, I will give you fifty thousand pounds on the day you deliver it to me; is it a deal?' Atkinson held his hand out.

For a long moment only the omnipresent ticking of the Victorian mantel clock could be heard and then Mutton gave his hand plus his answer in a low voice full of bile.

'I'll kill the bloody bastard for that amount, your Honour –,' he whispered in a conspiratorial tone. ' – and give you his head.'

'Just the book, Mutton, that will be quite sufficient, thank you.' And the criminal judge gave the hardened criminal his business card. 'Call me when you've got it.'

Mutton nodded and as he showed Atkinson out he recalled how he was forced to thumb a lift for more than three hours before a vehicle slowed down and didn't, like the rest, accelerate when it drew near enough to see he was virtually naked; it was a truck driver who had finally taken pity on the big man. He came to a halt with loud hissing from the airbrakes and with a flattering wink offered to take Mutton to London if he would perform a personal favour at the next transport stop.

This was the last straw and no sooner had the truck entered a truck park and stopped amongst a dozen other heavy vehicles than Mutton pushed the man into the curtained bunk behind the seats. The driver's expression of sexual eagerness changed abruptly when Mutton strangled him and removed his coveralls. He had been of similar build and apart from being tight across the chest the garment fitted perfectly and Mutton was soon back on the main road to London.

His vivid recollection of this incident gave impetus to his hatred of Dozer and he slammed the door behind Atkinson.

CHAPTER 13

GERALD WAS SLOWING DOWN for two trucks, one passing the other at a snail's pace, when Reg decided to mention the post office raid again. 'It would be a piece of cake and may solve your problem in one fell swoop,' he encouraged. This completely by-passed the matter concerning the bible and immediately posed the original problem of raising twenty-three thousand pounds and seventy pence within days; the Shady Trees deadline had now become a major issue.

'Don't do it, you'll be caught and go to prison, we'll all go to prison,' Elizabeth argued to which Reg tut-tutted and asked how she thought Gerald could pay the care home and stop his mother from being thrown out on her ear. He had to do something drastic, something like robbing a village post office or another bank.

'He's right,' Ali said and received an elbow in the ribs from his sister. 'It's a lot of money,' he protested. 'How else can he do it?'

The truck finally passed and pulled in front of the slower one and Gerald put his foot down. He accelerated past the fully loaded vehicles before moving over to the inside lane while listening to his companions continue arguing. Suddenly he made a decision and a sharp turn onto a slip road to leave the highway and head for a small village that had been signposted as having a post office. Elizabeth and Margaret both expressed their anxieties but were ignored and Gerald pulled up outside a tiny building amidst a tiny group of cottages that claimed to be the post office as well as the village shop and run by charitable volunteers.

'Make sure the Purdeys are empty,' Gerald instructed. 'We'll be using them for show and intimidation only.'

Reg groaned. 'Spoilsport, I've always dreamt of storming into a bank, like they do in the movies, and firing into the ceiling.'

'Has anyone ever considered the people who might be upstairs?' Margaret asked ruminantly.

'What do we do about masks?' Ali asked ignoring the question. Gerald said 'oh' and the car fell silent until Margaret reached beneath her dress, wriggled about to the amusement of Ali and the titillation of Reg and lifting her legs produced a pair of tights traumatizing a silver-topped pensioner who happened to be pulling her shopping trolley past the car. Elizabeth followed Margaret's example and quickly rolled fine nylon down her long legs and handed the tights to Gerald.

'Use them,' Margaret said to Gerald and handed him a pair of nail scissors. He quickly cut three short pieces from the thigh part of the garments and pulled one over his head.

Elizabeth nodded unhappily at the squashed nose twisted to one side on the distorted features of her lover. 'I wish you wouldn't do this, Gerry,' she murmured. 'It makes you look so ugly in so many ways.' Gerald shrugged his hopelessness.

The men left the car and, watched by a very bemused pensioner who had stopped to watch them, pulled on their disguises and retrieved the two shotguns. Reg checked both, handed one to Gerald and surreptitiously slipped cartridges into the other before they ran to the shop door and crashed in. That had been the plan but three men carrying two long shotguns trying to enter a narrow doorway at the same time had predictable consequences. The two customers, shop assistant and postmistress were initially shocked and then entertained by the predicament the robbers found themselves in. It was a few moments of taking turns to enter the shop first before they finally managed to untangle themselves and wave the guns in the faces of the onlookers.

'Hand's up, this is a robbery,' Gerald shouted and then regretted shouting for spittle collected on the silk material pressing against his lips. He turned to the postmistress and for the first time saw that she was behind a defensive curtain of thick glass with only a small opening for exchanging money and pension books. She was middle-aged and had a smile that was more of a sneer as she observed the antics of the three men.

Ali went to the small door that gave entrance to her cubicle and she shook her head in mock sadness. 'Can't help you, dearie, it's got a solid steel lining with a combination lock.' Ignoring the irritating smile he studied the twelve buttons on the keypad before accepting they were defeated.

'Let's go,' he muttered and Gerald nodded and went out.

Reg threatened the volunteer shop assistant who, on looking into the end of the barrels, was now regretting that he have ever listened to his wife and been press-ganged into doing his bit for the village.

'Give me all your money,' Reg demanded. 'And that includes you,' he said as he glared at the two women and pointed the gun, first at them and then at the ceiling. The urge to be Warren Oates playing Dillinger had come upon him and he pulled the trigger. Ali had been halfway out of the shop when the deafening explosion of both barrels compressed his eardrums painfully and he turned in time to see ceiling panels falling followed by a deluge of water. Reg snatched the few bank notes from the shop assistant's trembling hand and hurried after Ali. They all piled into the Mercedes and Margaret put her foot down as a white-faced Elizabeth looked at Reg in shock. He was saturated and water was being squeezed out onto the leather upholstery as he held the smoking shotgun.

'What happened?' Elizabeth demanded to know.

'How much did you get?' Margaret asked.

'Reg put a big hole in the ceiling and the water tank sitting above it.' Ali answered.

'Lucky it wasn't some old biddy watching Coronation Street,' Elizabeth observed philosophically.

'Seventy-five pounds,' Reg answered miserably.

'That was a waste of time wasn't it? Now we need to get rid of this car.' Elizabeth said being practically minded.

'What's wrong with it?' Reg asked as he fumbled in his pocket for the twist of paper he had put there earlier.

'Remember the little old lady with the shopping trolley? Well, I saw her jot down our number after you three made your intimidating entrance into the shop.' All three men accepted the sarcasm without a word and had the good grace to blush. Even Reg, dripping into his lap, couldn't help but be embarrassed by the debacle.

'There's a small railway station up ahead, I'll check the car park for something that's easy to nick,' Reg mumbled on spotting a familiar road sign. The others mumbled their agreement and Margaret pulled up fifty yards short of the station. It was only a matter of minutes before they saw Reg running towards them with an officious looking railway man hot on his heels and brandishing a stout-looking cane. Margaret started the car and Ali threw open the rear door just as Reg arrived to jump in with one breathless, explosive word. 'Drive!'

'What happened this time, Reg?' Gerald asked after they had left the village behind and were heading for the nearest town.

Having got his breath back Reg said, 'Would you believe it, I found the perfect car, a Volkswagen that was big enough for us all, and had it opened in a flash. The problem came when I drove it to the exit and found you needed a special card, coded to the car's registration, to open the barrier. It didn't look too strong so I tried heaving the pole up with the hope it would snap off but as luck would have it a guy in the station saw me and came out waving that bloody big stick. I had to leg it or he would have bashed my head in.'

'I don't think he would have killed you but I've a good mind to do just that, you stupid git,' Ali barked. 'Why didn't you read the sign by the exit before you went for a car?'

Reg couldn't come up with a suitable answer and remained silent until they entered Chelmsford and began looking for an alternative target.

They had passed the Odeon cinema four times before Gerald began doubting Margaret's navigation skills. 'I'll check the sat-nav,' he said. It might be quicker than acting like sightseers.' He tapped the screen until a post office was indicated four streets from where they were. Margaret followed the robotic vocal instructions until they were parked outside a small branch office. The frontage was no wider than twelve feet and there was a cash point machine in the wall next to the door. Once more the three men put on their tights and rushed into the shop and an inappropriately placed lotto display stand crashed to the floor drawing the attention of the postmaster and postmistress behind what appeared to be a normal counter. There was no armoured glass to foil the robbery.

'All the money, now!' Reg shouted, waving the shotgun in their faces and it was his turn to gather wet phlegm on the inside of the disguise.

The couple raised their hands in the air and an elderly couple turned from perusing a rack of birthday cards to stare angrily at the intruders. As Ali and Reg snatched the bundles of banded banknotes from the postmaster the old lady, who was the spitting image of Geraldine McEwan as Miss Marple, picked up a glass paperweight and tested it's weight in her hand. Gerald saw what she was doing and had time to rugby tackle Ali to the ground before the glass projectile flew across the post office and shattered against the wall behind the postmistress.

Reg turned, amazement on his face, in time to dodge a snowman encapsulated in an eight-inch diametre ball of glass. 'Shit,' he exclaimed and ran outside closely followed by Ali, Gerald and another snow-scene that punched a sizeable dent into the Mercedes. Once again Margaret did a Bonny and Clyde style of getaway driving and they soon turned a corner and raced from the scene of their latest fiasco.

'What happened this time?' Elizabeth asked despairingly.

'An old biddy, that's what happened,' Reg exclaimed angrily as he rummaged for another paper twist to calm his nerves.

'It was one of those have–a-go good senior citizens who looked like she wouldn't say boo to a goose,' Ali said. 'She started lobbing heavy paperweights at us just as the postmaster was behaving himself.' He held up a small bundle of five pound notes and Gerald did the same. 'This was all we could get and judging by what's written on these bands we've got a grand total of six-hundred pounds.'

'Eat your heart out Edward G Robinson,' Margaret muttered.

Twenty-two thousand, three hundred and twenty five hundred pounds and seventy pence still to go, Gerald thought to himself. His ability at mental arithmetic showed that they still had to rob another forty-four post offices. They rushed past a sign that pointed the way to a railway station and he began directing Margaret until they pulled into the car park. After cruising around for five minutes they found that every bay was occupied. Commuters to London tended to fill every parking bay by 6.30 a.m.

'Stop,' Gerald snapped and told everyone to get out. 'We leave the car here.' He then opened the boot and, after wrapping the two guns in an old oilskin coat, slammed it shut and walked towards the station ticket office.

'It's blocking the access,' Margaret observed in a concerned tone of voice usually associated with an moral, tax-paying senior citizen.

'Damn the access, let's go catch a train.'

As coincidence would have it Inspector Cooper had opted for a faster method of transport and had boarded a train in Norwich that only stopped at five stations en-route to London. One of those was Chelmsford where Gerald and his companions were waiting on the platform having just abandoned the Mercedes in the car park. As his train pulled into the station Cooper saw two patrol cars, with lights flashing, and a large group of police officers congregated around a large black Mercedes that seemed to be inconveniently parked.

'Bloody rich bastards, think they have the right to park anywhere,' he thought.

The inspector was tempted to leave the train but assumed it was an insignificant local matter like an inconsiderate commuter late for work, and slumped back into his seat in time to see a small group of people pass his window. The two women seemed vaguely familiar and he squashed his face against the glass in an effort to catch another glimpse but they were gone and the train jerked into motion.

Cooper arrived in Liverpool Street Station and caught sight of the two women again. Margaret Montague and her friend, Elizabeth Shanks, were with three men in a black taxi that left the station rank in a hurry and by the time he had commandeered a cab of his own it had long gone. He made a mental note to investigate the Montague family; especially Alistair Montague who he assumed was the taller of the three men and who had been sitting erect in a very military manner. He was holding a long item between his legs that was wrapped in a mud-stained coat.

He arrived at the office and no sooner had his skinny backside hit the hard leatherette chair than the phones began ringing. The first call concerned finding the car that had shot out of Montague Hall and removed the mirror on his patrol car. It belonged to a notorious man called Andrew Lawson and that it was currently parked at the owner's address. The second call confirmed that the Mercedes S-Class that had been found in Chelmsford Station car park was the second vehicle and the inspector mentally kicked himself. One simple call and the rogues could have been rounded up on their arrival in London; he had let them slip through his fingers and their whereabouts was now a mystery.

Detective Constable Teal had not been negligent for while his boss had been running round the farmyards of Norfolk he had used the connection between Elizabeth Shanks and Crampton Bank to obtain a search warrant for her apartment. After wantonly tearing the place apart the team of heavyweight constables found nothing to incriminate the suspect. Even Elizabeth's personal things, including her summer-wear, winter-wear, under-wear and sanitary-wear, had been left strewn throughout the flat. The abandoned Mercedes at Chelmsford had also interested him and officers on the scene had sent him the car's registration and an image from a blank notebook with the name Dozer, followed by a question mark, scrawled across one page in pencil. Teal had checked the DVLA to find the Mercedes was owned by Rasmus Psomas, a Greek national; he sent both registration and address by e-mail to Inspector Cooper and mentioned Dozer's name, followed by a question mark, as well

'Bloody hell!' was Cooper's reaction on reading it. 'Why on earth did this villain let Alistair Montague use his car?' He was very familiar with the name Rasmus Psomas for he had arrested the man on a number of occasions and given testimony in court to have him banged up. Unfortunately, the inspector had never been able to prove that the man had ever disposed of his competitor by dropping him from Tower Bridge onto a Thames barge; killing him and the barge owner's pet chihuahua. Disappointment and suspicion hung heavily in the air every time Psomas' name was mentioned in the squad room.

'What's his connection with the bank robbery?' he asked himself when Teal entered his office, 'and what is his connection with Andrew Lawson?'

'Lord knows, sir.' Teal said, thinking that his boss had spoken to him.

'Well, let's go and find out.' Cooper stormed from his office with Teal hurrying to catch up. The journey to Rasmus' penthouse apartment in the rush hour traffic was tedious, to say the least, and Cooper was well and truly exasperated when Rasmus didn't, or wouldn't, answer his doorbell. He decided to pay a visit to Dozer, followed by a question mark, to clear up the matter of his link with the missing assassin.

The first place the friends went to was Elizabeth's apartment and they hurriedly left on finding the chaos the police search had left behind. Reg made the point that 'pigs' could still be watching her place and hugging his jar beneath his jacket was the first down the stairs and onto the street. They walked purposely away and at the first opportunity caught a bus to go to Gerald's home on the premise that the police hadn't identified him yet.

They agreed to approach the house singly, with a ten-minute gap between arrivals, so as not to alert the neighbours to anything unusual. 'Naturally, I'll go first,' Gerald said holding up his keys and walking away from the bus stop. The others sat in the shelter as though waiting for the next bus and Reg, who had asked to go last, went behind the shelter to sit on the pavement. He spread a copy of the Daily Mirror he had found in the shelter and carefully tipped a little of his precious powder into the centre crease. The sides of the newspaper were raised forming a narrow line which he snorted using his faithful tampon applicator. This was repeated a few times until he was floating six inches above nothing one moment and submerged in the sea, swimming with dolphins, the next. Suddenly everything went out of focus, including the picture of Boris Johnson cycling past the Houses of Parliament, and Reg let himself be absorbed into a kaleidoscopic fantasy world.

Ali stood up to go but a silent warning in his head sent him round the bus shelter to check on the whereabouts of Reg. He needed to let him know that he only had to wait five minutes more. He found his street companion lying silently on the Daily Mirror with the small jar tipped over, spilling the contents close to his head. A light wind was whipping up the powder and while Reg had been breathing, for he no longer was, he had inhaled large quantities of cocaine that had blown into his nostrils. Ali knelt and found there was no pulse and instantly recalled his military field training. He quickly rolled Reg onto his back, cleared his airway with his fingers and carefully pinching the nostrils together he began cardiopulmonary resuscitation. It took three minutes of filling lungs with secondhand air and chest thumping before there was a reaction. Reg coughed, unfortunately into Ali's open mouth, and resumed breathing. Ali spat out the phlegm and picked the lightweight man up using a fireman's lift. He carried him round the shelter just as a number forty-two bus pulled up and the doors opened with a wheeze of air.

Is he okay, guv?' the driver inquired. 'Wanna hand?'

'Naw, he's had a skinful of lager and I'm getting him home.'

'Far to go?'

'Just down the road, thanks for asking.' Ali walked away and the driver shrugged and looked round at his passengers with a grin that was shared. It took Ali ten back-breaking minutes to arrive at Gerald's front door and, on ringing the bell, it opened in an instant.

'What the hell kept you?' Gerald exclaimed, his eyes fixed on the comatose figure draped over Alistair's shoulders.

'About half a jar of pure cocaine,' Ali said as the door was closed behind him. They went into the front room and Reg was unceremoniously dumped on the settee. 'He nearly killed himself snorting the filthy stuff,' he said looking at his sister accusingly. 'I got him breathing again with a bit of mouth to mouth and chest thumping.'

'Well done, Ali,' Elizabeth said. She had taken Reg's hand and was checking his wrist for a regular pulse. 'Looks like he'll be okay if he ever comes out of this coma.'

The four friends stood around the settee looking down at the pathetic figure who had begun snoring with moist noises.

'What will he be like when he wakes up?' Gerald asked nobody in particular.

'Bloody furious,' Ali said.

'Why's that,' Elizabeth asked.

'I left his damned jar behind the bus shelter.'

Gerald volunteered to get it and he left the house and strode down the road to the bus stop. He had covered half the distance when a squirrel leapt out of the hedge to land on the pavement where it proceded to run in circles as though chasing it's own tail before rushing along the pavement and under the wheels of a mobility scooter. The elderly driver grimaced, shrugged his shoulders and rattled past Gerald with a brief greeting as though nothing had happened. Gerald strode on past the flattened remains without looking down.

There were no people waiting at the bus stop and he went behind where Ali mentioned he had found Reg and was confronted by a rather weird sight. Two crows were lying beak to beak next to the jar and twitching the most peculiar manner; seemingly conducting a low intimate conversation. The alien sounds they made and the fox that had been feasting on a large black cat that was decidedly dead chilled Gerald's blood. The vixen, sprawled across a copy of the Daily Mirror, was still alive with eyes rolling every which way and her handsome brush swept from side to side. He cautiously leant over the assorted wildlife and picked up the jar to find that there were only four or five lines of the drug remaining. Reg will be more than furious when he learns that squirrels, cats, foxes and crows had flown higher on his precious cocaine than he ever did, Gerald thought as he trotted back to the house.

Ali rolled about with laughter on learning Margaret's gift to Reg had been made a gift to urban wildlife. Even the women were mildly amused although Elizabeth was a trifle squeamish about the tragic incident involving a mobility scooter and a wildly tripping grey squirrel.

After the judge had left his place Mutton immediately began laying plans for terminating Dozer and recovering the book. Fifty thousand pounds was not a sum to be sneezed at and he immediately lifted two floorboards in the bedroom and took out a cheese-cloth wrapped .45 Sig Sauer automatic, two fragmentation grenades and three double-edged combat knives which he placed in an old sports bag. He thought this would be quite sufficient to convince Dozer to give up the Guttenberg Bible.

With his old Ford abandoned at Montague Hall Mutton was compelled to take a bus to the nearest supermarket car park where he selected a Volvo estate that an air-headed shopper had neglected to lock. While she swore and argued with the delicatessen assistant about the thickness of her sliced ham Mutton was swearing at her ignition until the right wires were sliced, joined and the car started.

Mutton was only two blocks from Dozer's house when an earsplitting cry sounded behind his left shoulder and made him swerve from side of the road to the other. A quick glance in the mirror revealed a cot lying on the back seat in which lay a tiny scarlet-faced Churchill that had decided to scream one long note like the Golden Arrow flying through Clapham Junction. Mutton pulled up and quickly rummaged about beneath the blanket only to find the infant's nappy was full to bursting point. The seepage at the legs, which was now on his fingers, was making him gag and he quickly checked the large bag standing on the passenger seat for a clean nappy. It was a thirty-minute crash course before he succeeded in producing a perfectly clean baby and a bundle of toxic waste that needed to be disposed of quickly. He had just dropped the evil-smelling object into the gutter when a middle-aged couple paused to give loud tut-tutting sounds until he picked it up again. Mutton waited until they had continued on their way and he was in the act of putting it down again when they turned and he quickly stood up, opened the boot, and tossed it in.

As he resumed driving towards Dozer's address he became aware that the baby was now making contented gurgling noises and hard-hearted as he was about adults he knew he had to return the infant to its mother. The supermarket was still crowded and the mother was now arguing about the ripeness of the Stilton cheese when Mutton parked the Volvo in exactly the same vacant bay. Taking his sports bag he went into the supermarket and told a pimply-faced teenager at Customer Information that a baby had been left unattended in a silver Volvo. That's a unforgivable case of neglect and should be reported, he said, then gave the registration and hurried out to seek another unfortunate's car.

Mutton slowed the black Audi as he turned into Dozer's street and slammed on the brakes. A police officer standing in the centre of the road in full riot gear was holding his hand up to stop Mutton. Beyond him there were a dozen more, most carrying lethal weapons, entering the gate to Dozer's front garden. The officer studied Mutton through the windscreen in a manner that made him feel extremely nervous and he slipped the car into reverse and accelerated. As he hadn't checked his mirror he had been unaware of the car that had pulled up behind him and there was a horrendous sound of tortured metal and Mutton's head hit the headrest and then recoiled forward into the inflating airbag. For a few moments he was totally disorientated before pulling the deflating material to one side, putting the car into drive and putting his foot down.

Three things happened in quick succession.

One, the face of the policeman who had adopted a concerned expression on seeing the collision now changed to one of fear as the Audi leapt towards him, leaving little time to spring to one side. The front wing caught him in the hip and spun him over the bonnet and into the kerb where he fell, cracking his helmet on the pavement.

Two, the group of SWAT officers cautiously grouped around Dozer's front door looked round on hearing the cars impact, saw their comrade being run down and, as one, turned to open fire with Heckler & Koch submachine guns at the Audi racing past them.

Three, the officers were too late to aim accurately and the car zoomed past without acquiring a single bullet hole. However, three houses opposite were perforated with 9mm ordinance that shattered sixteen double-glazed windows, killed one pet Siamese dozing on a window sill, smashed a porcelain collection of Staffordshire horses and creased the buttocks of a teenager who was about to lose his virginity to his next-door neighbour.

Scotland Yard inquiries were begun as to why weapons were fired in the first place and secondly how could ten armed, professionally trained policemen miss a target as big as a car that was passing so close to them. Cooper was also in the firing line and to protect his job he decided to revisit Montague Hall and carry out a thorough search of the place.

Mutton kept driving, wondering how the rapid response team knew he was coming to Dozer's place.

CHAPTER 14

DOZER ENTERED THE OLD CHURCH carrying the small suitcase and headed straight for the lectern. He stepped up to look at the book that was open at Proverbs and murmured a few of the words to himself. 'To know wisdom and instruction: to perceive the words of understanding; to give subtilty to the simple, to the young man knowledge and discretion.'

'Can I help you?' a voice said, startling Dozer and he stumbled down two steps and almost dropped the case. He looked round to see the same priest who had taken his confession two days before walking towards him. For a moment he was tongue-tied and was unable to say anything intelligent that would suit the occasion.

'Is there something I can help you with, my son,' the priest repeated as he stopped and looked at Dozer with eyes that spoke of kindness and spiritual love. He then recognized the big fellow looming over him as the same Devil's right hand man who had confessed to so many murderous crimes not so long ago; his face had lost its angelic gentleness and his eyes were now flint hard.

'Yes, Father,' Dozer managed to say even though he didn't quite know what to ask and he reacted by grabbing at the only verse he had just read and remembered in order to say something, anything at all. 'What is subtilty?'

A little taken aback by the nature of the question and its source the priest said, 'That means the quality or state of being subtle, as in the subtlety of air or light, my son.'

Dozer thought for a moment and then took the heavy bible from the suitcase and asked the priest if he could find the Proverbs reference in it; the same verse as the one he had seen in the well-used bible on the lectern. The hand-tooled leather of the ancient tome immediately astounded the priest when it was placed in his hands and on opening it he gave a further gasp of amazement.

'This is a copy of the Guttenberg Bible,' he exclaimed as he reverently ran his eyes over the open book.

'No, it's an *original* Gutenberg Bible.'

'Original.' The priest could hardly believe what he had just heard.

'Yes, yes, of course it is,' Dozer said impatiently. 'Now find me the same bit in here that mentions subtitly?'

'I'm sorry, my son, but this is in Latin and I'm a little rusty in the language.'

'You can't read Latin?' Dozer was amazed at the man's inability. 'I thought all priests read, ate and slept Latin.'

'The Latin in this bible is from 380AD which is difficult for anyone who has studied the language whether at University or in a seminary. A bible of such beauty as this would possibly be used by a scholar and unquestionably those people would be found in cathedrals throughout Italy and many other Latin countries. But here, a humble priest such as myself can only use the King James bible; my congregation can only understand what I'm saying if it is read in English from that version of the Bible.'

'So, when your bible says "to perceive the words of understanding" your congregation can only understand what the good book is saying when it's said in English?'

'That's a very rough interpretation of the holy verse although it really means . . .'

'So, giving this bible to your church would really be a waste of time?' Dozer was disappointed and it had begun to show on his face, alarming the priest who hurriedly tried to mollify the thug.

'As a rare curiosity piece, to put on display and bring in worshippers, it would be a most generous gift.'

'But you wouldn't read from it?'

'No, as I said, I cannot . . .'

'Then I'll bugger off and give it to a priest who will.' Dozer took the book back, placed it in the suitcase and began walking down the central aisle, leaving the shocked priest standing in the nave. He was not only left in awe of what he had just held in his hands but had been left extremely curious. He dearly wanted to know how a man whose sins of violence took hours to confess came to be in possession of such a fabulously priceless treasure; he suddenly had an idea.

'While you are in my church can I take your confession,' the priest called out, his voice echoing in the barrel-vaulted roof and Dozer paused as did the prayers of three senior citizens kneeling in the pews.

'But I only did that two days ago why would I want to do it again?'

Three curious pensioners waited for Dozer's reply.

'You may have sinned since then.'

Dozer thought for a minute, changed his direction, and went between the pews towards the confessional; the priest hurried after him with robe rustling on the flagstones and prayers were resumed in the front pew.

'Bless me Father, for I have sinned.' Dozer said as soon as the priest was seated and had opened the grille; he was getting into the swing of religious rituals fast and before the priest could say anything he went into a detailed listing of everything that had happened since his last confession. An hour later the priest had learnt a part of the story about the bible, and a lot more beside, but was unable to do anything with the information because sanctity of the confessional forebade it and he decided to wrap things up quickly.

'I absolve you of all your sins, in the name of the Father, the Son and the Holy Spirit,' he said without taking breath. 'And for goodness sake, when I say go in peace I hope you do, my son.' The priest also dobted that a thousand Hail Marys could ever forgive the villainous stranger of his numerous sins.

Dozer left as quickly as he did last time and that particular church would never see him again for Dozer had decided that if only the top priests in their fancy cathedrals bothered to read bibles in Latin then he would go to the biggest cathedral in the country and present the Gutenberg Bible to the head honcho; he had decided that Canterbury Cathedral would be his next port of call and bugger the thousand Hail Mary's.

The Audi sped away from the church with the priest watching from the steps and wondering which unfortunate cathedral Dozer would choose.

It wasn't that the High Court judge mistrusted Mutton but that it was in his character to always have all the facts of a case before making any kind of decision. It was this aspect of his character that compelled him to contact his police informant. When the return call came, ten minutes later, he took down the address and car registration details of the owner, Andrew Lawson, aka Dozer, and decided to pay the man a visit to ensure that Mutton was telling him the truth. The drive took him until mid afternoon and as he turned into the street two dark, official looking vans rushed past and were soon gone. Atkinson stopped outside the house and saw, on walking through the front garden that the front door was hanging open. The lock had been shattered in the frame and he put his head inside and called out. There was no response and he went in to find the front room had clearly been searched, as had the kitchen and the dining room. He didn't bother going upstairs for he knew he would find the same chaos in every room. He called his contact and learnt that there had been a police raid on the address; his blood pressure rose rapidly.

'Why couldn't you tell me before I wasted two hours driving here?' he shouted and there was silence until the officer snarled back that he didn't know about it until fifteen minutes ago and when he rang the judge there was no answer. Atkinson didn't bother to apologise and simply hung up and stormed out to his car to find a group of curious neighbours peering through its windows.

'What's it all about, guv?' one of the men asked as Atkinson got in behind the wheel. Atkinson shrugged, started the engine and was about to drive off when a vehicle stopped immediately behind him and Mutton got out.

'Didn't expect to find you here, Your Honour,' the villain said, stopping by Atkinson's open window. 'Don't you trust me or summat?'

'I heard there'd be a police raid and I wanted to see if Dozer was being arrested and if it had anything to do with the book,' Atkinson lied. 'What have you heard?'

'I've only just got here and if Dozer's not around I can only think of one place where he might have gone.' Mutton explained that Dozer had forsaken doing the Devil's work and was now living with the fairies, or in his case the angels, and believed he was the only one who could save the book from capitalist exploitation by giving it to the church.

156

Atkinson laughed. 'You're telling me that vicious bastard, that killer, wants to follow the path of righteousness and will kill anyone who gets in his way?'

'Too right, sir, and I think he's gone to St Marks. It's the nearest church to where he lives.'

'Where's that?' Atkinson asked but was talking to himself for Mutton had already returned to his car and was now rapidly pulling away. 'You bastard,' he shouted after him as he started the car. 'One can never trust a thief sent to catch a thief,' he muttered beneath his breath and the onlookers jumped out of the road in alarm as he pulled away with screeching tyres.

St Marks was only a few streets distant and Mutton was already parked outside and running up the steps when the judge arrived. He hurried after his retained thug, his blakey-heeled shoes ringing on the flagstones as he entered the solemnity of the church. He walked down the central aisle after Mutton who was wildly looking round, hoping to find Dozer in one of the pews.

'He's not here, you've been wasting my time,' the judge said when he caught up with the big man standing in the nave.

'Can I help you gentlemen?' a voice called and they turned to see a black robed priest leaving a confessional and hurrying towards them as though to stop them from leaving before he had saved their souls.

'Has a big man been here recently,' Atkinson asked. 'He may have been carrying a large book.'

The priest looked from one man to the other, taking in the well-educated and clearly professional man standing beside someone who was clearly of the same ilk as the big stranger who had given such blood-curdling confessions.

'You mean carrying a bible don't you?' he said with suspicion growing.

'That's right, mate,' Mutton said. 'Where did he go?'

'Can't help you with that.'

'What my companion meant was did the man give any indication of where he might be going next,' Atkinson said in a velvety tone as he stepped up to the lectern and eyed the battered volume that was still lying open at Proverbs. 'For clearly he didn't leave the book with you.'

'No, he didn't think this church, or come to that, myself, was worthy of such a glorious book.'

'And . . .'

'He said he was going to take it to the head honcho.' The priest's nose wrinkled when he said the words Dozer had used to describe an Archbishop and he watched the educated man's reaction that was extreme to say the least. Atkinson went white and sat down in the nearest pew, his hands shaking, for he knew if the Guttenberg Bible was ever put in the hands of a Bishop or Archbishop then he could say goodbye to ever seeing it again.

'Where's this head honcho live?' Mutton asked in vague tone.

'In the Vatican in Rome,' the priest said and devoutly crossed himself.

With a muttered 'thank you, Father' Atkinson stood up and left the church with Mutton hesitating before hurrying after him to catch up with the judge at his car. The priest watched them go and wondered if he was in any way involved in a crime that had happened or was about to happen.

'Where are you going?'

'You're going to Canterbury Cathedral to get the bible and I'm going home to put fifty thousand pounds together and wait for you to come to me with the book.'

'Why Canterbury, the priest said it was Rome?'

'Because your former colleague in crime doesn't know the difference between one head honcho and the next, that's why. The priest wasn't referring to our Archbishop but to his Pope.'

The car quietly accelerated away leaving Mutton puzzling the whereabouts of Canterbury. The well-enunciated sat-nav lady soon put him on the right road and as the sun began to sink Mutton drove towards the county of Kent and one of the world's most famous cathedrals.

After a tedious train journey from London Detective Inspector Cooper read all the background case notes on Rasmus Ptomas while Detective Constable Teal drove him from the police station in Norwich to Montague Hall. A squad car with four more officers skilled in forensic investigation followed and on arrival they all began a systematic search of the house for any clues relating to the presence of Ptomas or either the bank robbery or the hi-jacking of the armoured van.

The temporary panels were levered off, the door opened and the holes blasted through the oak door, along with that in the hallway painting, were studied minutely while Copper and Teal searched the living room and the library. The entrance to the secret priest's hole remained a secret and it wasn't until they heard a shout outside the house that they had anything worth investigating. They followed the sound of the shouting until they found two excited officers standing by an old well in the farmyard. Cooper went to the rim and stumbled back on finding two faces leering up at him. There was another shout and he was informed that a dark green Citroën C3 had been discovered parked in one of the garages. 'It's the one stolen from the cathedral car park at Ely,' one of the officers reported after he had checked the vehicle's registration.

'I think Sir Alistair needs to answer a lot of questions,' Cooper murmured to himself as he watched the recovery of the two bodies.

One of the officers with expert weapon knowledge went to Cooper. 'The smaller of the two men was shot with a 12-gauge shotgun and the other, the big fellow, had drowned. Strange thing, half his foot was missing and it looks like an enormous gun did the damage.'

'Any identification,' Teal asked before his boss could say a word.

'They both carried wallets and the driver's licenses showed the shot man to be Rodney Walton and the big man was Rasmus Psomas.'

'Ah,' Cooper said in a deeply profound manner and if it was possible a light bulb would have lit up over his head. 'Rodney has been regularly pulled in for drug peddling and Rasmus was our old friend who got away with multiple murder.'

'The rumour has it that the judge was nobbled,' Teal said sourly. 'Can't remember who was sitting.'

'I can, it was Judge George Atkinson and, whether he was bent or not, at least justice finally caught up with Psomas.' Cooper gave one last glance at the swollen corpse and went back to the house to help himself to a large measure of Alistair's brandy. He offered the cut-glass decanter to Teal who shook his head and mimed driving. Cooper had started to recall the trial and how Judge Atkinson kept over-ruling the prosecution counsel and a sneaky suspicion crept into his mind and grew larger with every returning memory. Knight of the realm, High Court Judge and foreign assassin, 'I think they're all in it together,' he said with a satisfied nod of the head. 'Montague, who's down and out and needs money learns something about the judge and Psomas, possibly what happened at the trial, and blackmails the judge who sends Psomas and Walton to kill Montague. Only the good knight gets the better of both and hides their bodies and the car Walton stole in Ely.'

Teal could see that his boss had the same satisfied look that always came after a case had been well and truly sewn up but he had a niggling suspicion that the whole thing wasn't quite that simple.

'Where do Miss Shanks, Reginald Barnett and the mystery man come in to this, sir?' he asked and received an airy wave of the inspector's hand who was helping himself to another generous measure. 'Also, what about Alistair Montague's sister and Andy Lawson, how do they all tie in?'

The constable's constant nagging was now irritating the inspector and ignoring his subordinate he left the room and the house still holding the glass and climbed into the car. When Teal got behind the wheel he instructed him to drive back to Norwich and drop him off at the railway station on the way.

'You can get a later train once you've got the coroner's report and the forensic study on the damage to the house and any unusual contents found there.' Cooper said tersely and sunk into a broody silence clutching the glass.

CHAPTER 15

'SHOULDN'T WE TAKE REG to a hospital?' Margaret asked as she looked down at the comatose man and, as if to answer her question, one bleary eye opened.

'No bloody hospital for me,' he croaked, closing his eye again, 'If anything I need to confess before I die from this damned headache,' he murmured before slipping back into sleep.

'That's it,' Ali suddenly said. 'The man called Mutton mentioned St Marks and I wonder if that isn't the church Dozer is interested in.'

'Dozer? Going to church? You must be potty.' Elizabeth was amazed that anyone would suggest that a killer such as Dozer could ever be considered a churchgoer. The thought of the villain parking his bulldozer in the church car park brought a smile to her lips that Gerald noticed.

'What's so amusing?'

'Dozer confessing after every murder he's committed and being told to do a number of Hail Marys.'

Despite her black sense of humour Gerald laughed and added, 'he'd be a hit at funerals when he uses his experience to dig graves for the deceased.'

Elizabeth grinned and Ali scowled. 'After you two have finished your standup routines there may be a very good reason why he went to a church called St Marks. Did you consider that in his new frame of mind he might be considering giving the Guttenberg Bible to the priest.'

There was a stunned silence until Reg opened one eye again. 'St Marks is a catholic church that's very close to where Dozer lives.' He closed the eye and almost immediately opened it again accompanied by the other. 'Isn't anyone going to offer a sick man a beer?'

'You'll have tea like the rest of us,' Margaret declared firmly as she felt his forehead before going to the kitchen. 'At least you haven't a fever,' she called out and there was relief in her voice for she was rather attracted to the addict and had secretly vowed to wean him off the habit.

'Should we all go and find out what interest Dozer had in that particular church?' Gerald asked.

'No, we should be careful we don't meet Dozer by chance or, if he has already donated the book, make a priest decidedly nervous.' Ali said with a thoughtful expression. 'I'll go, and no offense to anyone here, but with my title I'll be able to allay any fears when I present myself as a potential parishioner.'

Elizabeth looked at the shabby appearances of both Gerald and Reginald, especially Reg and nodded. 'You're being a trifle sexist but I agree you should go, just in case Dozer is in St Marks giving confession.'

They all laughed, including Reg who had closed his eyes again and was impatiently awaiting his cup of tea.

Ali walked from the bus stop to the church and by the time he reached the steps leading to the entrance he was feeling a little damp and miserable caused by the misty rain that had persisted most of the day. He entered the dimly lit vestibule, brushed his jacket with his hand to rid it of surface moisture and pushed the glazed door open to enter the sixteenth-century. The few parishioners sitting in the hand-carved oak pews were quietly contemplating their lives and sins as they waited their turn in the confessional. Ali walked down a side aisle to the rood screen and stood waiting for any signs of a clergyman. The sound of brass rings on a rail travelled across the church and the velvet curtain of the confessional parted and, to Ali's astonishment, Dozer emerged with an angry expression on his face and stalked out of the church without crossing himself or giving a backward glance. Ali wasn't sure but he seemed to be carrying something under the arm obscured by his large frame. Another rattle of rings and the priest emerged to stare after Dozer with a sad expression.

Ali hurriedly crossed the church to accost the priest before he noticed the woman who wished to confess to having impure thoughts about a new milkman and returned to the confessional.

'Excuse me, Father,' he said, louder than necessary, and a couple of heads turned his way, including the priest. 'My name is Sir Alistair Montague and I wish to ask you a couple of very important questions.'

The priest, whose name was Jeremiah, invited Ali to sit in the pew outside the confessional with him. 'Everyone who comes in here has very important questions, my son,' he was obliged to say, even though he was twenty years younger than Ali.

'Mine doesn't concern my faith, Father, but a villain who stole a very precious family heirloom on the misunderstanding that he should give it to his own church. It has been in my family's possession since Henry VIII reigned.'

Jeremiah nodded solemnly. 'I do believe I know to what you refer.'

'You do?' Ali tried to conceal his excitement. 'And you have it?'

'I regret to say that the man who claimed it was his did not leave it here. He was exceptionally disappointed that I couldn't use it in any of my services and took it away with him.'

'The bible is part of my heritage and it's recovery is imperative to maintain family honour. Did the man say what he would be doing with it or where he would take it?'

Jeremiah had been nodding knowingly as Ali spoke and was about to say something when the velvet curtain was jerked to one side and the waiting woman glared at Ali.

'I also have very important questions to ask the Father,' she declared coldly and devoid of any Christian charity.

'I will be with you very soon, sister,' Jeremiah said softly and turned to Ali who had just realized that the smartly uniformed woman was in fact a nun. 'The man did say he would be taking it to the head honcho to read from in *his* services.'

'What did he mean by head honcho?'

'I assumed, being catholic, he meant the Pope but I have a feeling he was a little misguided in his religious knowledge and that he believed a bishop or archbishop would be the correct person to go to.'

That means he's going to Canterbury Cathedral, Ali thought. 'Tell me, Father, was that the man I saw leaving the confessional a few moments ago?'

'I'm sorry, my son, but I cannot give you any more information; especially as you are a Protestant, apart from warning you that there was another man making the same enquiry as yourself,' the priest said sorrowfully.

'What did he look like?'

'A big man with a hearing aid.'

'As a matter of interest, how did you know I wasn't a . . . ?'

'Catholic? It was the moment I saw you cross the church without showing reverence and bowing towards the altar.'

'Stop playing Father Brown, Father, and come and listen to the confession of a true catholic,' a muffled voice complained behind the velvet curtain.

Both men grinned, stood up and Ali shook the priest's hand with an unspoken thank you and left. There were no signs of Dozer in the street and he turned his collar up and strode back to the bus stop.

'How did it go?' was Margaret's first question when he entered the house and Ali gave them his conversation with the cleric verbatim. He then suggested that he and Gerald should go to Canterbury and try to apprehend the bible before it passes into the possession of the church.

'What about me?' Reg complained.

'We can't take a chance while you're still so ill and I'd like Margaret to care for you while Gerald and I return to Montague Hall.'

'Why do you have to go home,' Margaret asked.

'We need transport that hasn't been stolen by Reg and can't be picked up by the police.'

'Old Faithful,' Margaret declared happily.

'The Rolls will be stylish enough for visiting the cathedral and less likely to be recognized by either Dozer or Mutton.'

Gerald then realized three days had passed since he had last seen his mother. 'I'm sorry, I can't join you, Ali, I must go and see that Shady Trees is taking good care of my mother. It's just a brief visit but I cannot go to Norfolk and then drive to Canterbury before seeing her and reassuring myself that all is well.

'I'll go with you, Gerald,' Elizabeth said as she took his hand and squeezed. 'It's time I met your mother and this is as good a time as ever.'

Apart from Reg, who continued to complain about being confined to the settee despite having the company of an attractive woman, everyone agreed to Ali's plan and decided on the following morning as it was getting rather late for travelling anywhere.

Ali left at first light to catch his train to Norwich after taking some money from their meager funds for expenses. It was mid morning when Gerald and Elizabeth also took their leave to travel to Shady Trees. It took three bus changes before they arrived and walked up the gravel path to the forbidding entrance with numerous CCTV cameras turning to follow them until Gerald pushed the button on the complicated door lock. A stern voice demanded to know who they were and whom they expected to see and Gerald gave the required details. After a few moments there was a click and the door sprung open a fraction of an inch.

The lobby was cold and impersonal as was the white uniformed woman sitting at the reception desk. 'Name,' she inquired briefly and when Gerald told her that he had just given his name to the door he was sternly reprimanded. 'That was the entry phone, I'm the Matron of Shady Trees and I need you to give your names personally so that I can record them here.' She pointed with a well-chewed biro at a large tome embossed on the cover with *Visitor* in a cursive typeface. Gerald sighed, gave their names once more and asked to see his mother.

'Oh, yes, that Stephanie Latimer.' The woman sniffed disdainfully. 'I'll see if she's in any condition to receive visitors,' she said and picked up the phone. After murmuring briefly so that neither could hear what she was saying she pointed to a swing door and said, 'Room number thirteen,' and went back to reading *The Premature Burial*, something she had always thought a number of residents could benefit from.

Gerald led the way to find his mother sitting in an armchair with a travel rug draped over her lap. Everything was exactly the same as his last visit as if someone had taken a photograph and replaced reality with a giant print. The only difference being a slovenly looking nurse standing at the window and glaring at them both suspiciously.

'No point in talking to her, she's not coherent today. She has these spells quite often and it's best to leave her alone,' the young woman said dispassionately.

'She is Stephanie or Mrs Latimer. She is *my* mother and not the cat's mother,' Gerald snapped. 'Now I would appreciate it if you would leave us.'

The nurse was shocked and stormed from the room in silence.

'Well done, Gerald,' Elizabeth murmured as she went to take Mrs Latimer's cool hand. It jerked away and then settled to remain within the gentle warmth when Elizabeth took it again. 'I'm Elizabeth Shanks, Mrs Latimer, a very good friend of your son,' she said and waited for a response. The grey eyes stared vacantly through the young woman and the window as though seeking a different world beyond the high-rise office blocks that blocked out most of the sky.

'Hi, mum, it's Gerald,' he said softly taking her other hand and gently squeezing it in greeting. Her eyes continued staring beyond the couple for a few moments and then flickered and looked from one to the other.

'Lovely name,' Mrs Latimer whispered. 'Are you a resident here, my dear?'

'No, I live with Gerald,' Elizabeth said with a smile. 'I'm Gerald's girlfriend.'

'That must be nice for you. Who's Gerald?'

'He's your son, mother.' Gerald said as he leant closer to help her focus on his face but all he saw were eyes that recognized nothing from the past or in the present. He now knew that the poor memory loss that started when she was at home and had necessitated special care had now developed into full-blown Alzheimers. Tears formed in his eyes and trickled down his cheeks for there was a good chance that, although she lived, she had lost all memory of them all and they stayed like that for a few minutes until Mrs Latimer suddenly spoke in a loving manner that echoed of a distant past. 'Gerald, it's so lovely to see you, it's been far too long.' She turned her head and smiled at her son.

Gerald was amazed at the moment of clarity his mother was experiencing. 'I'm sorry, mother, there have been so many things happening lately that . . . '

'I understand, Gerald. You've met and fallen in love with a beautiful girl and that takes precious time that I'd rather you devoted to Elizabeth than to an old fogey like me.'

'You remember my name?' Elizabeth said with eyes prickling.

'My dear Elizabeth, of course I do and I'm so happy that Gerald has found such a wonderful person as yourself.' Mrs Latimer raised her hand and stroked Elizabeth's smooth cheek that was damp with tears. 'But why do you cry?'

'Happiness, Mrs Latimer, I cry from happiness.'

'Stephanie, you must call me Stephanie if you are to be my daughter-in-law.'

'Yes, I will . . . Stephanie,' Elizabeth was emotionally torn from joy to sorrow as she leant in to kiss the woman's cheek.

'We will try to see you as often as possible,' Gerald said and his mother's hand jerked away.

'Who are you, what are you doing in my room. Where's my son?' Mrs Latimer shouted. 'And you, who are you?' This was addressed to Elizabeth who quickly realized what had transpired and burst into tears. Although she had only known Gerald's mother for a few minutes she suddenly felt a great emptiness, a deep loss, and was driven to leave the room.

'I'm Gerald, your son, mother, and I'll make sure to come back very soon.' He followed Elizabeth down the corridor as the door to number six closed on the shrill voice ordering him 'out of the room before I call the police'. Those unkind words would soon be forgotten but he would frequently remember that one sane, unrepeatable moment of motherly love forever. The couple walked down the corridor, returning to the mad world of uncaring nurses and matrons whose only interests lay in profiting from the undignified ending of life.

CHAPTER 16

―――――――――

T HE TAXI DROVE UP the drive and on emerging from the trees Ali saw bright orange tapes now encircled the forecourt of Montague Hall.

'Looks like you've had the cops up here,' the cab driver commented.

'Does, doesn't it.' Ali paid and got out from the taxi and after ducking under one of the tapes climbed the steps to the door that was standing ajar. The taxi left as he entered the hall and he found plenty of evidence that the police had done a thorough job of investigating every room in the residence. Grey powder coated every surface designed to be touched and every door, cupboard, drawer and wardrobe had been opened and the contents either explored or scattered randomly on the floor. Ali found his favourite brandy decanter had been emptied and knew it hadn't gone to a forensic lab for drug testing but down a few policemen's throats. Fortunately he had a cellar that Margaret had been guarding while he'd been away doing his time on the streets of London.

The police had also toured the outbuildings and yet the garages had been left untouched and the green Citroën was still there. He went to look down the well and it was clear that the police had recovered the bodies of the two villains which made it imperative he left the hall as soon as possible.

Ali opened the second garage and the *Spirit of Ecstasy* gleamed proudly in the gloomy interior. The family Rolls had been left intact and apart from some messy fingerprint powder it was immaculate. The fuel gauge read full and the engine burst into subdued power at the first turn of the ignition key. With the engine murmuring smoothly he drove it to the back of the hall and left it idling whilst he unlocked the outside door to the cellar. Ali was amazed to find that there was no indication that the police had been in the huge brick-vaulted area that, even when the single hanging bulbs were switched on, stretched away into darkness. This was the place that he and Margaret used to visit often when children. They played hide and seek amongst the wine racks and giant oak barrels, scaring each other with homemade Halloween masks. Ali reflected on those times as he took two cases of Merlot, a case of Chardonnay, two brandy bottles and stowed them in the trunk of the car before locking up the hall.

The 1952 Rolls Royce Silver Dawn had no sooner whispered away from the stately gates than two patrol cars turned into the drive and rushed towards the house in answer to a tipoff that the owner had returned. The taxi driver had taken umbrage to the size of the tip given by Sir Alistair Montague.

Whilst Mrs Latimer was briefly recognizing her son and Ali was well on his way to Montague Hall, Margaret had been tending to the recovering addict. Reg lay on the settee with a light woolen throw covering his body as he sipped hot chocolate and nibbled a Wagon Wheel, long past its sell-by date, which Margaret had found on a top shelf in the pantry.

'Is there anything else I can get you?' she asked in a low, throaty voice as she tucked the throw beneath his legs and hips, lingering longer than necessary under his hips.

He looked into her big eyes and thought he detected more than a little concern for his health. 'I think she likes me', went through his mind as her hand pushed the throw under his backside and he wriggled slightly feeling the warmth of her hand.

'A couple of lines would be nice,' Reg said with a smile.

Margaret's face dropped. 'Let me tell you something about myself, Reg. I was introduced to drugs when I was twelve years old by my fourteen-year old boyfriend. It was peer pressure and the first time I tried it I only had half a joint which as you can imagine didn't have much effect. The second time it did and I really felt cool and agreed to go to a party that was being organized in a girlfriend's home. Her parents had gone to a rock concert in Milton Keynes for the weekend. There were five or six of us and after having a joint I became a little nauseous and dizzy. I didn't want to go on but my friends insisted and encouraged me to smoke more and more.'

Reg was only partway listening for he was recalling a similar scenario that hooked him on cannabis when he was fifteen. It was only one small step to the big day when the same mate introduced him to cocaine.

Margaret continued. 'Although I threw up that night, found it hard to breathe, and felt like I was dying I had to try it again on the following day and my boyfriend helped me with a small bag of weed he had stashed in the garden shed at home. I grew to like the happy and relaxed feeling that started producing weird hallucinations that excited me at the same time as scaring me like hell.'

'I remember my experiences with weed as well,' Reg murmured, his eyes closed as he drifted amongst memories of Hieronymus Bosch landscapes.

Margaret nodded and continued. 'I was eighteen when my new boyfriend, an Italian waiter, introduced me to cocaine. The high was so powerful I was hooked straight away and had to have a snort at least twice a day. At first, my boyfriend bought what I needed and I was in heaven for a year until one day I caught him in bed with his chef.'

'He had a female chef?'

'That wouldn't have been so bad but it was a male chef.'

'He was in bed with a man?'

'That's right, Reg. Orlando had finally decided he was gay when realizing he really did fancy the chef big time.' Margaret laughed. 'I decided on revenge and took his coke supply which was kept in a large jar with the flour, rice and sugar jars in his apartment kitchen. I left London and returned to Montague Hall, which was when Alistair came to my rescue. He hid the jar and for a whole month kept me locked in the house, talking to me about all my problems. He eventually told me where the jar was but by then I was no longer addicted and was disgusted by the thought of ever using again and left it alone until I saw the terrible condition you were in. You were in a terrible state.'

'And you were an angel, Margaret. Can I have those lines now?'

'Sorry, Reginald, but if anything serious is going to happen between us then this is the time to give up drugs forever. I know it'll be hard because I've been there but, believe me, you'll feel a lot better for it.'

Reg looked deep into Margaret's eyes. 'Do you think something serious could happen between us?' he murmured.

'I do, but only if you want it to happen enough to give up drugs.'

'Help me, Margaret, I do want it to happen.' Reg held his arms up and Margaret bent over to accept his embrace and to hug him close.

'Let's start now, follow me,' she said and taking Reg by the hand led him upstairs to her bedroom where she laid him on the king-size bed and covered him with the duvet. She went and drew the heavy drapes but not before he saw the windows had been left open to air the room.

She noticed his wary glance. 'Alistair put heavy bars on my bedroom window at Montague Hall to stop me escaping at night. You needn't worry, Reg, I'll be by your side all through the night.'

Reg's face registered mixed emotions. On one hand he was held a prisoner, unable to seek the hiding place of his drug, and on the other he'd have a warm loving body to keep him company. 'Will the door be locked too?'

'I'm a very light sleeper.'

Reg nodded and let himself fall into a deep sleep. Margaret left, after watching his face for a while, and then locked the door before going down to prepare the evening meal.

Time wasn't on Ali's side for he knew Dozer had a massive lead which would grow bigger if he had to delay in picking up Gerald. He decided to drive to Canterbury by himself and apprehend the villain before he had a chance to enter the cathedral. A steady run on three different motorways took him to the outskirts of the ancient city and he didn't have to use sat-nav to find the cathedral for it soared above all else. Ali parked the Rolls in a street close to the main entrance, even though double yellow lines threatened a stiff fine, and walked the rest of the way.

Evensong had ended and Holy Communion was just beginning when Ali entered the cathedral to be immediately overawed by the nave with its vaulted ceiling, soaring eighty-two feet above his head. Walking as lightly as he could he went towards The Crossing, checking every pew as he went for any sign of Dozer. Ali was nearing the front of the gathered congregation when two things happened at once. The first was the priest starting the service with his normal welcoming speech and the second was a bear of a man rising from the front row and striding to the high pulpit; it was Dozer and he was holding the Gutenberg Bible above his head. This was quite a feat of strength as the volume weighed thirty pounds.

'Latin, do the service in Latin,' he boomed and his words echoed among the magnificent columns throughout the cathedral. The Dean, for it was the Dean who was taking the service, was startled by the interruption and the giant of a man approaching him. Two attending clerics hurried to intercept, closing in on each side of the man, but were brushed aside by a tome to the side of the head for one and a back-handed slap on the other. There was a subdued intake of air from everyone in the congregation.

'Why not Latin,' Dozer insisted.

The Dean recovered and smiled benevolently, as though to a child, and spoke slowly to give clarity to his words. 'My dear sir, the choir may sing the Eucharist or the Magnificat in Latin but this is the cathedral of the Archbishop of Canterbury, leader of the Church of England, and all services are conducted in English.' The two clerics were beginning to recover and more robed assistants and lay members were approaching cautiously.

'I have here the very first printed bible and it is in Latin explain why you do not use it?' Dozer shouted as the front pews began to empty.

'Because the majority of worshippers would not understand a word of it and the word of God must be made clear to all who listen.'

Dozer was a little confused by the Dean's reply and while trying to think of a suitable riposte Ali leapt forward, snatched the Gutenberg Bible from his half raised hand, tucked it under his arm and dashed down the nave and out of the cathedral. Dozer said one word that shocked all who heard and ran after him, scattering worshippers with his outstretched hand like a rugby forward.

The whole ridiculous scene had been witnessed by one worshipper kneeling in the back pew with a silenced Glock automatic resting on his forearm. Dozer had been moving so much that he was unsure of his accuracy as the nave was one hundred and seventy-eight feet in length and when Dozer approached the Dean threateningly the whole congregation had risen to their feet to block his view. He put the weapon under his jacket as Ali rushed past with the bible clutched beneath his arm. Mutton watched Dozer following him and then left the cathedral to see where they had gone.

Ali sprinted down the street and round the corner where he leapt into the back of the Rolls and ducked down. He was trusting that Dozer wouldn't recognize the car in his haste to find a running man. Ali listened and heard heavy footfalls rapidly approaching and then passing the car and he breathed a sigh of relief. He was about to raise his head when there was a tap on the window and a policeman's puzzled face looked down at him. Ali opened the window and asked if there was a problem.

'What are you doing down there?' the officer asked as he looked beyond Ali at the floor.

'Searching for a cufflink, constable.'

'I see, sir, and what's your name?' His suspicion was growing and he took his little black book to begin making notes.

'Sir Alistair Montague D.S.O, MBE of Montague Hall, Norfolk,' Ali said in a haughty tone and the book was snapped shut and put away.

'My apology, sir,' the constable exclaimed, making a mental note to remove the page in his book, and began walking away hoping his collar number hadn't registered with the knight. He had walked twenty paces when he suddenly remembered that he had checked the car because it was illegally parked. Being a very fastidious man when it came to his duty he turned just in time to see the Rolls pull away and keep going. He also missed the illegally parked Audi that also pulled away from the kerb to shadow the Rolls.

Ali didn't stop driving until he arrived back at Gerald's house and when he knocked on the door Elizabeth opened it and a look of delight appeared on her face. She wasn't aware of the black Audi that quietly cruised past and parked a hundred yards down the street.

When Gerald saw the bible under Ali's arm he simply groaned. 'What on earth are we going to do with that?' he complained. 'We can't sell it and no doubt we've got a few nasty people out there wanting it back.'

'They will but they don't know where we are so we're safe while we consider what to do with it.' Ali said soothingly as he placed the heavy tome on top of the Welsh dresser.

Elizabeth began making tea as Ali related what had happened at Canterbury and Gerald groaned again when Dozer was mentioned.

'That thug will do anything he can to find us while in the meantime I'm still short a large sum of money for Shady Trees.' Gerald took the hot cup and passed it on to Ali.

'I have the answer to that little problem,' Ali said with a secret smile as he stepped out of the kitchen.

'No more bank or post office robberies,' Elizabeth snapped. 'If it comes to the crunch I'll stay at home and look after Stephanie while you go to work Gerald.'

'No need to do that I've got these,' Ali said, reappearing and holding up a beautiful monogrammed gun case.

'This is a 1937 James Purdey side-by-side 12 gauge shotgun.'

'No more robberies I said,' Elizabeth exclaimed.

'Absolutely, girl, this gun has a resale value of approximately thirty-one thousand pounds which is more than enough to solve Gerald's problem and . . .'

'No way, Ali,' Gerald interrupted. 'That's a family heirloom you can't possibly sell it.'

'Not sell, my friend, pawn,' Ali said as he laid the case on the kitchen table. 'I will simply pawn this gun at a reputable broker for twenty-three thousand and seventy pence and then recover it later; that gives us an extra thirty days to raise the money legitimately'

'But they're irreplaceable, Ali, why not the car?'

'The car has been valued at sixty-two thousand but I cannot sell or pawn it as the car was bequeathed to Margaret and I would never ask her to take any chances of losing it; after all, our mother took pride in telling her she was conceived on the back seat during a daytrip to Great Yarmouth.'

'But . . .'

'No buts, it's the gun and I'll be off early tomorrow.'

'What a perfectly ingenious and generous gesture on your part, Ali,' Elizabeth said and kissed him on the cheek.

Gerald was too embarrassed by the man's generosity to comment and he opted to smile while thinking of something to say. 'Which pawnbroker will you use?' he asked finally. 'It's a very valuable gun and a disreputable broker could swindle you,' Gerald asked.

'I'll play it safe and go direct to the Purdey showroom in Audley Street tomorrow and see if I can get them to agree an arrangement that is mutually and financially beneficial.'

While the friends discussed pawnbrokers in the living room, Margaret cooked dinner and Reg slept in her bed while the door of a dark Audi parked outside opened and Mutton got out and started walking back towards Gerald's house.

He paused outside the house whilst noting all the lit windows and strolled on for he had no idea how many people were inside or how they might be armed. He decided to wait until the next morning before he made any move to recover the bible and returned to the car.

Mutton woke with a start, a stiff neck and an aching back. Car seats, it seems, weren't designed for a full night of sleeping and he struggled out of the vehicle to stretch his arms above his head much to the amusement of an early riser who was taking in milk from his doorstep. Mutton pulled a face and resumed his seat behind the wheel just as an old Rolls Royce went bowling past with two people inside. For three sleepy seconds he watched it drive away and then turn right at the junction before it registered. 'Sir Alistair,' he exclaimed as he started the engine and accelerated away in pursuit. He caught up with the Rolls at the main A13 and then followed it all the way to central London. They passed St Paul's Cathedral and soon were averaging seven miles per hour as they made their way through to Mayfair. The Rolls finally slowed and pulled into a vacant parking bay and Mutton was forced to drive on and park illegally on double yellow lines. He watched Ali, carrying a long object, and Gerald leave the car to enter a large showroom on the street corner; Mutton immediately left his car and hurried to discover it was the world famous gunsmiths.

'Why would he bring his gun here?' he murmured to himself as he tried to peer through window after window to identify their position and business on the premises.

Unaware of the face peering anxiously through the glass Ali requested to speak to the manager privately and was shown into an office where a rather kindly man in his fifties stood to shake their hands. Ali explained his need to raise money urgently and this was received rather favourably. He unzipped the leather case to show the shotgun and the manager called in one of the staff who examined the gun minutely before nodding his head in admiration for the seventy-nine year old side-by-side. Ali was then advised on which company in the neighbourhood would have the reputation to negotiate such a contract.

Ali left the premises still carrying the gun and followed by Mutton drove to the recommended establishment where an agreement was drawn up, formalities such as the original receipt, maintenance history and proof of identity checked and, in exchange, Ali was given a banker's draft for twenty-three thousand pounds and eighty pence.

They returned to the Rolls and drove to Berkeley Square where Ali's bank had its head office and were fortunate to find parking nearby. Mutton returned to his car to find it being clamped by a woman in overalls. The closer he got the bigger she grew and, big as he was, he realized he had no chance of winning an argument with a woman who tossed a five kilogram wheel clamp from one hand to the other like a tennis ball. As he had stolen the car he decided retreat was the better option and he waved a hand at a cruising taxi and asked to be taken to Waterloo Bridge. Once there he walked the streets until he found an unlocked Volkswagen Beetle and drove back through London and into the suburbs to park near Gerald's address. What was running through his mind was that two men had gone to London leaving one man and two women in the house. Those were odds he could handle and he left the car and walked up the drive to push the doorbell.

Margaret was upstairs administering to Reginald's needs after a long sleepless night of performing the same duties when the doorbell rang and Elizabeth shouted that she would get it. She opened the door wiping her hands on a tea cloth and instantly recognized the big man.

'Why hello Mutton,' she said with a smile. 'What brings you to this part of the world?' She gave no indication of her shock at seeing the man again so soon.

'You have something that belongs to me,' Mutton growled in a rather unfriendly fashion. 'A book my boss would like to read.'

'A book? Your boss?' And who might that be?' She gripped the edge of the door to stop her hands from shaking.

'Judge Atkinson doesn't like to be kept waiting on doorsteps,' Mutton said, then bit his lip at the slip and pushed himself past Elizabeth and into the hallway. 'You have the bible, where is it.' An automatic pistol materialized in his hand and she felt a sudden need to alleviate the pressure of her bladder.

'I must go in here,' she said opening the door to the guest toilet.

'You'll go where you've hidden the book,' Mutton cocked the weapon with a distinct metallic 'click' that was echoed by a very loud 'clock' as the second Purdey was snapped shut and the safety flicked to the fire position.

Mutton looked up into the twin barrels being held by a totally naked Reg who was slowly descending the stairs. Without the dark suit, sunglasses and fedora hat favoured by Chicago hitmen the element of deadly threat seemed to be missing but the look on Reg's face and the shotgun more than made up for the humorous sight of his nakedness and the hypnotic swaying of his family jewels with each step.

'Put the gun away Mutton,' Reg said. 'I won't hesitate to pull the trigger if you don't do it within five seconds.'

Mutton suddenly grinned. 'Only joking, mate,' he said slipping the Glock into his belt. 'Wouldn't hurt the little lady, would I?'

'Put it on the hall table and then we'll have a little talk,' Reg said and waited until the gun was within Elizabeth's reach. She took it and backed away as Reg descended the last few steps and indicated, with the barrels, that Mutton should enter the living room.

When everyone was seated, except for Reg who kept the shotgun trained on Mutton, Margaret appeared in one of Reg's dressing gowns. 'Anyone for tea and chocolate biscuits?' she asked as though it was a typical meeting of the Woman's Institute. Nobody nodded and Margaret sat in the vacant armchair.

'What now?' Mutton asked with a slight smile.

'You'll leave and never come back is a pretty good start,' Reg said.

'My boss wouldn't like me to do that.'

'Your judge, is he a real judge?' Elizabeth asked out of curiosity.

'Yes, a High Court judge and very powerful,' Mutton said. 'He's offered me fifty thousand pounds for the return of the book and I'm willing to give you ten thousand if you give me the book.'

'Twenty-five,' Reg snapped back. 'And no less.' He had suddenly realized that Mutton had shown a way to pay the Shady Trees fee for Gerald without Ali having to risk losing part of his family's heritage. It was also a perfect way to rid themselves of the albatross that has given them nothing but bad luck.

Mutton thought for a while before speaking. 'Very well, give me the book now and I'll go straight to the judge and get your money.'

'Not so fast, Mutton,' Reg snapped. 'We're not imbeciles, if we give you the book you'll disappear fifty thousand pounds richer.'

Margaret suddenly interrupted. 'I think a better idea would be for you to go and get the money and return here or, failing that, you persuade the judge to bring the money to St Paul's Cathedral where we can make the exchange without fear of being assaulted and robbed.'

'A very appropriate venue, Margaret,' Elizabeth said with a light laugh. 'And the judge wouldn't try to cheat us in such a holy place.'

Mutton chewed his lip and nodded despite knowing that the judge had the power to retrieve his bible, destroy them and not lose a penny by enlisting the aid of the police and charging them with burglary; he wasn't to know that the judge wanted to keep possession of the book a dark secret. He stood up, took the slip of paper that Margaret had scrawled a mobile number on, and left to return to the judge with the terms.

CHAPTER 17

TIM HOLT HAD KEPT a tight lid on the boiling hate he had felt from the moment Judge Atkinson had pronounced his sentence and like an insidious poison it simmered within waiting to be released. The cessation of his drug was only the beginning of his nightmare from the first night he spent in the holding cell at the police station to when he was transferred from the court to Brixton Prison. The moment he entered his senses were assailed by the silence and the smells of disinfectant and cannabis. He was swiftly stripped, washed, dressed in prison grey and taken to the cramped and dingy cell that was to be his home for the next ten years; there he met his cellmate, Peter Pidd.

The cell had a small television, a small cupboard, kettle, sink and a toilet that stood, waiting to be flushed. The window was bar-covered with wooden shutters to repel the wind, rain and the light.

As Tim dumped his blanket and spare prison clothing on the lower bunk a long hairy arm reached out pulled them onto the floor. 'In 'ere, you'll find there are strict rules to be followed and one of them is always do what I tell you to do,' Pidd said pointing to the top bunk. 'You'll be up there and bloody like it.'

Since entering the prison gates Tim had been spoiling for a good fight and he looked closely at the Neanderthal sitting at the small table. He took in the ridged forehead, broad nose and deep set eyes and decided he'd better follow the rules; he clearly couldn't be alpha dog in this cell. Pidd wore regulation grey briefs and when he stood up he wasn't much higher than Tim but was definitely three times his size in hard muscular development. Brawny forearms writhing with inked serpents in the matted hair fleeing from a giant eagle with outstretched talons that spread across his barrel of a chest.

'I'm Peter Pidd but the screws call me Peepee.' A large forefinger poked Tim in the chest. 'You can call me sir, but if I ever catch you using Peepee I'll beat your head to a pulp, understand?' he growled and then held out a gorilla's paw and on taking it Tim felt as though every finger in his hand was being fractured.

'I understand,' Tim said rubbing his assaulted hand. 'My name is Tim Holt, ten years,' the younger man said as he gathered up his things and threw them up onto the top bunk.

'For what?'

'Accused of dealing but I'd only ever used,' Tim replied nervously.

'I got twenty for returning big H to a dealer and taking my money back,' Pidd said with a twisted grin.

'Twenty years for handling, that's a lot.'

'Sir.'

'Sir.'

'Not for handling but for shoving half a kilo of the baking powder he tried to sell to me down his throat.'

'You killed him, sir?'

'What do you think?'

Tim remained silent.

'Don't worry, Tim, you've come to the right place. Brixton is a training prison for screws and you'll find things are a little more laid back here than the class B lockups. We can get as much cannabis as we want.' Tim had already smelt the distinctive drug that permeated throughout the prison. 'There's plenty of heroin, cocaine and crystal meth as well so you'll be all right provided you keep your nose clean.'

'How does it get into the prison, sir?'

'Soft shit like cannabis is brought in by the day-release prisoners.'

'Harder drugs, sir?'

'You don't normally ask that question and I'll kill you if you finger me but you look like an honest lad so I'll tell you that I use drones.'

'Flown over the wall, sir?'

'Right, every Saturday night, at eight o'clock. That's when the screws are having their nosh. It hovers outside the cell window and I unhook my lovely presents and it flits away like my own fairy godmother. What's your particular trip?'

'Cocaine,' Tim said. 'But without any money I guess I'll be climbing the walls within a week.'

'Sir.'

'Sir.'

'You've got no worries there my lad,' Pidd said, leering up at the newcomer. 'I wasn't on any drugs when I first came here but the boring routine of twenty-one hours a day in this cell, year in, year out, drove me insane and like most of the other guys in here I found a little heroin made things more exciting and now my time passes a lot faster.'

'Will I have to stay here, in this cell, for that long each day, sir?'

'Naw, you can volunteer to work in the kitchen or laundry or join the fairies who go to art classes but you'll be glad to know that you will still be with me for at least fifteen hours each day.' Pidd winked. 'No what I mean?'

'I hadn't planned to stay here any longer than I have to, sir,' Tim answered and reeled back, head spinning, as the same paw that had shaken his hand earlier swiped the side of his head.

'You'll stay here for as long as I want you,' Pidd snarled and went back to reading his paperbook. Tim arranged his things on the bunk, including the small breakfast pack of cornflakes and milk carton that had been given to him with the bedding.

Tim climbed up and stretched out with his hands behind his head and began to think of how he could escape. When the drone had been mentioned it had sparked a small idea but he knew he would have to get Peepee's permission to carry out any plan. However, his comment about staying for as long as 'I want you', the accent being on those three words, and the accompanying leer Tim knew he had other plans for his cellmate and they didn't include escaping. It was then he became aware of the dozens of pictures blue-tacked to the wall. They were all of semi-nude young men in provocative poses and Tim shuddered, dreading the moment the lights went out.

'Do you want something to help you sleep?' Pidd asked suddenly.

Tim looked at him suspiciously and nodded. 'I told you, I don't have any money, sir.'

'Think of it as a loan against services to be rendered.'

Tim didn't bother to ask what he meant by that and took the length of rubber hose offered and wrapped it round his forearm while Pidd took a spoon and candle stub from a small tin box. He lit the candle and took a pinch of crumbly dark brown substance and heated it in the spoon until it became a bubbling liquid.

'Have you ever tried H before?' Pidd asked with one eyebrow raised as he drew a small quantity up into the hypodermic syringe before holding the needle tip over Tim's arm.

'No, but I'll try anything to get rid of the way I'm feeling at the moment.' Tim winced as the needle went in.

'You should get into your bunk before the rush begins.'

Tim did as he was told and had hardly laid his head down when he was overcome by an intense feeling of euphoria. His mouth went dry and his skin became warm as he entered a state of drowsiness and wakefulness. He heard Pidd say something but couldn't make sense of what he was saying for his mind was now working in a hazy fashion as though trying to think in a dense smog.

'Can you hear what I'm saying?' Pidd repeated and then grinned at the idiotic expression on the young man's face. He removed the rubber tubing and wrapped it around his own before using the remainder of the drug in the syringe.

The guards turned the lights off thirty minutes after the two men in cell 48C had switched themselves off.

Tim was woken by a strange dream, filled with weird apparitions and explosive sounds and immediately rolled over, with eyes still closed, and projectile vomited into space. Fortunately, it missed Pidd who was reading a paperback whilst on the toilet but landed on the small table. Another loud evacuation of gas greeted Tim as he jumped down with leaden limbs and used the sink to wash his mouth and face.

'You'll clean that lot up, right now,' Pidd said without even lowering his book.

'Yes,' Tim mumbled with a head that felt filled with molten lava.

'Sir.'

'Sir.' Tim spent the next fifteen minutes mopping up the mess that had accurately landed on his breakfast box and along with Pidd's morning read, was filling the cell with obnoxious odours.

'What happened last night, sir?' Tim asked timidly.

'Nothing lad, we both had a fabulous rush and went out like lights.' All signs of the drug taking had been hidden away. 'However, if you want another hit you'll have to pay for it.' Pidd finished his toiletry, poured milk on his cornflakes, and proceeded to eat without another glance at Tim. He watched the brute for he hadn't been fed since lunch at the courtroom but his hunger had been suppressed by a growing fear. He knew how he would have to pay and the thought made him rush to the toilet to throw up again.

'You'll be alright after a stroll round the exercise yard,' Pidd said and he was right. The cell was opened for one hour and Tim hurried out and asked one of the guards for directions to the yard. A size ten boot showed him the way and the relatively fresh air and open sky above his head provided a brief moment of exhilaration until he looked round at the heavyweight collection of pumped up testosterone that had paused in their workouts to eye the newcomer.

One particularly large bruiser with tattoos covering most of his upper body strolled across the yard and poked Tim in the chest. 'And who might you be, girly?' He laughed while slowly studying his victim from head to toe.

'I'm Tim Holt and I'm in Mr Pidd's cell,' Tim stuttered.

The man's hand dropped away and he took a step back while looking around the yard, half-expecting to see Pidd charging towards him with a shank in his hand.

'You're Peepee's girl?'

Tim didn't like the term the prisoner used but he nodded and the man moved away a lot faster than he approached. Soon everyone in the yard knew Peepee had a new 'vic' and they steered away whenever Tim jogged close which amused him and he started teasing the muscle men by deliberately changing directions and moving towards them. After five minutes of breathless exercise he stopped to survey the forbidding walls that surrounded the yard. They were exceptionally tall and beyond climbing but Tim began to think of his original idea and he checked how the guards were placed and their behaviour until he came to the conclusion that it was possible; but only with Pidd's cooperation which judging by his last words wouldn't be forthcoming.

Judge Atkinson opened the door and with an angry look at the big man's empty hands told Mutton to go into the library and explain what happened and why he didn't have the bible. Mutton told him what had transpired and then relayed the terms on which the book would be returned.

'They don't trust me, do they?' Atkinson said with a humorless chuckle.

'Looks like it, guv,' Mutton replied handing the judge the slip of paper.

'Then I'll call a couple of my friends first and then agree a time with these upstarts on when we can meet.' Atkinson waved Mutton beyond earshot, swiftly dialed and murmured a few words before repeating himself in a second call.

'It's all arranged, no thanks to you.' he looked at Mutton with a smirk before calling the number on the scrap of paper. 'Ah, Sir Alistair Montague I presume?' he said with exaggerated bonhomie. 'Ten, tomorrow morning, by Wellington's monument?' There was a slight pause. 'Yes, I'll bring the money, just make sure you have the book.' Atkinson hung up with a broad grin on his face.

'How will you get the book without giving them the money?' Mutton asked.

''I'm not giving them any money but I will give them four nightclub bouncers who'll wrestle the book away from them in seconds and be on their way before any possible ruckus is noticed by security or the tourists.'

Mutton nodded. 'Do you want me to be one of the heavies?'

'No, I want you to be outside, armed and ready to cut down anyone trying to escape with the book.' Another chuckle. 'You'll be my failsafe solution.'

'In broad daylight on the steps of St Paul's Cathedral?' Mutton was astounded by the temerity of what he had been instructed to do.

'Of course you'll do it in daylight, the meeting is scheduled for ten o'clock in the morning, did you think it would be dark with a full moon aiding your aim?' Atkinson glared at Mutton without chuckling at his own joke this time.

Mutton turned his head away and simply nodded.

At ten fifteen on the following day Gerald and Ali left the taxi at the foot of the steps and as they climbed they looked round for any suspicious characters. With so many tourists of different nationalities it was difficult to tell who was suspicious or not. They entered the cathedral and were immediately blanketed by the respectfully subdued mumble of voices and slowly walked down the nave. They turned into the North Aisle and approached Wellington's tomb to find a small group of Japanese tourists being shepherded around the monumental sculpture by a guide holding a flag in the tour company's colours. They could occasionally detect the words 'Jiang jun Werrington' in her non-stop history lesson until they moved on to view the 'gland organ.'

Gerald checked the four sides of the marble memorial and appropriately stopped beneath the impressive sculpture entitled Truth and Falsehood. The book was feeling heavier with every passing second and the thin handles of the plastic Tesco carrier was cutting the blood flow to his fingers. Ali had wandered back towards the centre of the nave and was inspecting everyone moving towards the monument. A dapper looking man in a three-piece suit caught his attention and he watched as he walked purposefully towards the monument. Gerald had also spotted him at the same time as well as the four men that appeared to be following him and he knew the judge had sprung his trap.

'You don't appear to be carrying any money with you,' Gerald said when the judge stopped before him.

'You must be a fool if you think I'd give you fifty-thousand pounds.' Atkinson replied as he held his hand out for the bag. The four burly men, one with a broken nose, closed in.

Gerald placed the bag on the stone floor and back away. 'You must also be a fool to think me a fool to turn up with the book on our first meeting.' He pointed above his head. 'I'm standing, rather appropriately beneath Truth and Falsehood. You've demonstrated you're a liar while I've been true to my word.'

'How could you without the book.' Atkinson said angrily.

'It's very simple, I've put the book somewhere in this cathedral.' Gerald waved a hand airily to encompass the vast vaulted and domed interior. 'All you have to do is give me the money and I'll tell you where it is.'

'I could get my men to start looking for it.'

'And they'll never find it.'

Atkinson peered into the carrier bag and saw the bundle of old newspaper. He thought for a while and then waved to one of the bruisers who came forward and handed him a small briefcase. 'There's your money,' he declared. 'Now where's the bible?'

Gerald snapped the catches and looked inside. Small stacks of banded fifty-pound notes filled the case and he didn't have to count to know it was the right amount. Ali appeared from the other side of the monument and took the case from Gerald.

'My friend will now take the case while your men stay here. When he reaches the main entrance I will reveal the hiding place,' Gerald said. When the judge said 'yes' Gerald gave Ali the nod and the tall man strode away swiftly.

'You think you're so smart, Mr Gerald . . . Mutton never told me your surname.' Atkinson's smile twisted into a smirk. 'However he does know what my briefcase looks like and he's outside waiting to retrieve it.'

'I don't think so, your honour. Mutton called us last night and told us what you were planning to do. It seems he hadn't the stomach for gunning down people on the steps of St Paul's Cathedral.' Gerald handed the Tesco bag to the astonished judge and walked away.

'Quick, get after him. Get my money,' Atkinson shouted and the blank-faced heavies began shambling at a respectful speed out of the aisle, into the nave and straight into a large coach party of Estonians going in the opposite direction. 'What about the book, where is it?' he called out to Gerald.

'What book, judge, I haven't got any books with me, on my honour your honour.' Gerald gave a cheery wave and he also disappeared into the crowd of happy Estonians.

Atkinson felt a white-hot rage coursing through his body and he smashed his arm against a plastic charity box releasing a stream of coins onto the marble floor. Every one striking the stone with a ringing sound that echoed throughout the vast interior.

Security men appeared from nowhere and Atkinson was bundled through a door to await the police and face charges of willful damage, theft and possibly sacrilege. His four bruisers clumsily extricated themselves from the tourists after shouts of 'out of the way!' which was answered by 'aurama!' which means bugger off in Estonian, and looked for their employer who seemed to have magically disappeared from the spot where a number of tourists now seemed to be scrabbling about on their hands and knees looking for something.

The bruisers gave up the search and left the cathedral to drink cappucinos at the Starbucks across the street and lick vanilla ice-cream cones bought from the Polish vendor at the foot of the Cathedral steps.

Atkinson gave up struggling and allowed himself to be transported from the cathedral to Wood Street police station where he had the misfortune to be instantly identified by Detective Inspector Austin Cooper, a policeman he had often crossed swords with in the courtroom.

'What a pleasant surprise, your honour,' he said loudly as Atkinson was bundled into the charge room, turning all heads with bemused expressions. 'What did this high court judge do to warrant handcuffs, constable?' he asked the arresting constable who was also grinning broadly.

'Petty theft, sacrilege and resisting arrest in St Paul's Cathedral, sir.'

'The charity box was broken by accident,' Atkinson protested as the sergeant behind the desk entered the charges into the book.

'Witnesses claimed his honour raised his hand and brought it down in a karate chop to deliberately shatter the box,' the constable said to Cooper.

'Tut, tut, sir. As you know, we come down heavily on anybody committing an offence in a church, especially a cathedral. It's a crime that verges on sacrilege.' Cooper added smugly as Atkinson was led away to the cells.

CHAPTER 18

ALI TOOK A CIRCUITOUS route using the underground, bus and another bus to join Gerald just as he was entering the house. Both women were overjoyed to see them arriving safely and decided to celebrate with a builder's brew of tea, cheese scones, strawberry jam and double cream before venturing to open the case and divide the money.

Ali put the money he had been paid by the pawnbroker to one side to redeem his family heirloom sooner than the date agreed and Gerald counted out precisely the same figure from the case to cover the fees for his mother's continued residence at Shady Trees. The remainder, twenty-six thousand, nine hundred and ninety-nine pounds and twenty pence, was divided between the five friends and according to Margaret, armed with pencil and paper, it came to five thousand three hundred and ninety-nine pounds and eighty-four pence each. They all cheered and agreed that it warranted another pot of tea and, damn the waistlines, fresh scones.

It was much later, when Gerald and Elizabeth were cuddling beneath the duvet, that Gerald realized that they had forgotten Mutton. 'We're still in trouble, Elizabeth.' He had decided to use her full name ever since his mother, during that one lucid moment, had used it herself. 'Mutton is still out there and he knows where I live; we can expect him to knock at our door at any time.'

Elizabeth mumbled something into the pillow and slept on totally exhausted by their amorous activities.

The next morning the slate grey sky threatened rain as the friends came together in the kitchen for breakfast. Gerald voiced his fear again and Ali nodded his agreement. 'We should prepare ourselves and have the second Purdey to hand at all times,' he said.

'No violence,' Elizabeth exclaimed. 'I suggest we take the bible to the police and simply say that we found it in a bus shelter.'

'That wouldn't do, Elizabeth.' Margaret said. 'They'd want to know our names and addresses and as soon as they knew that they'd arrest us for what happened at Montague Hall. Don't forget we left two dead men in the well and the fresh corpse of a young woman in the family crypt.'

Elizabeth fell silent.

Gerald overcame the awkward silence with the first thing that came to mind. 'One place where difficult questions wouldn't be asked is St Marks church. I'm sure Father Jeremiah would love to put such a beautiful thing on display for the local parishioners to view. Sir Alistair Montague could claim that it's a poor copy that had been in the family for two generations and he would now like to bequeath it to St Marks as he fears for it's safety.'

'And when Mutton arrives to demand it for himself?' Margaret asked.

'We tell him the truth, that we've given it to the church to keep safe in perpetuity.'

'Then he'll go and terrorize poor Father Jeremiah until he gets it.' Margaret said glumly.

'We won't say we gave the bible to St Marks but parcel posted it to the Pope at the Vatican.'

'I do like that, Gerald.' Elizabeth said and there was a happy note to her voice. 'It's the sort of thing I'd hoped you would suggest. No more running from villains and no more violent thoughts.'

Gerald hugged her and Ali shrugged. 'Let's do it as soon as possible because we don't know when Mutton will turn up.' They all nodded and the Gutenberg Bible, worth thirty million pounds, was placed in yet another Tesco Bag For Life shopping bag. Gerald had collected dozens over time and he always ended up stuffing them under the sink.

The journey to a street behind St Marks took Gerald, Ali and Elizabeth twenty minutes in the Rolls and after parking they walked the rest of the way. On stepping into the cool sanctity of the sixteenth century building they were immediately seen by a shadowy figure sitting behind the wheel of a black BMW that had the registration D10ZER. He had been parked most of the day, building up courage to enter the church and, completely out of character, pray for a miracle. Now, before he had had the opportunity to fall to his knees and put his hands together, one had been granted. 'There is a God,' he thought as the very people who had cheated him and run off with the bible had just entered the church. Dozer crossed himself and left the car to follow them for he had a distinct feeling that the plastic bag being carried by the taller man contained exactly what he wanted most.

Father Jeremiah watched the three people coming down the centre aisle and greeted them by asking if they would like him to take confession and Ali smiled at the kindly priest. 'Father, I am Sir Alistair Montague M.B.E, and I have a gift I would like to present to St Marks.' He withdrew the heavy tome from the plastic bag and as Gerald removed the old bible from the lectern he replaced it with the Gutenberg and opened it. The priest stepped up to look and once again was overawed by the sheer beauty of the oldest printed bible known to Christendom.

'I . . . wha . . . ' he tried to exclaim on recognizing the same volume that had been offered to him by a murderous looking thug.

'Please accept this poor copy that my great grandfather brought back from Mainz in Germany in 1875. It was found in the ruins of an old farmhouse he was thinking of purchasing but it really belongs in a church. Although it is in Latin I'm sure the words are just as holy as any English translation.'

'This is generosity beyond the pale, young man,' Jeremiah said breathlessly as he turned one and then another page. 'I will gladly accept your gift and will give it pride of place on the altar.'

Gerald suddenly saw movement and instantly recognized Dozer walking slowly down the aisle towards them. 'You'll not give away what is mine,' he boomed startling all present including, Marcia, the teenager waiting to confess what she had been doing with Eric, her brother's mate, on the park bandstand, before a drunk tripped over them causing coitus interruptus on the first stroke of midnight.

Gerald slipped the old bible into the Bag for Life in such a manner as to draw Dozer's attention and sure enough the big man stepped in, snatched the bag, and after waving a fist at the group standing by the lectern, stalked from the church.

'My goodness,' the priest murmured. 'Is it really his, because I remember he had it in his possession when he last visited St Marks?'

'He brought it to you?' Gerald was surprised beyond belief. 'He only wanted it to make a great deal of money.'

'You're mistaken there, my son. He wanted me to read from it in my services but I told him that English was the language I had to use. He then became very angry and said he would take it to the head honcho, whatever that meant.'

That's why he was at Canterbury,' Margaret exclaimed. 'He wanted the Archbishop to use it.'

'So it isn't really his?'

'Not at all, Father, he originally stole it from Montague Hall and we were able to recover it,' Ali explained. 'I would suggest that you hide it for now and if he comes back tell him that you've sent it to Westminster Abbey by special courier. In a few weeks time you will be able to display it where it belongs.'

'I am quite tempted to dispatch it to the Cardinal Archbishop.'

'It's only a copy, Father, I don't think His Excellency will feel it is quite suitable for the pulpit of the Mother Church in the land.' Gerald countered and saw that his argument had swayed the cleric. 'We'll purchase a new bible for St Marks as soon as possible,' he added.

'Do not concern yourself. I have a number of spares tucked away. I also have the perfect place to hide this work of absolute beauty,' Jeremiah said with a grin that lit up his face.

'Could you do that immediately, Father, and is there a side entrance we can use?' Elizabeth prudently asked, knowing that Dozer, after a good look at what he had run out with, would come thundering back into the church at any moment.

True to Elizabeth's prediction Dozer leapt into the car, took the book from the bag, stared at it for ten seconds in total disbelief, leapt from the car and rushed back to St Marks. He ran in, saw there was nobody in sight and checked every niche until he came to the confessional. When he yanked the door open he was aurally assaulted by a young woman's shrill scream. Marcia had just reached the crucial part in her confession, when she had allowed Eric to slip a hand inside her knickers, when the door was flung to reveal a huge brute of a man. She instantly cringed back into the furthest corner and wet herself.

'What's wrong, child,' Jeremiah called out and then, on hearing the faint sound of water trickling, he left the confessional to investigate.

'Where's my bible?' Dozer shouted into the priest's face as soon as the door opened.

Jeremiah managed to keep calm and replied in a quiet voice and a slight smile. 'As I told you before, I felt it was too perfect for a humble church such as St Marks and as I had a messenger waiting in the sacristy I sent it to the Cardinal Archbishop in London and asked if he would keep it safe at Westminster Abbey.'

'Damn.'

Jeremiah ignored the blasphemy. 'While you're here, would you like to confess your sins?'

'Damn,' Dozer repeated, mentally retracting his earlier thought that there was such a thing as God, and hurried from the church hoping to catch the trio and give them a damned good hiding. The light drizzle had now become a torrent and he saw nobody he recognized before he was saturated and had to run for the cover of his BMW. Gerald, Ali and Elizabeth watched him accelerate away as they sheltered in the porch of the side door.

'I guess we can return home now,' Gerald said as the BMW disappeared from view at the same time as the rain eased and stopped.

'If Mutton turns up we can tell him the same story as Father Jeremiah has just told Dozer,' Elizabeth said as they headed quickly to the Rolls and once more she was correct in her prophesy for the big man was waiting across the road from Gerald's home and as soon as they turned the corner and strode down the street towards the gate he crossed over and held his hand up.

'Where's the bible?' he demanded. 'I did you a favour by not turning up at the cathedral and gunning you down as I was ordered.'

'By Judge Atkinson?' Ali asked.

'Yes, so it's your turn to return the favour.'

'We're all so sorry, Mutton, but we've just given it to St Marks church and the priest has sent it to Westminster Abbey for safekeeping,' Elizabeth said in a mock apologetic tone of voice.

'So if I asked to search your house you'll tell me I wont find it there?'

'That's right, mate,' Gerald said.

'Damn,' Mutton murmured, replicating the same response Dozer gave at the church. He thought for a while, studying the three faces and then the house before asking where the money was.

'Atkinson refused to give it to us at St Pauls which is why we refused to give him the bible.' Ali said and he could see that his answer seemed logical to a thug like Mutton and he nodded slowly, turned away and returned to his car with shoulders slumped. He was thinking to himself that the judge most probably took the money home with him and this brightened him up for it presented an opportunity to at least get something for all the trouble he'd been put through. He pulled away and headed for the High Court judge's house unaware that his target was currently tucked up, safely awaiting Her Majesty's Pleasure.

The friends went into the house and voted to celebrate the end of their dangerous adventure with something a little harder than tea and Margaret's scones, as delicious as they were. As they were settling down to open a bottle of twelve-year old malt Mutton was turning into the long drive that led to Atkinson's substantial residence.

The garage stood open and he could see it was empty of vehicles. He braked hard on the shingles scattering little stones in all directions, some striking the windows and front door. He got out, pushed the bell with one hand and thumped on the wood with the other. He had noticed the CCTV camera so the Glock automatic, with silencer fitted, was already tucked into the back of his trousers for quick retrieval when the door opened. As Atkinson knew Mutton he didn't anticipate the judge refusing not to answer it. All remained quiet and he banged on the door harder until he heard the faint sounds of footsteps inside.

Mutton readied himself and when the door swung open he reached behind to pull the Glock from out of his trouser belt. Two things happened almost simultaneously; first, Mutton had forgotten he'd already moved the safety to 'fire' and as he tugged at the weapon the silencer caught against his belt making him tug again. Second, he had carelessly curled his finger round the trigger. Consequently, the gun fired with a dull 'thwock' and Mutton felt a searing pain across, or was it through, his left buttock. This made him reactively leap three feet to the right thereby avoiding the shotgun blast aimed at him by one of the bruisers Atkinson had hired for the St Pauls job.

Mutton fell to the ground and before the shotgun user could adjust his aim Mutton managed to extricate the Glock to shoot the fellow in the crotch. This didn't mortally wound the man but it did, with extreme pain, render him incapable of keeping his bloodline going into the future. He fell to his knees, screaming like a wild boar while clutching his groin with one hand and trying to aim the shotgun with the other. Mutton ended his misery with another round, this time in the head, which silenced the newly made eunuch and made him fall sideways. Everything was instantly silent and Mutton listened carefully for any other movements within the house as he stood up and probed his backside; the material was wet which he knew could only be blood.

He cautiously entered the house and after searching the ground floor he made his way upstairs to complete his exploration. Mutton soon found the bathroom and he went to drop his trousers and sodden shorts in front of the mirror. He explored the wound and found it was nothing more than a deep groove in the flesh that was four inches long. He opened all the cabinets until he found a box of dressings and after washing the seeping wound he covered the gash with two of the larger waterproof plasters.

Mutton found a pair of chinos in the bedroom that more or less fitted if he exhaled. It was as he was descending the stairs that he heard a loud 'bloody hell' and a man appeared at the open door, looking down at the dead man. Mutton kept his Glock aimed at the man as he finished the last steps and when the man looked up they both gave a start; Mutton on seeing it was the judge and the judge on looking into the muzzle of a rather formidable weapon.

'Where's the money, judge?' he asked the horrified Atkinson, who had recently been released from Wood Street police station on a two-hundred pound police bail and was now staring down at the floor again.

Atkinson ignored the question and pointed at the corpse redesigning his seventeenth-century Safid Kerman carpet with his blood. 'Did you do that?' he shrieked. 'Do you know how much that carpet is worth?'

Mutton briefly looked down at the elaborate 'vase' design that had taken a craftswoman in the Iranian Dasht-e-Lut region two years to weave and then repeated his question with threatening jerks of the Glock.

'What money?' Atkinson said innocently.

'The money you were going to give for the bible,' Mutton said his impatience reaching a critical point.

'I gave it to those bastards I was meeting in St Pauls, they were able to walk away with every penny and all because you missed them when they came out of the cathedral carrying it.'

Mutton grunted and admitted that he wasn't there. 'I said I wasn't keen on firing guns in the street so I didn't turn up. What with all the street CCTV cameras these days an armed response team would soon be shooting holes in my ass and when they shoot at a man they know is armed they tend to shoot to kill and only ask the corpse their questions later.'

'So, I don't have the bible and I don't have my money, what are you going to do about it?' Atkinson shouted, ignoring the threatening gun with his eyes still fixed on the precious carpet.

Mutton lowered the Glock and thought for a few moments before answering. 'I'm going straight back to ask Gerald Latimer what his game is and if he doesn't come up with the cash I'll shoot his bloody head off as well as those of all his friends.'

'Gerald Latimer,' the judge murmured to himself as he watched the big man storming out of the house. 'Hey, what about this?' he shouted and Mutton turned to see the judge pointing at the corpse.

'I'm not your housekeeper,' Mutton yelled jumping into the car and accelerated away, leaving deep furrows in the normally immaculate driveway. He also left the judge frantically using his smartphone to locate someone to tidy up before his overly house-proud housekeeper arrived. He knew she would be dangerously curious about the three pint puddle of blood on the hallway carpet he was always telling her to be careful about.

After he had arranged for one of the other 'hired help' to come immediately to carry out the disposal work he called his police mole and asked him to do a search on somebody called Gerald Latimer. It was only minutes later that he learnt, amongst the usual details, that Latimer held a bank account at the same branch of Crampton Bank that had recently suffered an attempted robbery and a hijacked security van. Atkinson read the address for the third time and decided to pay Mr Gerald Latimer a surprise visit.

It was pure coincidence that five minutes after Teal had left the station to fetch Atkinson one of the men standing by Wellington's Monument was identified as Gerald Latimer. His face had matched that of a Crampton Bank customer who had applied for and been turned down for a substantial loan. His face had been recorded on CCTV when he caused a bit of a fuss and had to be ejected from the bank. Gerald's address was given by the bank, for the second time that day, and rather than wait for Teal to return the inspector decided to pay Mr Latimer a visit, which would possibly be more surprising than that of the judge. He told the sergeant to prepare an armed response team to be ready in fifteen minutes. The team of officers fully clad in armoured vests and carrying automatic weapons was waiting for him and eagerly anticipating some action when he went down to the car pool to join them.

CHAPTER 19

———————————

GERALD HAD DECIDED to go to Shady Trees to pay the debt and abstained from drinking any of the whisky but the rest were happily halfway through the second bottle when there was a loud knocking on the door. It was as though a jackhammer was being used and they all looked at each other knowing it could only be Mutton or Dozer and by the noise reverberating in the hallway it couldn't be interpreted as anything other than an unfriendly caller.

'Where's the Purdey,' Gerald asked and Ali pointed to where it was standing in the corner of the room. He grabbed it and checked to see if it was loaded and was shocked to find both barrels empty. 'Where are the cartridges?' he demanded and Elizabeth looked at him guiltily.

'I'm sorry, I threw them in the wheelie-bin,' she confessed. 'I didn't think there would be any need for them.

'The bin was put out front for collection yesterday,' Gerald said with a sigh as he closed the useless weapon.

'Pretty dangerous thing to do, Betty,' Margaret said admonishingly. 'There were twenty-three cartridges in that box which could cause a bit of trouble if dumped into an incinerator.'

This was a rather visionary prediction for at that precise moment their previous day's waste was being tipped into a landfill that had developed a number of 'hot spots' where exothermic reactions had created small fires below the surface. A bulldozer pushed orange juice cartons, yoghurt pots, Tesco Bags for Life, well-used nappies and the unused cartridges around until a large pocket of noxious gas was released at exactly the same time as the driver carelessly flicked his cigarette into the air.

The flames shot high into the air and spread over a large area in seconds. The bulldozer hastily retreated from the fire and the amused driver sat looking at the roaring flames that would, over the next hour, reach twenty feet in height before dwindling down to a smoking layer of household detritus. Unfortunately, the driver wouldn't see the end of this brief conflagration for a twelve-bore cartridge shot his throat away and he fell from his seat dying. Four waste-pickers who had been salvaging reusable materials saw the fire and the driver falling and ran towards the big machine. One was suddenly surprised to find he had lost three fingers on his left hand. Another suffered a serious gunshot wound in the thigh before the remainder threw themselves down upon the fetid surface to contemplate what to do next. There were another twenty detonations before the landfill fell silent apart from the crackling of flames and the rumbling of the bulldozer's engine. The waste pickers took no chances and remained prone until a landfill site manager turned up to ask why one of his bulldozers wasn't working.

'This is what I'll do,' Gerald said. 'I'll pretend the gun is loaded and behave threateningly like Reg did before.' He went to the door and peered through the side window to see a large group of heavily armed police officers in full battle gear standing in the street.

'On second thoughts we'll all sneak out the back and get as far away from here as possible.' He ran down the hall, followed by the others, just as there was another bout of banging on the door.

Thanks to an oversight by Inspector Cooper no armed response officers were at Gerald's back gate and they ran down the service lane until they found another gate. They yanked the door open and stormed into a large garden shed only to find a naked Marcia and Eric in the act of resuming coitus interruptus on the workbench.

'Not again,' she cried as she pushed Eric off and jumped down to gather up her dress and hold it against her pubescent chest. On the sudden intrusion of five adults Eric had become white with shock and everything to boast about had instantly shrivelled. The shed was now packed from wall to wall and Gerald put his finger to his lips. They all fell into an amused, shocked, embarrassed silences that were suddenly broken by the pounding of heavy boots running down the service road.

When the boots had faded to silence Gerald, keeping his eyes above neck level, apologized to Marcia and Eric for the rude interruption and Margaret, boldly looking down, gave the young lad a verbal lashing for not wearing a condom. Reg couldn't help but laugh as they filed out of the shed leaving the traumatised couple unable to continue with what they had been doing then or ever again. Eric did eventually marry Marcia but whenever they attempted to make love his eyes always wandered to the door in dysfunctional expectation.

'Let's try my car,' said Ali as he led the way to the end of the service road and peered into the street beyond. 'Looks all clear in Fiesta Avenue he reported and there's no guard on my car.'

'They most probably didn't check the ownership of the vehicles in the street,' Reg said not realizing that it was yet another oversight by Inspector Cooper. They hurried down the street and climbed into the Rolls that Ali had had the foresight to park a few doors away from number six.

'Where do we go now?' Elizabeth asked.

Gerald shook his head. 'Lord knows but I'd better drive as I haven't had anything to drink.'

'He may not but I do,' said Margaret. 'The police have undoubtedly finished searching Montague Hall so I suggest we return there, hide the Rolls in the garage and then lay plans for getting ourselves out of this predicament.'

'I wouldn't have anyone else for a sister,' Ali murmured and, remembering the original reason for making the money, instructed a grateful Gerald to set course for Shady Trees. The large black saloon that had been parked near the corner of Fiesta Avenue pulled away and followed the Rolls at a discreet distance.

The Victorian frontage loomed over them like a malevolent being as Gerald parked the Rolls. The same severe looking woman, who had demanded to know what they wanted before, opened the door but only let Gerald, Elizabeth and Margaret enter after it was explained he had come to visit his mother and pay her fee for the coming year.

'I normally only allow two visitors at a time so think yourselves lucky,' the manageress growled as she led them to the office to deal with finances first. After astounding the woman by handing her twenty-three thousand pounds and eighty pence in cash, she wrote a receipt and then took them, floor after floor, up the old staircase.

'Isn't my mother's room on the ground floor,' Gerald complained as they breathlessly arrived at the top floor to find there were only three doors.

'We had to move Mrs Latimer when the fees were increased.'

'What do you mean increased?' Gerald demanded to know. 'I've just paid you.'

'You paid for the cheapest room available. Her previous suite on the ground floor now costs forty-six thousand per annum.' The door was unlocked and Gerald, fearing the worst, entered a tiny room that was almost filled by the bed and one small wardrobe. His mother seemed to have shrunken since last seeing her and she was now huddling beneath the faded coverlet and watching the newcomers with the eyes of a cornered fox.

'Who are you, what do you want?' she shrilled and Gerald recoiled in shock.

'It's Gerald, your son, Stephanie,' Elizabeth said softly as she sat on the bed and took the lined hand. Margaret looked on in horror at the conditions her friend's mother was subjected to and simply shook her head. The manageress left, closing the door behind her and Gerald, lost for words, went to sit on the other side but didn't attempt to take his mother's hand for fear of rejection. Tears prickled his eyes as he looked upon her face, seeking some flicker of recognition but Stephanie was wary of the strange man. She turned her head to study Elizabeth's face and suddenly a warm smile lit up her face.

'Elizabeth, it's Elizabeth isn't it?' she said in an excited tone and Elizabeth smiled back and stroked the hand lying in hers. 'And you must be Gerald?'

'Yes, mum,' he replied. Gerald realized that Elizabeth had acted as a mental trigger, bringing his mother back to the real world. They began talking all at once about what had transpired since their last visit while Margaret prowled the small room until she angrily stopped on seeing the remains of a meal standing on a tiny table at the foot of the bed.

'Is this what they feed your mother?' she asked softly in Gerald's ear. He looked briefly and saw what could only be described as a workhouse meal. A form of a greasy gruel with small shreds of indeterminate meat floating amongst the fat forming on the surface half-filled a soup bowl. Next to that were a glass of water and a small packet of shortbread biscuits.

'What's this, mum?' he asked and Stephanie peered down her length at the table.

'It's my lunch, dear. I wasn't very hungry so I've left the rest for later.' There was no hint in her voice that something was wrong and Gerald knew that this had become an acceptable meal for his mother.

One hour passed and the door suddenly opened and the manageress announced that visiting time was over. Gerald pointed to the table. 'Is that what you serve to all residents in this place?' he asked harshly.

'Of course not, your mother is on the economy package.'

'More like starvation package,' Margaret hissed through tight lips.

'You can always take your mother elsewhere,' the manageress retorted as she stood to one side to let them pass. Gerald leant over to kiss his mother and whisper that he would be back soon and Elizabeth gave the thin hand one last comforting squeeze before turning away to hide the tears she couldn't stop.

When they reached the lobby Gerald told the manageress that she had better take more care of his mother and move her to a larger room with proper facilities or he would make sure the authorities investigated Shady Trees thoroughly. Margaret held her smartphone aloft. 'I have pictures of Mrs Latimer's room showing the lack of space, storage facilities, casual seating and close-ups of her last meal should you wish to argue.'

The white-faced woman remained silent and simply nodded, for they had gained an audience of assistants and carers. Gerald stormed out after his friends and they set out for Ali's family home followed by the black car.

Two hours later they cautiously drove past the entrance to the hall with five pair of eyes looking for any signs of possible danger. The gates had been closed and on their returning pass Ali had to get out to open and then close them again after the Rolls had entered the drive.

The black car slowly rolled towards the gates until the driver could read the brass plate. 'Montague Hall,' he murmured. 'This I've got to see.'

The Rolls purred softly as they progressed along the drive to emerge from the trees and finally catch sight of the deserted house. There were no cars waiting, police or otherwise, and Gerald drove round the house to the garage block. The car was parked and once inside the house the women went to make a meal from whatever food was still edible in the kitchen while the men permanently barricaded the front door. 'I'll get it properly repaired when this is all over,' Ali said and suggested that they use the rear door whenever they had to leave as that was capable of being locked

Gerald had been thinking throughout the journey and no sooner had they sat down to eat the unsophisticated stew Margaret had thrown together than he told them what he intended to do.

'I've paid the care home and returned the Gutenberg Bible to a proper home which means it is now time for me to pay the piper.' Gerald's face had adopted its original sad look. 'I tried to make drugs and blew up a house and a gasometer. I robbed a bank, stole an armoured van and held up a post office for which I must pay the penalty.'

Elizabeth stood up and squeezed his hand. 'I'll go with you and tell the police how I helped you.'

'You don't have to do that, Elizabeth.' He released his hand and made her sit. 'They can't link you to anything that I've been doing so you can keep quiet and continue with your life as though nothing had happened.'

'I can't do that without you, Gerald. Anyway, there must have been many witnesses who would come forward and identify me as an accomplice."

'Oh, for goodness sake.' Margaret threw her hands up in despair. 'Nobody is going to give up and confess to crimes; especially not you two ninnies. All we have to do is get proof that Judge Atkinson was secretly in possession of a priceless item without any provenance and that he used assassins to try and hold on to that item and keep his personal wealth growing.'

'How on earth are we going to prove that?' Reg asked with one eyebrow arched.

'Let's sleep on it,' Elizabeth said with the suggestion of a wink at Gerald who was unable to prevent himself from blushing.

After the fiasco in Fiesta Avenue inspector Cooper, in an attempt to get a new lead, instructed Detective Constable Teal to check every CCTV camera in and around Canterbury Cathedral and St Pauls. Four officers spent the night running through gigabytes of digital film until two characters matching those held on police files clicked onto the screen.

The results, along with his customary double espresso, were given to the inspector as soon as he entered his office in the morning. 'Well, well, well, Andrew Lawson, disturbing the peace in Canterbury cathedral, and Cyril Catchpole waiting outside St Pauls when His Honour was creating chaos within.' He smiled a genuine smile that surprised Teal, for he was only ever used to brief twitches at the corner of his mouth that neither meant pleasure or displeasure. Atkinson now had his lead; a positive link between all three men and he only had to put one of them under pressure to wrap up the whole case. As he summoned the sergeant he couldn't help wondering about the large book that Dozer had been waving under the Dean's nose. The cameras had shown a tall man of military bearing snatching it from him and hurrying away. He told the sergeant to call the Dean and ask him for enlightenment before issuing a general call to all units in the area to be on the look out for the two villains.

While this was happening constable Teal was taking a call from Marcia Watson who reported being assaulted in a confessional at St Marks church by a big, nasty brute. She also sobbed that five strangers had pushed into her father's garden shed and threatened herself and Eric, her boyfriend.

Police Constable Deborah Parks was sent to interview Miss Watson and, after eliminating Father Jeremiah as the sexual pervert in the church, she was able to get a good description that fitted Dozer. During her questioning of the priest P.C. Parks learnt that the thug had found religion and not only wanted to confess but had insisted that the priest use Latin in all of his services. Jeremiah didn't mention the Gutenberg Bible as he felt this might affect the nice people who had presented the book to the church. The shed incident related by the girl gave two more descriptions that approximated people who had been standing by Wellington's Monument in St Paul's with Judge Atkinson at the time His Honour began his very public criminal career.

P.C. Parks was bright enough to figure out that the garden shed was only a few houses down from where the abortive armed response raid was carried out by her boss. She took every detail involving the two assaults before informing Marcia that her boyfriend would be charged with the rape of a minor; the girl was only four weeks shy of her sixteenth birthday. On hearing this Marcia burst into tears again and told the officer that Eric was only fourteen. To avoid a mountain of paperwork on her desk and the extra time she would have to spend in court she took four condoms from her own purse and ordered the girl to practice safe sex for at least the next four times; the couple's carnal activity in the garden shed was then erased from P.C. Parks report.

The inspector was delighted even more when the final, edited report arrived on his desk and he wasn't sure what to do next; bring the judge in for further questioning or wait until Dozer and Mutton were apprehended? In his normal professional way he tossed a coin and instructed Teal to get Atkinson.

At nine o'clock the judge pulled out of his drive and was on his way to Fiesta Avenue when constable Teal arrived at nine fifteen to find two burly men standing at the front door, frozen to the spot by the squad car's headlights. They were holding a long heavy package between them and the look of total surprise on their faces told Teal they were up to no good. He leapt from the car with his driver and ordered the men to put what they were carrying down and explain their presence on Atkinson's property.

'The judge asked us to get rid of this carpet and some other rubbish.' The bald-headed man at the heaviest end of the rolled carpet answered.

'What is it?' Teal asked as he prodded the roll they were slowly lowering. This sudden prod took the man at the lighter end by surprise and he lost his grip. This had the unfortunate effect of making the skinhead drop his end and the package landed on the hard porch with a heavy thud and unrolled onto the gravel not unlike the myth of Cleopatra. The sight of a man with only one staring left eye and a bloody crotch lying on a blood-stained seventeenth century Persian carpet shocked the officers into immobility. The 'disposal experts' took this as their golden opportunity to jump into the van and drive away. The rear doors had been left open and they clanged from side to side as the vehicle raced erratically for the gates without any lights showing.

'Who the hell were they?' the police driver asked watching the van's stoplights briefly flashed before disappearing through the gateway.

'More to the point who the hell is he?' Teal responded as he poked the body with the toe of his boot. His driver contacted headquarters to report their findings and to put out an alert out for the black van with open rear doors. Teal entered the house to check whether he would also find an emasculated High Court Judge with only a right eye.

Teal had to wait thirty minutes after checking the house was clear before homicide officers turned up with a full forensic team. He gave a description of the two men and the van that had driven away and after his driver had confirmed his statement they left to report back to the inspector.

Another piece had dropped into Cooper's puzzle when the sergeant reported on his call to the Dean at Canterbury Cathedral. It appeared that the book Dozer had been waving angrily was a Gutenberg Bible and that the villain wanted the Dean to use it in his services.

The inspector quickly surfed the net to find, with a sudden intake of breath that hissed between his yellowing teeth, the phenomenal value of such a book. 'Small wonder all the villains want it,' he murmured as he doodled three million, with a halo over the pound sign, on his blotter.

'Has Teal returned with the judge yet?' he demanded to know and the sergeant simply shook his head. Cooper swore beneath his breath for he now knew why Dozer originally went to St Marks and he decided to personally pay Jeremiah a visit not realizing that Dozer had determined to do exactly the same for, like the inspector, he suspected that the priest knew a lot more than he had let anyone know.

'One more thing, sir,' the sergeant said. 'Detective Constable Teal has just reported that the judge wasn't at home but that a dead body wrapped in a blanket had been. Two unidentified men had been carrying it from the house and had scarpered in a white van before D.C. Teal could apprehend them.

'Idiot.' Cooper muttered under his breath and then ordered his car to be downstairs immediately to take him to the church. The journey was frustratingly slowed by the end of the day traffic and on arriving at St Marks he took the steps two at a time and entered the church slightly out of breath.

'Father,' he called out and the priest left the confessional with an eyebrow cocked.

'How can I help you, my son.'

'It's Detective Inspector Cooper, Father,' Cooper replied tartly. 'Tell me everything you know about the Gutenberg Bible.'

Jeremiah sighed inwardly for he was now over a barrel. He would be unable to lie within the confines of the church and he may be forced to reveal the bible's hiding place. 'A gentleman came in here yesterday and asked if I would like to use that holy book for my services.' He sat down in one of the pews. 'I told him that I couldn't because it was in Latin and all services in St Marks were always given in English. I advised him to show such a valuable book to someone in the cathedral.'

'Canterbury?'

'Yes, and that was the last I saw of him.' Jeremiah held Cooper's icy stare until the officer looked away and scanned the rest of the church as though expecting to see the book amongst the hymnbooks on the pew shelves.

'Did the policewoman manage to catch the man because he really upset one of my young parishioners mid confession?' the father asked, hoping the question might hinder the inspector's current line of questioning.

'Was the man who asked you to use the book the same man who frightened one of your parishoners?'

'Yes.'

'We're still looking for him.' Cooper didn't wait for any criticism of police performance and stomped from the church without another word followed by the sergeant who shrugged apologetically at the priest. Jeremiah smiled, waved and hurried to brief the locum who had arrived to take over during his forthcoming vacation. He then returned to the confessional where he had hidden the bible under the seat. It can't stay here another minute, he thought. It'll have to go to the Vatican where Latin bibles belong. He wrapped the book in a black silk cloth and, using the side door, hurried from the church to begin his journey to Rome.

Twenty minutes after the priest had left by the side door Dozer entered at the front of the church and looked for the absent priest. Father Rogers, the locum, emerged from the sacristy and with hands folded approached the confessional. 'Would you like to confess, my son?' he asked poised to draw the curtain open to check that the cubicle was unoccupied.

'Why is it every time someone comes into a church priests assume they've sinned and have to tell them all about it?'

'Then how can I help you, my son?'

'You can tell me where Father Jeremiah is.' Dozer grabbed the priest by the front of his vestment and lifted him into the air. 'Now!'

'I'm sorry I cannot divulge that inform . . . ' Which was as far as he got before a hairy-knuckled fist the size of a ham hock broke his nose. Father Rogers squealed with pain and rather than lose some teeth he spoke rapidly, 'Father Jeremiah said something about Heathrow and going to Rome.'

A violent rage overcame Dozer and he pummeled the priest two or three times more before the confessional curtains were opened a little and a small white face appeared in the gap.

Marcia had come to confess that, despite Eric being her boyfriend, she had been unable to say no to the handsome barista at the coffee bar who had invited her into the storeroom and didn't suffer from erectile dysfunction. Marcia took one look at the blood-stained face of the priest, screamed and closed the curtain. Dozer let the man collapse into the nearest pew and, muttering what the priest had finally confessed, went to his car to set the sat-nav for Heathrow not realizing he had been misled and that Jeremiah was on his way to Gatwick.

Marcia emerged from the confessional sobbing and using the freshly filled font she wet her handkerchief and began dabbing at Father Rogers face. At that moment Mrs Trotter, the organist, entered the church with the baptismal party. The father of the baby ran down the nave and, on seeing the state of the locum's face, immediately phoned the police. Marcia, who was now rapidly losing all faith, was led away by one of the kindly grandparents and a distant cousin took over the task of tending to Father Rogers. The mother, holding the sleeping infant, took one look at the pink water in the font, gave an 'eeeek' like a baby otter and woke the baby. This resulted in the church reverberating to the sound of young, lusty lungs. As one, all the relatives and friends of the parents clapped hands over their ears and awaited the arrival of the ambulance.

Inspector Cooper had just arrived in his office when he received a message that a large man, fitting the description of Dozer, had rearranged the features of the locum at St Marks and that after pounding the priest into unconsciousness had left, repeating the word 'Heathrow' over and over again.

The sergeant had anticipated any order from his superior and the inspector's car was ready and filled with armed officers by the time it left Oakwood police station. Airport police had already been instructed to apprehend Dozer and to await the arrival of Detective Inspector Cooper.

CHAPTER 20

S IR ALISTAIR MONTAGUE, sunk deep in his armchair, thought deeply about their situation for a few seconds and came to a conclusion that despite no longer having the Gutenberg Bible they were still at risk from the thugs. Using his smartphone Ali called St Marks after finding its number on the Internet and Father Rogers answered. He was on the point of leaving the sacristy to take a confession but when Ali introduced himself and explained he had given Father Jeremiah a Gutenberg Bible the reason for Jeremiah's rapid departure became clear to the locum.

'The Father has gone to Rome to present that bible to the Vatican,' he whispered.

'When did he leave as I believe he may be in grave danger,' Ali began whispering back until he realized how foolish he sounded.

'He should be arriving at Gatwick about now.'

'Does anyone else know?'

'No, I was asked to keep it secret from everyone but yourself. He said that you were the only one he could trust.'

'Thank you, Father.' Ali hung up and told Gerald where the bible was. 'It should be taking off shortly and I have a very good feeling that it'll never return to this country.'

'Once the Vatican have it you can be sure it never will.' Elizabeth had come into the room at the tail end of Ali's report and she gave a deep sigh of relief. 'So, if anyone threatens us we can tell them to have words with the Pontifical Swiss Guards.' Elizabeth had no sooner finished than they heard the sound of a car approaching on the shingle drive.

Ali went to the window and watched as a dark car came to a stop and a familiar figure got out. 'It's that guy Reg calls Mutton,' he said. 'I think we'd better be ready to convince him that the Gutenberg is on its way to Rome.'

Reg entered the room. 'Guess who's knocking at our door?' he said as there was a loud pounding on the temporary repair.

Ali went into the hallway. 'Who is it?'

'You know bloody well who it is, mate. Now, where's the damned book?' Mutton shouted before thumping again.

'This door is sealed, you'll have to go to the back to be let in,' Ali shouted in reply. There was silence and then they heard the sound of boots on gravel as Mutton began circling the house.

'What'll we do if he doesn't believe us?' Reg asked and Gerald answered by picking up the useless Purdey.

'We'll bluff him.'

Ali went down the hallway and in a few minutes returned followed by a scowling Mutton. 'In here,' he said and went into the drawing room where he resumed his seat in the armchair. Mutton followed Ali and was in turn followed by Gerald holding the shotgun in a threatening manner.

'Where's the money?' Mutton growled, watching the barrels follow him as he walked across the room to sit facing Ali. 'The fifty-thousand pounds that were never returned to judge Atkinson?'

'We know nothing about the money and the bible should now be making its landing approach at Leonardo Da Vinci-Fiumicino Airport.' Gerald said in a firm voice.

'Leo-what airport?' Mutton asked incredulously.

'It's Rome's airport and where Father Jeremiah has gone to donate the Gutenberg Bible to the Vatican.'

'Why the hell would he do such a thing?' The surprise on Mutton's face was clear but it soon turned to anger. 'You're lying,' he snapped.

'It's where Latin is commonly used in all church services and a natural place for a priest to take such a book.' Ali explained, as though to a child.

'You're lying about the money.'

'Uh huh, I think you'll find that Dozer had something to do with that,' Reg said, grinning at his ex-colleagues bewilderment.

Mutton was silent, lost for words, as he thought about what had been said until an invisible light bulb went on inside his head and his eyes gleamed dangerously. He leapt to his feet. 'I'll kill the bastard,' he yelled. 'He's got in my way for the very last time.' Mutton rushed from the room and they heard his feet pounding down the hall and out of the house. They waited with bated breath until the car started and roared away, spraying gravel over the front porch.

Suddenly the phone rang.

'Is that Sir Alistair Montague?' a voice inquired and when Ali confirmed his identity the phone clicked and went dead.

'Wrong number but his voice sounded familiar.' Ali said replacing the antique receiver on its cradle as a figure raced from the cover of the trees and sprinted across the wet lawn towards the house. Margaret caught a brief glimpse, shouted a warning and everyone went to the big window to follow her pointing finger. The strange figure was wearing a long black dress that flapped around the runner's legs wildly.

'It's a man,' Gerald cried out as the stranger drew near.

'A transvestite?' Reg was puzzled.

'No, it's Father Jeremiah.' Ali had turned away from the window on recognizing the priest and went into the hallway to await his arrival. The doorbell, which none of the official or brutalist callers had bothered to use, chimed melodically and Ali shouted his instruction to use the back door and walked down the hallway as Gerald appeared at the living room door holding the shotgun.

'You won't need that,' Ali called out as he released the lock and opened the door. He shook Jeremiah's hand, pulled him into the house and quickly relocked the door.

'You're supposed to be in Rome, Father. What happened?' Ali asked after he had introduced the priest to everyone present in the living room. The bulky attaché case hadn't escaped his notice and he raised an eyebrow.

The priest sat down and put the case between his feet. 'I arrived at Gatwick and was about to purchase a ticket when I had second thoughts about giving the bible to the Vatican.'

'Why was that?' Elizabeth asked as Margaret knelt by the coffee table and began pouring the tea.

'The discovery of such a book can be seen as a significant find for religion, mainly for Catholicism, which was why you suggested that I take it to the Vatican. However, it can also be considered an extraordinary historical find and that's what stopped me from flying to Italy.'

'Surely, being such a beautiful bible printed in Latin provides the fundamental reason why it should be at the centre of the Catholic faith.' Margaret argued, passing a cup to the priest.

Jeremiah shook his head. 'The bible was the first major book to use moveable type and it began what was called the Gutenberg Revolution. It began the new age of the printed book in the West. Books could now be mass-produced and this created a monumental social change that has had profound effect through the centuries, including this one.'

'So where do you think the blooming thing should go?' Reg asked as he added a shot of rum from his hip flask to his cup under Margaret's disapproving gaze.

'A museum,' the priest declared. 'The Victoria and Albert Museum to be precise.' There was a collective intake of air. 'I wanted your approval, Sir Alistair, before giving the bible to them. I also want to know how you would go about it as I have no legal provenance to offer the museum other than your word that it belonged to the Montague family for centuries before it was bequeathed to St Marks Church.'

The friends sat in silence for a few moments, apart from an embarrassed burp from Reg before Gerald volunteered a solution. 'Reg, you know a lot of people with artistic abilities?' Reg remained silent and his eyes followed Gerald as he walked around the room in deep thought. 'What if we create an eighteenth-century receipt for the sum of one hundred guineas showing that a member of the Montague family purchased the bible from a Spaniard deserter during the War of Spanish Succession?'

Elizabeth was listening with eyes brightening in admiration. 'What a brilliant plan, Gerald, nobody would be able to trace a deserter.'

'Not during the civil and military chaos that must have taken place in 1714 when Gibraltar and Minorca were ceded to Britain.' Ali said, recalling his history lessons at school and the raps across his knuckles by Mr Farthingale's ruler for passing notes in class. He was known as Fart-in-Gale ever since trying to make himself heard during one particular morning assembly.

Reg waited until the hubbub of voices had calmed down before giving his answer. 'There's one chap who, when sober, can turn out bonds and letters of credit that can fool the governor of the Bank of England himself.'

'Did he?' Gerald asked suspiciously.

'Not once but ten times until, when working on a five-thousand pound letter after two bottles of claret, he ran out of black ink and used a blue ballpoint to finish the bank signatures. He got three years porridge for that and, unfortunately for us, he decided to go straight the very day he was released.'

'Could you convince him to do one simple letter?' Margaret asked as she took the hip flask from his pocket.

Reg shrugged. 'I can but try asking him,' he sighed, 'but it'll need cash.'

'I'll pay,' Ali volunteered.

'And I'll go with you.' Margaret went to get her coat. 'I'll drive the Rolls,' she added before anyone could raise any objections. Reg hurried after her with a little more enthusiasm now that Margaret was his partner.

The Rolls started first time and soon they were smoothly returning to London to find the wizard of Quink ink and quill pens. Following Reg's directions and ignoring his hand when it occasionally rested on her thigh they arrived in a narrow street lined with shabby two-up and two-down houses.

'What's his name and how did you get to know him?' Margaret asked as they stepped onto the covered porch that boasted two gnomes guarding the door with their fishing rods.

'Spinks but everyone at Goldenstein's place called him Inky.'

'Did he do work for him?'

Reg nodded and as the door buzzer didn't work he used the tarnished lion's head knocker until they heard footsteps approaching on the other side of the door. They counted four bolts being shot back, a chain being unhooked and a deadlock turning before the door opened two inches and a bearded face appeared in the gap and looked up at them suspiciously.

'Is that you, Reg?' a voice croaked. Another chain was unhooked and the door was opened sufficiently for them to slip inside before it slammed shut again. They watched as the man, who reached no higher than Reg's chest, stood on an upturned bucket to re-lock, re-bolt and re-hook the chains on the door.

'You're not expecting anyone are you, Inky?' Reg said as they were led into the front room. The man simply shrugged as with deep-set eyes overhung with bushy brows as he studied Margaret shiftily until Reg introduced her.

'Never know these days, what d-ya want?'

'A simple job, an eighteenth-century receipt.'

'As long as it's not *too* illegal how much?' Inky rubbed his thumb and forefinger together.

'How about two hundred?' Margaret said with a warm smile.

'How about four hundred?' Inky came back, enamoured by her beautiful eyes.

Reg looked at the forger with a look of dismay.

'All right, three hundred.' Inky threw his hands up in surrender. 'Give me the details.'

Margaret ran through the period, the nature of the transaction and how much the receipt was for while Inks listened attentively, admiring the thoroughness of the briefing and the woman's full lips as they moved.

'The right paper may be a problem, I'll have to go down into the cellar and rake through what I've got, but the rest is simple. I have the right pen style and inks and I've perfected document ageing for any period, including continental early seventeen hundred; come back tomorrow morning with the money.'

With a friendly slap on Margaret's rear Inky shooed them from the house until they found themselves standing on the pavement listening to Inky's routine of pulling up the drawbridge. It was only then that Reg noticed the tiny CCTV camera mounted beneath the eaves. Inky takes no chances it seems, he thought as they got into the Rolls and drove to Gerald's house to stay the night. They had bought pizzas on the way and they hungrily devoured them with a dust-covered bottle of Merlot that Gerald had stashed at the back of a kitchen cupboard. Margaret then complained about being tired after such a long journey and they climbed the stairs. Reg watched her enter the bedroom and was about to return downstairs to sleep on the settee when Margaret paused and beckoned. Reg's pulse raced as he slowly went and took her hand. He was jerked into the room and the door kicked shut behind him; it seemed that Margaret could bat for both sides.

It had been while the Rolls was arriving at the house in Fiesta Avenue that Detective Inspector Cooper arrived at Heathrow and entered the terminal packed with confused tourists searching for their right departure gates. He checked the departure board for likely flights, noted the gate numbers and struggled to cross the hall to the check-in desks without having his shins barked by the numerous pull-along suitcases. He spotted a small group of uniformed police and a discreet flash of his warrant card and a brief enquiry told him that Andy Lawson hadn't been seen. Cooper looked round, told the men to stay alert, and returned to the main entrance in time to see his quarry getting out of a black cab.

'Mr Andrew Lawson, I arrest you for the aggravated assault on – ' he never finished for Dozer, on recognizing the inspector, dropped his overnight case and sprinted out of the terminal; a noteworthy accomplishment for a man of his size. Cooper ran after him but too many iced buns and chocolate éclairs in the police station canteen had taken their toll and he was forced to come to a gasping stop and watch Dozer disappear into the multi-storey car park. 'Damn, I should have brought Teal,' he wheezed as, with hands on knees, he tried to catch his breath; three of the uniforms who had seen their superior running outside caught up with him and between gasps he instructed them to search every level of the car park.

Cooper decided to return to his car after a thorough search failed to find any sign of the man. The space where he had left his vehicle was empty for the unmarked yet illegally parked squad car had been towed from the zone reserved for ambulances. Two hours later it was returned from the airport car pound with two broken headlights; a hammer-wielding parking attendant had noticed the police equipment inside. The choleric detective returned to London after issuing instructions to the local officers to keep looking out for Andrew Lawson returning to the departure hall.

The officers who had checked the cars on every level were not to know that Dozer, thinking he had found the perfect hiding place, had climbed into the boot of his car and on closing it had engaged the lock. He was locked in and didn't become aware of his situation until he felt sufficient time had elapsed for the police to complete the search and pushed up. Nothing moved and he pushed again and again but he had no leverage, for his legs were awkwardly trapped beneath him, and the lock remained steadfastly locked despite the cheap materials used in its manufacture.

It was a bright, sunny morning when Reg and Margaret woke, passionately made love yet again and then shared a simple egg and bacon breakfast with a cafetiere of their friend's finest ground coffee. They were cozily cuddling on the settee watching a repeat of *Spooks* and reluctant to get dressed when there was a knock at the door. They looked at each other in surprise and Reg went to the door and used the spyhole. He immediately recognized the dapperly dressed man who impatiently stared at the spyhole. The glittering eyes made Reg recoil and he knocked the jardinière with his elbow.

'Open up Latimer, I want a word with you,' Judge Atkinson said, his words muffled by the door separating them. Reg remained still but the vase rocking on the jardinière didn't and it fell to shatter on the parquet floor. On hearing the sound of fine pottery breaking into a myriad of pieces the judge repeated his demand, more loudly this time, and Reg was unable to keep up the pretense that nobody was at home; he unlocked and opened the door.

'Reginald Barnett!' the judge exclaimed. 'I should have known you'd be involved.' He pushed the door wide open with the palm of his hand. 'Where's Latimer, he's got something of mine.'

'Involved in what, Mr Atkinson,' Reg said innocently as he pulled his dressing gown together and stepped forward to block the doorway, preventing the man from entering.

'The theft of my book you damned thief; and you'll address me as Your Honour,' Atkinson snapped as he tried to push past the young man.

'Excuse me, who might you be?' Margaret said wafting up behind Reg in her filmy nightdress to successfully provide a further barrier.

'I'm a high court judge who wishes entry,' Atkinson blustered, trying to avert his eyes from what clearly wasn't concealed by the delicate silk.

'Which you won't get without an official court order.'

'I *am* the court and who might you be?' Atkinson had changed colour and was clenching and unclenching his hands.

'Lady Margaret Montague and I wish you to go away before I call the police.'

Atkinson looked into her steady gaze and wilted. 'I will be back with a warrant, you can be sure of that, madam.' He turned on his heel and strode back to his car with stiff shoulders and head held haughtily high. Reg laughed but after closing the door his face became serious again.

'He'll be coming back,' he stated and Margaret nodded.

'Let's go an pick up our receipt,' she said briskly.

Inky had been standing on his upturned bucket, sliding the last bolt to open the door when it began to wobble and the little man's last words were 'Oh, Christ' before falling backwards to break his neck on the black and white tiles.

'Oh, Christ,' were Reg's first words on entering and finding their forger sprawled on the floor. Without touching the man he knew Inky was dead by the unnatural angle of his head. Margaret pushed past Reg, saw Inky and put a hand to her mouth to stifle a cry of alarm. Reg turned her away and went to fetch a throw from the front room. When the corpse was respectfully covered the couple went into the small room Inky had always used as his studio. Examples of his legal work were pinned to a corkboard and they searched, hoping the receipt had been completed. It was Margaret who opened a drawer and found a tattered piece of sepia stained paper.

'I think I've found it,' she declared as she carefully lifted it out on the palm of her hand.

'Are you sure, it looks like it's been burnt.' He peered at the scorched edges and then at the exquisite copperplate penmanship that had been faded artificially.

'It's a real work of art, Reg,' Margaret whispered as she checked the amount. Inky had changed her brief to substantiate the period by changing one-hundred pounds to guineas. Inky had even described the book by its title *Biblia Sacra Latina* showing how much research the little scribe had completed in the course of designing the receipt. 'He must have worked on this all through the night.'

'And he'll be paid, Margaret,' Reg said taking a blank envelope from the stationery rack and writing *To Mr Spinks with thanks for a job well done. R.* He then tucked the agreed three hundred pounds into the envelope and left it on the workbench. 'It should cover some of the funeral costs.'

Margaret hugged him and after diligently wiping the surfaces they may have touched they left the house and returned to Montague Hall.

Ali greeted them at the back door after the Rolls had been safely tucked away in the garage. 'Any luck?' he asked as they hurried to the kitchen to make a warming drink of chocolate.

Reg carefully took the specially folded receipt from his pocket and handed it to him. 'Inky did us proud and if that doesn't fool the experts then nothing can.'

Ali took the piece of aged paper, carefully opened it and gave a low whistle of admiration. 'Looks like the millstone that's been hanging round our necks for the last few days is off to the Victoria and Albert.' His sister nodded and handed him and Reg steaming mugs.

Gerald and Elizabeth entered the kitchen, admired Inky's skill and then Elizabeth asked what they should all do when Father Jeremiah went to London. Ali suggested that they return to Fiesta Avenue and await Jeremiah's call. Despite half-hearted protests from Reg Margaret decided to continue with his cold turkey treatment at Montague Hall and that they would hide in the priest hole should anyone else turn up.

Jeremiah entered the room and being told they now had the essential provenance to approach the V&A he told the friends that he would take the bible immediately and after the curator had accepted the bible he would return to St Marks to resume pastoral care of his parishioners. He fingered the stubble on his chin and thanked Ali for the use of the nineteenth-century four-poster, despite the discomfort of the lumpy mattress that felt as old as the bed. Using his mobile phone he called Father Rogers to tell him of his plans. He then learnt of Dozer's visit to the church and that the locum had told him that Father Jeremiah had gone to Heathrow to fly to Rome. Not knowing the state of the young priest's face or that he had only just arrived back from hospital Jeremiah thanked him.

Reg, who had kept quiet while Margaret made the decision concerning themselves, now spoke. 'I shall be going with Father Jeremiah,' he said softly and Elizabeth asked him why he thought that was necessary. 'We still have some pretty nasty people out there who are dying to retrieve their fifty-thousand pounds.' The group fell silent. 'So, I'm going to act as Father Jeremiah's security guard while you all hold the fort here.'

Margaret suddenly clasped Reg to her as though she feared never seeing him again. 'Do you really have to, Reg,' she whispered.

'Of course he doesn't, I will be perfectly okay by myself,' the priest said as he picked up the small attaché case containing the bible and tucked the receipt into the side pocket.

'I do and I will, Father, and that's my last word.' Reg went to the knife rack and selected a small paring knife that had a bright orange plastic scabbard; he tucked it into his jacket. 'Shall we go now, Father?'

The priest frowned and left the kitchen and Reg gave Margaret one last squeeze before following him.

'Don't worry, Maggie. Nothing's going to happen,' she heard him say as he strode down the hall to the back door.

Much to Jeremiah's relief Reg threw the paring knife away as soon as they were out on the road.

CHAPTER 21

DOZER HAD ALMOST BREATHED the last lungful of clean air and was choking on the carbon dioxide that filled the confined space when a group of North Korean tourists noisily passed the rear of his car. The thumping on the lid had become rather sporadic, a result of Dozer's dizziness and waning strength, when one of the chattering party held up his hand for silence. They all stopped and the car park became deathly quiet apart from two feeble thumps from inside the boot. With wide-open curious eyes they stared at the car until a man, wearing a policeman's helmet and carrying a Harrod's shopping bag, put his ear to the boot lid just as another thump and a faint cry was heard. The resourceful tourist fumbled in his jacket of many pockets until he found his prized Korean Army knife with twenty-five different tools. There were admiring intakes of air from the whole group, like deflating tyres, and then cries of *seoduleuda* that loosely translated meant 'get your finger out' for it took precious seconds to choose the right tool, break two fingernails while opening it and then manipulating the lock.

The lid sprung up and the Korean recoiled from the foul air that rushed out followed by a gasping head. More tyres were deflated accompanied by cries of *ileon jenjang*, or, bloody hell, as they watched Dozer extricate himself, slam the boot shut and stagger to the driver's door. He weakly nodded to the man in the policeman's helmet, relieved him of his Korean Army Knife with twenty-five tools and drove away. The group was stunned into silence and when their guide, holding up the little flag for them to follow, was unable to say anything and just looked at them with blank eyes they all began talking at once.

Now knowing the police had the airport covered Dozer chose to return to London and go straight to St Marks Church to have another friendly chat with the locum; there were a few questions he wanted to ask the young priest. It was midday when Dozer arrived and the church was empty, except for a solitary figure kneeling before the altar in deep prayer. A single shaft of sunlight, shining through a stained glass window, bathed Father Rogers in a pool of many colours. The thug walked the length of the nave and grabbed him by the scruff of his neck. He dragged the terrified young man to the first row of pews and forced him to sit.

'You will now tell me the truth,' Dozer thundered. 'Did Father Jeremiah go to Heathrow Airport or not?' He pulled a lead-weighted cosh from a trouser pocket and rested the warm tip gently against the swan-white cheek.

'Yes, he did go,' the young man stuttered.

'With the book?'

'Yes, he took the bible with him.'

Dozer raised the cosh.

The locum raised his hand defensively. 'But . . . but . . . I've just had a phone call and he said that he was going to the Victoria & Albert museum to see the curator before returning to St Marks.'

'Liar!' The single swipe on the temple drove splinters of bone into the brain and Father Rogers slumped sideways. Dozer felt his pulse, muttered a brief 'damn', the strongest word he dared use in a church, shrugged and left just as a young woman was entering to try once more to confess her sins. It was only after Dozer had stormed past that Marcia Watson reacted by falling to the stone floor in a dead faint. She would wake, remember the brutish face she had seen twice before and then faint once more on discovering Father Roger's body; it was from that day onward that Marcia Watson became an ardent atheist convert.

Dozer sat in his car for a few moments until the sense of what Father Jeremiah was doing crystallized and he could see that he would need some help if he was to recover the bible successfully. He ran through some of his more trustworthy associates and decided on Beaky, a pickpocket who, when employed by Goldenstein, had used his dexterous fingers to obtain blackmail material from unsuspecting business rivals. Dozer had occasionally worked with him as a 'stall' to enable Beaky to 'dip' without being noticed. Moving queues were generally favoured as they enabled Dozer to suddenly bend down to tie a shoelace causing the mark to bump into him permitting Beaky to legitimately bump into the mark. This gave Beaky the opportunity to 'pick' what he had been told to get by Goldenstein. It was in kindergarten, when some of the children noticed he repeated things when he was nervous and that his nose was a little like a parrot's bill; and because they thought parrot was a cute name they decided to call him Beaky; children will always cruelly choose less flattering sobriquets.

The phone was answered immediately and familiar nasal tones asked; 'Who's calling. Who's calling?'

Dozer sniggered. 'Dozer here, Beaky, I've got a little job for you that has to done now, are you available?'

'Dozer, me old mate. Course I can. Course I can.'

'Meet me on the steps of the Victoria & Albert museum and I'll give you the details as soon as I arrive.' Dozer hung up.

He drove towards central London and after averaging fifteen miles per hour in the lunchtime traffic he arrived in the Cromwell Road and at the museum. He walked from where he had parked the car to the main entrance and immediately spotted the small man in a shabby raincoat standing on the top step and to one side of the main entrance.

Dozer looked around as they shook hands to check whether the Father was outside. 'Our target is medium height, greying hair, wearing a tweed jacket and dog-collar and carrying a black attaché case that is thicker and heavier than average.'

'Our mark's a priest. A priest?'

'Yeah, and it's the case I want,' Dozer said as he led the way into the museum. 'He is most probably with a young man who we both know very well. Reginald Barnett.'

'Reg, Reggy the druggie, the druggie?'

Dozer nodded and then indicated that Beaky should go to the right while he went left to begin the search.

Reg, the drug addict no more, had been waiting just inside the door for Jeremiah to finish explaining to the security guard that what he had in the attaché case was a priceless bible and not thirty pounds of Semtex when he saw Beaky standing on the steps. He then spotted Dozer approaching the museum as an assistant curator appeared and after a brief glimpse inside the case led the priest away with evident excitement on his face. Reg turned his back and strolled behind the information desk as Dozer met Beaky and the two entered the museum.

Reg couldn't see which way the Father had gone and made a point of keeping his eyes fixed on Dozer who had now stopped on the other side of the circular reception desk and was studying the visitors. It would only be a matter of time before he spotted Reg who quickly went down the stone steps to an exhibition titled Faiths & Empires. It seemed appropriate until he saw the items on display were dated between 300 and 1250 AD. This was clearly a period too early for Gutenberg and Reg checked a wall guide and found Renaissance Art and Ideas, a period closer to the 1450 bible was on level two and, to avoid bumping into Dozer, went to the side of the museum until he reached New Europe and climbed the stairs where he emerged in Chinoiserie. He hurried round all the displays until he entered the right exhibition. He studied every group of visitors but there were no signs of the Father or the young curator.

It was as Reg was going down the staircase that Dozer turned and recognized him. He knew Reg was undoubtedly with the priest and followed him. As one man followed the other through New Europe and up the stairs the door to a study room opened and the Father came out, still carrying the heavy attaché case, and climbed to the main entrance to look for Reg. As the Father went out of the main entrance to search the steps Reg, realizing that the Father must have been taken to an office to discuss the bible, had turned and walked straight into Dozer. The two men recoiled and it was the smaller man who reacted first and darted under the big man's flailing arms and sprinted back the way he had come.

Dozer was no match for the lithe young man who sprinted through the displays and down the stairs until he reached the entrance. As Reg went out a hand grabbed him by the forearm and he recoiled away until he recognized the Father holding him tight.

'Quick, this way, Father,' Reg said in a loud whisper and pulled the priest behind one of the large display signs. 'Dozer's inside and he has help with him.' He put a finger to his lips and they both waited until they saw their nemesis run down the steps looking both ways. Dozer stopped on the pavement, looked back up the steps and when Beaky came out shaking his head they both stomped back towards Dozer's car.

'I've been told we must go to the British Museum, Reg,' Jeremiah explained. 'The curator here said that they already have two copies and the V&A couldn't possibly compete with that and recommended we talk to Mr Denison, a senior archivist and expert on Renaissance books.'

'Sshhh!' Reg pointed down the road to see Dozer pause, turn and head back to the V&A while Beaky continued walking to his own car. They tucked themselves behind an exhibition display board and discreetly watched as the man made his way through the throng of visitors and re-entered the museum. 'He has either decided to search the museum for either of us or –'

'Or?'

'As he hasn't got his friend with him I reckon he's going to find that curator I was talking to and ask if he has the bible and if not where it may be now.'

'That means they'll also be going to see Mr Denison.' Jeremiah was horrified at the thought and with the attaché case heavily pulling on his shoulder he hurried after Reg who was rushing down the steps to hail a taxi. The nerve-wracking slowness of the journey preyed upon both men's nerves and Reg kept looking through the rear window until the driver, unable to stand it anymore, asked them if they were escaping from the law.

'I believe we are being followed by someone who wishes to steal a precious artifact we are planning to donate to the museum,' Jeremiah said and he saw the driver use his mirror to inspect first the dog-collared man and then the attaché case.

'Is that it, Guv?' he asked.

'Yes, it's one of the few remaining Gutenberg Bibles worth three million pounds,' Reg added.

'Then don't you worry, I'll get you there before you can say the Lord's Prayer.'

Reg and Jeremiah looked at the traffic suffocating their snail-paced cab and then at each other with forlorn expressions until they were thrown to one side as the cab cut through a gap in the traffic and shot into a small mews. With unerring skill their driver chose lane after lane, bypassing anything that resembled a high traffic street until they entered Piccadilly

Circus. The two men gripped the leather straps hanging beside them and watched fearfully, and in awe, as they were expertly threaded through the traffic to emerge on Tottenham Court Road. Two more hair-raising corners and they thundered along Great Russell Street to the main entrance of the imposing neo-classical building that was the British Museum.

The wonderful glass domed roof was lost on the two men as they hurried into the main hall and went directly to one of the information desks. Reg asked to see Mr Denison and was told that he saw nobody without an appointment. Jeremiah interrupted the ensuing argument by placing the attaché on the counter and showing the museum guide the book. She gasped and looked from one man to the other and then at the book again before the Father suggested she tried to contact Mr Denison before they decided to take the bible to the Vatican.   Two minutes of muted conversation followed before they were invited to follow the guide down to the anteroom to a suite of offices in the basement.

'Mr Denison is currently attending a meeting in the Ancient Japan exhibition but is coming straight down to meet you in his office. Would you like some coffee while you wait, gentlemen?'

Reg shook his head and turned to the Father. 'I think I'll return to the main hall to keep a lookout for you know who,' he said and the priest agreed. He climbed the stairway with the lady who smiled and shook his hand on entering the vast space. Reg watched her return to the information desk and then looked round to instantly recognize Beaky watching him from the far side of the hall. Reg turned away but it was too late and Beaky began walking towards him. He went out to the smaller entrance hall and ran up the marble stairway to the first floor. He looked down to see Beaky beginning to climb and Reg went on until emerged in the Chinese ceramics display room on the second floor. He hurried between the illuminated glass cases until one particular Yuan Dynasty blue and white vase he was passing suddenly exploded. Reg stopped and looked round in surprise to see a neat hole on one side of the case that was repeated on the opposite side. The 1350 AD vase lay in a score of pieces and Reg didn't wait to lament its destruction but ran for his life as yet another priceless display was reduced to sherds. Beaky was using a silenced 9mm Beretta and apart from the low 'thwock' the only other sound was shattering glass and ceramics.

Reg turned into the next gallery and then went up the stairs to the Mesopotamian display room. Beaky had discovered a round had jammed the Beretta and he had paused briefly in an effort to clear it before throwing it at a fencai-enameled flask of the Qing period and hurrying after Reg.

'I'm going to cut your throat when I get you, get you,' Beaky called out and turned the corner in time to see Reg disappear through a doorway. He followed to find that his quarry had trapped himself by going over the glass-bridge, bypassing the two curving staircases that led down to the Great Court, and had been considering whether to backtrack when Beaky appeared with his knife.

'You've made Dozer really mad and he wants that attaché case or else. Or else, Reg,' Beaky hissed.

'I don't have it, Beaky.' Reg held his empty hands out for inspection and walked towards the pickpocket.

'Where is it, where is it?' Beaky waved the knife as Reg walked even closer. 'Is it the priest, does he have it, have it?'

'What priest, I don't know any priests,' Reg said as both men reached the middle of the bridge. Reg was not unfamiliar with knife fights and without any hesitation he feinted a move to the right and when Beaky slashed that way, across his own body with the razor sharp knife, Reg then danced to the left and grasped Beaky's wrist; using the pickpockets own momentum he spun the small man round and thrust him against the chrome railing. Beaky was unable to stop himself toppling over the rail and falling two storeys onto the hard marble floor below.

A number of feminine shrieks of shock filled the cavernous court and Reg was galvanized into action. He ran back through the Mesopotamia room, dodged the museum security staff who were inspecting the damage in the Chinese ceramic gallery and went down the stairs. He slowed down as he reached the last flight so as not to attract attention to himself and then, with one brief glance towards the people flocking to see the mess Beaky had made of himself and the immaculate marble floor, went out the main entrance and strode to the gates on Great Russell Street to hail a passing black cab.

In Mr Denison's office Jeremiah had finished telling the archivist the history of how the bible came into his possession and was now, in turn, being told the receipt was insufficient provenance and that the museum could only accept such a generous gift when more evidence of ownership was produced.

'I think you'll appreciate the position we're in, Father?' Denison said as he slid the book, with obvious reluctance, across the table to the priest.

'I do?' Jeremiah placed the bible back in the attaché case and stood up. 'I will see if the Montague family can give me more assurances of the bible's origin.' The two men shook hands and the priest left the office to return to the Great Court where he became aware of the excited crowd gathering beneath the glass bridge. Ambulance men, carrying emergency equipment, were running through the main entrance as museum guards attempted to clear a passage through the chattering visitors trying to catch a glimpse of the victim.

Jeremiah could vaguely see that there were two people lying on the cold marble. One was perfectly still and twisted in an unnatural pose while the other was angrily waving his hand at the rubbernecking crowd and shouting obscenities at them. The priest hurried from the museum before the villain caught sight of him and on seeing no sign of Reg made his way to the nearest tube station.

Dozer had spotted the priest and his foul language was primarily directed at him. It was sheer coincidence that Dozer had positioned himself beneath the bridge as it gave him a discreet vantage point from which he could observe the whole concourse. He knew Beaky was moving through the display rooms one by one and he hoped this would flush their quarry. He hadn't expected Beaky to drop his knife before dropping from the bridge himself. Dozer had glanced up on hearing a shout above his head and the blade sliced off his ear and impaled his right buttock as Beaky appeared beside him on the marble to the sound of a wet sack of potatoes.

A party of women, who had coached up to the city from Weybridge, shrieked in pitch-perfect harmony on seeing Beaky plummet to his death. Two museum attendants ran to kneel at the dead man's side and were greeted by foul language from the man kneeling on the other side of the corpse.

'He's dead and I'm not,' Dozer shrieked pointing to the earless side of his head and the handle of the knife sticking out of his trousers. Blood was now running freely down the side of his head and seeping through his chinos. One of the attendants used his walkie-talkie while the other went to try and hold the gathering crowd back. It wasn't long before a museum guide pushed her way through the people and produced a box of plasters from her pocket.

'What's that fucking for?' Dozer exclaimed, followed by yet another expletive.

'It's all I have until the ambulance arrives,' she explained apologetically. She touched the handle of the knife and Dozer shouted in pain as he pushed the woman away.

'Touch that again and I'll stick it in your arse,' Dozer growled and then cursed again as through the forest of legs surrounding him he saw the priest sidle out of the main entrance; he was still carrying the attaché case. Two paramedics put their equipment bags beside Beaky and on realizing he was dead moved them to beside Dozer who was pointing to the knife handle.

The younger of the two men carefully tore the material to expose Dozer's buttock and a few giggles came from the women craning their necks to get a better look. The senior paramedic frowned and waved them back before instructing the museum staff to provide a screen.

Dozer groaned. 'Can you get that out?'

'Can't do that here, sir,' said the young paramedic. 'The blade may be sealing the superior gluteal artery and this area needs to be x-rayed before any removal can take place.'

After his head had been temporarily bandaged Dozer allowed the men to lay him face down on the stretcher and carry him out to the waiting ambulance. As no weight, not even a blanket, could be placed on the knife handle his right buttock had to remain exposed for everyone to goggle and giggle at.

Dozer swore to himself that he would slice Reg's ears, nose and testicles off before burying him alive.

CHAPTER 22

DETECTIVE INSPECTOR COOPER CLOSED his eyes and tried to sleep as the car sped along the motorway towards the fenlands on the bleak Norfolk coast. Detective Constable Teal was at the wheel and had memorized the route he had to take while at the station. He remained in the fast lane, occasionally flicking on the blue lamps hidden behind the front grill to shift the drivers hogging the lane until he reached the off-ramp and took the road to King's Lynn. Cooper woke to check their progress just as Teal was approaching the gates of Montague Hall.

'Here, sir,' Teal said needlessly and the inspector grunted and watched the windows of the hall as they drew to a halt outside the door. A curtain briefly moved and he knew the place was occupied and he shifted the holster beneath his armpit to a more comfortable position. He had armed himself and Teal should the impending interview with a suspected murderer get out of hand. The door remained closed when he pounded on it with his fist until a woman's voice instructed them to use the door at the rear of the hall as the front door had been sealed.

Margaret Montague greeted the two officers and led them to the front room where the curtains remained drawn and asked them to be seated. 'How can I help you, Inspector?' she asked pointing to the sherry decanter.

Cooper shook his head. 'I wish to know if your brother or Gerald Latimer are here and if so I wish to question them.'

'I'm sorry, but neither are here. There's just Elizabeth, my friend, and myself' Margaret lied as Elizabeth entered the room carrying a tea tray for she knew ears were listening on the other side of the bookcase. 'You will take tea with us, won't you, Inspector?'

'If we searched the place we wouldn't find Mr Latimer would we?' Cooper asked with one eyebrow raised and a touch of sarcasm.

'There's just the two of us, one lump or two?'

'What do you know about the Gutenberg Bible?' The question was totally unexpected and Margaret's hand shook as she tipped the teapot, spilling a little into the inspector's saucer. 'So you do know something,' he added with an edge of triumph in his voice.

Teal smiled at the two women. 'It would be better if you told us the truth,' he said and Cooper frowned at losing temporary control of the interrogation and glared at the junior officer.

'As the *constable* said – ' he laid stress on Teal's rank '– you must tell us everything you know about the bible, who has it and where it is now or I will be forced to continue this interview in London.' Cooper looked from one woman to the other and waited.

Elizabeth spoke first. 'I think we have to tell the Inspector before anyone else is hurt.'

Margaret nodded. 'It all began when Elizabeth's friend lost his job and was refused a loan by his bank to pay his mother's care home fee and –'

'And he sought help from a man called Goldenstein who said he could make his mother's fee if he stole a single bible page from a high court judge,' Elizabeth continued. However, what he found was not a single page but a whole book, the Gutenberg Bible, which Goldenstein said he didn't want as he couldn't sell it without proper provenance.' Elizabeth paused to take a sip from her cup. 'He had a customer who could only afford a single page.'

'Then what?' Cooper demanded impatiently.

Margaret took up the story. 'Two of Goldenstein's men decided that they wanted it. One they called Dozer, suddenly became religious and wanted the bible to be used in a church – ' Cooper grunted as the pieces began coming together. 'The other just wanted it for the money he could get.'

'Dozer, the religious freak, took it to a church in East London – ' Elizabeth added.

'St Mark's?' Teal asked.

Margaret nodded. 'Yes, and a kindly priest called Jeremiah told him he never used Latin for his services and that the book was too priceless for him to keep in his church; he suggested that it would be a lot safer in a cathedral.'

'That would explain the fracas in Canterbury, sir,' Teal said, writing furiously in his notebook. Cooper frowned again as his subordinate revealed what the police knew.

'The book was snatched from Dozer in the cathedral by Alistair, my brother, and it was returned to Father Jeremiah who decided to take it to the Vatican. Father Rogers, a locum, was asked to care for St Mark's while he took a flight from Gatwick but when Dozer returned to the church the young priest cleverly told him that Jeremiah was leaving from Heathrow.'

'That would explain –'

'Shut up, constable,' Cooper snapped.

'But he didn't fly,' Elizabeth said.

'Why? Where is he now?' Cooper snapped.

Elizaebth was tiring of the man's attitude and snapped back at him. 'Father Jeremiah came to the conclusion that the bible was more important as a piece of social history and had decided to place it in a museum.'

'Museum?' Teal asked.

'Putting it in the archives of the V&A was considered the most apt place for the bible and that's where he took it.'

'We don't know what's happened since he left,' Margaret concluded and the two women sank back into their armchairs and waited for the officers next move. They were both hoping that Gerald wouldn't interpret the silence as the police leaving the hall and decide to make his appearance from behind the bookcase.

'You have been very frank, Miss Montague,' Cooper said as he took the cup of cold tea, sipped and immediately replaced it on the saucer. 'We had reports from a curator that the priest did take it to the V&A but that they couldn't accept it because it would be better in the British Museum's Gutenberg collection.'

'We should have thought of that ourselves,' Elizaebth said to Margaret with a deep sigh. 'I did vaguely read somewhere that they already had two copies.'

'Father Jeremiah did go straight to the British Museum in the company of another man whose identity we do not know but maybe you can enlighten me.' The inspector looked at both women accusingly. 'You haven't told me everything have you?'

Elizabeth shrugged. 'That would be Reginald Barnett who has been helping us,' she said in an apologetic manner.

'Therefore he would most probably be the man who threw a pickpocket commonly called Beaky to his death in the Great Court.' Teal said.

'The Great Court?' Elizaebth asked, creasing her forehead.

'It's the vast central area in the museum,' Teal explained and then fell silent as Cooper glared at him again.

'Reg would never do a thing like that,' Margaret said abruptly.

'You know him well, Miss Montague?' Cooper asked with a knowing look.

'Enough to know that he isn't a murderer.'

'Unlike Gerald Latimer,' Cooper snapped. 'Didn't he kill the two men that were found in a well; your well, Miss Montague, which is not more than a hundred yards from this very spot.'

'No!' Elizabeth exclaimed angrily. 'One of those men was an assassin sent by the judge to recover the Gutenberg Bible and the other was Dozer's partner. Both deaths were the result of self defense and an accident.'

'Explain!' Cooper stood up and pointed at Margaret. 'It was your brother wasn't it.'

'Sir Alistair was in the house at the time,' she replied coolly. 'It was Reg who was shot at when he went to investigate a noise. He was hit in the side and when he fell back the shotgun he was carrying went off, hitting the man who had been hiding in the shadows.'

'Rodney Walton,' Teal clarified referring to his notebook.

'The assassin was called Rasmus Psomas and he was sent by Judge Atkinson. He was creeping round the stables when I crept up in the dark and surprised him when I pointed a shotgun at him. He was so startled he accidentally shot his own foot and fell backwards into the well.'

The inspector switched off the tape recorder he had in his pocket and signaled to Teal that they should leave. 'I think you've given me enough for now but it will have to be corroborated by Mr Latimer, Reginald Barnett and Sir Alistair.' He handed Margaret his business card. 'Please inform all three that they have to contact me immediately or I will have to issue an arrest warrant. I will also need to talk to you both in a more formal manner later.'

They both nodded and with relief watched the officers preparing to leave.

Cooper was walking from the room when he turned. 'You may be interested to know that another man was hurt at the museum and taken to hospital. He left after his injuries had been seen to and before any police officers could question him. His description matched that of a known felon called Mr Andy Lawson. You may know of him by his popular pseudonym of Dozer so if I were you I'd lock the doors and windows tonight.'

The officers left by the back door and Margaret peered through the chink in the curtains until she saw the squad car drive away before giving the all-clear wave. Elizabeth went to the bookcase, swung it open and Gerald appeared with a grim expression upon his face.

'You've practically put me and your brother away for a lifetime sentence,' he said as he dusted himself down and then threw himself onto the settee. 'I heard everything you said.'

'We had to lay the ground for later, Gerald,' Elizabeth said as she sat beside him and took his hand. 'It will all come out in the end but at least if we have to call for help we're guaranteed of getting it faster.'

'Why would we need help?' Gerald said without thinking.

Margaret laughed. 'Have you forgotten that Atkinson, Dozer and Mutton are baying for our blood; they want fifty-thousand pounds and the bible.'

'Sorry,' Gerald mumbled. Elizabeth gripped his hand tighter and planted a kiss on his cheek.

'I'll brew up some more tea, this has become cold.' Margaret took the pot and tactfully left the room to make her way to the kitchen.

'That priest's hole is bloody cold,' Gerald murmured as he snuggled up to Elizabeth and they kissed each other with a passion that only comes from being apart for too long. They had just come up for air when they heard the sound of a car approaching the hall. With a muttered 'they haven't come back have they?' Gerald leapt up and went to the window and carefully pulled the curtain until he could just see the drive. It was a strange looking car, one he didn't associate with anybody they knew, and he waited until the door opened before deciding whether to head for the priests hole or not.

Reg climbed out of the stolen car and waved at the drawn curtains knowing full well he was being watched. Gerald told Elizabeth who it was just as Margaret was entering the room with the tea tray. She gave a squeal of delight, thrust the tray into Gerald's hands, and ran to the back door to let him in. They entered the living room arm in arm; a grin on Margaret's face and lipstick on his.

'The knight-errant returns triumphant!' Margaret declared.

'What about the genuine knight?' Elizabeth said with a laugh. 'When is he coming home?'

'Ali's not here?' Reg asked.

'No, he said he had to do something and that's the last we've heard from him.' Gerald said looking at his watch and the group became ominously silent.

'I hope it's nothing foolish,' Reg muttered.

'What happened at the museum, mate?' Gerald asked and Reg gave a blow- by-blow account of what had taken place, including Beaky's death.

'Father Jeremiah, did he manage to get the museum to take the bible?' Margaret asked as she handed him a glass of brandy.

Reg sipped gratefully before replying. 'He called me at Gerald's house and said that Denison couldn't take the bible without more authenticated records of its history and how it came into the Montague family's possession. The Father left the museum saying he would check with Sir Alistair.'

'So he still has the bible?'

'Yes, he has it on him.'

'Thank goodness.'

'Yes, but there's more. The reason he called from your place, Gerald, was that when he arrived at St Marks he found the whole area taped off by the police and when he asked one of the constables what the problem was he was told that Father Rogers had been murdered in the church.' There were gasps from the listeners. 'Not only that but there was one eyewitness a young girl who had been in the confessional. Father Jeremiah guessed he knew her identity and went round to her home. She was still in shock but grateful for the priest's visit and was able to tell him it was the same man who had scared her twice before.'

'Dozer!' Gerald exclaimed.

'Yes, and we can bet it was Dozer getting information about Father Jeremiah's whereabouts.' Reg sat down and let a long sip of the fiery nectar slip down his throat.

'Where's the Father now?' Margaret asked.

'Coming here.'

'Another gathering of the clan.' Elizabeth said in a serious voice.

'With the clan leader, my brother,' Margaret added softly. 'Where the hell has that silly fool got to?'

CHAPTER 23

TIM HOLT HAD BEEN UNABLE to do anything but study his cellmate during the weeks of close proximity and he now knew the big man's routine as intimately as himself. To prevent being caught by the guards Pidd had arranged for a friend on the outside to visit Tim each Friday so that notes, with instructions on what was required at the next fly-by, could be discreetly passed on. Pidd wrote these messages on the eve of visitor days, which gave Tim the opportunity to secretly read and copy them in the morning when Pidd was taking his habitual ten-minute jog around the exercise yard. Most of the notes just listed the drugs required and with dedicated practice Tim had soon mastered Pidd's scrawling handwriting.

Tim was now able to plan his escape and he intended to make use of Pidd's own people. His first step was to ensure Pidd was unable to stop him and Tim knew he would need a weapon, a knife. Tim's first idea was to write a postscript on the next note but then rejected the thought for Pidd always took charge of recovering the deliveries and would wonder why the knife had been included.

Long before Tim had arrived in Brixton Pidd had removed a length of wire from under the mattress of the top bunk. This he had fashioned with a hook at one length and then put it back in the same place he had taken it from. At the agreed fly-by time, which was usually after midnight, Pidd always stood on the lavatory to open the window. When he heard the low sound of the drone approaching he would extend his arm between the bars, holding the length of wire, and snag the fishing line holding the small bag of drugs. It was a simple matter to gently tug the bag towards the window until Pidd was able to grasp the bag and unhook it. This released the drone that flew back over the prison wall; because Pidd included some of the guards as his customers there was very little attention paid to the strange whirring noise in the middle of the night.

Frost was beginning to paint roofs white and each breath Pidd expelled created a new cloud that drifted out of the open window where he waited patiently for the drone. Tim huddled beneath the thin blankets as the temperature in the cell dropped fearing the moment when Pidd, drugs recovered and tested, would want to warm his gross body by sexually abusing Tim's. He had tolerated this nightly rape because he knew that without Pidd's protection he would be fair game for any body builder(s) in the showers.

This night was different because the drone never appeared to deliver dreams of forgetfulness. Pidd waited until even he couldn't stand the cold anymore and he angrily slammed the window and roughly shook Tim's shoulder to wake the young man who was only feigning sleep.

'What's going on!' he growled, his lips only millimetres from Tim's ear.

'Wha . . . wha . . . ' Tim croaked, as though returning from a deep dormancy.

'The drone didn't come, did you give Bert the note?'

'Yes, of course I did.'

'I thought I heard something but it didn't come. What happened?'

'How the hell would I . . . ' Pidd slapped Tim's face hard and pulled him out of bed and threw him onto his own.

'You don't talk to me like that, girl,' he snarled and Tim knew when he was called 'girl' that he was in for a very rough night; Pidd was going to work out all his frustration on Tim and it was a long period of extreme pain before the sadist eventually rolled over and started snoring. Tim slipped out of Pidd's bunk and retrieved a toothbrush from under his own pillow. He had used the concrete floor where it met the wall beneath the bunks to sharpen the end to a point. He had done this during the short times when Pidd was out of the cell and now by the faint moonlight filtering through the window glass, he looked down at his snoring rapist with revengeful eyes.

Tim had practiced his next moves in his mind, over and over again, until when it came to executing them for real it happened so smoothly even he was amazed at how simple it was to take the man's life. He hovered his steady hand over the broad forehead and aligned the sharpened end of the toothbrush with the left nostril then using the heel of his hand he rammed the makeshift weapon upward while pressing down on the forehead with the other hand. Pidd jerked once, with surprised eyes wide open, and was still. A small trickle of blood came from the nose with the toothbrush when it was slid from brain and nasal cavity. Small nose plugs he had fashioned from tissue paper were firmly pushed into the nostril until they couldn't be seen and all signs of blood was sponged away. Tim closed the accusing eyes and arranged the bedclothes so that the dead man couldn't be seen easily by anyone in the doorway. The wire hook was replaced beneath the bed and the toothbrush was broken into small pieces and flushed down the lavatory. Tim returned to his bunk and slept the sleep of an avenged angel.

Prison routine meant that breakfasts, collected the night before, were to be eaten in the cells and Tim ate both bowls of cornflakes and drank the cartons of milk dry. This would be the day he would taste freedom and he checked the time before tidying his bunk and leaving the cell. There were five prisoners trying to keep warm with extreme exercises in the yard and they moved away from Tim as though he were a leper when he started jogging round the perimeter. He did this four times before noticing the fine thread of fishing line lying on the ground. His eyes flicked up to follow the line and knew that his escape plan had been taken seriously. What Pidd didn't know was that the drone *had* visited the prison but its only cargo was an almost invisible line that it released over the wall before flying off. The substitute note had worked and Tim paused next time he approached the line and crouched down as though recovering his breath. Nobody seemed to take any notice and he surreptitiously took the end of the line and began winding it around his hand behind his back until he felt resistance. He tugged and the end of a heavy rope came over the fifteen-foot wall. Tim stood up and pulled as hard as he could before anyone realized what he was doing. The rope came down and then stopped with a jerk. It had conveniently placed knots and Tim discarded the fishing line and began scaling it. The five prisoners exercising stopped what they were doing and froze with mouths agape. They watched, fascinated, as Pidd's 'girl' climbed hand over hand until he reached the top and disappeared. One wearing running shorts and scant tee shirt came out of his shock first and he ran to the rope and began climbing. He had only covered ten feet before the rope was released on the other side of the wall and he fell, splintering his coccyx on the hard concrete.

On reaching the top of the wall Tim spotted the open truck parked beneath him. It was loaded with empty cardboard boxes and he jumped to crush them with his body, reducing the impact of his fall.

'Get under the boxes,' a man in a flat cap said as he cut the rope tied to the back of the truck with a long knife and climbed into the cab; there was a short cry of agony from the other side of the wall.

The truck pulled away and using a maze of back streets it headed west with Tim rolling painfully under the boxes until the vehicle came to an abrupt halt.

'Put these on,' a different yet familiar voice instructed and a set of clothes including, strangely enough, the right size shoes were tossed into the back of the truck. Tim quickly discarded the prison garb and dressed himself within the privacy of the high walled sides. A face appeared over the edge and Tim, in the act of slipping on a rather smart tweed jacket, recognized the man who always visited the prison to take Pidd's orders.

'How's my brother?' he asked handing a wallet that appeared to be stuffed with ten pound notes to Tim.

'I left him sleeping like a baby,' Tim said.

'You're rather young to be chosen by Peter as his assassin,' the man said with questioning eyes.

'I'm very good at what I do.' This was said with the conviction of truth for hadn't he just cleverly assassinated the prison's worst inmate.

'You must be. The plan worked perfectly and I'm surprised that Peter didn't escape with you.'

'Two would never have had the time to clear the wall and your brother wanted me to do this particular job for him so I had to be the one to escape.'

'Makes sense to me.'

Tim recalled what he had whispered to Pidd's brother at the last visitor's day and what he had written on the substitute note;

Drone. 9.30am. Drop line into exercise yard
with rope attached. Have clothes and cash waiting.
Make sure Tim gets what he needs to complete hit.

Address of target essential. Peter.

'Did you get everything asked for?' Tim asked.

'Of course I did and I've got the other thing Peter asked for here.' The man patted the long leather case before handing it to Tim.

'Where are we?' Tim asked

'Clapham South tube station is just around the corner and the target's address is in the wallet.'

Tim climbed out of the truck to the amusement and ribald comments from a group of schoolboys trooping to the station for a museum visit; the teachers in charge shrugged and grinned at Tim in apology. Pidd's brother wished him good hunting, handed him the long leather case and Tim followed the school party to put part two of his revenge plan into action.

When Alistair slipped away from his friends he had one goal in mind; to make sure that Judge Atkinson was publicly exposed as the nasty criminal he was. He had quietly driven the Rolls from the garage to the main road and on reaching the motorway he took the south on-ramp and put his foot down. Allowing his mind to shift into autopilot Alistair let the car find its own way to London while he pondered his next move.

The car purred along Fleet Street to where it became The Strand and Alistair turned down Bouverie Street to park in the Green Parking garage. From there he walked the short distance to The Royal Courts of Justice and decided to see if Atkinson was sitting. He strode into the huge Victorian edifice of a thousand rooms and nineteen courts and after passing through security went to the list posted on the wooden cabinet in the Main Hall. His eye ran down the various courtrooms until he read Atkinson's name. He was sitting in an open court, hearing a case of aggravated assault, and he entered quietly, bowed his head towards the bench and took a seat at the rear.

It was Alistair's intent to get a good look at the man's face for identification purposes later and when he studied the face buried within the archaic, short wig he saw pinched, shrewish features and eyes so cold they would strike fear into any defendant brought before him whether guilty or innocent. The tightly pursed lips moved slightly as though repeating the prosecuting counsel's words that were summarizing the case for the Crown. Alistair had seen enough and, without even glancing at the poor wretch in the dock, left the courtroom to return to the Rolls. He had previously learnt Atkinson's home address during a casual discussion with Gerald and he entered the postcode into the sat-nav and soon he was driving out of London.

After being instructed by the dulcet tones from the sat-nav to leave the main road, Alistair found he was on a narrow country road that wound between thick hawthorn hedges. Blackbirds occasionally swooped from one side of the road to disappear into the other and after a few minutes the sat nav spoke again,

You have reached your destination.

The hedgerow on his left suddenly changed into a tall brick wall with razor wire strung along the top and after two hundred yards this was interrupted by a large set of wrought iron gates. Alistair pulled up and through the heavy bars he could see a large Lutyens styled house at the end of a long drive. As he edged closer to the gates he spotted the CCTV camera and intercom set into the stone pillar on one side and a brass name plaque on the other etched with the name *White Friars*.

Deciding to return later that night to confront the judge he drove on to the nearest village pub and ensconced himself in a snug corner away from the noisy group of locals who were challenging each other in a drinking contest. He passed the time with a palate searing Vindaloo curry and a contrasting glass of chilled Italian lager. It took two more pints to douse the fire in his mouth and for the sun to set before he left the hostelry and drove back to *White Friars*.

The gates were still locked and Alistair decided to try a rear entry and took a small lane that followed the high wall surrounding the property. He switched off his lights so as not to attract attention in the house and as he approached the last corner he stopped and left the car to continue on foot. As he crept along, tight to the wall, he saw a dark shadow move away from the wall and become the silhouette of a man against the low moon rising. He was holding something that looked very much like a long rifle with a sniper scope and Alistair froze. He had interrupted what could only be an assassination attempt on the Atkinson's life.

Although Alistair sought justice the last thing he wanted was the cold-blooded murder of a High Court Judge on his conscience. The silhouette was now resting the weapon on something and as Alistair moved away from the wall he could see it was a crossbar in an iron gate.

Tim Holt, for that's who the assassin was, tried to steady his breathing as he aimed at a shadow he could see moving about on the curtains of the library. The Vortex Viper scope on the M40 sniper rifle accentuated every muscle movement he made and the image flickered uncontrollably in the viewfinder. He was not sure who his target was and ideally he wanted to be in a prone position to steady his breathing and make sure of the shot.

Tim was taking up the first slack of the trigger and anticipating his target's move when he heard a twig snap. He turned his head and saw a tall man hurrying towards him. The shock of realizing he wasn't alone on the back path was sufficient to make him jerk on the trigger causing the rifle to fire. The butt recoiled hard against Tim's unprepared shoulder and Alistair heard him grunt with pain.

Alistair had heard the gun's report and now he stopped to watch as the man leapt to his feet and ran towards the tree line edging the freshly tilled field. He considered chasing the assassin but knew he would be a perfect target in the middle of the open field bathed in the silvery moonlight. Alistair chose to go to the iron gate and see if anyone had been hit but when he looked between the bars he saw a middle-aged woman wearing a pinafore running towards him brandishing what appeared to be a gun. She was holding something in the other hand but was unsure what it was. The angry woman paused to bring the weapon up and aim at Alistair who stepped to one side before she could fire. The bullet struck a gate bar and fragmented, spraying the field beyond with small pieces of lead. Alistair who had stepped behind the wall felt a sharp pain in his arm and without waiting for the woman to bring the gun any closer he ran back to the car. The Rolls started first time and with reckless abandonment he drove back along the track until he had reached the minor road and then headed towards King's Lynn.

Mrs Parker, the housekeeper brandishing the gun, was stopped by the locked gate for in her haste to catch the shooter she had left without the key. She could only shout obscenities after the fleeing man while still clutching the pedigreed Persian Blue she had been holding when the 7.52mm bullet punched a hole through the window, heavy drapes and the cat. She returned to the house to change her bloodied blouse, call the police and to let Judge Atkinson know that she had used his gun during an attempted burglary. After cleaning the gun and replacing it in the judge's desk drawer she phoned again to tell him that, unlike every year past, he wouldn't be winning the county fair trophy for Best in Show this year.

Tim kept running through the wood until he found the clearing where he had left the car he had stolen in Norwich. He drove along the foresters' track until he reached the main road and it was at this juncture that he decided to make his next attempt in London when the judge was arriving at the Courts of Justice.

'It would be so much more appropriate,' he murmured.

This wasn't what Alistair thought on glancing at the arm that had been hit and had become decidedly soggy with blood. He definitely needed immediate medical attention and instead of going to a hospital where awkward questions would be asked Alistair went back to Montague Hall. The two women immediately chided him for disappearing without a word and then, on seeing his blood stained jacket sleeve they became overly solicitous, stripping him to the waist and inspecting the small entry wound that was still seeping a little blood.

'Oh, you poor dear' and 'Trust my brother to go and get himself shot' comments flew around his ears as they tended the wound. The most painful moment was when Margaret used turkey-plucking tweezers, which had been sterilized with vodka, to probe for and extract the piece of lead. This was capped by the searing agony of a liberal splash of iodine before the arm was swathed in bandage. It was while the women were working that he related the events leading up to being shot.

Gerald, who had been sitting quietly throughout finally spoke. 'You said you couldn't identify the man with the rifle?'

'It was a bit gloomy but I'm sure he was a stranger.'

'Then we can only assume that the judge has other enemies apart from Dozer and Mutton.'

They all nodded and, as if keeping time with their heads, there was knocking at the front door. Gerald went to the window and saw Father Jeremiah standing beneath the porch and he was carrying the same black attaché case.

'The albatross has just returned, people,' he said as he left the room to tell the priest to use the rear door. Gerald was greeted with a very grim expression when he opened the door and Jeremiah thrust the case into his hands, as though the man of God was trying to distance himself from an unspeakable disease.

'Take it back, I want nothing to do with it,' he exclaimed as he stormed past Gerald to confront Alistair. 'How many more will die because of that book?' He then noticed the bandaged arm. 'Looks like someone has already tried to kill you for it, too.'

Alistair shook his head and explained how he had been wounded while Elizabeth poured Jeremiah a large measure of malt whisky. 'It's not too serious and we doubt it will become infected,' she added.

Gerald opened the attaché and took the bible out. 'I think we'll have to find a really good place to hide this.' He looked at the bookcase.

'Mutton already knows about the priest's hole,' Reg said. 'We'll need to find something new just in case he returns.'

'The wine cellar,' Alistair said and his sister agreed.

'There are a few hiding places where our father used to keep his best whiskies.' Margaret grinned. 'He thought nobody knew about them and only went by himself when he needed to take a bottle out for special occasions.'

'Was he ever wrong,' Alistair chimed in. 'Margaret and I used to play down there and we found every bottle. We were only small kids at the time and we never touched a drop.'

'However, you did on your eighteenth birthday because I followed you that night.' Margaret laughed. 'That's when father gave you hell for opening one of his best years.'

Alistair led Gerald into the kitchen and opened an innocuous cupboard door that exposed a flight of stone steps descending into darkness. A light switch just inside the door illuminated a vast cellar that had three long wine racks standing six feet in height. They went down the steps and Alistair strode to the far end where there was an open inglenook fireplace with benches on both sides of a large grate that was a work of art by the local blacksmith. It was heaped with grey wood ash and Gerald looked round to see matured logs stacked against the wall.

'My father used to bring his friends down here to discuss estate business and to empty a bottle or two.' Alistair pointed at the empty racks that were no longer filled with the finest vintages apart from a few lonely bottles closer to the steps. 'Those were the days when Montague was a name renowned throughout the county for the finest cellar and the generosity with which it was shared.' Alistair sighed. 'Unfortunately my father was too generous and he literally drank the estate into the ground as well as himself.'

Gerald's sad look had returned as he listened to his friend.

'It was a surfeit of Burgundy, Port and Spey River whisky that saw him off. Our doctor was more clinically inclined and put cirrhosis of the liver on the death certificate.'

'I'm sorry, Ali,' Gerald murmured and his friend shrugged and stepped into the inglenook and peered up the blackened chimney. With his head half hidden he clicked his fingers and Gerald passed him the attaché case. He rose up on the tip of his toes, reaching up as far as he could and placed it on a small ledge. Small lumps of soot fell into the grate to puff dark clouds into the air.

'That should do it, Gerry,' Alistair said as he brushed his jacket and slacks with one hand that was surprisingly clean while the other grasped a dust-covered bottle of whisky. 'I think we should down a drop or two of this in memory of my father who supplied us with the perfect hiding place.'

'And the unbelievable taste of a Glenlivet XXV twenty-five year old.' Gerald added as he studied the label with a look of amazement.

'He only ever drank the best.' Alistair sat on one of the short, stone benches and Gerald sat facing him as his friend reached into a nook in the wall behind him and magically produced two cut-glass tumblers that were so clean the facets sparkled in the light from the single light bulb. Alistair explained that it was a family ritual to clean them every week as he broke the seal and poured healthy measures of golden pleasure into each glass.

'To your father, may he rest in peace,' Gerald said and they both drank and continued drinking until a voice shouted from the far end of the cellar.

'What the heck are you two doing down there?' It was Reg and another glass was produced and a measure poured. It was received with a surprised look and then closed-eyed rapture as he sipped a glass of history. The three men relaxed and the level in the bottle fell fast until Father Jeremiah appeared to ask what was taking everyone so much time. Yet another glass materialized and the bottle was drained before Reg remembered why he had come down into the cellar.

'The girls have prepared the food and you are to come immediately or it will be cold.' He said, hiccupped, and said again.

'You came down an hour ago, Reggie,' Alistair rebuked, peering at his watch.

'It'll be cold,' Gerald commented with a grimace.

Four plates had been set at the kitchen table and as predicted the cottage pie, cauliflower, peas and carrots were stone cold, as were the expressions on Elizabeth and Margaret's faces.

Father Jeremiah gave his apology and said that he had to return to St Marks to give consolation to his parishioners and to revisit Marcia Watson and talk to her before she became totally traumatized by her encounters with Dozer. He was unaware that she no longer accepted God as a solution to all her problems. The group was sorry to see him leave for he had helped them when it really counted and in the process had become a good friend; Gerald's normally sad-looking face became downright miserable.

CHAPTER 24

DETECTIVE INSPECTOR COOPER AND Constable Teal were heading for *White Friars* at the same time as Atkinson left court to begin his journey home. His clerk had passed him a note, while the court was in session, informing him that someone had slaughtered Madame Saroya II while trying to break into his house. The case he was trying coincidentally dealt with extreme animal cruelty. Tears filled his eyes and ran down his cheeks as he sentenced the defendant to prison for a period that far exceeded the stipulated period for such a misdemeanour. The press gallery immediately linked the judge's tearful outburst to the prisoner's crime of kicking a dog and the gutter-press editors had a field day.

JUDGE CRIES OVER CANINE CRUELTY!
JUDGE BLUBBERS OVER A BITCH!
BARKING MAD JUDGE JAILS DOG OWNER!

Atkinson left the court in a hurry, brushing aside all questions thrown at him by a slant of reporters gathered on the pavement. He didn't notice a leading Times journalist slumping to the pavement and drove as fast as legally possible back to *White Friars* to bury Madame Saroya II and to dismiss Mrs Parker without references.

As the Mercedes glided up to the front porch Atkinson was annoyed to see a police car where he usually stopped and two officers standing at the open door. His housekeeper was greeting them and about to lead them inside when she saw her employer's car approaching. She waited until he had got out and entered the porch before Sergeant Quirt stepped forward and introduced himself and Constable Howard.

'We are here to investigate a call relating to a possible burglary and a shot being fired that has killed a cat,' he said.

'Narrowly missing me,' Mrs Parker said with a quaver in her voice.

Atkinson ignored the woman. 'You had better come in and we'll check if anything is missing.'

'They didn't get into the house, Judge.' Mrs Parker said proudly. 'I saw them off with your revolver.'

'You have a firearm in the house, sir?' Quirt asked with a raised eyebrow.

'My father brought it back from the war.'

'May I see it, sir?'

The group walked into the living room and Atkinson went to his desk in the corner and removed the gun from the drawer. Despite his housekeeper's diligent cleaning he could still smell the cordite on it and he broke it before handing it to the officer. 'Only one bullet fired it seems, Sergeant,' he said giving his housekeeper a dirty look.

'So I see, sir,' Quirt said checking the chambers. 'Do you have a license for this weapon.' He handed it to his constable who placed it in a plastic evidence bag.

'I told you, it was my father's and I don't know if he had a license. Why are you taking it?'

'If your housekeeper hit anyone this will be checked for forensic evidence and possibly be used in court, sir. Is your father still alive.'

'Of course not, he died of a heart attack while placing a wreath at the Cenotaph last year,' Atkinson snapped. He then went on to give the sergeant a lecture on his father's war record including the battles and all the decorations awarded.

'A great man, sir,' Quirt agreed. 'However, the license, if he had one, would have been cancelled on his death and you should have applied for a new one.' He pointed at the bag his constable was holding up. 'However that seventy-year old weapon would have been classified as dangerous and not given a permit; it would have been destroyed.'

The sergeant had wandered across the room to the window while talking and he pointed at the small hole with radiating cracks in the glass. 'I will assume that was the entry point.'

Mrs Parker interrupted his train of thought. 'The curtains were drawn at the time, Sergeant.

Quirt pulled on the silk cord and the floral decorated drape was drawn, instantly reducing the room light. A spot of bright light could now be seen on the curtain and Quirt pulled the material aside to reveal how it lined up with the hole in the glass. 'Did you have the lights on Mrs Parker?' he asked and she went to the light switch. Three crystal shades hanging from the ceiling were lit instantly illuminating the room.

'The shooter still wouldn't have been able to see his target, Sergeant,' the constable said, which was answered by a single nod.

'Just a shadow,' Atkinson murmured. 'Without any identification he took a gamble on hitting the right person.'

'Who I'm guessing would be you?'

Atkinson shrugged. 'Possibly. Or my housekeeper.'

'Can you think of anyone who would like to see you or your housekeeper dead, sir?' Quirt asked as his constable scribbled non-stop in his notebook.

'I'm a High Court Judge, Sergeant. There must be scores of villains who'd like to settle a score of one kind or another.'

'Nobody wants to kill me, officer, everyone likes me.' Mrs Parker said drawing herself up to her full height which wasn't that high.

The sergeant had the same opinion. 'We will be taking the cat with us as well as the gun as the autopsy will give us the bullet and therefore the type of weapon used to fire it.'

The constable was taken into the kitchen by Mrs Parker and shown the bloody corpse. Using a slightly larger evidence bag he bundled the cat into it with gloved hands and wrote on the tag. They both returned to the living room where Quirt was still trying to elicit a lead from the Judge on possible suspects. Atkinson started on seeing his cat rolled up in the polythene bag like last years fur fashion.

'Do handle Madame Saroya II with great care,' he said in a broken voice. 'She's won seven Best in Show trophies and comes from a long unbroken line of pedigreed Persians.'

The constable looked at the bag he was holding and couldn't equate the bloody bundle of cat with the words. He shrugged and walked from the house to place both evidence bags in the car.

'Forensic will be coming soon and I would appreciate it if you could close and lock the door to this room for them,' Quirt instructed and then waited until Atkinson gave his agreement before joining the constable in the car and leaving *White Friars*.

'Right, Mrs Parker, who gave you permission to use my father's revolver?' Atkinson barked. He sat at the desk and took a chequebook from the drawer.

His housekeeper looked at him in shock. 'A murderer tried to kill me but apart from that I felt it was my duty to defend your property,' she snapped back. 'What did you expect me to do, let them take what they wanted and leave me for dead?'

Atkinson tore the cheque he had written from the book and held it out to the housekeeper. 'No I expected you NOT to contact the police, now take this and leave the premises immediately.'

'You're firing me for reporting a crime, Your Honour?'

'Can I make it any clearer?' He waved the cheque impatiently.

Mrs Parker, who had been Atkinson's housekeeper for a number of loyal years, took the slip of paper and with total disbelief in what had transpired she went into the hallway to collect her coat.

The judge sat at his desk until the sun had long set and the first barks of courting foxes began to sound across the fields from the woods beyond. His mind kept returning to the Gutenberg Bible despite his grief over Madame Saroya II's death. His first suspicion was that Reginald Barnett had tried to shoot him but discounted that theory when he recalled the young man's character. 'He's no killer,' he thought aloud. 'But he and his friend and Sir Alistair must know where the bible is being kept.' It was at that point he made the decision to return to Montague Hall and forcefully get some answers.

The armoury his father had kept, just in case the enemy invaded Britain, was sealed in a large box buried in *White Friars'* stable block. Colonel Montague had confided its whereabouts to his son during the height of the Cuban blockade, in preparation for the Cold War developing into something hotter. He picked up a shovel from the garden shed on the way and began digging in the far corner until metal struck metal.

The steel box was of military origin and when he at last managed to unlock the corroding catches and open it he was amazed to find enough firepower to arm a large platoon. Unfortunately the weapons were museum worthy and the ammunition doubtful as to its ability to fire. He unpacked three Webley Mk.VI .45 Automatics and a 9mm Welrod silenced pistol. Four Mills bombs wrapped in brown wax paper were taken from the box and added to four boxes of handgun rounds. His father had warned him that some of the Mills had either seven or four-second fuses but he was unable to remember which was which.

Atkinson carried the weapons to the house and placed them in a backpack. He then changed into a black tracksuit, put a balaclava helmet in with the pistols and went to the garage where he kept his 4 x 4 Jeep Renegade for rough country.

The constable that had been put on protection duty at the gate saluted as Atkinson went through the gates.

The run to Montague Hall was quick and he circled the estate until he found the ideal spot where he could abandon the car. He switched off the lights and set off through the dense copse on foot. As he was wearing light clothing the briars snagged and scratched as he pushed his way through the dense undergrowth. Atkinson was beginning to perspire when he finally reached the other side of the copse and the swathe of open meadow that stretched to the ha-ha and the Hall beyond.

Dozer lay face down on the gurney as the staff nurse, five second-year students and a first-year doctor compared an x-ray against his exposed backside. His trousers had been swiftly cut away on his arrival in the hospital, a local anesthetic injected and the area around the embedded blade swabbed with antiseptic before he was taken to radiology.

'There doesn't seem to be any arterial damage, Mr Lawson and therefore it is quite safe for us to remove the object,' the doctor said. 'It may hurt a little more but I will be quick.'

'Quicker than the guy who put it there I hope,' Dozer muttered through clenched teeth and involuntarily clenched his buttocks too.

The young man gripped the handle, gave it one hard yank and the blade slipped free with a wet slurping sound yet very little blood was released. The nurse immediately stepped forward to clean, stitch and dress the wound while the students politely applauded the doctor's skilful withdrawal.

'This ain't the bloody Palladium, fuck off,' Dozer shouted at the youngsters.

'You must moderate your language, Mr Lawson. There are women and children in the emergency department,' the doctor admonished as the nurse applied the last big plaster and Dozer swung his legs round, slipped off the gurney, stood up and sent the doctor flying with a solid punch in the face.

'Sod off,' he said and the staff nurse and five medical students fled from the cubicle. Dozer pulled the curtain open to the next cubicle and after checking that the patient, a survivor of a motorway pile-up, was close enough in size to Dozer quickly put on shirt, trousers and tweed jacket before returning to his own cubicle to slip on his loafers and collect his wallet. Alarm bells were ringing and the staff was running in all directions as he casually walked out of A&E. Pain stabbed through his buttock like a fresh knife with every step he took, and he climbed into the first taxi that had drawn up to off-load a day patient. The journey to his apartment building was punctuated by frequent Anglo Saxon expletives as his wound was jolted by the poor road surfaces.

The driver scowled at his fare in the mirror. 'Could you tone it down a bit, Guv?' he asked for the tenth time and Dozer replied with a scowl and said nothing. When the cab arrived he thrust the right money through the sliding window and left the cab without adding the mandatory tip. It was the turn of the cabbie to curse as he watched the big man limp into the tall building.

Mutton watched the big man climb out of the taxi from the cover of a parked removal van and shadowed him into the apartment block. He held a Beretta .25 that was no bigger than the palm of his hand. A deceased nightclub bouncer had donated it to Mutton after his neck had been broken for trying to use it on him. He paused at the entrance when he saw Dozer standing before the bank of lifts and waited until he had entered one before running across the lobby and stepping in just as the doors were closing. Dozer was totally unprepared and froze when the muzzle of the gun was placed against his cheek.

'Mutton, what a surprise!' Dozer said as he watched his assailant push the right button.

'I'm sure it is, mate. Specially as you owe me half the money.'

'Look Mutton, I don't have the fifty grand. The holy book is the only thing I want.'

The doors opened and Mutton waved Dozer out and followed him to the apartment. Once inside they went into the main living room and Mutton couldn't help admiring the view of East London that was spread out before him.

'Nice place you've –'

He was interrupted by a door opening and a scantily-clad pole-dancer coming into the room. 'Hello, darling,' she said and then gave a small cry on noticing the automatic pistol being aimed at her pimp.

'Come out, Sheila,' Mutton shouted and a second girl entered the room. She was completely naked apart from a small hand towel that was inadequate for regaining her complete modesty. Mutton knew both girls worked in Goldenstein's club and that they were lovers.

'Shut up and sit down,' Mutton instructed and the girls slouched across the room to where Dozer had already seated himself on a settee and sat on either side of him with crossed legs. 'I'll ask you one more time, Dozer, where's the money?'

'I'll tell you one more time that I don't have it and if anyone does it'll most probably be those bastards at Ali's place in Norfolk.'

'I've been there and tried them –'

'And they said I've got it, right?'

Mutton was now in a state of confusion with a nasty feeling that Dozer was telling him the truth. He went to the French window, slid it open and stepped out onto the balcony to think by himself.

Dozer surreptitiously slipped his hand down the back of the settee to where he kept his backup and withdrew the Walthar P5. The girls looked down at it with fearful eyes and shook their heads but Dozer squeezed Sheila's thigh cruelly before rising to his feet and aiming the weapon at arms length at his ex-colleague on the balcony. Mutton caught movement in the corner of his eye and spun round to find it was his turn to look into the muzzle of a gun.

It was apparent that Dozer had the more powerful weapon and that his own .25 ladies gun could never match the mess a 9mm parabellum round would do to his head. Mutton let the tiny Beretta drop onto the balcony where the shock caused it to discharge with a sharp crack. Doris, the other girl on the settee, gave a brief 'oooh' and fell back against the armrest. Dozer looked round and his mouth tightened with anger on seeing her lolling head with blood trickling down the side. Sheila simply looked at her lover in disbelief holding a fist to her mouth. Dozer strode towards the shocked Mutton who was staring past him at where the stray round had gone and Dozer ordered him to turn round. As soon as the dazed Mutton was facing the city Dozer swiftly bent, grabbed his ankles and with one almighty heave lifted him up an over the railing.

As Mutton's terrified scream diminished and abruptly stopped Dozer stepped forward to look down at the broken bag of bones nine storeys below. People began to gather as blood trickled slowly across the pavement and into the gutter. Before mobile phones could finish fighting for the most macabre angles and be tilted upward he ducked back inside the apartment to see to the disposal of the girl's body. To his relief, Dozer found that Doris had only fainted when her overly pierced ear acquired an extra XL piercing. Sheila bathed and bandaged her lover's ear and later, when they were all in bed basking in the afterglow of their efforts, Dozer instructed Doris to tell her visiting clients that she had nipped it with scissors when trimming her hair. She was a practical girl and to avoid any publicity that could affect their sideline as a part-time call girls she washed the cushion covers, where blood had been spilt, cancelled two of her regulars and gave the same nipped-ear story to the constable who was questioning tenants in all apartments over seven storeys high; the medical examiner had determined that this would be the right height to inflict such fatal injuries.

As the luxury apartment had been leased in the girl's names no suspicion was aroused until much later when the cab driver and hospital staff were questioned and Dozer's description and name rose to the surface. Detective Inspector Cooper was notified and with a squad of armed response officers he rushed to the apartment building that after a thorough search revealed he had missed the fugitive by minutes. Two girls found and questioned in one apartment on the ninth floor stuck to the same story; they had been alone yesterday and all night and didn't know anyone called Andy Lawson. Doris elaborated on their story by adding that she thought something had fallen past their window yesterday at four o'clock. Cooper looked at her and caught the flicker of an eye movement suggesting a cock-and-bull story.

'Did you hear anything, Miss?'

'No, I don't think so.'

As Sheila had been conscious at the time of Mutton's departure she realized the man had started screaming the moment he cleared the top rail. 'There was something, Doris. Don't you remember how we heard a noise and you said it was seagulls nesting on the roof?'

Doris understood instantly. 'You're right, darling. That's what it was.'

Teal who had been quietly eyeing both girls while his boss did the questioning found all lascivious thoughts vaporize on hearing that the sexy duo in skintight yoga leggings wouldn't be interested in male detective constables. Cooper asked more general questions about other tenants before getting more personal.

'Where do you both work?'

Without thinking Sheila said, 'Goldenstein's. It's a club –'

'I know what that is and where it is,' Cooper snapped. 'Maybe Andy Lawson doesn't mean anything to you but how about the name Dozer?' As a piece of his puzzle dropped into place he could have heard a pin drop for both girls had fallen silent.

'Did Dozer throw Mutton off that balcony,' he barked and the girl's cringed into the slightly damp settee cushions; they remained silent which was the answer Cooper sought. 'There'd be no point in asking where he is now, would there?' With much misguided loyalty the girls stayed quiet and were led from the apartment by Teal for further interrogation back at the station. The inspector returned to his car and decided to question Sir Alistair about his role in the missing bible.

CHAPTER 25

NOW SURE THAT BOTH the money and the Gutenberg Bible were in the hands of Reginald Barnett and Ali Montague, Dozer rose very early and set out for the Norfolk estate to exercise divine retribution on all those gathered there. He was positive in his mind that it was God who intervened at the British Museum and diverted the knife to inflict pain only. Pain to remind him that he had yet to recover the holy book and take it to the Vatican for the Pope's use only. He crossed himself and then blew the horn to clear a very old Morris Minor convertible out of his way. The middle-aged church elder was on her way to assist the vicar in raising funds for the new organ and was determined to overtake the large container lorry, albeit very slowly. Dozer grew impatient and he closed the gap until he could see the woman's panic stricken eyes in the mirror. He waved his hand to get her to move over but she was unable to drop back or to go any faster. She was obviously unable to move over and the veteran car was making very little progress. Dozer drew back and then accelerated to ram the Morris increasing its speed by five miles per hour. It shot forward a few feet before fishtailing out of control and spinning into the gap between the huge lorry's front and rear sets of wheels. Dozer hit the brakes and watched as the topless car and driver, rammed under the lorry, caused it to jackknife.

Dozer pulled back further and then stopped on the hard shoulder as the lorry, now minus its container, flipped over into the central reservation while the giant steel box, filled with previously owned automatic washing machines destined for the Central African Republic, slid along the highway with a peacock tail of flaming sparks spraying into the dawn sky. More cars pulled up behind Dozer and people ran to see if they could help the drivers. Unfortunately, the church elder wouldn't get any older but the lorry driver was climbing out of his cab window with one arm broken as the rescuers arrived.

The man in the car directly behind Dozer got out to have a word. 'My, God, look what you've done you bloody fool!' shouted the businessman who was on his way to an AGM at his head office in Norwich.

Dozer got out and the executive poked him in the chest to emphasize his revulsion. Dozer responded with a sharp poke in the face with his hammer-like fist. The executive slumped to the ground unconscious with blood pouring from his broken nose and Dozer got back into his car and drove along the hard shoulder until he came to an off-ramp. The sat-nav voice instantly protested at the change of route but soon re-plotted a new one and Dozer followed the instructions, ignoring all directions to rejoin the highway, until he was nearing the Montague estate.

The executive being attended to by ambulance men gave nasal-sounding descriptions of the car and the big man to the police investigating the fatal accident and these were routinely sent back to Central Traffic. Inspector Cooper had already initiated an APB on Dozer and when this was cross-linked to the information received from the scene of the accident it set alarm bells ringing. The inspector was notified of the fugitive's latest crime and a rough location and he put two and two together which coincidentally added up to Sir Alistair Montague. An armed response team was put on standby in King's Lynn and a police Eurocopter was requisitioned to take the inspector and D.C. Teal to the Hall as fast as possible.

Tim Holt was four hundred yards from the Royal Courts of Justice and had been waiting patiently for more than an hour for his target to appear. He had spent two days reconnoitering the area until he found an office building that was within visible range of the main entrance to the courts. It was an old Victorian structure with an open steel cage lift and a marble staircase that went up to what was originally a solicitor's office. Tim had forced the lock at night and, with a padlock he had purchased, relocked it again until he needed to gain entry. He was now lying on the roof between two sandstone buttresses with his favourite M40 aimed along The Strand to where he expected Justice Atkinson to emerge.

The Vortex Viper scope brought everything at the entrance to the courts into sharp reality and he watched barristers and legal secretaries coming and going. There was a group of reporters waiting for someone of significance to appear and Tim wondered who it might be. His stomach protested at the lack of food and as the distant Big Ben began booming out that it was lunchtime there was a stir at the doorway and a figure strode out into the light. It was Judge George Atkinson and Tim recognized the man who had blackmailed him and then not kept his promise to keep him out of the hell he had suffered in prison.

The crosshairs were fixed on the man's narrow chest as Tim levered a round into the chamber and took a deep breath. The tripod held the barrel steady and he lightly squeezed the trigger. As the gun lightly kicked back into his shoulder a tall man holding a tape recorder stepped into the line of fire and the steel jacketed bullet shattered his spine. Tim quickly levered another round but he was too late for Atkinson had moved on and climbed into his car. Cursing to himself he quickly bagged his weapon, picked up the expended cartridge and hurried down the stairs without touching anything. Tim casually left the building after locking it and strolled up The Strand and past the Royal Courts of Justice where a group of excited men were gathered round a dying man. They were all reaching out with their recorders, trying to catch the man's last words, and not one had considered calling for an ambulance.

Tim knew where the judge lived but realized that he couldn't try again at that venue and he decided he would have to shadow the judge until he settled in a place that enabled him to execute the man. The previous day, when the judge was sitting in court and in the event of any miscalculation with the shooting he had placed a tracking device under the wheel arch of Atkinson's car and Tim switched on the mobile phone he had taken from the late Peepee and activated the app he had bought on line.

Atkinson was heading out of the city and it wasn't long before Tim was keeping a steady three miles between them. He had passed Stanstead Airport when he encountered a tailback and was reduced to walking speed. At one point the traffic ground to a halt and he got out of the car to view the road ahead. The app had shown that he was close behind the judge but didn't realize how close until he saw the familiar figure standing beside his Mercedes only ten cars ahead of him. Tim ducked down and got back into his car but not before he had seen that two cars shunting into the back of a lorry had caused the hold-up. One lane had just been cleared and the traffic slowly filtered by the wrecks, the drivers trying hard to get a glimpse of any victims.

Contrary to Tim's initial belief Atkinson did return to *White Friars* and he watched the app as the blip stopped and then disappeared. Tim slowly cruised into the avenue and cautiously drove past the gates, guarded by a solitary police constable, before turning into the next street to park and wait to see what happened next.

Atkinson wasn't very long until he saw in his mirror a 4 x 4 rush past the street he was waiting in. Realising that the judge had changed vehicles, Tim turned his car and began following until it became clear that the new vehicle was heading in the direction of the Montague estate. Instead of entering the main drive to the hall the Renegade circled the property and came to a halt a fair distance from the residence. Tim spotted the abandoned 4 x 4 in the roadside undergrowth and he pulled up behind, checking for any signs of his quarry. The sound of rustling leaves and the loud curse coming from the depths of the copse when Atkinson tripped over a surfacing root gave him the clue he sought. Tim took the M40 and began to slowly track the judge. He roughly calculated the position of Montague Hall and set off in that direction with the assumption that Atkinson was also going there to surprise someone.

'You'll be the one getting the surprise,' Tim murmured as he left the copse to see the judge striding purposefully towards the hall with a long barreled pistol in one hand and something like a ball in the other. He lay down in the damp grass and flicked out the bipod legs attached to the end of the M40's barrel. The stock was pushed snugly into the shoulder and the protective caps removed from the scope. Tim took his time lining up the cross hairs on Atkinson before pulling the bolt back to bring the first round into position. He slowly pushed it forward to ease it into the firing chamber, flicked the safety to the 'fire' position he took a deep breath and slowly squeezed the trigger.

Margaret and Reg were in the living room when they both spotted the figure walking across the meadow towards them. They went closer to the window and attempted to identify the man who appeared to be wearing some kind of backpack. It wasn't until he had cleared the ha-ha and was approaching the terrace that Reg saw who it was.

'It's Judge Atkinson, Margaret,' he exclaimed. 'I'll go and get Ali – ' Reg saw the silenced pistol being raised to point at him through window. ' – and the shotgun. Get down on the floor,' he shouted and as he turned to run from the room the whole world seemed to explode; there were sudden, excruciating pains in his back and neck as he was thrown to the ground with a severed carotid artery and punctured lungs.

Tim had squeezed the trigger and the round, covering the distance in 1.2 seconds, had torn into Atkinson's backpack and destroyed the detonator in one of the grenades. All three bombs went off together in a giant ball of intense heat and black smoke. The concussion reverberated across the meadow to shock Tim into immobility as he tried to see his target. This would have been impossible, as the judge had been blown into pieces no bigger than a quarter-pound burger with onions.

The large one-piece window overlooking the terrace had been transformed into a thousand pieces, some of which struck Reg like flying scalpels while the rest shredded the room and flew over Margaret who had, on Reg's shout, dropped to the floor behind the settee.

Ali ran from the kitchen and into the devastation that was once a drawing room and, oblivious to the pain from the carpet of broken glass, fell to his knees beside his sister. Gerald and Elizabeth also ran into the demonic chaos of overturned chairs, lacerated walls, the stench of high explosives and a fatally lacerated friend. Elizabeth knelt beside Reg and took his bloodied hand as he gave his final cough and died. Tears filled her eyes and Gerald lifted her up and held her tight with her face averted from the sight of what was once the only person to offer him help when he needed it most, the best friend he had ever experienced. Ali had cleared the slivers of glass off the settee and was lowering Margaret into it when she became aware of Reg and his shredded back.

'Reg!' she cried and tried to stand but Ali restrained her until Gerald used the Belgian lace cloth from the side table to cover her lover.

'What was it?' Gerald asked.

Ali shrugged. 'Lord knows,' he said putting a comforting arm around his sister who began to murmur between her sobbing.

'What!' Ali exclaimed with surprise on his face. 'Judge Atkinson?'

Gerald crossed the drawing room. 'What's that about the judge?'

'Margaret said he was on the terrace outside and that he had a pistol. Reg told her to drop to the floor and that's when it happened.'

'What happened? Elizabeth asked softly.

Margaret didn't acknowledge that she had heard the question and when Alistair asked her again it became clear to them all that the explosion had deafened Margaret. Ali hugged her and asked Gerald to get them all some brandy while he telephoned the police. As they sat in a state of shock sipping the warming spirit they heard, apart from Margaret, the sound of a helicopter and Gerald stepped through the broken French-window and looked up to see the aircraft directly overhead.

'It's the police,' he said.

'That's bloody quick,' Alistair said. 'I've only just put the phone down.' He left Margaret and joined Gerald and Elizabeth on the terrace as the helicopter with clear police markings swooped over the house and headed towards the copse. As it hovered over the trees there was the sound of a rifle and the aircraft turned and pulled away to land in the middle of the meadow. There was another distant report and Ali pointed to the small puff of smoke rising on the edge of the copse.

'I reckon the judge must have been carrying something and that the gunman over there wanted it and him dead.' Gerald said as a group of armed response officers emerged from the drive and began fanning out across the lawn and into the meadow, advancing on the helicopter.

'As the police are here already it must be assumed that they have been chasing the judge and the gunman,' Elizabeth guessed incorrectly.

'You could be right.' Gerald shaded his eyes as the mystery shooter fired again from the thin cover at the edge of the copse and an armed response officer fell to the grass; the remainder flattened themselves and began returning fire.

'It's like watching a live battle,' Margaret said as she joined them and then pointed at three men leaping from the helicopter and running towards the hall. 'That's Detective Inspector Cooper,' she observed. 'The second one could be Constable Teal but I don't know the third.' One of the men stumbled and fell, shot through the right calf muscle and was picked up and helped by the officer Margaret had identified as Teal. They circled the shallow crater that had been a High Court Judge and Cooper was the first to step through the missing windows into the drawing room. Teal helped the pilot over the sill and Elizabeth went to lend a shoulder to help get the wounded man to the settee.

Cooper looked around the ruined room and saw the covered figure. 'Would that be one of the bloody people I need to question about a bank robbery and a few other things?' he asked brusquely.

This caused Gerald to bristle. 'That is Reginald Barnett, son of a bank manager, who has just been killed by a terrorist,' he snapped.

'And you're Gerald Latimer who I need to question about the same crime.' The inspector was unperturbed by Gerald's attitude and after picking up a small chair and dusting it with a cushion he made himself comfortable.

Elizabeth had only looked up briefly to glare at the officer before returning to her task of applying a clean bandage to the leaking hole in the pilot's leg. 'I'm Elizabeth Shanks who used to work at the bank and Mr Latimer was one of my customers,' she called out.

'You helped with the bank robbery, did you?'

Teal frowned at his senior officer's lack of sensitivity during, what seemed to be the centre of a war zone.

'No, I did not,' she exclaimed angrily. 'And the robbers wore masks, they couldn't be identified.'

'That's very convenient. You also stole a security van.' Cooper aimed this at Gerald and Alistair.

'Who told you that fairy tale, Inspector?' Alistair asked with his best face of innocence.

'I read in the paper that they were also masked,' Margaret said, her hearing now restored. Using her hands she began dusting herself down and in the direction of the inspector.

Cooper knew he hadn't any evidence or anything that could positively link the group to what had been happening over the last few days. The man who had tried to donate a Gutenberg Bible to the V&A and then wounded a man who matched the description of Andy Lawson, aka Dozer, at the British Museum was now lying dead at his feet.

'What about the bible, Sir Alistair?' Teal quietly asked. 'You apparently gave it to the priest at St Marks church.'

Ali turned to face the constable with the same fixed look of innocence. 'The book was stolen from Mr Barnett by a man I didn't know and I was able to recover it from him at Canterbury Cathedral.' Ali turned to face Cooper. 'At Mr Barnett's request I then went to St Marks, which was his local church and gave it to Father Jeremiah.'

The inspector grunted but due to CCTV evidence he couldn't dispute Ali's account of events.

'Where is it now because we know your deceased friend took it to the museum and also left with it?'

'He was followed and threatened with a gun by Judge Atkinson,' Gerald said off-the-cuff.

'That was the last we saw of it,' Ali added.

'Threatened by a High Court Judge?' Teal asked with a look of surprise.

'Yes, he had hired two gunmen to get it and when they didn't he took it himself.' Ali said innocently.

'Would that be Mr Lawson and Mr Catchpole?' Cooper's mistrust was evident.

'Mr Latimer informed me that they were called Dozer and Mutton,' Ali said, maintaining his innocent demeanour.

Another dissatisfied grunt and Cooper went to check the pilot's condition. He used his walkie-talkie to ask the leader of the armed response team what the current situation was before turning to address the friends. 'You will all remain here and not touch a thing until the medical investigator and forensic team have finished.'

'Will that be long?' Ali asked.

Cooper grunted and without another word left the same way he came while Teal simply shrugged and said, 'They are on their way and should be finished within two or three hours. We'll most probably want to see you all again.' He then followed the inspector out and across the meadow to where a small knot of heavily armed officers were conferring.

'He's in a very bad mood.' The friends were startled when the pilot spoke. He was a slightly built man with fair hair and a very pleasant face. 'A motorist we were chasing had caused a fatal crash on the motorway and we had tracked his car to a point not far from here when we saw a massive fireball, that explosion. The inspector thought the man had committed a serious crime in London.' Pointing to the small, charred crater in the scorched terrace he added, 'That gave us no choice but to deviate and investigate and that's how we lost track of him.'

Gerald looked at Ali and they both thought the same thing; Dozer.

'Do you know why the inspector was after that man?' Gerald asked.

'I heard from the constable in confidence that he'd murdered a man called Munton, Murton or somebody with a name like that.' He winced as Elizabeth checked to see if the wound was still seeping through the bandage.

'The paramedics will be here soon,' she said as she tenderly covered his legs with a car blanket to keep him warm. 'They were on standby for the officers who now seem to be flushing out the pheasants very successfully, but not much else.'

As though on cue an ambulance screeched to a halt on the drive and on seeing Elizabeth beckoning two men ran to the French-window. Open-mouthed they stared at the carnage the judge had inconsiderately wrought by exploding on the Montague's terrace. They speedily inspected the pilot's leg and then complimented Elizabeth on her fast thinking before putting him on a stretcher and leaving the hall. They watched as the ambulance raced away and disappeared into the tree-shrouded drive.

The four friends then turned their attention to the police officers that had fanned out and were approaching the copse with weapons pressed into their shoulders.

'Who do you think that is?' Elizabeth asked nobody in particular.

'It can't be Mutton and it's definitely not the judge,' Gerald said looking at the terrace. 'May he rest in pieces.'

'Could be Dozer,' Margaret murmured.

'No, it couldn't be him,' Ali said. The inspector was still following his car when whoever fired from the copse hit whatever was in Atkinson's backpack. It must be a stranger to us all but one who knew Atkinson and wanted him dead.'

The stranger they referred to had watched the object of his hatred disintegrate before his eyes and his jaw dropped as he watched the flame and smoke rising into the sky. Movement caught his eye and he saw a helicopter suddenly bank and fly over the neighbouring sugar beet farm towards the hall. It descended to hover in the middle of the meadow before landing and three men jumped out. Tim used the scope and saw that two were in official uniforms and the other was in civilian clothes. His first assumption was that they were prison officers searching for him and he quickly lined up on the leading officer and as he squeezed the trigger a lone blowfly flew into his face. The barrel jerked, the gun fired and the civilian fell to the ground. Knowing he had given his position away he quickly readjusted his aim to the leading officer who had jumped over the ha-ha and was racing towards the hall. He was at the point of squeezing when he noticed a score of men pouring from the main driveway and spreading out across the meadow. Tim swung the scope and saw that they were heavily armed police officers and that their weapons were now firing in his direction. He lay as tight to the ground as possible and took out the lead man forcing the others to drop to the ground. The prison escapee had no intention of being returned to a Brixton hell for life and decided to get back to his car as quickly as possible. Tim had achieved what he set out to do, a little more dramatically than a hole in the heart, but nevertheless he was vindicated.

Tim began crawling through the brambles and stinging nettles to slowly make his way parallel to the line of the advancing police. No sooner had the officer at the end of the line entered the copse than Tim was clear by fifty yards and he stopped to remain perfectly still as the officers advanced further into the copse. It soon became apparent that he had stopped on a nest of red ants; they crawled over his hands, up his trouser legs and shirtsleeves, biting all the way until he was forced to continue crawling. When he had reached the road he stood up and slapped his body until he was sure nothing was living under his shirt or trousers. Tim then trotted along the lane until he reached the car he had stolen in Kings Lynn. He checked Atkinson's Renegade and saw with some relief that the judge had left his keys in the ignition. As the 4 x 4 would be a lot safer than a car whose registration had undoubtedly been circulated throughout the county he got in and drove away. He had only driven one hundred yards when he noticed another car that appeared to have been abandoned by the side of the road. He shrugged thinking it was a poacher's car and he drove on without giving it another thought.

The sun was trying to break through the thin cloud cover and Tim was smoothly moving through the countryside when he began thinking seriously about maintaining his freedom. He came to signs indicating the way to the port of Felixstowe and chose to leave the country by ferry and work his way across Europe. The Renegade responded throatily when he accelerated on the on-ramp to match the flow of traffic on the highway. Tim switched to cruise control and began to relax when there was a fearful pain in his crotch. A large bull red ant had been caught between cotton brief and skin and had chosen the delicate skin of the scrotum on which to use his jaws.

Tim grabbed at his crotch and lifted himself up off the seat, inadvertently pressing the pedal to the metal with his foot and sharply turning the steering wheel to the right with his upraised thigh. The Mercedes leapt out of cruise control and shot across two lanes and straight into the oncoming traffic on the other side of the highway. A Fiat 500 was swatted out of the way like an annoying fly before a much larger tourist coach using the inner lane ran headlong into the side of Tim's vehicle. It was his turn to be swatted out of the way and the Renegade shot off the highway and cartwheeled down the banking and into a farmer's fuel bowser parked by a field of green peas.

The Renegade was welded into the metal tank, sparking one thousand gallons of lead-free petrol. The car was engulfed in a fiery explosion that the young, semi-conscious man was unable to escape and within seconds had been reduced to tiny charred fragments not dissimilar to a High Court Judge.

CHAPTER 26

D OZER HAD BEEN AWARE of the helicopter that it had been tracking him for the last ten miles and was taken by surprise when it suddenly veered away and headed off in a totally different direction. Dozer knew it would return and he turned off at the first opportunity and from that point made sure he only drove on the narrow lanes that wound through the dense woodland. This provided leaf cover and despite confusing the sat-nav equipment, which frantically kept reprogramming his route, he was still able to head towards Montague Hall. He passed two parked cars and on being informed by the mellifluous electronic woman that he was close to his final destination he pulled over and left the car to continue on foot.

The copse on his right thinned and then ended and Dozer dropped to the ground. The helicopter had landed in the middle of a meadow and three men were getting out. He watched as they started to walk towards the distant hall and was startled by the sharp sound of a rifle nearby and one of the trio fell over. Dozer remained flat and saw a group of black clad men rushing towards the copse from the far side of the meadow. The rifle sounded again and the man leading the group dropped like a stone and didn't move. The others followed suit and lay with weapons firing at someone in the trees.

Bloody hell, Dozer thought, as he identified the shooter's position by a small tendril of smoke rising from the undergrowth at the edge of the trees, I'm in the middle of a fucking war. As the men started crawling forward and firing their automatic weapons Dozer rose to his feet and keeping low trotted along the lane until he had circled the property and had the cover offered by the hall.

Dozer ran to the rear gates, swiftly climbed over and rushed across the open courtyard to the stable yard. He paused and after realizing that no one was around he darted across to the back door to the hall, slipped an automatic from his belt and entered. There was a smell of cordite in the air as he sidled along the hall, peering into each room he passed, until he looked into the drawing room and saw the carnage that had been wrought by the grenades. Margaret Montague, covered in dust, was sitting on the settee with her brother and he could see Latimer and the girl standing by the window watching the unfolding action across the meadow. Dozer then looked down at the motionless figure, lying in a pool of fresh blood that was slowly creeping towards the doorway, and stepped into the room.

'Don't move, stay still,' he barked and showed his weapon to give emphasis to his order when their heads turned to register surprise at his sudden entrance. 'What happened here?' he asked Gerald who had stepped between Elizabeth and the automatic pistol.

'Judge Atkinson exploded on Alistair's terrace.' Gerald said this in a matter of fact manner that implied such things regularly occurred in the country.

'Exploded?' Dozer looked through the French-window at the scars on the stone and then surveyed the damage in the room. 'What made that happen?'

'He was carrying something that was hit by a rifle bullet from the woods over there,' Alistair said pointing towards the copse where small figures were pushing through the perimeter undergrowth.

'And who brought that here?' Dozer pointed to the Eurocopter where Inspector Cooper, Teal and the head of the armed response team were still in deep conversation about the next moves to be made in identifying the unknown assailant in the copse.

'You must know who that is, Dozer,' Alistair said. 'It's your old friend Inspector Cooper. 'He was trailing a car that had caused a fatal accident on the highway when he spotted the explosion and landed here. Was that you by any chance?'

Dozer nodded. 'Is he going to come back here?'

'Naturally, he has a lot more questions he wants answers to and in the meantime we have been told to wait until the forensic people and the medical examiner arrive to study the site of the explosion and Reg,' Gerald said looking across the room to his friend's body.

'Reginald Barnett?' Dozer exclaimed turning to look once more. 'Young Reggie is a bloody mess isn't he. He's dead, I take it?'

'Of course he is,' Elizabeth retorted.

'Pity, I would have liked to have done it myself.'

Elizabeth wanted to strike the big man but Gerald held her arm and squeezed it as a warning.

Dozer thought for a moment and then, denied the opportunity to seek revenge on the one who had knifed his backside, he said, 'So, who has the bible, is it that priest from St Mark's?'

'No, we have it,' Alistair said.

'Give it to me now or I'll kill your friends slowly and painfully.'

'The police would hear your gun,' Gerald observed and then bit his tongue as Dozer took a silencer from his pocket and dramatically screwed it onto his automatic one thread at a time.

'I don't think so.' Dozer smiled with humorless eyes.

'Alright, I'll tell you where it is,' Elizabeth said and squeezed Gerald's arm to keep him quiet as he had squeezed hers. Dozer asked her where it was and she pointed out of the window at the small granite folly on the other side of the lawn. 'It's been hidden in the mausoleum.'

Gerald was unable to understand why Elizabeth would direct the villain to a place that could be so easily searched to prove her a liar. Then the penny dropped and he backed up her story by adding that the bible had been sealed in an empty casket where it was thought it could remain forever. Dozer listened to them both and when Alistair added that Dozer couldn't go in there and disturb the peace of his ancestors he was convinced that it was *the* hiding place.

'If it's locked I want the key and one of you will accompany me,' Dozer pointed to Elizabeth. 'You'll do.'

'No!' Gerald tried to restrain Elizabeth but the silencer pressed firmly against his forehead prevented him from trying too hard and he let go of her arm.

Dozer watched the trio talking by the aircraft and when they had their backs turned to the hall he grabbed Elizabeth by the wrist and tugged her through the non-existent French window. 'We go now,' he exclaimed and began running, pulling the girl across the terrace and the lawn until the mausoleum stood between them and any observer in the meadow. The closer they got the less chance that they could be seen and they arrived at the door without incident.

The friends watched as Elizabeth unlocked the well-oiled door with the key that had been thrown to her by Alistair before the pair left the room. Elizabeth was thrust through the opening into the darkness beyond and Dozer followed her. With breaths held the trio waited, hearts pounding until Elizabeth suddenly reappeared and slammed the heavy door shut. She trotted back to the hall beaming from ear to ear and her friends simultaneously let out a deep sigh of relief.

'Can he shoot the lock?' Gerald asked Alistair.

'Impossible to do that, old boy,' he replied with a grin. 'Only the key can activate the ten steel bolts that slide into the cast iron doorframe. It's a unique system that was designed, patented and installed by my great-great-great grandfather to trap grave robbers and only the master key can deactivate the deadlock and withdraw the bolts.'

It's a fabulous invention,' Elizabeth exclaimed as she stepped back into the drawing room to be hugged by a much-relieved Gerald.

Dozer also found that to be true.

On entering the gloomy vault and breathing the mustiness of old bones Dozer felt a flicker of fear enter his mind. 'Where is it?' he shouted and Elizabeth pointed up to an alcove in the wall where a large porcelain urn stood.

'It's in there,' she explained.

'I thought your boyfriend said it was in a casket.'

'Gerald doesn't know the difference between a casket and a burial urn.' Elizabeth said, hoping he couldn't hear the lie in her voice.

'Okay, then go and get it!'

'It's too high up and heavy for me, you'll have to get it,' Elizabeth shouted back just as angrily and Dozer raised the automatic and placed the silencer between her eyes. They stood for a few seconds in silence like two statues in a contemporary Greek tragedy. Only their heavy breathing prevented total silence and Dozer finally accepted that he would have to climb up to the urn himself. He went to stand beneath the alcove and began climbing, using a lower opening in the wall as a foothold. As he reached up he heard a quick clatter of heels and looking over his shoulder he saw Elizabeth disappear through the door. He fired after her, missed and then the next round struck the door that closed with a resounding thump, hurting his ears as the air was briefly compressed within the vault.

Dozer jumped down and ran to the door and searched, in what little light there was, for a handle. There was no handle to find or any sign of a locking device and he realized the pretty young woman had led him into a trap. He looked up at the four very small apertures near the ceiling. They were high above the alcoves that only held urns and were only intended to help refresh the air as human remains that had been recently interred decomposed. They were big enough for the passage of a little light and air but not for any body wishing to escape his Last Judgment.

Dozer removed the silencer and holding the gun as high and as near to one of the apertures as possible he pulled the trigger in the hope that the sound would carry to the three men at the helicopter. The sound was deafening and the bullet ricocheted off the concrete wall, concrete ceiling and concrete floor before being spent and lightly dropping onto a long bundle of material lying on what appeared to be some sort of dais. Curiosity aroused Dozer pulled the cloth apart and jumped back in shock when the eyes of Lilly-Ann flicked open to stare up at him. The bloody patch on the side of her dress told it's own story and he shuddered and quickly recovered the girl's corpse.

He waited for a few minutes to see if anyone had been alerted to the gunshot but when nobody came he held the gun up and pulled the trigger again. Nothing happened and on checking the clip he found it was empty. He began to pound the metal butt on the wall that had been built two-feet thick by ancestors determined to make their remains remain sealed in forever.

Sweat was pouring down his face when he collapsed onto the floor, exhausted by his efforts. It would only be a matter of time before the gases building up in the corpse would begin to escape, the only substance that would escape the mausoleum.

'When will we let him out?' Elizabeth asked three grinning faces as she handed the key back to Alistair.

Margaret's mouth suddenly grew thin and grim and the normal warmth in her eyes changed to glitter coldly. 'It's my intention to never let him out, Betty,' she said and everyone knew she meant it.

'He'll die slowly and horribly,' Elizabeth exclaimed in a frightened voice. 'Can we do such a thing?'

'Yes,' Alistair said abruptly. 'You are forgetting Father Rogers.'

Gerald was about join Elizabeth in her argument against murdering the man when two men dressed in green coveralls entered the drawing room by the door. The medical examiner had been briefed as to the position of Reg's body and chose to come through the back door to begin his study of the dead man. Another group of men similarly dressed appeared on the terrace and began systematically gathering evidence with tweezers and cotton buds. The friends fell silent to watch them at work, lost in their own thoughts about the end Dozer faced. They tried to justify condemning a man to die slowly without water and food whilst breathing air that grew more foul as Lilli-Ann's body began it's decomposition processes.

They were all gathered on the long settee in various positions of sleep when the inspector returned with Teal trotting behind like a faithful hound. The medical examiner had finished with Reg and he had been taken away in a black body bag to the coroner's van. The forensics team was wrapping up the operation and after a few muttered words with the inspector they also left to return to the police laboratory to begin their technical investigation.

'It would seem that two specific explosives had been detonated. One was called Baratol and used in world war two hand grenades and the other was Semtex, popular with terrorists' Cooper said. 'Now why would the carrier, whoever he was, be bringing high explosives to Montague Hall?'

'To kill us?' Margaret predicted with a raised eyebrow.

'But why?'

'Damned if we know, Inspector.' Gerald stood up and went across to the side table to hide the lie on his face and to rescue an unbroken bottle of whisky. He poured a drink and then held it up for the inspector who shook his head. Gerald gave the glass to Ali and then poured three more for his friends. Teal looked at his inspector and then at the glasses being handed out and received a scowl of disapproval that a junior officer would even think of drinking on duty. With a final nod to the group Cooper strode from the room and went to investigate the two cars that had been found parked in a nearby road. Without a pilot he was stranded and with constable Teal's skill in locks he planned to use one of the cars to return to the police station in King's Lynn. Teal smiled goodbye to the group and hurried after his boss.

'Now what do we do?' Elizabeth asked and her question hung in the air for a moment before Gerald answered.

'Our first priority will be to dispose of the Gutenberg Bible,' he said this firmly and looked at everyone as though challenging them to argue the point. Margaret was the first to agree and then suggested that they follow a very simple plan that Elizabeth had already put forward.

'What was that?' Alistair said.

'We wrap it up carefully to protect it from the weather and then leave it in a public place to be found by the first curious person.' Margaret crossed her hands in her lap.

'What sort of place?' Elizabeth enquired.

'How about a police station?' Gerald suggested. 'At least it is less likely to be vandalized or destroyed by a police officer if it is found on their doorstep and they will know who to take it to for safekeeping until they find the real owner.'

'Which they won't be able to do as the book originally belonged to the judge and he is no longer around to put in a lost property claim,' Alistair said with a dry laugh.

'I think he's very much around.' Gerald waved an arm to encompass the room and the terrace but nobody laughed.

'But where did Atkinson get the bible from, surely he obtained it from somebody somewhere, either legally or illegally,' Elizabeth said.

Gerald put his glass down. 'It has to be illegally obtained because who else would buy such a famous tome and then keep it a secret to be viewed only by himself in a special room.' The group nodded and it was generally accepted that the police would never be able to find a claimant for the bible. The discussion then moved on to which police station and a number were suggested before Ali put his hand up.

'I think the best station would be Inspector Cooper's lockup.' He had spoken with an impish expression and they all laughed despite the tragic events that had just taken place in the hall.

Elizabeth suddenly changed the subject and the mood. 'I'm still concerned about Dozer. It would be cold-blooded murder if we leave him in there.' A chill descended on the room and they thought of the consequences should they set him free.

'As soon as we've disposed of the bible I'll return here and let him out,' Ali said with little conviction that it would be a safe thing to do. 'His first act would be to hunt us all down and use his bloody bulldozer.'

'Not if we handcuff him at the point of a gun, take him to Mutton's apartment in the middle of the night and chain him to the railings.' Gerald said and waited for their reaction.

'The police would soon arrive on the scene if we stripped him first.' Margaret suggested and then giggled like a young girl. Alistair remembered that when they were children she had run off with his clothes as he was skinny-dipping in the village pond. Water hyacinth leaves barely maintained his dignity as he ran down the high street and out across the fields chased by some of his younger school friends who were pelting him with acorns.

'It's a great idea, sis,' he said with a chuckle and he left the room to go and fetch the bane of all their troubles.

'We can also use the Citroën and leave that there so that the police believe he stole it.' Elizabeth suddenly suggested and Gerald gave her a hug and told her that it was a great way to dispose of the stolen vehicle. They stood and watched as the armed response officers emerged from the trees with despondent faces; they hadn't apprehended the shooter and critical questions would be asked back at the station. They slowly grouped together as they crossed the meadow and the lawn and made their way into the drive. As the last man disappeared into the trees Ali returned carrying the big book and they all set to in wrapping it in some bubble-wrap Margaret found in the kitchen and a roll of stout brown paper before sealing it in a plastic supermarket carrier bag.

'I'll use the Rolls and take this to London while you all try and get some sleep. He left and Gerald watched the Rolls drive away before taking Elizabeth by the hand and wearily leading her upstairs. Margaret suddenly felt very alone and she went into the kitchen and attempted to mask the memories of Reginald's death by preparing the evening meal.

Three hours later, the slow-cooked leg of lamb had been removed from the stove and was resting on the carving tray when Ali returned and flung himself into a kitchen chair. 'There was nobody around so I took a chance and stood it in the doorway of Oakwood police station,' he explained as Margaret put a hot mug of coffee in front of him.

'I'll go and get the sleepy heads and then we can eat,' she said and left to fetch the couple who had fallen asleep on top of the duvet the moment they had put their heads down. Margaret knocked, entered in the bedroom and found them locked in each other's arms. Margaret felt guilty waking them but knew that the food would soon become cold if she didn't.

The trio entered the kitchen where Alistair was already picking delicious pieces off the leg. He explained once more what he had done and then they all satisfied their raging hungers with full plates of food. At one point, when Gerald had a crisp and fluffy roast potato halfway to his mouth, Elizabeth voiced her guilt about Dozer having nothing to eat but nobody was listening as they enjoyed Margaret's cooking skill.

It was when they had adjourned to the library; the drawing room held too many bad memories, that Alistair raised the subject of Dozer as he raised his glass of vintage port. 'I suggest that we dispose of our friend out there tomorrow night,' he said between sips. Gerald and Margaret were in favour despite Elizabeth's protest that the man would freeze if he slept on the stone floor.

'That bastard is so heartless he'll use the duvet we wrapped poor Lilly-Ann in,' Margaret said with some misgivings about keeping Dozer for the night which might force him to desecrate the corpse. She was unable to know that Dozer had already deprived Lilly-Ann of her place of rest and was cozily sleeping on the dais, above any drafts.

It was a long night and the temperature had dropped sufficiently to spread a sparkling hoar frost over the lawn and hedges. They all got together in the kitchen and while Elizabeth made breakfast for everyone they discussed their futures.

'Mine looks a bit desolate, Elizabeth,' Gerald said. 'I've no work and it won't be long before I have to raise another twenty-three thousand pounds and seventy pence.

'You have your share and mine of the twenty-five thousand we got the judge to pay.' Elizabeth answered trying to sound optimistic.

'I would like to put that towards a good send off for Reg.'

Margaret looked up and smiled gratefully. 'You don't have to do that Gerald,' she declared. 'I will take care of putting my darling to rest. He can also sleep alongside Lilly-Ann after we've got rid of that brute in the family vault.'

'What about his father, won't he want to give his son a funeral?' Alistair asked and then remembered everything Reginald had told him about his father.

'I don't think he could give a fig about Reg,' Gerald said. 'However, we could invite him to the church service –'

'Given by Father Jeremiah,' Elizabeth interrupted.

'– right, Father Jeremiah would be the natural choice, but we shouldn't involve Mr Barnett in any of the other arrangements.'

They finished breakfast and spent the rest of the day estimating the cost of repairing the damage done to the sixteenth-century manor house. Alistair explained that because it was listed everything had to be repaired or replaced with the right type of seasoned wood and that the walls had to be in the traditional lime plaster. The amateur estimate Alistair put together took their breaths away.

Gerald stated the obvious by pointing at the shattered French window. 'You've got to make that weatherproof first and as soon as possible otherwise the central heating will be wasted and very soon damp will creep into what plaster does remain.'

Alistair and Margaret nodded with mournful expressions. 'It's a bloody fortune and will take us a very long time to get together.'

'What about insurance?' Elizabeth perked up.

'I don't know if we're covered for terrorist attacks.' Margaret said. 'But I'll check. In the meantime, if you can suffer a cold bedroom you are both very welcome to stay with us for as long as you wish.'

Elizabeth smiled gratefully and hugged the woman who winked at Gerald over Elizabeth's shoulder. 'I don't think you and Gerald will be cold during the night, dear' she whispered into Elizabeth's ear and then giggled.

Elizabeth blushed but didn't pull away. 'Thank you Margaret,' she whispered. 'We'd be very happy to accept your invitation.'

Gerald suddenly stood up. 'Darn! I'd completely forgotten it's time to visit my mother again.'

'We'll take Dozer in the morning and after we've dealt with him you can stay in London at your place and in the afternoon go and visit your mum,' Alistair proposed and Gerald agreed and was glad when Elizabeth insisted on joining him.

They spent the rest of the day thinking up wild-cap ideas to raise capital with Elizabeth interrupting whenever a plan appeared to be fringing on illegal. 'Spoil-sport,' Alistair said after one particularly good idea was vetoed on the grounds that pyramid selling had already been declared a financial fraud and highly immoral.

'What we need is a lucky lotto win,' Margaret said with a sigh as she left the library to prepare the evening meal.

This seemed to stir a distant memory with Elizabeth but when nothing came to mind she shrugged and went to the kitchen to give Margaret a hand with the vegetables.

CHAPTER 27

A DENSE FOG HAD DESCENDED on the Montague estate as the unseen sun ascended and visibility was reduced to thirty feet and in some places even less. Gerald and Ali approached the mausoleum listening for any signs of life within the stone edifice. Not a whisper came from the small apertures and Ali turned the key and pulled on the door that suddenly flew open throwing him to the ground. The Purdey flew from his hand and Gerald snatched it from the air as Dozer ran past and into the fog. He turned and fired after him but the target had been instantly swallowed by the whiteness covering the land.

Ali stood, holding his head where the door had whacked him hard, and swore heavily. 'We'll never find him under these conditions,' he muttered as he checked his hand to find a little blood had seeped from the cut on his forehead.

'We'd better get back to the girls just in case Dozer returns to the hall,' Gerald said on emerging from the mausoleum and closing the door. He handed the shotgun back and the two men, taking their bearings from the mausoleum hurried in the rough direction until they saw what was left of the French windows and went inside.

'We'll have to stand guard until the fog lifts before you can even think of leaving for London to see your mother,' Ali said as he cradled the Purdey and sat in a winged armchair that faced the broken window.

'I must go some time today,' Gerald insisted as Elizabeth, followed by Margaret, entered the room.

'What's wrong,' Elizabeth asked.

'Dozer escaped and is out there in the fog somewhere,' Gerald said.

'What has he done to Lilly-Ann?' Margaret started walking towards the window.

'Stop,' Alistair ordered. 'You can't go outside with that maniac roaming the grounds. Wait until the fog clears and then we'll check in what condition he left the poor, unfortunate girl.' They all gazed out at the white wall that appeared whiter the higher one looked up. The sun's pitiful light was trying to penetrate the suspended water drops and it wasn't until midday, when the wind changed direction, that the fog began roiling to the west and the sky cleared to a pale, china blue.

'I think it's safe to check the mausoleum,' Gerald said as he went outside and strode across the lawn. The key was still in the lock and he went inside, not forgetting to use a paperback he had brought with him to prevent the door from closing completely. After his eyes had become accustomed to the gloominess he saw Lilly-Ann's sprawled figure on the floor beside the dais and the duvet on the other side. He had just finished laying the bedding on the dais and placing the girl on it when Margaret entered the vault and went to stand by his side.

'Is she alright?' she whispered and laid a hand lightly on the pallid cheek.

Gerald raised each side of the duvet and placed them over the girl leaving the face exposed for Margaret's last kiss. They left together and the door was locked for the next time a Montague passed away.

'We must get going as it will be mid afternoon before we get to Shady Trees and I'll have little visiting time left,' Gerald told Alistair as he entered the kitchen where his friend was switching on the coffee machine.

Alistair nodded, 'Margaret and I will wait here until you return. Although Reg stole it, take the Citroën. It's not as conspicuous as the Rolls and the chances of you being stopped will be reduced if you avoid the main highway and stick to minor roads.'

Elizabeth had already packed her small overnight bag and they left Montague Hall and headed south. Avoiding the highway added time to their journey and they arrived at Shady Trees at teatime which was later than expected. Gerald went to the reception desk and was starting to sign the visitors' book when one of the nurses told him that Mrs Latimer wasn't in.

'What do you mean, she isn't here?' Gerald was confused as his mother was incapable of going anywhere without someone to care for her.

'Her Nephew signed her out,' the nurse said with concern creeping into her voice. 'He said he had promised his aunt a shopping trip to find a particular book.'

Elizabeth frowned and looked at Gerald with questioning eyes.

'Your cousin knew you were coming to visit today and he asked me to tell you not to worry and that as soon as he had the book he would bring your mother back to Shady Trees.'

'My mother doesn't have a nephew and I don't have a cousin,' Gerald exclaimed. 'Did the man give you his name?'

'It'll be here.' The nurse turned the visitors' book round and ran a finger down a short list of signatures for the day. 'Here it is.' She pointed to one and Gerald leaned closer to read the scrawled name and could just make out the words *Andrew Lawson*.

'Dozer!' Gerald jerked back in horror. 'He's taken my mother! You stupid woman you've let a perfect stranger, a known murderer, abscond with my sick mother.' Elizabeth held on to Gerald's arm in an effort to restrain him from striking the nurse who went chalk white and pressed the panic button under the counter. Bells sounded along corridors and more nurses appeared in reception led by the matron of Shady Trees. They were told what had happened and the matron reluctantly used the phone to call the police.

On his return to London, Inspector Cooper was met with a number of reports, one being a major car accident that involved a Jeep Renegade and a petrol bowser on a farm. There was nothing unusual about that except for the blackened remains of an M40 rifle with telescopic sight that had been lying in the boot.

'Our mystery sniper,' he murmured to himself and sent instruction for DNA samples to be taken from the burnt remains of the man and compared with those in Central Filing. The second report was of a kidnapping from a care home called Shady Trees. His attention was grabbed by reading the names Stephanie Latimer and Andrew Lawson.

'I saw these reports and thought they might be of interest to us both, sir,' D.C. Teal said and he received a terse nod from his boss.

'We'll go and check with the care home first,' Cooper said as he grabbed his coat and left the office. On leaving the station Teal spotted a parcel on the top step wrapped in brown paper and tied with string.

'What's that, sir?' He said in all innocence.

Copper snatched at the sleeve of his jacket and pulled him away as he signaled to a uniformed constable just coming into the entrance lobby. 'Anonymous package?' he shouted pointing to the parcel by the officer's feet. 'If it's not expected make sure you alert the bomb squad and get it seen to.'

The officer made a strange little sound, went white, turned and ran into the building as the two detectives hurried down the street to put as much distance between them and the mystery parcel as possible. Cooper's car was parked outside the steps and he judged it a bad risk to return to it. He kept running and snapped. 'We'll go to the train station and take a taxi from the rank there.'

He and Teal were driven south to Shady Trees and on arrival they noticed a green Citroën parked outside which rang a very faint alarm bell. They went into the reception area to find Gerald and Elizabeth still waiting for news of Mrs Latimer.

'Ah, Mr Latimer, I presume,' Cooper said on spotting Gerald and then turned to the matron to introduce himself.

'Nurse Andrews signed the missing woman out,' the matron said pointing to a blushing girl of about twenty in a blue and white stiffly starched uniform. Cooper instructed Teal to take a statement and turned to Gerald and Elizabeth.

'Pure coincidence that you're here?' he asked with arched eyebrows.

'Not at all, Inspector. This is one of my regular visits to check on my mother's health and general well-being.' Gerald stared meaningfully at the matron when he said this. The middle-aged woman dressed in a three-piece navy suit from Aquascutum and reeking of Chanel No 5 looked away with her nose in the air.

'You thought it was Andrew Lawson,' Teal said, opening his notebook. 'You shouted "Dozer" after inspecting the visitors' book,' he read and Gerald grudgingly nodded. Cooper went to the book and soon found the villain's signature.

'So, it was your friend who took your mummy for a ride?'

Gerald, knowing Dozer's character, winced at the expression. 'Of course it was him,' he snapped impatiently as though addressing a small child.

'And why would he do such a thing?' One eyebrow remained cynically arched.

'I haven't the faintest idea.' Gerald looked at Elizabeth as if to warn her not to mention the bible. This was unnecessary because the inspector's next question went straight to the point.

'He wouldn't by any chance have been looking for the Gutenberg Bible and is now threatening to do harm to your mother unless you give it to him?'

'We know very little about the bible,' Gerald replied knowing full well that the darn book had been placed in the entrance lobby of Inspector Cooper's very own police station. What he didn't know was that the bomb squad had arrived and was currently assessing the potential risk in opening the package.

'The little we do know, Inspector – ' Elizabeth interrupted, squeezing Gerald's hand to keep him quiet, ' – is that someone had taken the wise decision to give it to the authorities who'd know precisely what to do with it.'

'And which authority would that be?'

'The police of course.' Elizabeth smiled at the inspector. 'The last we heard was that the book had been very safely packaged and left in the care of Oakwood Police Station.'

Cooper looked at Teal and then at Elizabeth and suddenly went white. 'That's where we're stationed,' he gulped. 'Is the package about this size?' He held his hands apart like a fisherman describing his catch.

'Having not seen it wrapped I can only assume it would approximately be that size.' Gerald fought to suppress the smile that threatened to break out while watching the Cooper's face turn paler than that of a three-day old corpse.

'Get on the phone, Teal,' Cooper said, with a falsetto edge of panic. 'Tell them to cancel the bomb squad.'

'Bomb squad!' exclaimed Gerald.

'Bomb squad, Inspector!' Elizabeth echoed.

'D.C. Teal saw a package that had been left in the lobby and because of the increase in security alerts he ordered it to be investigated.' It was a blatant effort to shift the blame before anything happened that would most certainly require a blameworthy candidate.

Detective Constable Teal looked at his superior with narrowing eyes. 'I recall you instructed Constable Avers to phone the bomb squad as we were leaving the station to come here.'

'What about my mother?' Gerald grabbed the inspector's sleeve.

'I could take that as assault on my person, sir,' Cooper said in a soft, dangerous voice and Gerald instantly released his hold. 'D.C. Teal will be initiating a full search for Mrs Latimer as soon as he gets back to Oakwood and ensures the safety of the package.'

Cooper waved his hand dismissively and repeated his order to Teal to cancel the bomb squad as he hurried out to the waiting taxi. Teal used the phone on the reception desk and then rapidly followed Cooper. As the two officers were driven away the constable explained that there was no answer at the station and that he didn't have the bomb squad number on him.

'What do you mean there was no answer, it's a bloody police station, there's always someone there to answer the phone.' Cooper snapped.

'No answer whatsoever,' he said. Then another thought came to mind. 'The building may have been evacuated, sir.'

Cooper leant forward and tapped the driver on the shoulder. 'Make this heap go as fast as you can and I'll take care of any speed cameras,' he snapped. The driver murmured something derogatory beneath his breath about the arrogance of British police these days and the taxi spitefully decreased speed by one mile per hour.

Cooper chewed his nails and watched the speedometer remain fixed below the legal speed limit. I'd better bloody get there in time, he thought.

Unfortunately, he didn't.

The call about an anonymous package left in a police station alerted the Metropolitan Police who then had to pass the responsibility on to the army because Counter Terrorism Command were on full alert at every London international airport.

It was revealed later by an investigative journalist that a geeky adolescent had hacked into MI5's computer; a list of fictitious terrorists were flying from a number of European cities to all major airports in Britain with undetectable explosive devices about their persons.

Sergeant Evans and Private Benson of the Explosive Ordinance Disposal Regiment were the only members of the team on duty when the call from Oakwood came in. Evans checked with his captain, who was en route to Iran, and was angrily ordered to 'handle the poxy little package yourself, Sergeant as I have my bloody hands full with twenty possible IED's waiting for me in the bleeding desert.'

The best sniffer dogs had all been commandeered and flown out with the captain and Benson was stuck with Crapper. So called because he seemed to spend most of time fouling the kennels despite having his diet drastically reduced to dried food laced with Imodium tablets. He had originally been one of the finest sniffers in the regiment but the soldiers reckoned that it was his constant bowel movement that now confused his olfactory abilities.

The two soldiers loaded the van, tied Crapper in the back and raced to Oakwood with sirens blaring to clear the road. They found the road closed with police tape and the station building and street totally evacuated; something Crapper had been practicing in the back of the van all through the journey. Two constables kept the curious at bay while a third directed them, with pointed finger, to the object wrapped in brown paper that lay seventy yards away.

Crapper was immediately set to work at sniffing the package on which he deposited a rather large stool. The constables looked at the soldiers with expressions that asked if that was part of the investigation procedure. Benson pulled Crapper away mid second stool that unfortunately dropped onto the toecap of Evans boot.

'If he does that again I'll shoot the bastard,' he growled as Benson towed the useless dog back to the van and used his lead to tie him up.

'What do you reckon, Sergeant?' Benson said on returning to stand beside his partner who was methodically scraping his boot on the edge of the kerb.

'We don't take any chances, we blow the bugger up.' Evans mumbled with lips and teeth clenched against the smell. They both nodded and the sergeant then instructed the private to unload the robot and prepare a minor 'shaped' charge while he questioned the constables and inspected the package closely for any wires. He then stacked shock-absorbing sandbags around the package, leaving an opening for the robot arm to enter and place the charge.

The familiar whine of the robot's electric motor heralded it's approach and the sergeant backed a good distance away as Benson remotely controlled the long boom to delicately place the charge on top of the object. The dog stool was slowly flattened and a further pungent wave of obnoxious gases was released into the air. Despite being twenty yards from the sandbags the two men rapidly backed away even further than was absolutely necessary.

'I suggest you retreat seventy paces up the street before I detonate the charge,' Evans advised the constables and they hurriedly trotted away, more from the stomach churning smell than any threat of bomb injury.

Evans and Benson returned to the van and Evans connected the cable, checked the police were well clear and then triggered the charge. There was a thunderous explosion that deafened all those within one hundred yards and the front of the police station disappeared in a dense cloud of white dust.

'Christ, what size charge did you use, Benson?' Evans said but received no answer despite the private's panicking lip movement. Benson realizing that his superior couldn't hear him resorted to pointing to a steel munitions box and Benson saw with horror that he had chosen a charge normally reserved for large terrorist IEDs.

'That one, you should have used that one,' he shouted pointing to another box containing charges used to disconnect and destroy small devices. They were now being showered with dust and fragments of paper, one of which the sergeant picked up and tried to identify. There was some large print on the larger pieces that was impossible to decipher.

'Looks like Latin to me, Sarge,' Benson said looking over Evans shoulder. 'Do you think the bomber was Italian?'

With his hearing restored Evans said, 'Why the hell would an Italian want to target a small cop shop in a boring place like Oakwood?'

It was at this point that the two constables, coughing their lungs up, came running into view through the dust cloud. 'What the hell was that?' one declared pointing back at his place of work where damaged parts of the building were becoming visible.

'Must have had a pretty nasty bomb in your package.' Evans didn't get his sergeant's stripes for slow thinking. Picking up the evidence kit he walked towards the destruction that was once a smart entrance lobby. The kit was normally used to identify small parts of a bomb to enable the source to be pinpointed by the forensic staff. This time Evans pretended to pick up pieces with Benson realizing what he was playing at. He also looked far and wide for small pieces of parchment and leather binding to complete the appearance of having destroyed a lethal attack on the police station. It was while a part of the façade was collapsing, creating an open-air lobby, that the police tape stopped a taxi at the end of the road and two officers alighted.

'Close call, sir. Most probably IRA in origin,' Evans said as Detective Inspector Cooper stopped before his ruined police station with his mouth wide open.

'You blew up one bloody book with enough explosive to drill a hole to China.' Cooper was near to exploding himself as he watched the soldiers storing the robot and other assorted pieces of equipment in the van.

'Wouldn't know about that until after the forensic report, sir.' Evans said in all innocence as he climbed into the van and Benson started the engine. They drove away and it wasn't until they had reached the end of the road that the officers noticed a forlorn looking spaniel tied to a lamppost. Crapper had been abandoned along with the mound of excrement he had uncontrollably evacuated when the controlled explosion, which was more of an uncontrolled explosion, had occurred.

Cooper and Teal cautiously entered the station and were confronted with the shattered remains of the Duty Officer's counter. The latest in switchboard technology now resembled a bombed spaghetti factory.

'Use the car phone and put out an alert for Dozer and the Latimer woman,' Cooper said as he stomped down the passage to his office and suddenly stopped. 'Did you notice the bright green Citroën at the care home?'

'Yes, sir.'

'Did you take its number?'

'No, sir. Should I have?'

'Just check the stolen car listings for a green Citroën and add its number to the all-points bulletin. Maybe I can get that damned Latimer lad for something after all.'

Teal nodded and then asked in all innocence, 'Was that the Gutenberg Bible, sir?' He jerked a thumb over his shoulder at the devastation behind him.

'That was a three million pound balls-up, Constable,' Cooper confirmed and slammed the door behind him.

CHAPTER 28

D OZER HAD CLAIMED HE was a very good friend of her son and that he had promised Gerald he would take his mother for a day at the seaside. 'He thinks you need some nice sea air,' was the only plausible reason that convinced her to get into the car. She had eagerly agreed for although she didn't know who Gerald was she was keen to have some ice-cream and a paddle in the water as she did with her mother yesterday; at least in her mind it was yesterday despite overlooking fifty two years that had elapsed.

It was when they were smoothly running south on the motorway with the sounds of André Rieu lulling the old lady to sleep that the red light began to blink on the fuel gauge. Dozer cursed beneath his breath and at the next service station he used the slip road and parked at the pumps. There were few people about and he confidently got out of the car and filled the tank. Stephanie was still sleeping when he finished and replaced the filler cap so he went into the shop without taking her with him and after paying browsed the sandwich bar to allay the hunger he had started to feel.

It was only three minutes later, while chomping into a cheese and cucumber sandwich. that he went to the car to find it empty. The passenger door had been left wide open and he tossed the remnants of his sandwich onto the seat and looked round wildly to see where she had gone. It was a shout from the driver parked behind him and his pointing arm that drew his attention to Mrs Latimer standing fifty yards away on the motorway central reservation. Traffic was heavy and Dozer couldn't understand how she could have got where she was without being hit by a truck or a car in the fast lane.

'She just walked across,' the man behind him shouted as explanation and then seeing the big man's determination added, 'I wouldn't try it mate, the traffic is far too heavy. You'd better call the cops.'

Dozer ignored him and ran down the slope to pause on the hard shoulder of the south moving lanes and wait for a gap to appear in the traffic. He saw Mrs Latimer step off the central reservation and walk slowly across three busy lanes, miraculously being missed by wildly swerving vehicles. The elderly woman, now crossing the far side lane, was his only key to being forgiven for his sins and gaining salvation. Only Stephanie could provide him with the emotional leverage to force Gerald Latimer to return the bible so that he might have peace of mind when he placed the holy tome into the hands of the Pope in the Vatican.

The man who had warned against taking any action now watched in horror as Dozer made his first and last move to catch up with Mrs Latimer. He told the investigating traffic police that he thought it was the most foolhardy yet heroic rescue he had ever seen anybody attempt. An eavesdropping reporter used the exact same words in his story for a late edition of The Messenger. The writer also gave an eyewitness account of the incident that was subsequently slashed by the editor in order to make the article acceptable for the newspaper's family readership.

The following incident was very brief. An airport coach was approaching fast and Dozer ran across the first lane and into the second, carelessly putting himself in the path of an overtaking low-loader. He had 1.2 seconds to decide whether turning back and being struck by a freshly washed coach would be preferable to a dirty truck but time proved faster than muscle reaction.

If the pathologist found it difficult to identify the gender of the mangled pieces delivered to him for autopsy he only had to read the logo stamped into the squashed torso to clarify his confusion. *MAN* was neatly, and paradoxically, stamped beneath the fresh impression of St Christopher's bullet-dented medallion.

Stephanie Latimer, unaware of the chaos on the motorway behind her, trotted along the hard shoulder whilst three cars and a supermarket van hurtled into the low-loader that, ironically, was delivering a bulldozer that had just been repaired and was being returned to the owner, Mr Andrew Lawson.   Stephanie was now single-mindedly fixed on one image, a young man with a pleasant, yet sad expression, whose name she could not recall. She had an unaccountable desire to see him again and the large, not unpleasant man who had promised to take her to the seaside and a young man called Gerald, had rung a familiar bell. However, he had driven in a direction she had begun to doubt was correct and when Stephanie had expressed her concern she had been rudely ignored.

After a while Stephanie had fallen asleep and on waking up in a petrol station she decided to get out and make her way to where she thought the young man might be living. She was able to extract one clear memory from the fuzzy filing system in her mind that had grown fuzzier after each day had passed; 6 Fiesta Avenue.

Emergency vehicles racing to the scene of the traffic pileup failed to notice the stooped figure shambling along on the other side of the motorway until a rather observant Sergeant Tate instructed his driver to slow the police car, use a convenient gap in the central reservation and make a U-turn to apprehend the reckless woman.

'Are you okay, love?' he called out on leaving the car and trotting after the woman.

Stephanie turned and waited until the sergeant was close enough before answering. 'Perfectly all right, officer,' she said. 'I'm on my way to visit my … my err … young friend.'

'You do realize you're breaking the law by walking on the hard shoulder of a motorway?"

'I'm sure my young man will pay the fine, if there is one.'

While the sergeant kept Stephanie occupied by reciting every law concerning motorway usage by pedestrians and the accompanying penalties for breaking those laws the constable who had remained in the car had been checking recent reports and had found one concerning abduction from a care home. He scrolled the screen and a picture of Andy Lawson, aka Dozer, came into frame. A snapshot immediately followed this. It had been taken twenty- five years ago when Stephanie, Arnold her husband and little Gerald had spent a Bank holiday in Southend. Constable Hawkins looked through the windscreen and saw the similarity between the sun-touched youthful figure on the screen and the grey, lined features of the woman being bored by his sergeant's lecture.

Sergeant Tate saw the constable's signal. 'Would you like us to give you a ride to where your young man is waiting?' he asked and was replied with a smile. 'What's his address?' he enquired and watched as she hesitated on approaching the open door before nervously entering the car.

'Number 6 Fiesta Avenue,' she suddenly declared, proudly recalling the nine syllables.

'What town would that be, ma'am?' the constable asked over his shoulder as he accelerated and shifted across into the fast lane.

'Town?'

Tate saw the confusion and fear appearing as she entered her fuzzy filing system and he quickly reacted. 'Don't worry, Mrs Latimer, we know the address very well.' Using the keyboard he quickly entered the woman's details and waited until a page of information flashed onto the screen. 'Rainham, Constable,' Tate directed in a low voice and Hawkins nodded.

Messages were relayed and Inspector Cooper was able to notify Shady Trees and Gerald Latimer that Mrs Latimer had been found and was currently being driven to her home.

It hadn't been too long after the inspector and his team had left Shady Trees that Gerald and Elizabeth realized the peril of continuing to use the stolen, bright green car and on leaving the care home had abandoned the Citroën near Tilbury docks, after carefully wiping everything they had touched. They had then taken a taxi to Fiesta Avenue.

The police car stopped outside and Tate led a puzzled Stephanie to the front door. 'Where have you brought me?' she asked anxiously as she looked up at the house that had once been her home for thirty years The doorbell sounded in the hallway and a young man with brown hair, hazel eyes and a sad expression opened the door; his face altered on seeing his mother smiling up at him.

'Mum,' he exclaimed with a broad grin and threw his arms around her. 'Thank God you're okay.'

Stephanie was confused and withdrew with an alarmed expression until a smiling Elizabeth appeared behind her son.

'Elizabeth,' she cried and pushed a surprised Gerald to one side and hugged the young woman tightly. 'Who's this man?' she whispered in Elizabeth's ear.

'That's Gerald, Mrs Latimer,' Elizabeth replied. 'He's your son.'

Sergeant Tate was becoming a trifle embarrassed by this peculiar reunion of the two family members and muttering a few words about returning later to obtain a statement from Mrs Latimer he withdrew, closing the door behind him. Elizabeth led Stephanie to the kitchen and poured tea for them all while a deeply concerned Gerald watched his mother for any signs of recognition. There were none and he was wondering what he should do next when Elizabeth provided the solution.

'I think it would be a good idea if your mother stayed here, in her own home. That way I could stay and look after her.'

Gerald nodded enthusiastically. 'And it's time I started taking care of you both by getting a job to put food on the table and pay for the wedding,' Gerald exclaimed.

'A girl does like to be asked,' Elizabeth scolded with the suggestion of a smile.

Gerald dropped to one knee, took her hand and without any signs of sadness asked, 'Elizabeth Shanks, would you do me the honour of becoming my wife?'

Elizabeth looked down into his hazel eyes and failed to detect any mockery, only adoration. 'Do you truly mean that, Mr Latimer?' she whispered.

'Wouldn't you agree we need a roof over our heads and something to eat every day?' His eyes now twinkled mischievously and his mouth had turned up at the corners.

'Don't play with me, you know what I mean, Gerald,' Elizabeth answered and then she laughed.

Gerald nodded. 'Of course I mean it, Elizabeth,' he said.

Elizabeth then also knelt and placed a forefinger across his lips. 'Then ask me again.' Her voice was soft and tender.

'Elizabeth Shanks, will you marry me?'

She took his face in her hands and kissed him hard. 'Does that answer your question,' she murmured. They were suddenly startled when Stephanie began clapping her hands.

'Of course it does, Elizabeth,' she said. 'You love the damned fellow. Anybody with opened eyes can see that. You and Gerald will make a perfect couple.'

'You remembered my name, mum,' Gerald said with a look of surprise as he stood and put an arm around his mother's shoulders; he kissed her on the cheek.

'Kiss your bride to be, not me,' his mother said, playfully pushing her son towards Elizabeth. 'She's a beautiful girl and I'm truly happy that I'll be able to see you wed before I lose complete control of my mind.'

'I'll make sure you don't lose anything, errr . . . mum,' Elizabeth said with a nervous smile. 'I'll keep you so active you won't have time to forget a thing.'

'You have a kind heart, Elizabeth, one I could very easily love.' Stephanie declared and hurried off into the kitchen to start preparing a meal for them all and to hide the flush of embarrassment on her face.

'What about Dozer, what should I do about him?' Gerald murmured more to himself than anyone present as they followed her. 'That man doesn't believe we gave the bible to the police which means he's bound to return here and demand we return it to him.'

'Who's this man Dozer?' Stephanie asked on appearing at the kitchen door. 'He has a very funny name.'

'You needn't worry about him, mum,' Gerald said quickly as he sat at the table. As though to contradict his reassurance the doorbell rang and Elizabeth started, looked at Gerald and raised a concerned eyebrow. He stood and went down the hall studying the shadow on the frosted glass strip beside the solid wood door. It was the outline of a large man and Gerald took a Malacca cane from the hallstand and opened the door.

Detective Constable Teal smiled at the makeshift weapon gripped tightly by the slender man. 'That wouldn't scare a real villain, Mr Latimer,' he said as a relieved Gerald waved him in and closed the door. 'I've come to give you some good news, sir,' he added as he was led into the living room.

Elizabeth smiled on recognizing the constable. 'Nice to see you again, constable,' she said and quickly introduced Gerald's mother who stared at the policeman as though trying to recognize someone she had known long ago.

'We've been able to identify the man who kidnapped Mrs Latimer,' Teal said. 'At least we were able to tell by his DNA who he was as he was in a bit of a mess after a truck hit him on the motorway.' He apologized for upsetting the ladies who had both reacted to his description of Dozer's remains. 'Andy Lawson was trying to rescue Mrs Latimer after she had escaped from him at a service station and ran across the motorway.'

'Dozer tried to rescue Mrs Latimer?' Elizabeth gasped in disbelief.

'My mother ran across a motorway?' Gerald said incredulously.

'Well, actually she walked rather casually across all six lanes without any trouble at all and then Lawson tried to do the same thing,' Teal explained and then turned to address the older woman. 'You were very fortunate, Mrs Latimer,' he said but Stephanie wasn't listening for she was still trying to remember where she had last seen the officer.

'I can't believe Dozer wanted to rescue my mother, he wouldn't rescue a drowning cat even if it was within his reach,' Gerald murmured.

'Nevertheless he went after Mrs Latimer.'

'Amazing,' Elizabeth said. 'Wouldn't have thought he had it in him.'

'Two other late developments are that the Gutenberg Bible has been identified and like Andy Lawson it was also in a number of small pieces.'

'What do you mean?' Elizabeth asked mystified.

'It had been considered a security risk by Detective Inspector Cooper and the bomb squad destroyed it with a controlled explosion.'

'My God, it was blown up?' exclaimed a horrified Gerald.

'I'm very sorry to say that it was, along with a large part of the police station, and we're still trying to find the person who imprudently wrapped it in brown paper and, without saying a word to anybody, left it in the lobby of a police station.'

Gerald and Elizabeth looked at each other and remained silent.

'You do realize that since the latest bomb atrocity the whole country has been alerted to any terrorist activity?' Teal asked as he studied the pair with suspicion. 'And that includes mysterious packages.'

'I would only assume that Dozer had put it there as an act of contrition after killing the priest in St Marks church.' Gerald said unconvincingly.

'He mentioned giving it back to the church the last time he threatened us,' Elizabeth added quickly. 'As no church or cathedral would take the book maybe he saw leaving it with the police the only way to gain God's forgiveness.'

Teal couldn't prevent himself from laughing and could only regain the power of speech after a period of uncontrollable mirth. 'It's difficult to imagine a cold-hearted thug like Dozer, a man who takes pleasure in killing and inflicting pain, suddenly finding God and becoming penitent.' He spluttered into laughter again. 'I have to admit, you two are good.'

Gerald frowned. 'I'm convinced he did want to give the bible to a church that would use it,' he said resolutely.

'Whatever, sir.' Teal gained control and shook Gerald's hand. 'Glad you managed to dispose of the green Citroën.' His expression remained unchanged. 'I would have disliked having to charge you with something as petty as car theft, sir.'

'Citroën, officer?' Gerald said with wide-eyed innocence.

'Sorry, I must be confusing you with somebody else.' Teal allowed the corners of his mouth to curl as he let Gerald lead him from the room. 'I'll let Inspector Cooper know that it was pure coincidence.'

The two men held each other's gaze for a few moments before Constable Teal nodded, turned, and went down the path to his car.

Gerald returned to tell Elizabeth that he had gone and they both smiled with relief when they realized that their Sword of Damocles, Dozer, was no longer poised above their heads. He returned to the phone to let Ali and his sister know that their nightmare was over. Ali was shocked and then happy, in a peculiar way, to learn of the bible's violent end for it felt as though a heavy load had been lifted from his shoulders. Gerald returned to the kitchen after promising to see them both in a few days time and hung up

'I knew who that man was,' Stephanie said to her son. 'He's a constable, Constable Teal who came round to the house to tell me of your father's accident.' Her eyes moistened for she could clearly recall her husband's smile and the touch of his hand upon her cheek.

'That's wonderful, Mrs Latimer,' Elizabeth said as she took her hand.

'Mum,' Stephanie corrected.

'Mrs . . . Mum . . . if you can remember that policeman's name it means you'll be able to remember many more things and I'm determined to help you.'

Gerald had read that a sudden change of circumstance could have a positive effect on patients suffering from Alzheimer's disease and came to the conclusion that his mother should remain at home in his and Elizabeth's care. He gave his considered opinion to them both and although Stephanie wasn't clear on what was being decided she smiled broadly on seeing the happiness on the two youngster's faces.

'I still have the problem of getting a job,' Gerald confided when he and Elizabeth had finished getting his mother ready for bed and were themselves buried beneath the duvet. He pounded the pillow and tried to get comfortable as he considered the list of expenses in keeping the house and themselves going. 'It will have to be a bloody good salary,' he muttered to himself and Elizabeth listened with the growing fear that her husband to be might resort to criminal solutions again.

'You'll find something she whispered and put an arm around him. He subconsciously stroked her hair and then her shoulder as he lay worrying and it wasn't long before his hand had slowly worked its way lower and lower. Elizabeth shifted her position to encourage him, knowing that making love would help to distract his mind from their present financial situation. Gerald was aroused and with their passion growing he kissed and caressed her wildly until they were united as one and fell into exhausted sleep.

They rose early and after Elizabeth had checked on Stephanie and found her still sleeping peacefully she returned to the bedroom and began dressing. It was as Elizabeth took her purse from the bedside table that a small piece of paper slipped out and fluttered to the carpet unnoticed. Gerald was dozing when she went down to begin making the breakfast and was only just stirring when she returned with the tea tray. The smell of bacon and fresh coffee soon woke him and he sat up with a look of pleasure as the tray was placed on the bed and Elizabeth joined him under the covers.

'Is mum okay?' he mumbled around a slice of buttered toast that was half in and half out of his mouth.

'She got up while I was dressing and has made this feast as well as porridge for herself.' Elizabeth tucked into the other plate of eggs and bacon that she had placed on her lap and poured milk into their coffees. They both ate in silence like a typical married couple until the tray was cleared of every morsel and then Elizabeth lowered the tray to the floor before rolling back to snuggle into Gerald's arms. The next forty minutes was spent in a repeat performance of the previous evening's performance and after cessation of all activity they both rose to use the en-suite bathroom.

As Elizabeth swung her legs over the edge of the bed she noticed the scrap of paper and picked it up. A wave of guilt flowed through her as she realized it was the same lottery ticket she had taken from Gerald's wallet after his abortive bank robbery.

'Gerald, I have a confession,' she called through the open door and when her naked lover appeared, a towel draped about his loins, she told him about the lottery ticket.

Gerald laughed and sat beside her. 'I've had that quite a while and I doubt it's won anything. I've been using my birthday numbers for the last ten years and never won a penny.' He took the ticket, looked at it for while, then screwed it up and tossed it into the wastepaper basket. Gerald took a surprised Elizabeth around the waist and lifted her over his shoulder and carried the giggling girl into the bathroom.

The ticket was forgotten while they showered together and dressed for the day. It was as Elizabeth prepared to leave the bedroom and follow Gerald downstairs that she remembered the ticket and retrieved it from the basket with a plan to check it later in a web-cafe.

Gerald left the women and returned to Shady Trees by taxi to recover his mother's property and cancel all future payments. The surly matron became even surlier on learning about the loss of a client but dare not withhold the initial deposit for fear he would contact the press who had already given Shady Trees a tarnished reputation.

The taxi driver was asked to make a stop at St Marks church and Gerald entered and asked the cleaner if Father Jeremiah was available. A nail-bitten finger pointed at the sacristy and he found his friend with his nose deep in a religious tract.

'Gerald! It's so nice to see you looking so healthy,' he declared on looking up to find the young man before his desk. 'I heard what happened from Constable Teal when he came to ask if I knew anything about a green Citroën.'

'And?'

Jeremiah crossed himself. 'What Citroën, I asked and made a promise to myself to confess later.'

Gerald laughed. 'Father, I've come to ask if you would do me the honour of marrying Elizabeth and myself?'

The priest's jaw dropped and then a smile spread across his face. 'I would be delighted, Gerald. The honour will be mine.' He and Gerald then discussed the details required for the forthcoming marriage and a date was set that Gerald agreed to confirm after he had Elizabeth's agreement. They shook hands and Gerald returned to Fiesta Avenue to offload his mother's things and give Elizabeth the news that Jeremiah would be the officiating priest. She was overjoyed and agreed the date.

'You'll need this, my dear,' Stephanie said on overhearing the couple's plans. She had a simple gold band in the palm of her hand and held it out to the young woman.

'But that's your ring, mum,' Elizabeth exclaimed. 'I couldn't take that.'

'Oh, you will, my girl,' Stephanie insisted as she tipped the ring into Elizabeth's hand. 'It gave me many years of joy and I wish it to do the same for you.'

Elizabeth closed her hand around the priceless symbol of love, threw her arms around the older woman and kissed her on both cheeks. 'This must be the most precious wedding gift any girl could wish for; thank you, Mum.'

Gerald felt a lump rise in his throat and he turned away to hide the tears forming in his eyes and filled the kettle to make tea; the primary remedy for all emotional upwellings.

A rather unfortunate ending.

G ERALD REMAINED AT HOME to look after his mother while Elizabeth took the bus into town to purchase some essential groceries and a new lipstick. As she paid the checkout lady the lottery ticket slipped out of her purse with the bank notes and, as it had a habit of doing, it fluttered down to the floor. Elizabeth retrieved it, looked round to see a lottery display board and asked the shop assistant to check the numbers.

She had just finished packing her purchases in the bag when the elderly woman who had fed the ticket into the lottery machine gave a low squeal followed by a loud shout that drew the attention of every customer in the store.

'Oh, my God,' She had cried out.

Elizabeth was also startled and looked up to see the grey-haired woman studying the scrap of paper with a shocked expression on her face. She looked up and slowly proffered the ticket to Elizabeth.

'It's a winner, my dear,' she said. 'You've won.'

Elizabeth looked down at the innocuous slip of pink paper. 'Very much?' she inquired.

There was a long pause as the queue continued to back-up with other customers. 'Three million, you've won three bloody million pounds.'

A collective gasp arose from all people within earshot and while Elizabeth tried to assimilate the information the news spread, word of mouth, until everyone in the store knew of Elizabeth's incredible win. The checkout woman pointed at the ticket. 'I'd take great care of that if I were you,' she said in a conspiratorial tone and Elizabeth gripped the ticket tightly in the palm of her hand as she accepted her change with the other. She left the store amidst a babble of excited voices and envious looks.

The ticket remained clutched in Elizabeth's hand when she boarded the bus to return home and was still there when she alighted at the end of Fiesta Avenue. Fingernails were on the point of drawing blood when she opened the door and went into the kitchen to deposit the crumpled ticket on the kitchen table in front of Gerald.

'Three million,' she whispered still in shock. 'Your birthday numbers were worth three million pounds.'

Gerald stopped peeling the King Edwards and after checking the wall calendar that April hadn't begun he looked into Elizabeth's wide eyes that confirmed that what she had said was the truth and that they were now millionaires.

'We can employ the best nurse for your mother, holiday in the Bahamas and drink champagne every day,' Elizabeth said excitedly.

'We can leave Fiesta Avenue and . . .'

'What's happened?' Stephanie asked on entering the kitchen and seeing how excited the young people were.

'Gerald's lottery ticket has come up trumps,' Elizabeth said as she held it up and waved it in the air. 'No more money problems.'

'That's nice dear. Who's Gerald.' She ignored Elizabeth's startled expression and continued. 'Can I have that cup of tea you promised me, Elizabeth?' Stephanie sat at the table and took the ticket and studied it while Elizabeth began preparing the tea tray.

'Could you light the stove, mum?' she asked Stephanie. 'It's time I started making lunch.' Gerald took the ticket and scribbled down the various contact telephone numbers on a notepad before putting it back on the table.

'I'll go and give Ali and Margaret the good news that we can help with the restoration of Montague Hall and then call the Camelot lottery company with these numbers,' he said and left the kitchen. Elizabeth called out that it was a good idea and switched the kettle on while Stephanie took a newspaper from the table and twisted some of the pages tightly before feeding the old AGA. Kindling was placed on top of the paper and Stephanie began singing happily as she struck a match to ignite the fire. Gerald returned with some split logs and these were added and soon they were spitting and flaring merrily as Stephanie stared at his face, struggling to recall where she had seen the young man before.

The trio was happily discussing how they would spend the rest of their lives in the lap of luxury while sipping their third cup of tea when Gerald asked where the lottery ticket was.

'Where's the ticket, Elizabeth?' he asked with eyes scanning the tabletop.

'Yes, where's the ticket, mum?' Elizabeth echoed as she also looked for the pink scrap of paper that would render her pauper a prince.

'Where's the ticket – ' Stephanie asked as the young man's name suddenly came back, ' – Gerald?' And then it faded back into the fuzzy filing system. 'Didn't I give it to you?'

'You did, mum, but I put it back on the table – ' There was a slight pause that expressed his grasp of the disaster. ' – on today's newspaper where Elizabeth could see it.' Elizabeth sank back in her seat and gave a deep sigh of despair.

'Three million pounds burns rather well doesn't it, Gerald?' she murmured.

Gerald was silent for the return of his sad-look was sufficient answer.

Semper in excretia
sumus solim
profundum variat!

Lord de Ramsey, House of Lords

A brief biography of
Clive F Sorrell

C LIVE'S LIFE BEGAN AND almost ended in 1942 when a bomb detonated very near the hospital in Kent. His father demobbed from the RAF in 1948 and emigrated to Australia only to bring the family back to England when Clive was ten. The family nomadically trekked back to Australia in 1956 and Clive started work in a South Australian advertising agency. He changed water pots and cleaned brushes for artists whilst studying and was accepted by the Australian Advertising Institute as the youngest Licentiate Member.

Once more Clive's father was drawn back to England and in 1960 Clive joined a London agency as a trainee typographer. He progressed to become an art director, copywriter and finally executive creative director.

Clive gained awards for radio, television and print work during a career spent in Adelaide, London, Johannesburg, London (again), Jeddah and Dubai. He retired and returned to Suffolk and his wife Sophia in 2005, to continue writing, switching from faction to fiction.

The last ten years in the Middle East inspired Clive to write three crime thrillers; *Siddiqui*, set in Saudi Arabia, *Kawthar* set in the UAE and *Jumana* in Bahrain. As an unknown author he had to self-publish his work and Clive went on to write *DURESS*, another thriller set in 1960s England.

Keeping up his average of one book a year Clive completed *Ingrid's Children*, the first in a series of three novels featuring a narcoleptic private detective. *The Distant Cousin* and *The King's Charter* followed but it was while completing *The Sad-Faced Bank Robber* in 2017 that Clive's wife suddenly passed away.

Clive continues to live in a quiet Suffolk village and apart from writing his other interests include reading, film and travel.

Lightning Source UK Ltd.
Milton Keynes UK
UKOW08n1958030517

300414UK00003B/30/P